Selected as a

BEST BOOK OF THE YEAR

NEW YORK TIMES

SAN FRANCISCO CHRONICLE

WASHINGTON POST BOOK WORLD

BOOKLIST

A BOOK SENSE
BOOK OF THE YEAR FINALIST

A NEW YORK TIMES NOTABLE B

Finalist for

the MAN BOOKER INTERNATIONAL PRIZE,

the KORET JEWISH BOOK AWARD,

and the PATERSON FICTION PRIZE

Selected by

BOOKLIST as one of the

TOP TEN HISTORICAL NOVELS *of the* YEAR

Lavish Praise for Cynthia Ozick and
Heir to the Glimmering World

"An irresistible read. A trove of wonderfully imagined characters, brilliantly written—a dazzling performance."
—Alice Munro, author of *Runaway*

"A novel as scintillating as this one makes the world infinitely new, and it's the reader—every writer's ultimate heir—who walks away with the biggest fortune of all."—*Newsday*

"A wise, quietly magical book."—*Washington Post*

"Generous and entirely entertaining."—*Los Angeles Times Book Review*

"Lovely, smart . . . Every strand of this hugely ambitious novel is strange and original."—*Entertainment Weekly*

"Funny and witty and engaging on a pure what-will-happen-next level . . . A satisfying, well-plotted novel—one of life's old-fashioned pleasures, handily renewed."—*Chicago Sun-Times*

"Audacious . . . *Heir to the Glimmering World* is both a character nautilus and a haunted house—a fairy tale with locked rooms, mad songs, secret books, and stolen babies."—*New York Times Book Review*

"One of Cynthia Ozick's best novels . . . A captivating page-turner."
—*Miami Herald*

"A novel written with the vigor and strength of a literary artist in her prime, at the height of her powers, masterly not only in her prose but also in her ingenuity . . . One is left only wanting more."
—*Washington Times*

"Sparky, mischievous, witty, dazzlingly clever, properly dimensional, and written with such calmness so close to the foulness of history as to seem somehow beyond the world, almost mercilessly self-assured . . . It works, like all Ozick's fine, uncompromising, and paradoxical oeuvre, to leave both books and world at once more properly mysterious and better understood." — *Guardian*

"Aglow with fierce wit and passionate intensity . . . Lavish in invention and ideas . . . *Heir to the Glimmering World* has all the hallmarks of a permanent work of literature." — *Wall Street Journal*

"Virtuosic . . . delightful . . . a tour de force." — *Boston Globe*

"Her funniest and most elaborately patterned novel yet . . . dazzling."
— *Seattle Times*

"Masterful . . . an elegant marriage of the brothers Grimm and the greatest-hits-of-the-nineteenth-century novel."
— *Atlanta Journal-Constitution*

"Ozick writes eloquently, with smooth prose and beautiful use of language." — *Elle*

"A brilliant novel of ideas, but not of everyday ideas."
— *New York Times Book Review*

"An enjoyable novel on many levels. The characters are wonderfully eccentric and original." — *Rocky Mountain News*

"Inspired . . . [Ozick's] language alone . . . long ago earned her a position among the very first rank of American fiction writers."
— *New Republic*

"A consummately strange book, fascinating . . . [Ozick] can capture the feeling not only of a place but an era." — *New Leader*

"An unbelievably ravishing read . . . We talk of [the work of] Henry James, the Brontës, and George Eliot, and I think [*Heir to the Glimmering World*] is a tribute to that but it lives in that company."
— BBC2 *Late Review*

Heir to the
Glimmering
World

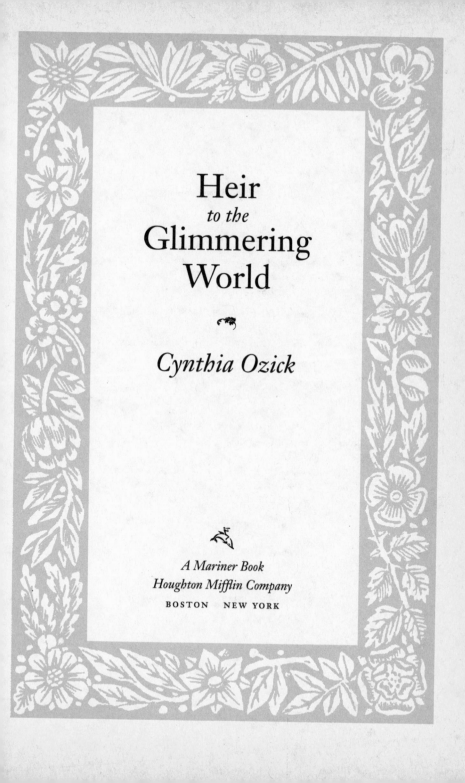

Heir
to the
Glimmering World

Cynthia Ozick

A Mariner Book
Houghton Mifflin Company
BOSTON   NEW YORK

First Mariner Books edition 2005

Visit our Web site: www.houghtonmifflinbooks.com.

LIBRARY OF CONGRESS CATALOGING-IN-PUBLICATION DATA

Ozick, Cynthia.
Heir to the glimmering world / Cynthia Ozick.
p. cm.
ISBN 0-618-47049-2
ISBN 0-618-61880-5 (pbk.)
1. Bronx (New York, N.Y.)—Fiction.   2. Inheritance and succession—
Fiction.   3. Children of authors—Fiction.   4. Refugees, Jewish—Fiction.
5. Jewish families—Fiction.   6. Benefactors—Fiction.   7. Rich people—
Fiction.   8. Nannies—Fiction.   9. Orphans—Fiction.   I. Title.

PS3565.Z5H45 2004
813'.54—DC22   2004042723

Book design by Anne Chalmers
Typeface: Janson Text

PRINTED IN THE UNITED STATES OF AMERICA

QUM 10 9 8 7 6 5 4 3 2 1

A portion of this book previously appeared
in the *Princeton University Chronicle Supplement*.

The absence of imagination had
Itself to be imagined.

— Wallace Stevens,
    "The Plain Sense of Things"

Yet the world is full of interpreters. . . .
So the question arises, why would we
rather interpret than not?

— Frank Kermode,
    "The Man in the Macintosh"

Heir to the
Glimmering
World

1

In 1935, when I was just eighteen, I entered the household of Rudolf Mitwisser, the scholar of Karaism. "The scholar of Karaism"—at that time I had no idea what that meant, or why it should be "the" instead of "a," or who Rudolf Mitwisser was. I understood only that he was the father of what seemed to be numerous children, and that he had come from Germany two years before. I knew these things from an advertisement in the Albany *Star:*

> Professor, arrived 1933 Berlin, children 3–14,
> requires assistant, relocate NYC. Respond
> Mitwisser, 22 Westerley.

It read like a telegram; Professor Mitwisser, I would soon learn, was parsimonious. The ad did not mention Elsa, his wife. Possibly he had forgotten about her.

In my letter of reply I said that I would be willing to go to New York, though it was not clear from the notice in the *Star* what sort of assistance was needed. Since the ad had included the age of a very young child, was it a nanny that was desired? I said I would be pleased to take on the job of nanny.

It was Elsa, not Mitwisser, who initiated the interview—though, as it turned out, she was not in charge of it. In that family she was in charge of little enough. I rode the bus to a corner populated by a cluster of small shabby stores—grocery, shoemaker's, dry cleaner's, and under a tattered awning a dim coffee shop vomiting out odors of some foul stuff frying. The windows of all these establishments were impenetrably dirty. Across the street a deserted gas station had long ago gone out of business: several large dogs scrabbled over the oil-blackened pavement and lifted their hind legs against the rusting pumps.

The address in the ad drew me along narrow old sidewalks fronting narrow old houses in what I had come to think of as the Albany style: part Hudson Gothic, part Dutch settler. But mainly old. There were bow-shaped stained-glass insets over all the doors. The lamps in the rooms behind them, glowing violet and amber through the lead-bordered segments of colored panes, shut me out. I thought of underground creatures kept from the light. It was November, getting on to an early dusk.

Frau Mitwisser led me into a tiny parlor so dark that it took some time before her face, small and timid as a vole's, glimmered into focus. "Forgive me," she began, "Rudi wishes not the waste of electricity. We have not so much money. We cannot pay much. Food and a bed and not so many dollars." She stopped; her eyelids looked swollen. "The tutor for my sons, it was you see . . . charity. Also the beds, the linens—"

She was all apology: the slope of her shoulders, her fidgety hands twittering around her mouth, or reaching into the air for a phantom rope to haul her out of sight. Helplessly but somehow also slyly, she was reversing our mutual obligation—she appealing for my sympathy, I with the power to withhold it. It was hard to take in those pursed umlauts sprinkled through her vowels, and the throaty burr of her voice was lanced by pricks so sharp that I pulled back a little. She saw this and instantly begged my pardon.

"Forgive me," she said again. "It gives much difficulty with my accent. At my age to change the language is not so simple. You will see with my husband the very great difference. In his youth for four years he studies at Cambridge University in England, he becomes like an Englishman. You will see. But I . . . I do not have the—*wie nennt man das?*—the idiom."

Her last word was shattered by an enormous thud above our heads. I looked up: was the ceiling about to fall in on us? A second thud. A third.

"The big ones," Frau Mitwisser said. "They make a game, to jump from the top of the . . . *Kleiderschrank*, how you call this? I tell them every day no, but anyhow they jump."

This gave me a chance to restore us to business. "And the littler ones?" I asked. "Do you need help with them?"

In the dimness I glimpsed her bewilderment; it was as if she was begging for eclipse.

"No, no, we go to New York so Rudi is close to the big library. Here is for him so little. The committee, it is so very kind that they give us this house, and also they make possible the work at the College, but now it is enough, Rudi must go to New York."

A gargantuan crash overhead: a drizzle of plaster dust landed on my sleeve.

"Forgive me," Frau Mitwisser said. "Better I go upstairs now, *nicht wahr?*"

She hurried out and left me alone in the dark. I buttoned up my coat; the interview, it seemed, was over. I had understood almost nothing. If they didn't want a nanny here, what did they want? And if they had had a tutor, what had become of the tutor? Had they paid too little to keep him? On an angry impulse I switched on a lamp; the pale bulb cast a stingy yellow stain on a threadbare rug. From the condition of the sofa and an armchair, much abused, I gathered that "the big ones" were accustomed to assaulting the furniture downstairs as well as upstairs— or else what I was seeing was thrift-shop impoverishment. A woolen shawl covered a battered little side-table, and propped on it, in a flower-embossed heavy silver frame that contradicted all its surroundings, was a photograph—hand-tinted, gravely posed, redolent of some incomprehensible foreignness—of a dark-haired young woman in a high collar seated next to a very large plant. The plant's leaves were spear-shaped, serrated, and painted what must once have been a natural enough green, faded to the color of mud. The plant grew out of a great stone urn, on which the face and wings of a cherub were carved in relief.

I turned off the lamp and headed for the front door with its stained-glass inset, and was almost at the sidewalk (by now it was fully night) when I heard someone call, "Fräulein! You there! Come back!"

The dark figure of a giant stood in the unlit doorway. Those alien syllables—"Fräulein," yelled into the street like that—put me off. Already I disliked the foreignness of this house: Elsa Mitwisser's difficult and resentful English, the elitist solemnity of the silver frame and its photo, the makeshift hand-me-down sitting room. These were refugees;

3

everything about them was bound to be makeshift, provisional, resent-ful. I would have gone home then and there, if there had been a home to go to, but it was clear that my cousin Bertram was no longer happy to have me. I was a sort of refugee myself.

(Some weeks later, when I dared to say this to Anneliese—"I some-times feel like a refugee myself"—she shot me a look of purest con-tempt.)

Like a dog that has been whistled for, I followed him back into the house.

"Now we have light," he said, in a voice so authoritatively godlike that it might just as well have boomed "Let there be light" at the begin-ning of the world. He fingered the lamp. Once again the faint yellow stain appeared on the rug and seeped through the room. "To dispel the blackness, yes? Our circumstances have also been black. They are not so easeful. You have already seen my nervous Elsa. So that is why she leaves it to me to finish the talk."

He was as far from resembling an Englishman as I could imagine. In spite of the readier flow of language (a hundred times readier than his wife's), he was German—densely, irrevocably German. My letter was in his hands: very large hands, with big flattened thumbs and coarse nails, strangely humped and striated—more a machinist's hands than a scholar's. In the niggardly light (twenty-five watts, I speculated) he seemed less gargantuan than the immense form in the doorway that had called me back from the street. But I was conscious of a force, of a man accustomed to dictating his conditions.

"My first requirement," Mitwisser said, "is your freedom to leave this place."

"I can do that," I said. "I'd like to."

"It is what *I* would like that is at issue. And what I would like is a certain engagement with—I will not say ideas. But you must be able to understand what I ask of you."

"I've done most of a year of college."

"Less than *Gymnasium*. What is this nonsense you write here about a nanny? How is this responsive?"

"Well, your ad mentioned children, so I thought—"

"You thought mistakenly. You should know that my work has to do precisely with opposition to the arrogance of received interpretation. Received interpretation is often enough simply error. Why should I not speak everywhere of my children? There is no context or relation in which they do not have a part. That is why your obligations will on occasion include them—but your primary duty is to me. And you will try not to disturb my poor wife."

It seemed, then, that I was hired—though I still did not know for what.

And it was not until a long time afterward that Anneliese confided that there had been (even in that period of crisis unemployment) no other applicants.

2

IT WAS MY FATHER'S habit to tell people that my mother had died in childbirth: it had a nineteenth-century intimation of Tragic Loss. He said this to account for what he admitted was the shallowness of his paternal devotion. "The shallowness of my paternal devotion"—that was exactly how he put it. He cared (though not crucially) about the opinion of his colleagues and acquaintances, and would send out a stream of self-castigation in order, he hoped, to nip their condemnation in the bud. His intention was to arrive at his own condemnation fast and first. It was a kind of exculpation.

No one condemned him; no one paid much attention. My father had, as far as I could see, no friends. I thought it was because he talked too much, elaborated and fabricated too much, and always took an exaggerated view of himself. He told so many stories that after a time he forgot the facts out of which his pessimistic romances sprang. It was even possible that he truly believed he had lost my mother the day I was born, though in reality I was almost three when she died of leukemia. I retain an uncertain memory of her lying on a sofa, holding my rag doll—or it may only have been a handkerchief. Years later, Lena, one of our series of housekeepers, informed me of my mother's enduring illness.

Of course it was my father who would refer to "our series of housekeepers." They were mostly neighbor women who would come to fetch our dirty laundry, scrub it on washboards in their cellar basins, and hang it to dry on their own clotheslines. Or sometimes one of these women would bring in a meal of hot cooked food, and while my father and I sat eating our supper, would mop the bathroom floor or change the sheets. It was all haphazard and irregular. The women were paid little; my father preferred to barter. He taught algebra and geometry at the high school, and would offer to tutor a pupil in exchange for a load of soiled clothing or two consecutive dinners. Disorder was our rule of life—disorder and my father's puffery. In the post office once, when a man buying stamps alongside my father struck up a conversation and asked what he did for a living, my father replied, "Professor of mathematics. Got my doctorate at Yale." He had no doctorate and had never set foot in New Haven; he liked to dream out loud. An invention of this sort was ordinarily harmless and evanescent, but the man in the post office turned out to be the uncle of one of my father's pupils; they met again at a school event, and my father was exposed. I suffered from such chronic embarrassments, but nothing troubled me more than my father's negotiations with those women. No one else I knew lived with our disorganization and dependence. My father was incapable of washing his socks or baking a potato. When no one was available to help out—around Christmastime, for instance—we ate dry cereal for nearly a week.

Despite fits of shame or irritation, I was not sufficiently humiliated by this system—or lack of system—until the night before my eleventh birthday, when my father uncharacteristically announced that he was arranging for a treat. This was extraordinary: usually my birthday was the start of a long spurt of gloom. "On this day," my father would say, "eight years ago, Jenny left me." And the next year: "On this day, nine years ago," and so on. It had been the same all through my earlier childhood.

"It's eleven years tomorrow," he began that evening, "since I lost my Jenny."

But this time I was ready to argue.

"Lena told me she didn't die on account of me. It was afterward, from leukemia. Lena said leukemia's a cancer that gets into your blood."

"Lena told you this? When?"

"Last week. When she brought back the wash."

"You shouldn't listen to any of these women," my father said. "Especially not that one."

"I think I even remember her a little—my mother. She was lying down. I think I remember that. Right over there," I said.

"You remember my wife?" My father's bald scalp reddened; he stared. "It's not possible. She was just giving birth. She gave birth on the sofa, before the doctor came. You shouldn't pay attention to a silly witch. These are all dishonest people—I see it in their kids all the time. They

7

believe in cutting corners, they're brainless, and they'd bribe you blind. If I could afford it, I'd get off their goddamn street, I'd move out of this one-horse goddamn town."

My father, even when I was included, almost never said "we."

"I wish I could have a birthday party," I complained. "Everyone else in my grade gets to have one."

It was then that my father said he would be sure to have some kind of treat for me, he couldn't figure exactly when—but it depended on my carrying a packet of papers down the street that very evening to Lena's house and letting her know it was my birthday.

"Tell her the stuff'll help the kid with tomorrow's test," he said.

I hated going to Lena's house—the rooms smelled of cat dung. Lena had two sons; the younger one wore corduroy knickers, and these too smelled of cat. Timmy, the older one, was in my father's geometry class. He was drudging but sluggish. In payment for Lena's tending to our laundry, my father now and then gave him private lessons.

A day or so later my treat arrived. "Treat": it was an odd word for my father to have used; it settled between his teeth with an ironic click. The treat was a crumbling, lopsided cake with urine-yellow frosting. It leaned like a fallen-in shack, and the artificial lemon icing was so bitter it stung.

"Now that's what I call cake cast upon the waters," my father said. "Isn't that fine? Lena made it for you, and Timmy brought it over before you were awake. Not that the kid was in much of a mood."

"It's not fine. It's not a treat. It's disgusting," I said.

He told me then that the packet he had asked me to deliver was a complete midterm geometry exam: it contained all the questions and all the answers. But it was a discard. It was not the exam he had intended to give the following day; it belonged to the year before.

The cake was still squatting on the table when Lena came storming through our back door.

"You did that on purpose!" she shrieked. "You sent over the wrong test, and my boy put in four hours breaking his head over it, and all the time you knew it was the wrong test!"

"Now wait a minute," my father said. "The wrong test, what are you talking about?"

"How could he pass it, if it wasn't the one you gave them in class? You gave them a different one! You got my son all balled up! See this thing?" She thrust her finger into the soft downward flow of collapsing yellow cake. "Give your kid an idea of what you did to my kid."

"Now wait a minute," my father said again. Pedagogical repetition was his way; it was a type of cunning. "Practice with an old examination is eminently useful, it's recommended. Practice makes perfect, yes?" A sly glint crept into his eye. "You didn't expect me to dishonor myself and my profession, did you? You didn't expect me to hand your son the contents of an examination in advance, did you?"

But I saw that she *had* expected it; she had assumed it, and my father had understood she would assume it. They were complicit: that was what lay in their agreement to barter—value for value. But my father had let down his side of the bargain. He had let it down in order to punish Lena for denying the hour of my mother's death. And she, in throwing together that travesty of a cake, was punishing my father for his betrayal of her boy. Wasn't he her son's teacher and helper? Shouldn't he have done what a man whose underwear she scrubbed, whose toilet bowl she cleaned, ought to do?

Lena had intended my cake to be ugly and bitter. And my father had intended to mislead her boy.

It was not strange that I could see all this: I knew my father. It came to me in a flood—the silliness and the malice, the pathos and the pettiness; a simple-minded vengeful woman, her inadequate son, my father's tiny preposterous plots; and then our household, our sterile and constricted small cosmos. A formal feeling, palpable and gossamer, fell over me like a skein. It was as if I had been caught in a fisherman's net and lifted out of a viscid sea. From then on I was able to resist my father at nearly every point.

My resistance took the form, at first, of a furious domesticity. I was old enough to do laundry and clean house, and every afternoon after school I taught myself a repertoire of easy meals. Because my father had long ago declared that we were vegetarians, I never had to touch meat. But I began to make order; my object was to rid us of those women. I scraped an aged layer of annealed oil off the inside of the oven. I stood on a chair and painted all the kitchen shelves. I shopped cautiously and hoarded pennies. The greengrocer, who knew me by name and often gave me, gratis, a basketful of back-of-the-store vegetables that were still usable but not quite salable, one day called out, "You're growing into a shrewd little thing, Rosie!"

I did not feel shrewd. I felt formal, even puritan. I had turned myself into a mad perfectionist. I lived by an inflexible schedule: school; homework; supper; and then, sometimes until midnight, ironing my father's shirts. My father had little to say about this change in our way of life. When I asked for grocery money, he silently handed over his wallet and let me take what I needed.

This skin of formality covered over my mannerisms and the pitch of my voice, and even the march of my sentences. I took over my father's typewriter and practiced typing with the help of a manual and became proficient—I was enamored of the methodical rows of letters. My speech was stilted. I had at that time been reading *Jane Eyre*, and admired the gravity and independence of a sad orphanhood. My own try at gravity and independence was a way of escaping the wilderness of my father's imagination. My goal was utter straightforwardness: it made me prim and smug. I fought chaos and sought symmetry, routine, propriety.

But it soon came clear that though I could make household order, I could not make order of my father's mind. One winter evening, without so much as a warning, my father's principal rang our doorbell and strode in, spraying snow.

"Now Jack," he said, "what's this about Euclid and the Hebrews?"

"We call the Mediterranean a sea," my father said, "which makes it sound insuperable. Better to think of it as a pond, yes?" It was his most serenely teacherly tone. "In ancient days the old sailing ships went back and forth and across, year in and year out, carrying more than goods for trade—"

"What in God's name," the principal roared, "did you tell your eleven o'clock geometry class this morning?"

My father continued mild. "I told them it wasn't merely goods that were traded. It was knowledge, information, education."

"What you told them was that King Solomon invented geometry!

You told them Euclid got it all from the Hebrews! From King Solomon!"

"It's perfectly possible," my father said. He was buoyant; he was thinking well of himself; he expected admiration if not confirmation. "All sorts of ideas traveled across the pond. Of course we can't be precisely certain of the timing—"

"Stick to the textbook! Stick to the problems in the text! Stick to the Pythagorean theorem! I tell you, Jack, pull something like this again, and you're out of a job."

This colloquy was unfolding in what passed for my father's "office"—his desk and chair in a corner of the foyer. I hid myself in the kitchen, huddled out of sight: I was in absolute fear. What if my father were really sent away? How would we survive? It seemed to me he was growing more and more reckless.

Three years later he was dismissed. King Solomon had nothing to do with it. I was then fourteen ("Fourteen years since my Jenny's gone"), and had almost finished my sophomore term in high school; the ignominy descended on both of us. Our school—Thrace Central High—was small. It served only our town, and a few students from the failed farms nearby, where old abandoned barns decayed on weedy miles of neglected land. Most of the farm people had long ago departed. Syracuse was to the north of us, Troy to the east, Carthage to the west. Our shabby Thrace, with its depressed Main Street, was the poorest of these nobly named upstate places. The others were more fortunate: Syracuse had its university, Troy its shirtmaking, Carthage its candy factory. Thrace had nothing of value—men out of work, or discouraged families on their way to Albany, looking for work. Most of the town boys tolerated no more than two years of high school; the girls went further. This annoyed my father. Girls, he said, though they were born to multiply, were incapable of doing mathematics; I was his prime example.

Thrace Central High employed only one other math teacher, a man who wore pocket handkerchiefs as if they were flags and flaunted three names: Austin Cockerill Doherty. He was unmarried and much younger than my father. The principal was impressed with him and thought him a superior teacher; my father took this as a preference and a slight and smarted over it. "I've got twice the brains," he said. He had chosen Austin Cockerill Doherty for an enemy, and dubbed him "the Tricolor," because of the bright handkerchiefs and the three names; and also because Doherty had inherited money and every year summered in the south of France. "That fellow's free as a bird," my father would mutter.

For some reason—my father believed the principal was behind it —all the available boys were assigned to Doherty's classes, while my father was left with the girls. This meant that his "load," as he called it (though sometimes this was transmuted into "my toad," which led to "my frog," and then "my hog," and finally "my pigs"), was three times heavier than Doherty's, and also, he claimed, three times stupider. His stupid pigs were all girls.

My father plotted his revenge and made me his accomplice. Now that I was in his school, we would—too often—run into each other during the day, which embarrassed us both. Usually, when I spotted my father heading in my direction, I would instantly change course and dart away. I hated it that my classmates might think me overprivileged, dangerous, in the camp of the enemy, because my father was a teacher. As for my father, he simply did not like to see me there.

But on this occasion, when we happened to pass in the corridor—it was late June, the last day of the semester—he whipped me aside and put a hand on my shoulder. His grip was hard. "Rosie," he said, "do me a favor, will you? I've got a curriculum meeting late this afternoon—got to sit in the same pew with the goddamn Tricolor, can't be helped. What I need you to do is go into the office and pull out the grade sheets for Doherty's Algebra 2-B. You'll find 'em right there in the file."

"You mean after school? Go in the office after school? But nobody's there, by then they've all gone home, it's all locked up."

"I'll give you the key. Just go in and get the stuff and take it home for me."

"If you've got the key, can't you get it yourself?"

"It has to be done while I'm in the meeting. So I won't be held responsible. Look here, Rosie," my father said, "it's *important*."

That night my father sat at his desk for two hours, comparing lists: his girls and the Tricolor's boys.

"You're not fiddling with Mr. Doherty's grades, are you?" I asked.

"Fiddling? What's fiddling? Of course I'm fiddling, can't you see? If those cretins in the office did what they're supposed to do, I wouldn't have to put in all this extra time, would I?"

"I mean tampering."

"Where'd you get an idea like that? I could get thrown out for that."

"Then what are you doing?"

"Improving my students, that's all. Giving the pigs their due."

It was my job to return Doherty's sheets to the file, again after the office staff had left; and then the term was over. Doherty sailed away for the summer, and I still did not know what my father had done.

What he had done (I learned this long afterward) was a cheater's dream. Whatever grades Doherty had set down for his boys, my father made sure his girls surpassed. He elevated every mark of every girl he taught. His aim was to mock the Tricolor and admonish the principal — to prove that a really fine teacher could take a roomful of sows' ears and turn them into silk purses. Despite stealth and theft, it was a harmless scheme. It pleased the girls, who thought they had performed better than they knew, and my father was certain there was no way he could be found out.

He was not found out. His dismissal came about because he had given passing grades in algebra and geometry — both of them necessary for graduation — to a student who had never set foot in either class.

I was that student.

"You can't go with the Tricolor," my father had announced early on. "Not in his class, no siree. I wouldn't give him the satisfaction. I've got a kid who can't do math? None of his business. And it's too goddamn awkward to have you in with me. Tell you what," he said. "I'll fix up the paperwork, no one'll ever know the difference. I'll slip you through the cracks, what d'you say?"

"But then I'll never know how to do algebra. Or geometry either."

"You'll never know how to do 'em anyhow, I guarantee you," my father said. "You can spend the time in study hall. You're big on reading, so you can go read in study hall. Don't worry about it. It's all bureaucracy, it's nothing but filling in the blanks. I'll take care of it." I must have looked wildly troubled—my whole head heated up—because he added, "I won't have you in with Doherty, and I can't have you in with me. So that's that, you understand?"

In this way I came to the end of my sophomore semester with a hole in my education. As he had predicted, it was simple enough for my father's deception to go undiscovered; and on my part, I was anyhow insulated from much of the life of the school. After classes, when the others went off to clubs or sports, I was on my way to the grocery store. I was mainly a watcher and a listener. No one invited me, and I invited no one. I felt apart; I felt the weight of the house and the mercurial weight of my father. For nearly two years, his fabricated records concerning my nonexistent math provoked no questions.

Yet finally he was brought down by an informer. It was my father's conviction that the informer was Austin Cockerill Doherty. With the friendliest smile, Doherty, to whom I had never spoken a word—and he had certainly never before addressed me—approached one morning and asked, "Aren't you one of those female math whizzes your dad manages to churn out?" My father took this to be a telling hint or a revengeful probe: it signaled that Doherty suspected I was not among my father's students; and since I was not among Doherty's, where could I be? But Doherty as informer seemed to me implausible. In my mind a more feasible candidate was Timmy's younger brother, who had grown out of his corduroy knickers and into a football uniform. He was—nominally—in my history class, always late, always inattentive. Sometimes he would get up out of his seat and swagger around the room, and on one of these excursions he stopped at my desk and whispered, "Come on, Rosie, how's about another birthday cake? I could get my ma to do you one in a minute." I thought his conspiratorial sneer less horrible than Doherty's ripened smile.

But these were speculations. We did not really know who had uncovered my father's crime; or how. The outcome was quick and not without mercy: my father was allowed to resign—but this, of course, was merely the language of dismissal. It was also the language of our humiliation. Soon afterward, my father sold our little house and moved us to Troy.

3

Troy in 1930 was larger and more attractive than Thrace. It had earned its thimbleful of fame through the manufacture of the detachable shirt collar; and because Ossip Gabrilowitsch, who was married to Mark Twain's daughter, had once conducted at the music hall, with Mark Twain himself in the audience. It was an excitable place, much given to religious stimulation: preachers came and went, sometimes performing miracles. A certain downtown street corner was admired as the site of an outdoor revival where, in 1903, a wooden pulpit had, all of its own accord, split in two, knocking the preacher unconscious. When he woke (according to the story, a fellow pietist spilled a bucket of ice water over his head), he claimed to have been "slain of the Lord," after which Troy had its portion of ecstatic fainters. The miraculously severed pulpit was kept on display in a local church.

Troy had its Jews, too—mainly immigrants who were brought straight from Castle Garden to work in the shirt factory. Newcomers summoned other freshly arrived relations; an uncle drew a nephew, a sister a sister-in-law. My father and I found ourselves living on the top floor, converted into an apartment, of a frame house abutting a rundown little building in what appeared to be an immigrant neighborhood. The building next door was a makeshift synagogue; it had once been a store. On Saturday mornings I stood at the window and watched the thin parade of worshipers heading there, mostly worn-looking young men in gray fedoras. Sometimes I could hear the singing, in a language I took to be Hebrew. Though I knew my father could read a little Hebrew, falteringly, and (he once admitted) had even gone through the bar mitzvah rite, he was indifferent. "I don't hold with it," he said. "I've got bigger troubles than worrying about who runs the universe." He was a stubborn atheist.

And by now I understood him to be a trickster. I saw that he was volatile and dangerously open to gratuitous impulse. He was, besides, innocent of cause and effect: he had believed that our move to a different town would mean an unblemished new beginning. Inevitably, the old events followed him. Because of his deception in Thrace, he was anathema in Troy. Teaching jobs were rare enough, and no principal would take him on. As for me, I was even more wretched in Troy than I had been in Thrace: again and again I was made to explain why, starting the junior year of high school, I was ineligible for trigonometry, having never been taught geometry. This led to a cumulative complication: while I was catching up on math, I was missing out on French. Consequently I was a year or two behind in one course or another, and was tossed into classes with students younger than myself. To me they seemed like little children; they had no fears. I watched the laughter and the horseplay with a melancholy so ingrained that it crept downward into my hands: often my palms were damp. I was afraid day and night. My father had joined the terrifying company of the unemployed.

He appealed finally to the man he called "our cousin Bertram," a name I had never heard him speak. Bertram, my father told me, was my mother's first cousin. He lived in Albany. He was a bachelor and a pharmacist; he worked in a hospital. Beyond these paltry items my father knew nothing about him; Bertram was a stranger. "But he might have some ideas," my father said, licking the stamp on his letter. "And he's a cousin, he owes it to me." I protested: how could a pharmacist get my father a job teaching math? As it turned out, Bertram knew a doctor in his hospital whose brother-in-law was the dean of Croft Hall, a boys' preparatory academy just outside Troy. It was nothing more than a private high school run on British mimicry; it was set among green lawns, with an artificial castle at its center.

No one at Croft Hall cared about my father's old transgressions; no one asked; what was needed—and right away—was a math teacher to replace a malcontent who had fled in the middle of the term. Overnight my father became a "master." He was delighted with his new status. The pay was low, considerably less than his salary in Thrace, but the boys were rich. They had vast allowances and were accustomed to tip the masters; on weekends they went off to Saratoga to bet on the horses. They concentrated on the crease in their trousers and were particular about the shape of their collars. My father acquired a second-hand car and drove every day to the castle and its lawns; after a time he began to drive some of the younger boys to Saratoga on Saturday afternoons. One evening he came home jubilating, clutching a roll of bills. It was three hundred dollars; I assumed he had won it at the track. "Nah," he said, "I got it off an upper-form kid. Wilson. A poker fiend, his mother's married to that German, Von Something, some kind of baron."

Bertram, our cousin in Albany, had saved us.

Toward the end of my last semester of high school—we had been in Troy nearly twenty-one months—my father divulged a new plan: "I'm getting out of this Yid place—just you watch me skedaddle." The headmaster, he said, had ruled against masters who commuted: there was too much disorder, more men were required to be on the spot, especially at night, to keep an eye out for mischief. There were rumors of boys gambling right on the property.

"Inviting the fox in to guard the chicken coop," my father chuckled.

"You'd better be careful," I said.

"It's high society over there," he said. "What do *you* know about it?"

In the fall my father was designated housemaster of Croft Hall's third form, and went to live in the fake castle; and I departed for Albany, where I moved in with my cousin Bertram.

4

FOR A LONG WHILE it was not clear to me why Bertram had taken me in. Sometimes I thought my father had reverted to his old habits and had arranged for a barter: housekeeping in exchange for lodging. Unlike my father, though, Bertram was orderly and self-sufficient; he kept a handkerchief in his breast pocket and wore dandyish suspenders. He was almost too fastidious, and never left a dish on the table for more than five minutes before he got up to wash it. His shirts were picked up by a laundry van, and the neighborhood storekeepers delivered bread and milk and vegetables and cheese. Bertram was skilled at making omelets. There was almost nothing for me to do, and if there was, Bertram would not allow me to do it.

"Go work on your Chaucer," he would say. This was a bit of comradely mockery. Chaucer had no place in my misshapen little college; literature, except for the pedagogical kind, was hardly wanted there. I had dreamt of Gothic arches and the worn flagstones of old libraries — where such a grand yearning came from, I hardly knew. Unaccountably, my heart was set on Smith or Vassar or Bryn Mawr; I imagined afternoon teas, and white gloves, and burning lips (mine, perhaps) murmuring out of a book. But all that was wistfulness — there was no money for such romantic hopes, and my patchy record in high school, my father warned, would never have won me a scholarship. I was only an average girl from Thrace Central, what was I thinking of? The right spot for me, he said, if I expected to earn my way, if he was ever going to get me off his hands, was Albany Teachers' College. He couldn't afford to keep me in the dorms, and anyhow they were famous for resembling dungeons. With luck he might manage to talk cousin Bertram into putting me up. "Makes sense, doesn't it?" he said.

I hated that college. There were classes in pedagogy and psychology and "early childhood and adolescence": these were taught like the tenets of a cult. I did not believe in any of them. I had no interest in becoming a teacher. I had observed enough of my father's predicaments to want to flee any reminder of schools. What I cared about was reading novels.

Bertram lived on the ninth floor of a modern apartment building, with fire escapes jutting from the window ledges. I discovered that if I climbed out and stood on our own fire escape—a kind of latticed metal balcony—I could just see the roof of the State House. This was impressive; it was a glimpse of history, of law; there was gravity in it. Sometimes, when Bertram was away, I sat on the windowsill, with my legs stretched along the cool slats of the fire escape, and smelled the rain. Albany rain was different. It smelled of excitement.

Bertram was away much of the time. Hospital shifts went halfway around the clock, and pharmacy hours conformed. Often he came home when I was already asleep. And once I was not asleep—I lay dozing, vaguely dazed: how had I arrived in this bed, in this room, in Bertram's big flat? I had a bedroom to myself, with a dressing alcove (Bertram had put a desk and a typewriter in there, and turned it into a tiny study), and my own bathroom. When my father forgot to pay my first quarter's tuition, Bertram instantly sent a check to the college bursar. I was certain my father had not forgotten; Saratoga, or poker with Wilson, had cleaned him out.

Bertram was quietly loitering at the partly open door of my room. I heard him breathing, and wondered whether he was listening for my own breathing. There was something maternal about his standing there, and I wanted to call out; I wanted to ask, out of the darkness, whether it was true that my mother had died in childbirth. But I held back. Bertram was my mother's cousin, though not as my father had made me understand this: he was not a cousin by blood. Instead he was a cousin to my mother's first cousin; it was a tenuous in-law connection. Laughing, Bertram had worked it out for me—he was the son of my mother's aunt's husband's sister. He was not really a relation. He had never known my mother. He had no stories to tell. But when, some days afterward, I confided my phantom memory—my mother lying on a couch and holding a rag doll—Bertram said, "That's what you should trust."

"My father says it's a hallucination. A wish-dream."

"That's why you should trust it. The world doesn't get better without wishes."

"My father doesn't care about the world." I thought of him crouching behind a closed door at Croft Hall, clandestinely gambling with his pupils.

Bertram said mildly, "Well, maybe you'll make up for him."

It was not only his work at the hospital that occupied Bertram's nights. He went to weekly meetings and occasionally to what he called "rallies," after which he was hoarse for days; sometimes he stood on picket lines. He was thinking, he said, of joining the Party, but he was still unsure. "It takes your whole life," he explained, "and I may not be able to give it the time. Got to pay the landlord. But they're on the right track, those people." I asked what the right track was; this made him smile. I had seen the half-turn of that smile before. It meant that he thought me as innocent as a savage.

"First we're going to abolish rent," he said, "and after that tuition. Shelter and education for everyone." Again the twist of a smile: Bertram was not above self-parody. "To each according to his need. That's how the poet puts it."

At that instant I discovered why he had let me come and live with him. It was because of my need. Or, at any rate, my father's.

Bertram was thirty-six. He had once been married, a dozen years ago, but she—he never said "my wife"—had left him after only two years. "She didn't like me," he told me; he never said her name. "I suppose I was too short." I could not imagine not liking Bertram, or finding him unbeautiful. He was not much taller than I, but his head was large, with crescents of unshorn brown curls sticking up from around his neck and ears. "Got to get a haircut," he would say. Or else: "Beginning to look like Karl Marx or Jesus Christ, take your pick." Or else, when he was actually on his way to the barber shop, "Goddamn hospital rules. Bad enough they dress me up in a white coat, like a dogcatcher."

Now and then he said, "Put the chain on the door, will you? Won't be home at all tonight, got a date."

I was seventeen and stabbed by jealousy. My jealousy felt literally like a stab: it resembled the quick pain I would sometimes feel in my groin on the left side, just before my period. Bertram did not hide from me that he had a sex life (his words). Toward me he was affectionate and perfectly chaste: his kiss touched my forehead or my cheek, or, comically, my nose. But he worried about appearances. "Honor is the appearance of honor," he recited. "I read that somewhere. So look, if anyone ever asks, you tell them you're my little sister away from home to go to school. Half of it's true anyhow. But don't say cousins. Nobody believes cousins."

When my father again neglected to send the money for my tuition on time, Bertram said, "There's no point to it, your pa's out of the picture, so never mind. From now on I'll take care of it. A dollar goes a long way these days. Trouble is," he added, "you've got to have the dollar." In my eyes Bertram seemed rich. I marveled that his apartment had a dining room with a glass breakfront and a spacious square table covered by a lace cloth. There were six carved mahogany chairs with green leather seats. All this heavy furniture, Bertram told me, had belonged to his mother. She had left him the dining set, her wedding ring, and his father's considerable life insurance. "I've got some leeway," he said. "You could even say I'm in the money, so don't worry about your pa's not coming through. It's hard times."

Bertram often spoke of hard times. His two themes were the Depression and what he called "the reformation of society." The hospital sweepers were agitating for a union, but more than half of them were afraid to strike. Bertram went out with the strikers. "Have a look at this," he urged me one evening—he was heading for a rally—and handed me a copy of *The Communist Manifesto*. It was a thin little thing, with a pale pink cover.

The next morning he asked me what I had made of it.

"It's like a hymn. A psalm."

"You could think of it as architecture. A blueprint."

"Oh, I don't know," I said. It was true that I did not know; what I knew was that I had been brought up to cynicism. I was not easily inspired or moved.

Bertram's head moved me—the brown ringlets rising straight out of his temples like a waterfall in reverse, the line of his nose with its gradual change of course, the virtuous motherly mouth. At times he caught me looking at him; this disconcerted him. "Hey, you're a kid," he would say. In my classes at the college I shut out the droning assault of lectures—Dewey, Pestalozzi, Montessori, Piaget, how to write a lesson plan—and filled the back pages of my notebook with Bertram's name, scrupulously inscribed over and over again. At night in my bed I shredded his name into mental anagrams, and the next day set them down: *at, am, are, ram, mar, tram, mart, tame, rate, mate, meat, eat, beat, rare, tear, bear, mare, bet, bat, tab, rat, ream, beam, team, art, tar, rear, tare, brat, bare, tea, me, be, ear, term, berm.* It struck me that some magical syllable might be hidden among the letters—a hint, an illumination.

I wanted Bertram's kiss to land just once, even if unintentionally, on my lips.

"What's this?" he said. He had found the paper with the anagrams. I had left it on the dining room table. "Berm? Tare? Is this some sort of test? Something from your psych class?"

"It's everything that comes out of Bertram," I said. "All the words."

"How about that. Rosie, I told you, to me you're a kid."

After that he began bringing his girlfriends home to supper. Sometimes all three of us would walk over to a nearby movie house, I feeling sullen and stifled, Bertram with his arm around whoever his date happened to be. Later he and the woman would march me back, right to the door of Bertram's flat, where the two of them would leave me. Once again I was alone for the night. "Remember to put the chain on," Bertram would remind me. He had a fear of break-ins. It was hard times, he said, not human nature, that promoted thievery.

Bertram thought well of human nature. The women he brought home did not. These were always women he met at rallies, or on picket lines; they all had short black or brown hair and fiery tongues given to malice. Most wore thick lisle stockings stuffed, whatever the weather, into thonged sandals. One dangled long earrings made of shells that clattered; another had nearly identical earrings, but arrived in work shoes and men's trousers. They were like no women I had ever known. They were zealots; they argued and theorized and wept with enthusiasm. I did not understand their talk, wave after wave of Bukharin, Lenin, Trotsky, Budenny, Stalin, Ehrenburg. They disputed over skirmishes, kulaks, trials, solidarity, scabs. I could not tell one alien phrase from an-other. It was not how Bertram talked or thought. In his dreamy water-color way, Bertram spoke of poverty abolished, the lion lying down with the lamb, the hopes of mankind: it was like a painting on the wall. You could contemplate it or you could ignore it. But these fierce political women spoke of men, living men, whom they despised and would gladly have torn to pieces. Bertram admired their rages and excitements, but I was afraid of them—of their clipped hair, the forwardness of their dress, their hot familiarity with far-away crises, their blurting passion. They were angry and omniscient. It seemed to me that they were in command of the age.

The woman who wore the shell earrings and dressed like a man (oc-casionally she turned up in overalls) was called Ninel. It was not her real name; it was a Party name, in honor of Lenin. "Just try spelling it back-ward," Bertram told me, grinning. Ninel enchanted him; the play of her name enchanted him, and I was stung: he had disliked my search for a secret signal in the letters of his own name. Yet Ninel had done the same, and it pleased him. Even Ninel's big work shoes and clumsy worsted pants with the zipper in front pleased and amused him.

Ninel disapproved of Bertram's flat. If she saw that I had already set the dishes out on the dining room table, it made no difference, we had to move back into the kitchen to eat. Bertram's mother's furniture sickened her: that china-closet thing with the glass doors, she said, whatever it had cost, could feed a famine. She asked Bertram how he could stand to live with it. With Ninel we never went to the movies. She was scornful of stories told by shadows. She maintained that movies were the new church, a diversion for the masses; she was too serious; she was combat-ive. Whenever Ninel came, I ate quickly and ran to hide in my little study with my book: Emma and Mr. Knightly were soon to unite. "Don't you see the *point*, Bert?" I would hear Ninel growl. I had chosen Bertram to be my own Mr. Knightly; instead he was being led away from his proper Emma by a woman who was conducting a revolution in his kitchen. "It's all about exploitation, however you want to look at it."

It turned out that they were arguing about Croft Hall. "You got the kid's father a job at a place like that? What were you *thinking?*"

"The man was out of work, and I knew this fellow at the hospital who had a connection over there. It seemed the right thing. Her father's a math teacher, where else could he go?"

"In this system he could go out and dig ditches, that's what. A decent government would provide something."

"Ninel, the fellow was in trouble, and he had the girl—"

"To keep a place like that in business! It's just a contamination. Posh kids, offspring of the oligarchy. They're being trained to exploit, that's all. A cadet corps for the banks. Schools like that should be burned to the ground."

Gradually the other women Bertram had been bringing home vanished. Now it was only Ninel. One night during our meal I asked her what her real name was. She hooked her thumbs into the loops of her woven-straw belt and blew out a sigh of disgust. "Miriam," she told me, "but don't you ever dare use it." This was hardly likely; we rarely had anything to say to each other. Her eye went ferociously to my book. "Jane Austen, wouldn't you know. Now that's what I call a provocation. Do you realize," she demanded, "how the servants in those big houses *lived?* The hours they had to put in, the paltry wages they got? Chicken-feed! And where the money to keep up those mansions *came* from? From plantations in the Caribbean run on the broken backs of Negro slaves!" It was as if she was leading a meeting.

"Mr. Knightly doesn't have a plantation," I said.

"What do you think the British Empire is? The whole *thing's* a plantation! The whole kit and caboodle!"

Bertram said quietly, "You should listen to Ninel, Rosie. She's right about that."

Ninel was angry at Jane Austen not only on account of the British Empire—she was angry at all novels. Novels, like movies, were pretend-shadows; they failed to diagnose the world as it was in reality. "Crutches," she said, "distractions. And meanwhile the moneybags and the corporate dogs eat up the poor." For Ninel, the only invention worse than novels and movies was religion. She hated her given name because it came out of the Bible. She railed against all varieties of worship. "If you want to get the real lowdown on, okay, let's take Christian-

ity," she urged, "try this out. You're a believing Christian of the twentieth century and you're transported by time machine back into ancient
Rome. You're walking around the main squares and it's all pretty impressive. Big marble cathedrals with columns. Huge statues all over the
place, and folks crowding into the temples, genuflecting and bringing
offerings. Plenty of priests and acolytes in fancy dress, the whole society
rests on this spectacular stuff. And then you ask what's behind it, what's
it all about. You sit down with a couple of these ancient Romans and
they start telling you it's Jupiter, the god who lives up in the sky and
runs the world. And you think, Jupiter? Jupiter? What's Jupiter? There
isn't any Jupiter, it's all imagination, it's all some made-up idea. You
know damn well that this sacred Jupiter that everyone's so devoted to,
that everyone's dependent on, that everyone praises and carries on
about, and writes epics and treatises and holy books about, and mutters
prayers to . . . you know damn well that their Jupiter is air, their Jupiter
is a phantom, there isn't any Jupiter, no Jupiter of any kind, the whole
religion's a sham and a fake and a delusion, no matter how many poets
and intellectuals adhere to it, no matter how many thrills and epipha-
nies people get out of it. Then you come back to the twentieth century,
and what you've seen and understood doesn't mean a thing, you're
blind as a bat, you figure you've got the goods on Jupiter but Jesus is
different, Jesus is for real, Jupiter is a vast communal lie but Jesus is a
vast transcendent truth. . . ."

Bertram was standing at the stove, heating up the kettle for tea. He
gave a pleasurable little chirp and poured the water into our cups. "Well,
now you've heard one of Ninel's flights. You don't run into talk like that
every day, it doesn't grow on trees."

Bertram, I was beginning to see, was intending to marry Ninel.

In the morning he denied it. "Not possible."

"But you want to," I said.

"What I want doesn't count. Ninel doesn't believe in marriage.
She's against it on principle."

Ninel was with us on a night in early March when Bertram opened
the door to a seedy fellow in uniform and cap. Bertram gave him a quarter, and the man handed him a yellow envelope. It was a telegram from

the dean at Croft Hall. My father had broken the rules: he had taken a group of four third-formers to Saratoga in his car. One boy sat in the front seat next to my father. The other three were in the rear. It was dusk when they headed back to school. A hard rain, propelled by a hard wind, hastened the dark and pelted the road. They drove through swiftly forming lakes, one of which concealed the heavy branch of a middle-sized fallen tree. The wheels, spinning through the black water, struck the branch; the car was brutally flung on its side. The windshield splashed out a fountain of glass splinters and two of the doors were crushed. The three boys in the back seat survived. My father and the boy nearest him were dead.

There was no funeral. My father was in posthumous disgrace; the dead child's parents called him a murderer. Bertram arranged for the burial with an undertaker in Troy, and with no ceremony at all my father's remains were dispatched. A week later the mail brought a package from Croft Hall: it was a box containing my father's papers. In it I found my mother's death certificate and a hospital bill dated February 15, 1921 —they were folded into the pages of a ragged children's book. Now there was proof: my mother had not died in childbirth. She had succumbed to blood cancer when I was three years old. Lena's disclosure, and my memory of the sofa and the rag doll, were vindicated.

I kept almost none of these papers. They were impersonal and faintly shaming—old grade books, wrinkled lottery tickets, racetrack stubs, a dirty pack of cards, two pairs of scratched dice. Not a single item hinted at my existence. I did not recognize the children's book as mine, though I knew its fame; it was the first of a well-known series. A pair of nearly new shoes was in the box; I wondered when my father had acquired these. They were not the kind of shoes he usually wore. An inscription on the inside of the heel read HAND-MADE IN LONDON. I imagined something horrible: had he thrown dice for them, had he won them from one of the bigger boys, had he taken them in lieu of cash? I was relieved when Bertram carried them away and gave them to an orderly.

It was Bertram's idea that I should compose a phrase or two for a headstone. On Bertram's typewriter I wrote:

JACOB NEHEMIAH MEADOWS

1887–1935

LOVING FATHER

FRIEND TO YOUTH

Words as conventionally sentimental as these ought to have scandalized me as I set them down, but the irony of their falseness did not touch me. It seemed right to attribute plain virtue to a man whose miniature vices could no longer do harm. I thought of my father's small life, and of Lena and the birthday cake, and the Tricolor, and my father's gambling. Most of all I thought of his lies. His lies took aim but had no point; they seduced risk; they were theatrical, though enacted on a tiny stage for a tiny audience. My father had been a kind of daylight robber. He robbed dailiness of predictability, so that my childhood's every breath hung on a contingency. Living with him had never felt safe.

In another three months my first year at the college would be over. In the classroom I sat self-enclosed, in a mist of indifference. Or else I recoiled. All those theories of pedagogy, I told myself, were no better than a shrine streaming with phantasmagoria. An alien faith, like Ninel's Jupiter. Its liturgy and rites were abhorrent, and whatever was declared to be truth was fakery. . . . But I knew I was only bored.

I was afraid to confide any of this in Bertram. My private wish was to abandon the college altogether. I had already seen Bertram send off my third quarter's tuition: I was obligated to him. I was, in a sense, his ward, as in those old English novels I was reading night after night, Dickens and Trollope and George Eliot, one after another.

Bertram picked up *Middlemarch* and opened to an illustration of Dorothea and Casaubon. Casaubon sat cramped with his candle, ringed by a heap of fly-specked books. Dorothea's finely molded neck arched backward. "Dorothea resists Casaubon," the caption read.

"Tell you what," Bertram began, "how would you like to move into the dorms for the rest of the term?"

"The dorms? You mean live at the college?"

"Sure. It's not that much extra, I can swing it. Then you wouldn't be alone so much of the time. You'd be with people your own age."

"My father said they're like dungeons."

"Oh come on," Ninel said, "from what Bert's told me your father never so much as set foot over there. He never even *saw* those dorms, he just didn't want to pay the fees."

Then I understood that Ninel meant to drive me out of Bertram's life.

This made me brazen. It made me rough. "Did you decide?" I asked Bertram. "About the Party, about joining?"

He twisted up his little smile; he hardly minded. But the smile was for Ninel. "Well, you can't hang around Ninel and not end up committed."

"But Ninel isn't committed to *you*. She won't marry you."

"Oh for Pete's sake," Ninel said.

"It's only an empty figment, Rosie. A piece of paper."

"Mumbo jumbo," Ninel said.

"Look," Bertram said, "we've got to figure out some sort of new arrangement—"

"It's already figured out," Ninel broke in. "Bert's selling the furniture and moving in with me. It doesn't make sense these days to keep up a big place like this, all full of monstrosities."

That night I answered Professor Rudolf Mitwisser's advertisement in the Albany *Star*.

And that same night—as a reward, I thought, for my promised departure—Bertram came into my bedroom, put his knee on my bed, and kissed me, for the first time, fully on the mouth. The pressure on my lower lip was heavy, painful, voluptuous. I felt I was being bitten.

In this way I was expelled from Albany's obscure and diminutive radical pocket.

5

EVEN AFTER two entire weeks, my position in the Mitwisser household remained amorphous. I could not fathom what my obligations were, and if I attempted to ask, the answer was dissolved in chaos. "Just fill those boxes with papa's books," the oldest child ordered. Her name was Anneliese; she spoke good English—she spoke it casually, familiarly—though with a distinct accent. Except for the youngest, all the children had been enrolled, for some months now, in the Albany public schools, and (so Mrs. Mitwisser had intimated that first day) they had had a tutor besides. They had already acquired a patina of the local vernacular. It was several days before I could arrive at exactly how many Mitwisser children there were. They rushed around on this or that mission (the whole house was packing for the move to New York); it was like trying to identify the number of fish swimming in a pond. At first I counted six, then four—the actual total was five. Their names were so many bird-chirps whirling around me: Anneliese, Heinrich, Gerhardt, Wilhelm, Waltraut. Waltraut was the easiest to remember, a round-eyed, curly-haired girl of three, who would cling to whoever happened to be passing by. Mrs. Mitwisser (I tried on occasion to call her Frau Mitwisser) was not often seen. She was hidden in a bedroom upstairs and appeared to have little to do with the fierce activity all around.

I could not distinguish Heinrich from Wilhelm, or Gerhardt from Heinrich. This was made all the more difficult because now and then they addressed one another as Hank, Bill, and Jerry, and then would rapidly switch back to Heinz, Willi, and Gert. "Papa doesn't like it when they do that," Anneliese instructed me. "Papa is a purist." Anneliese was sixteen, and regal. It came to me that it could not have been Anneliese who had jumped from the *Kleiderschrank* and loosened the ceiling plaster down below. She was tall, an inheritance from her father, and like him she gave out a formal strictness. She was hardly like a child at all; her hair was wound in braids on either side of her head, revealing tidy pink ears. In each lobe a bright dot glittered. Braided and earringed, she looked authoritative and amazingly foreign. She was almost formidable, and the three boys seemed more afraid of her than of their mother. They obeyed Professor Mitwisser, and they obeyed Anneliese. But when Mrs. Mitwisser appealed to them—usually it was to beg them to take charge of Waltraut—they laughed and ran away. "American savages!" Professor Mitwisser roared at them. "*Rote Indianer!*"

I too was careful to obey Anneliese. I felt my fate was in her hands: she alone, so far, had troubled to acknowledge my status as more than an intruder. The three boys never spoke to me, nor I to them. They flew past me, heaving bundles into the vestibule, where a growing mound of objects awaited the movers. But my dependence on Anneliese went beyond her occasional command. She was the sole source of my understanding, incomplete as it was, of the annals of her family. I was startled to learn that timid Mrs. Mitwisser, whose eyelids were so red, and whose thin nostrils trembled like a rabbit's, had held a senior fellowship at the Kaiser Wilhelm Institute in Berlin.

"They threw her out," Anneliese explained, "and they threw papa out of the University. The Quakers brought us over, that's why we're here. Mama says they saved us. Papa says sometimes mama acts as if she doesn't like being saved. But anyhow there was a mistake."

The mistake was comical. In their good-hearted intent to rescue a family of refugees, the Board of the Hudson Valley Friends College had requested its provost to invite Professor Rudolf Mitwisser, the well-known German specialist in the history of religion, to teach several seminars on the Charismites, a sixteenth-century mystical Christian sect, an offshoot of the Pneuma Brethren of northeastern Bavaria. The Board, businessmen mainly, had confused the Charismites—famous for their emphasis on the Spirit Within, akin to the Friends' Inner Light—with the Karaites.

I asked Anneliese who the Karaites were.

"Oh, they're just papa's people. But it didn't matter about the mistake, the Board got us out and gave papa the job. He didn't mind about the Charismites. And they rented this house for us. Here, look, I sent Gerhardt for the rope you're going to need."

She handed me a scissors and a rough hairy coil. I had been packing books all that day, as she had directed me to do. There were thirty-two boxes filled with Professor Mitwisser's strange indecipherable volumes, and in order to cram as many books as possible into each container I had arranged them in rows and towers, meticulously, according to their sizes and shapes. The rope scored and burned my palms as I tied the boxes shut.

Half an hour later Anneliese informed me that her father was not pleased, and after a moment he arrived to tell me so himself. His hands, with their great workman's thumbs, were soot-blackened. He had been sorting papers stored in the coal bin, he said; his eyebrows stood up furiously, like a forest of sooty straws.

"Why am I interrupted by such nonsense? Anneliese! This is how an intelligent creature organizes scholarship? By how tall and how short?"

I protested, "I had to make the books fit in the boxes."

"They must fit by idea, by logic. Ach, what cataclysm, what foolishness. You disrupt an entire library, Fräulein! And you, Anneliese, you permitted this?"

I was helpless: the books were in German and in what I supposed was Hebrew. There were other languages I could not recognize. I saw then that it would not always be safe to take orders from Anneliese; she was not above falling into error and disgrace.

"Anneliese," Mitwisser growled, "you must undo the boxes and begin again. Give to Fräulein Meadows a simpler task, one that she will not make into a wilderness."

This was how Waltraut came into my care; I was to be a nanny, after all. She was a compliant and affectionate child, and quickly grew attached to me. She chattered in her infantile German and seemed to think I comprehended; at the same time she showed signs of absorbing whatever I said to her. I had little feeling for her, though I was captivated by the interplay of our two languages, both expressed in the most primitive argot. Waltraut had her small charms—her frequent smile disclosed tiny square teeth shining with baby-spittle, and if she ever refused any direction from me, she would squeal out a soprano "*Nein!*" with a teasing slanted look that signaled eventual consent. I spent my days—these were the few days left before the move to New York—feeding and entertaining her and putting her to bed at night. I took her for neighborhood walks, and discovered a nearby playground, long deserted, behind an abandoned garage. The metal swings were rusty and the slides were filthy and impassable, clogged with mud and leaves and, inexplicably, several pairs of badly torn men's socks stiffened by weather. I assumed this place was a tramps' lair; there was an iron barrel lying on its side, with scarred evidences of old fires. Waltraut scampered here and there, poking in the weeds with a stick and swatting at the creaky swings to set them going, while I suffered from the tedium of observing her. It was a familiar tedium: this was the "early childhood" knowledge promised by all those chapters on Pestalozzi and Montessori. Waltraut was the future I had run from—she was what the Albany Teachers' College might have made of me. I was relieved to bring her home to her supper and her bath; but I dreaded the strained ritual of her mother's bedroom.

Waltraut slept in a low crib several feet from Mrs. Mitwisser's narrow couch. The crib would soon be hauled into a van, but the couch (it was not a bed) belonged to the house, like nearly all the furniture, and would remain behind. What I saw each evening when I carried Waltraut, already half asleep, into her crib, was Mrs. Mitwisser hunched on her couch, in the shape of a crescent, with a tray of partly eaten food on the floor beside her.

"Frau Mitwisser? Here's Waltraut to say goodnight."

She sucked in a wisp of breath, as if sipping some noxious fume, and raised a dismissive hand, drifting it like a curled leaf to a spot under her chin. Her gaze was inward. I thought she might be looking into the past. And I wondered whether, when the move was accomplished and we were finally settled in New York, she would resume sleeping in her husband's bed.

6

AT NIGHT I had a couch of my own: the dilapidated sofa in the parlor. The little side-table next to it was now bare—the old photograph in its silver frame had been taken away. Each day another domestic item joined the massive heap in the vestibule: the scenes that had seemed indelible to me at first sight—the arrangements of this dim cramped room especially—were being, particle by particle, erased. But the emptied table was useful: on it I set one of my two suitcases. The second, out of which I daily drew what I needed—it was clothes closet and toiletries shelf combined—I kept open on the thin carpet. Everything I owned was in those suitcases, and I did not own much. Before leaving Bertram I had disposed of all my school papers. Ninel took the fifteen or twenty textbooks Bertram had paid for and gave them to the Salvation Army, which struck even Bertram as perverse—but Ninel said they would be shredded and pulped and turned into something worthier than the psychological trash they were to begin with. (And for once I agreed with her.)

My suitcases held only the sparest handful of the books I valued, since it had always been my habit—privately I felt it to be an ecstasy—to enter, as into a mysterious vault, any public library. I was drawn to books that had been read before, novels that girls like myself (only their mothers would not have died) had cradled and cherished. In my mind—I suppose in my isolation—I seized on all those previous readers, and everyone who would read after me, as phantom companions and secret friends. The unprepossessing library in Thrace had itself been secretive, the habitat of frosty ghosts: there were darkened passages between the stacks, unaccountably cool, even cold, in summer. Troy's library loomed far larger, a white-columned Roman-style limestone edifice, brazenly civic; I had hardly lived there long enough to become intimate with it. And during my life with Bertram we had often passed, on our way to the movies, and before the reign of Ninel, the old brown Carnegie library that was a two-block walk from Bertram's apartment—but by now, I surmised, he was no longer there, and the library, like Bertram, was lost to me.

The morning of my departure, as I was filling my suitcases, Bertram quietly put into a corner of one of them a long blue envelope. He squashed it in beside the tattered storybook I had discovered in the carton they had sent from Croft Hall; the hospital bill and my mother's death certificate were still inside its torn covers.

"This was going to take care of next year's tuition," Bertram explained, "so it's yours anyhow."

I opened the blue envelope and looked in: he had given me five hundred dollars. It was clear that Ninel was not to know.

"And these are from Ninel. She picked them up from the Salvation Army last time she was down there. It's where she gets her clothes." He screwed up the wistful torque of his half-smile and handed me two books; they smelled of cellar. "She says she's read the Dickens, and it's not half bad, but she wouldn't touch the other with a ten-foot pole. Says it might as well be called *Vanity and Inanity*." Bertram was pleased with Ninel's joke; I saw that he believed the war between Ninel and me was over.

And it was. I was certain that I would never see the two of them again. I shoved *Sense and Sensibility* and *Hard Times* down among my slips and underpants. I had read them both long ago, and understood that Ninel regarded the one as an affront to herself and as a reprimand to me, and the other as a stern endorsement (in sugar-pill form) of her own insurgent outlook. My small store had nearly doubled. I had kept the unwieldy compendium of seventeenth-century Dutch paintings I had won for writing the best eighth-grade composition at Thrace Elementary ("But can you add two and two?" my father had remarked on that occasion); and also the pale little *Manifesto* Bertram had pressed on me; and here were Ninel's parting shots. Besides these and a dictionary, I had only the old-fashioned children's book my father had strangely preserved.

A meager cache; and then I was engulfed by an oceanic library of negation and mutiny, volume upon esoteric volume, a limitless kingdom of books—not one of which I could penetrate. The libraries of Thrace and of Troy, the weathered Carnegie brownstone of Albany, and even the fabled library at Alexandria, burned to the ground two thousand years before, could not have imagined what lay in Professor Rudolf Mitwisser's boxes.

7

THE DAY OF THE MOVE brought relentless rain. The household was up early; breakfast was scanty and cold, since the kettle had been packed and the ice for the icebox canceled. Professor Mitwisser could be heard upstairs, pleading with Mrs. Mitwisser to put on her street clothes. The plan was for all of us to go by train, while the van containing the Mitwisser possessions proceeded on its own. Anneliese was preoccupied with shouting orders to the boys, who ran upstairs and down, saying goodbye to the house. There was one last jump from the *Kleiderschrank* —shrieks from Anneliese, and "*Indianer!*" from Professor Mitwisser— and another shower of plaster chips over the parlor sofa, where I had lain sleepless most of the night, rehearsing every uncertainty I could think of. Leaving Albany, where at least there had been Bertram, felt obscurely unsafe.

The boys dashing here and there, the four wiry moving men appearing and disappearing on their route to the van and back again, the thumps and bumps of the heavier articles, the odd small cries of resistance bleated out by Mrs. Mitwisser as she came down the stairs carrying her shoes (which she was refusing to wear), had transformed mild little Waltraut into a frantic creature. She butted Anneliese like an angry goat; she ran after the boys, yowling.

"Get her out of the way," Anneliese commanded.

"But it's pouring. And all her things to play with are in the van."

"Do something this minute, or papa will come."

I caught Waltraut in the middle of a lurch and lifted her by the waist and tossed her on my sofa. She was panting furiously, like a dog after a chase. Half a chocolate bar was in my pocket; I gave it to her. Her black eyes swam with pleasure.

"There you are. Now you can be civilized again."

"*Nein*," Waltraut said.

"I'll show you something if you're good." But I could not think what.

"*Nein*"—mechanically: she was attending to the chocolate.

"I know! I've got a nice old storybook. There might be a bear in it," and Waltraut said nothing, because when I said "bear" she heard "*Bär*," and was all at once interested. I sat her on my lap and reached into the open suitcase on the floor and drew out the book that was my only inheritance, hoping for pictures of bears; but just then one of the boys rushed in to accuse me of malfeasance.

"You've got one left, they have to take it now! They have to take all the luggage now, they're leaving!"

"This one's coming on the train with me," I said. "They've already got the other."

"It's too big for the train."

"It's light enough. Now which one are you? Heinrich, isn't it?"

"Willi."

"*Bär*," Waltraut reminded me.

Willi stared. "How funny you have that."

"Have what?"

"That story."

"Do you know it?"

"We used to read it all the time at home. When we were little."

"You mean over there, in Germany? You read it in German?"

"At home it's famous for little children. When we came he was our tutor. They rented him for us."

"*Bär!*" Waltraut insisted.

"Hired," I corrected, searching for some sense.

"He gave us English lessons, Gert and Heinz and me. Anneliese only a little bit, she could speak already."

"Who was it gave you lessons?"

"The boy from the story, only he wasn't anymore a boy."

"Willi!" Anneliese called. "Where are you? Papa wants you." She came into the parlor; her face was very red. "What are you doing here?

You have to help look for mama's shoes, she hid them someplace." To me she said, "What have you done to Waltraut? She puts mud in her hair. And her hands!"

"It's chocolate," I said.

"*Lieber Gott.* Clean her up, please. The taxi is here, if we don't go now we miss the train."

8

THE NEW YORK we came to was hardly the New York I had expected. I was disappointed and astonished. I knew the city only from picture postcards and the movies, and in the movies (no one ever said "film" in those years) the opening scenes of airy skyscrapers and streaming crowds were always accompanied by syncopations of ascending horns and jazzy excitements. To me, and to all the world, New York was the peopled channels of Manhattan, and tall skies where no birds flew. And hadn't Mrs. Mitwisser, in that distracted attempt at an interview, hinted that the very point of the move to New York was her husband's wish to be near "the big library"? The big library of New York was on Fifth Avenue in Manhattan, fronted by two stone lions, like some Venetian palace. I had seen photographs of it.

The place we settled in had no big library. It had no library at all; it had nothing. Compared to Albany—or Troy, or even Thrace—it was an obscure little village in a remote corner of the sparse and weedy northeast Bronx. Strictly speaking, the Bronx was New York, or at least an official part of it; but I felt deceived. The subway line had only recently crawled to this huddle of small houses hemmed in by swamp and creek—and yet there was, despite the name, no subway either: rather, a raucous elevated track that further darkened the fly-specked stores below, and finally nosed its way underground toward Manhattan only after what seemed scores of miles. The true New York was far away. Infrequent trains—toys high up on a trestle—were our only conduit to the promised city. Where were we really? A modest bay flowing in from Long Island Sound, with a ragged fringe of mud and sand and seaweed-mantled rock, defined a neighborhood ringed by open fields: beyond the city's caring, and out of its sight. Here were uncombed meadows purpled and gilded by violets and dandelions, and the drooping heads, with their insectlike antlers, of wild tiger lilies.

Our house—rented and furnished—was one of a row of similar houses, with this difference: the others had two stories, ours had three. With a poor relation's imitation of suburban gratification, someone had added on a third floor, which stuck up absurdly, like a craning neck. Otherwise the house was identical to the few others on our street: stucco flanks, a stoop, a green front door leading directly into a sun parlor no bigger than a cube (where no sun could penetrate), cramped rooms. But the rooms were plentiful, thanks to the third floor, and within our first hour one of them—the largest, on the second floor and at the back—was designated as Professor Mitwisser's study, although it was clearly a bedroom. A wide bed stood against one wall. On the third floor, the three boys were distributed between two rooms; Gerhardt and Wilhelm took one, and Heinrich, the oldest, was put in with Waltraut. Anneliese had her own room on the second floor, across a narrow hall from her father. And on the third—she was still unfit for her husband's bed—I was made to join Mrs. Mitwisser.

By now I understood that the Mitwisser household held a secret: I thought it was Mrs. Mitwisser. She had sunk into an ongoing strangeness, something deeper than lethargy, and more perplexing. She was unwilling to be touched by anyone—she pushed Waltraut away from her like a contaminant. Waltraut had grown used to these rebuffs, and would shrink at the first sound of her mother's footsteps. At night, alone with Mrs. Mitwisser, I would listen to her whimper; she murmured and hissed in her own language, the choked gurgle of a dammed-up river.

"Did mama sleep at all last night?" Anneliese asked. "Papa wants to know."

Professor Mitwisser himself never approached with this question or any other. It seemed he had forgotten about me, or else he was lost in the repetitive clangor that now surrounded us: hammering, sawing, the slangy shouts of workmen. A trio of carpenters were building bookshelves: the bare boards covered every wall of Professor Mitwisser's study, and had begun to line the hallway.

During all this racket, Mrs. Mitwisser lay on her bed in her nightgown. Sometimes she pulled out a pack of cards from under her pillow

and idly shuffled them; or else she would lay them out in curiously un-
equal rows.

One afternoon I heard her singing:

> *Röslein, Röslein, Röslein rot,*
> *Röslein auf der Heide —*

She broke off and called me to her side.

"Röslein," she said, "that is your name, no?"

I said it was something like that, though in fact I could hear no re-
semblance.

"My husband told to me we have in this place a garden."

"There's a little back yard." There were only weeds behind the
house, and one unidentifiable tree.

"Then we go there."

But she would not get out of her nightgown or put on her shoes,
and Anneliese would not allow her to walk past the workmen as she was;
so she went back to her bed, sullen.

"Mama's very bad this time, but at home it was worse. When they
threw her out of the Institute she was *very* bad."

It was even more serious, Anneliese recounted, when they had to
leave Berlin, they had to run away practically, it was a miracle they could
ship out Professor Mitwisser's books, first to Stockholm, where they
stayed for a month with a great-uncle, and then, when the Quakers in-
tervened to save them, to Albany. In Albany their mother was almost all
better, and Waltraut was happy, and the boys behaved themselves, and
got funny new American names from their tutor, and everything was
nice for a while; but when the move to New York was decided on, little
by little she worsened. And now she was very bad. That was how it was
with their mother, she had a sickness, a private sickness—"Papa doesn't
let us talk about it to anyone, only to our own family, and the nurse we
had at home after they threw her out of the Institute, and then the law
came that no German could live with us, so the nurse had to go away.
And so did Waltraut's nanny, even though she was French."

"But you *haven't* moved to New York," I pointed out.

They almost had. A spacious apartment, prepared and accoutered,
with a real study for their father (they wouldn't have had to suffer the

clatter of all these carpenters!), an easy walk to the Reading Room of the great Library in Manhattan. But at the last minute their father had determined it would not be feasible, not with their mother so sick: what she needed was healing air, strolls, greenery. Sunlight and breezes. A quiet neighborhood, a backwater, a touch of salubrious scenery, no city swarms or city noises: it would be a kind of spa. And Professor Mitwisser could ride the subway to the Reading Room.

All this reminded me of money. I had not yet been paid my salary; I did not know what my salary would be.

"That apartment in the city," I said, "that would have been much more expensive than living out here, wouldn't it?"

Anneliese seemed offended; she turned aloof. Her cold eye told me I had transgressed. But my education in such matters had come from Ninel. Remembering Mrs. Mitwisser's melancholy warning about bed and board, I added, "I thought you could barely afford *me*."

The familiar redness flooded her forehead and ears. "At home we had things. At home we were all right."

It disturbed me that the Mitwisser children spoke of home. They were as homeless as I was. But I felt stealthily rich: the hot blue fact of Bertram's envelope warmed me. I had put it away, swathed in a sweater, in the bottom drawer of the dresser next to my bed.

"Here we have nothing. Papa's books we got out to Stockholm just in time, because of Uncle Sigmund. So now we have nothing if nobody helps."

"The Quakers—"

"Papa left his position. It's finished."

And so was our discussion; Anneliese made this plain. Her mouth tightened into a flat line, like an oscilloscope shut down. The Mitwissers' money arrangements were a subject closed to me: they did big things—Manhattan secured, Manhattan surrendered, this odd house in this odd neighborhood—but not little things; they didn't think of paying me.

"Go see about mama, please. If she puts on her shoes she can watch Willi. He's out in the back with Waltraut, planting seeds."

It came to me then that the Mitwisser family was an impregnable fiefdom, with guards at the borders. No one could be admitted. Yet how did they live? Professor Mitwisser went away every morning. Though it was late June, he wore his heavy black suit and his red-and-black-striped tie and his black fedora. He climbed the high stairs to the tracks; the train's screech bore him away to the Reading Room in the unimaginable city. Anneliese ran the household much as I had in my Thrace childhood; the difference was that my father had given me money out of his wallet. Among the Mitwissers, money was invisible.

The boys had discovered a pebbly patch of beach and disappeared for hours every afternoon. They returned salt-whitened, draped in strands of seaweed, smelling of low tide. Sometimes they took Waltraut with them on these excursions, and then, while Anneliese murmured at her mother's bedside, the house would feel deserted, desolate. The door to the room where Mrs. Mitwisser lived out her days, and where I slept at night, was shut against my intrusion; but I could hear fragments of these exchanges, partly in German, and often enough in Anneliese's high-pitched, persistent, irritable English.

"—they don't go to school now, it's summer—"

"*Wo sind sie dann?*"

"—gone down to the water. It's not far, it's only a little way. Come out and have a look."

"—*müde. Ich bin zu müde*—"

"—try, you can, papa wants you to."

"*Vielleicht morgen, ja? Wo ist der Vater?*"

"You know where"—exasperated. "In the city. At the Library."

"—*so heiss, ich bin so müde, ich muss ruhen,*" and it would end, Anneliese emerging with bright ears and flat angry mouth, her braid undone, as if someone had clawed at it.

"Go in there and get her *out,*" she ordered.

"If you can't, how can I?" I retorted. It was the first time I had ever dared to contradict Anneliese.

But one morning I was able to persuade Mrs. Mitwisser to put on her shoes. No one else was in the house—the boys and Waltraut at the beach, their father in the city, Anneliese gone to the greengrocer's.

From her bed Mrs. Mitwisser resumed her mournful singing: "*Röslein, Röslein, Röslein rot . . .*"

I said, "Is it a lullaby?"

She did not reply; the singing went on. "*Röslein auf der Heide . . .*"

"Do you ever sing it to Waltraut?"—though I knew that lately Waltraut would not come near her.

She was all at once fiercely alert. "*Natürlich*, the child must not make a noise. When we go with the chauffeur in the auto. We go in the streets around and around. Gert and Heinz and Willi, my husband gives to them *Spielkarten*—" She released a sly brown look and reached under her pillow. Out came the pack of cards. "Will you like a little to play?"

I despised cards; I remembered my father's gambling.

"I don't know how," I said.

"I teach you." A marvel: Mrs. Mitwisser rising out of her solitude.

I pressed my chance. "We would need a table. There's one in the yard behind the house—Anneliese put it out there for Waltraut. To draw on with her crayons."

Mrs. Mitwisser was indifferent to Waltraut and her crayons.

"Your shoes," I urged.

"No, no. No shoes!"

"Frau Mitwisser, please. You can't walk out barefoot."

"I put on my shoes, they become no good. They become holes, no? And I have not any more shoes, only these."

"When they wear out you can buy a new pair."

But now there was danger: fury assaulted her nostrils; they panted wide as a mare's. "We have no money, the money is not our money, like beggars we take! I do not agree to be a beggar for money!"

It struck me that it was only the family madwoman who would mention money.

Thrust over the side of her bed, her white legs trembled; she was relieved, spent; her eyes were grimly sane. She let me push her feet, swollen from disuse, into her shoes. When Anneliese came back, Mrs. Mitwisser was sitting under the single tree in the tiny back yard, instructing me in the rules of patience. To Anneliese she said, "What a pity the Fräulein cannot when she hears him recognize Goethe."

That night I asked about the chauffeured car.

"Papa hired it. It had smoked-glass windows, no one could see inside. Only important people would ride in an auto like that, big and black, and the driver had a black cap with a shiny beak, like a police-man." And so for a week they were—precariously—safe. All over Berlin, Anneliese said, there were impromptu raids; people were being arrested right out of their own apartments, or the apartments of relatives or friends, wherever they tried to hide. You could be picked up at any hour, you never knew when or where, and there were still seven days be-fore the ship to Sweden, they had their papers all ready, but where could they go in the meantime? Not home, not anywhere. "Papa gave this man, his name was Fritz, he owned the limousine, papa gave him the key to our apartment and told him he could take away anything he wanted, anything at all, if he would drive us around the city for a few days. Wal-traut was so little then, she cried all the time, and mama had to sing to her, and the boys played cards, and we went up and down the streets day after day, and no one stopped us because the auto looked so important and official and dark. Fritz brought us food to eat in the auto, and when we needed to use the toilet we would hold our heads up and walk into any fine hotel. It made us nervous to do that, even though we were wear-ing our best clothes on purpose, and Fritz would get angry when Wal-traut's diapers smelled bad, so we were afraid of him."

Anneliese spread her clean fingers into the shape of a fan and stared into the empty spaces between them. "He didn't trust papa about the key. Once he parked right in front of our own building and locked us all in the auto and went into the elevator and upstairs to make sure that it was really the key to our apartment. And when he came back down he told us that just next door he'd heard terrible screams, and when he looked in he saw some men beating an old woman and dragging her across the floor. Mama said 'Frau Blumenthal!' and papa said to keep quiet, and then Fritz said, 'Your place has paintings on the walls, what right do you people have to live like that?'"

She doubled up the fingers of her right hand into a fist.

"So we kept on driving round and round Berlin, until the last day before the ship to Sweden was due in Hamburg—it took six hours, that part, getting to Hamburg, and halfway there, when it was all country vil-lages and little towns, Fritz stopped the auto and said he wouldn't take us any farther unless mama gave him her wedding ring, and he made the boys and me turn out our pockets to see if we were hiding anything, and he tore off Waltraut's diaper. Mama was carrying her mother's picture in her bag, an old photo in a silver frame, and Fritz grabbed it, but mama lied and said the frame was only plate, so he threw it down. At the pier in Hamburg he asked papa for some more marks, and then he told us to get out finally, and that was that. Whether there was anything left in our apartment when he got back there with papa's key we never knew. —Waltraut will want some water, won't she, before she falls asleep, so take care of it now, please. I'm going up to papa's study to tell him how much better mama was today."

And after that Anneliese never again disclosed any part of her family's travail.

9

SOME PEOPLE THINK the Bear Boy is the most famous boy in the world—famous the way, in those early years of movie cartoons, Mickey Mouse was famous, or, to choose a more elevated example, the metaphysical Alice. These comparisons do not exaggerate. I suppose that nowadays there would be replicas of the Bear Boy in every imaginable manifestation: stuffed dolls, of course, and toys that move on their own, and songs and animated films, and all the rest of the detritus meant to attract the modern child. The Bear Boy was not a modern child. He did not look like a modern child; he did not speak like a modern child. He spoke, in fact, mainly in verse, sometimes rhymed, sometimes bounced into a clever beat of his own. He was called the Bear Boy not because he lived among bears, as Mowgli lived among wolves, and not because he was whimsically accompanied by a battered plush bear, like Christopher Robin. The Bear Boy may have *resembled* a small bear, as many old-fashioned children do: his ears were round and his eyes were black buttons with artistic wedges of light in their corners, and his too-long-on-purpose bangs suggested fuzzy velvet when it is rubbed into a furious furriness.

That, at any rate, was his author's conception of him; and his author was also his illustrator. His author's name was James Philip A'Bair: hence the 'Bair Boy, popularly transmuted into the Bear Boy, and ultimately surrendered to by the author himself. I was interested in that apostrophe; I was interested in everything the Bear Boy might reveal. It was he who lay among my father's miscellaneous belongings in the box shipped from Croft Hall. It was he who had delivered to me my mother's death certificate, and the news and nature of her last illness. A few days after the arrival of my father's things—and soon after Bertram had disposed of those London-made shoes—I ran down the street to the brown façade of the Carnegie library, to learn what I could about the Bear Boy.

It was true that I was already acquainted with many of the Bear Boy's characteristics—who was not? To be oblivious of him would have been as likely as never having heard of Peter Rabbit, and the Bear Boy and Peter Rabbit had the same—what to call it?—constituency. Little children delighted in the Bear Boy—all, it seemed, but me. My father had never read aloud to me; I could not imagine such a tradition, a father reading to a child. When I finally came to books on my own—and I came to them with a driven hunger—I was already too old for the Bear Boy. I had missed the moment, I had passed him by. He belonged to the very young.

The apostrophe, I discovered, was an elision: the name had once been apBair, and before that possibly apBlair, somehow corrupted from its Welsh origin—an oddly evolved country name on the style, for instance, of Prichard, condensed from apRichard. James Philip A'Bair, according to my source (a thick and dusty authors' compendium), was born near Cardiff in 1843, emigrated to Boston at the age of nineteen, and was married, late, to Margaret Dilworth, of Gloucester, Massachusetts, in 1887; their only child, James Philip Jr., was born in 1895. How far away these dates seemed! The author of the Bear Boy was long dead; he had sent into the ether three plays, some negligible verse ornamented with a border of birds and blossoms from the poet's own inkpot, and a pair of not very noteworthy novels, all the while supported in these mostly unremunerative strivings by Margaret A'Bair, who designed ladies' hats and eventually ran her own millinery shop.

It was one of those hats, in a period when women affected great swooping brims adorned by ribbons and feathers, that gave birth to the Bear Boy. Jimmy A'Bair, then age two and a half, plucked his mother's fabrication from the blank-faced dummy-head on which it was displayed for sale, and moved into it. He moved into it literally, like a hermit who has found an agreeable cave. The hat was certainly very broad, and very deep, and very green, and he could curl his entire body into its cavity, overhung, as by fronds in a forest, by waving green feathers. He slept inside it and he ate inside it; he reached up to play with its dangling bows, but he would not come out of it. If he drew together the two ends of its wide encircling brim, he effectively shut his door on any view of the outside scene. At first Margaret A'Bair was amused, and after some days vaguely worried; but James Philip A'Bair, who was already past fifty and had sparse affinity for small boys, was electrified. He took up his neglected watercolors and painted the boy who wanted to live in a hat; a strange and simple tale, made up of strange and simple syllables, tumbled out of him, he hardly knew how, but even as they jetted from his pen he felt them to be enchanting and unprecedented, like his wife's twisted-cloth flowers, the seductive forms of which existed nowhere in nature. From then on, greedily watchful, he kept his eye on the child, though in rather a distant way; he had no sympathetic insight into Jimmy, who nevertheless supplied all the bizarre tricks and curious marvels that the author of the Bear Boy could wish for. He almost believed that the child was his conscious collaborator.

The Boy Who Lived in a Hat was the first of the celebrated series (and included an actual bear, who was served ginger ale on a visit to the boy in the hat). This was followed by *The Boy Whose Thumb Was a Puppet* and *Six Times Two Is Thirteen Midnights*, the acclaimed volume of illustrated rhymes, in which the Bear Boy counts up all the blue-black spaces between the galaxies. Bear Boy book succeeded Bear Boy book—there were fifteen of them, translated into every European language. Riches quickly mounted. Margaret A'Bair gave up her hat shop, and devoted her skills to tailoring fanciful blouses for her son to wear and her husband to paint. By the time Jimmy was six years old, he had the most recognizable tiny chin and round ears and furry hair and scalloped collar of any child on earth. His face and dress and robust little legs—especially their rosy knees—had turned into legend; the Bear Boy was indistinguishable from folklore. And the author was eclipsed by the boy.

All this was recounted in a reference work in the Carnegie library two blocks from Bertram's flat—the flat he would soon give up for Ninel's sake. I was particularly drawn to those far-off dates of marriage and birth. The story of the hat-cave had disclosed my mother's true fate. Might the Bear Boy have been one of her childhood treasures, precious to her and therefore precious to my father? Cynical about everything else, he was never cynical about his Jenny.

"The timing doesn't work," Bertram pointed out. "Your mother must have been ten or twelve when the series got started. At that age she wouldn't care for all that Jellydrop stuff."

It was the Bear Boy's habit to call everyone, human or animal—even his own thumb—Jellydrop. It was a magical spell.

"If it had nothing to do with Jenny," I said, "my father wouldn't have saved a thing like that. A picture book! It makes no sense. And look how long he's had it—the cover's coming apart."

"Maybe your mother bought it with you in mind. And was too sick, so it got put away."

I was skeptical: would my father have preserved something meant for me? His sentiments extended no further than his protracted mourning for his wife.

"Or it could be," Bertram said (I felt his impatience), "that your father kept the Bear Boy for himself. Because . . . well, maybe because he just liked that sort of stuff. Some people do. Look, kid, I'm late. Just put the thing away and don't eat yourself up over it, what d'you say?"

He was kindly but restless. Ninel was waiting for him on a certain street corner with a placard on a tall stick; she was leading yet another march in favor of the downtrodden. But his words—they were, I saw, unserious, hasty, tossed out—opened a light before me. However my father had got hold of the Bear Boy, it was all at once possible that he had, on his own account, cherished the image of a child who lived in a hat. And why not? My mother was dead; being mortal flesh, he had to cherish someone. Since it wasn't going to be me, why not the make-believe Bear Boy? I could not discover—how would I ever know?—how a children's story came to rest among my father's few last things. He had been a reckless imaginer, a man of caprice, and his attachment to a chimerical boy was an explanation I was, for all my mistrust of him, willing to accept.

At night at the Mitwissers', when the briny smell of the bay traveled feebly on the summer wind, and when I could be sure that Mrs. Mitwisser was turned to the wall or asleep, I sometimes lifted the Bear

Boy, soiled and torn, out of the bottom drawer of my dresser—I had deposited him there, on top of Bertram's blue envelope filled with money—to watch him creep into that gargantuan feathered hat. In those wandering moments I tried to believe that my father, overwhelmed by his deceits, had in the same way wished to hide himself away from his own complexities. And then I would pull out Bertram's blue envelope, look into it, and count my fortune.

10

DAY BY DAY Mrs. Mitwisser improved. She had begun to walk out
with Anneliese in the mornings, at first as far as the corner, and then circling the nearby streets, observing (she was becoming more attentive)
the little houses of the neighborhood, each with its low hedges squared
off to mark a miniature front yard dominated by a single pared evergreen shrub or lilacs struggling to escape their enforced boundaries. She
had grown almost docile about putting on her shoes, and would complain only that she had no others. Except for this recurrent grumbling,
she seemed agreeable enough. Now and then I would take Waltraut by
the hand and join these modest walks; but Mrs. Mitwisser's newly awakened scrutiny, searching everywhere, continued to avoid the face of her
child. Instead she would stop to examine a bit of green stalk burst up
from a crack in the pavement, or a purple clover-head sprouting from
the curb; or else she would remark on the needling glints of mica in the
sidewalk, or the starlike configurations of straw caught in a puddle of
sun-melted tar. Her look was that of a microscope, enlarging with a relentless eye whatever fell under it, and I thought I might be witnessing
evidences—diminished though they were—of the scientist she had
been. The refugee physicist formerly attached to the Kaiser Wilhelm
Institute in Berlin suddenly sat down on the ground and picked up a lady-
bug and let it run companionably along her finger. But when Waltraut
came near, tentatively, distrustfully, drawn by the insect's tiny round
spotted back, Mrs. Mitwisser instantly blew it away.

The walks lengthened. If the day's heat was not too heavy, Mrs.
Mitwisser could be cajoled to the outer margins of the bay, untenanted
except by her own vagabond boys. They were generally bloody, their
feet and shins cut by shells and small sharp stones. A shower of butter-

flies, wave after wave of whirling white ruffles, splashed up like an inverted fountain around their heads; they dashed through the fluttering clouds, shrieking when thorny grasses caught at their bare legs—they were the captains of this half-wild ring of neglected marsh. Mrs. Mitwisser made no move in their direction. She stood gazing over the water, as if (but this may have been my own imagining) Europe, and not a distant extrusion of the mundanely inhabited Bronx, darkened the opposite shore; and then she bent to study a stray goose feather. Anneliese tried to take her mother's arm; she shook it off. She was enormously—excessively—concentrated. She fixed on a single object as if she could see into its molecular structure, or as if some luring being within it, god or lurking elf, was summoning. She had put on her shoes and awakened to the natural world: the botanical, the ornithological—that goose feather—seized her notice. Her children did not.

These were days almost pastoral. Professor Mitwisser departed in the morning, attired like an ambassador about to address an assembly of fellow diplomats. Five minutes after the green front door shut behind him, it was jerked open with a force that strained its hinges, and the boys shot out—three dervishes clutching paper-bag lunches and heading for cattails and empty watery lots. Then Anneliese and Mrs. Mitwisser would venture out on their wandering excursions, and usually I followed with Waltraut, who, when the trek began to tire her, rode high on my shoulders. There was a summer stillness in the streets; every few yards Mrs. Mitwisser halted our little parade to investigate a spray of leaves on a fallen twig, or a beetle swimming in a rain-channel. In the afternoons, while Mrs. Mitwisser fell into a doze on her bed, and Waltraut napped in her crib, Anneliese vanished to some other part of the house, shunning me. I understood that she no longer wished to be her family's historian: I had pressed her too hard. Or she feared I would again ask about money. In the motionless quiet of those shadowed hours I was perfectly idle, and perfectly alone.

This way of life—it had begun to feel exactly that, as immutable as if years were passing in these identical routines—was all at once ruptured. Three weeks after our arrival, Anneliese announced that her father was waiting for me in his study. "Never mind that," she told me (I was helping Mrs. Mitwisser into her nightdress; she had stopped to stare at the crossed threads of one of its buttons), "just go. Papa wants you right now."

It was ten o'clock at night. I had never before stepped inside Professor Mitwisser's study, even in daylight. Only Anneliese had permission to go in and out, and for the most domestic of tasks: she was to change the bedsheets and clear out the wastebaskets. The place was sacrosanct. Its very walls, with those scores of esoteric volumes arrayed on the newly carpentered shelves, declared their untouchability. I had been invited into a shrine. In its absolute center—presumably so that the books might be unobstructed and accessible—stood a small wooden desk, on which an old-fashioned typewriter rested. I had not known that such a machine was in the house; I had never heard it in use, and it seemed to defy everything around it.

Professor Mitwisser placed his large rough hand on the keys. "You will assist me here," he said, "immediately." He did not ask about my competence. He merely assumed it, which was logical enough in those years, when most young women without a university degree (and many with one) went to work as typists in offices. This, in fact, had been Ninel's advice when she drove me out of Bertram's life; she herself was a secretary for the AFL. She admitted that she admired my typing; she admired little else. She was familiar with the fierce and rapid rattle of Bertram's old Remington, on which I would sometimes copy out a paragraph from whatever novel was currently claiming me, partly for the bliss of seeing the words fly out of my fingers as if I were inventing them myself, and partly (or mainly) to drown out Ninel's voice, murmuring and murmuring into Bertram's ear. At other times—and then the keys would crack their little whips far more reluctantly, with long slow silences in between—I would be typing a letter to my father at Croft Hall: a letter he never answered.

"Please to duplicate what I have written," Mitwisser ordered.

I sat down at the typewriter and took a paper from him. I saw with relief that its language was English: a clear foreign hand. But when I struck the keys only the ghosts of letters appeared.

"The ribbon's worn out. This one must be ten years old, it's useless," and I stood up again.

I noticed now the color of his eyes—startlingly different from the brown intelligence of the rest of that family. Professor Mitwisser's eyes were acutely blue, as blue as the intensest blue of Dutch porcelain; they looked dyed: dipped once, dipped twice. I was shocked by their waver of bewilderment—like heat vibrating across a field—and it occurred to me that he scarcely knew what I meant by a ribbon, that the machine was as alien to him as the map of any mythical island. He was a man who had been much served. He was accustomed to privilege: at home in Berlin, at the University, he had been surrounded by a haze of attentive acolytes; his students bowed to him, waiters in restaurants recognized him from newspaper photographs and bowed to him, he was Herr Doktor Professor, esteemed lecturer before the Religionswissenschaftliche Vereinigung, honored by his colleagues all over Germany. And then—overnight—they threw him out. His poor wife, a respected senior fellow of the Kaiser Wilhelm Institute, her too they threw out—it unsettled her spirit, her spirit was unsettled, she felt herself emptied out, a pariah. The good Quakers had somewhat restored them, true enough, and they were grateful for their lives, but Inner Light could not comprehend Outer Darkness, and besides it was impossible to continue genuine scholarship at an insignificant provincial American college, however good-hearted their hosts were; nor were their hosts to be blamed for mistaking Karaites for Charismites, after all they had given him a house for his family and an office and a part-time secretary, and when it was incumbent on him, despite all their generosity, to leave, they were again generous, and presented him with the very typewriter the part-time secretary had used: it was his to carry away.

Here was a man—this severe paterfamilias, this formidable scholar of the Karaites!—who had barely spoken a syllable to me or even, as far as I could tell, of me, for nearly a month, since the day I had clumsily disorganized his library. And this looming large man, with his great ugly hands clapped on the body of a hapless half-obsolete typewriter, was numbering his losses in the full cry of inconsolable lamentation. He had, in effect, no wife, and though he had all those children, they were only children, and one no more than a baby. As for Anneliese, he said, her young shoulders were burdened enough, and though capable in two languages—unlike you, Fräulein—she was without capacity in relation to this accursed machine, this devil's contrivance, and what was he to do, how to proceed with his work if it could not be properly recorded? What was to become of his work?

The helpless hand on the typewriter curled into a hard white bloodless fist: Anneliese's fist. They were remarkably alike: she had inherited his big frame and his burning fury over Outer Darkness. But the daughter was colder than the father. Out of Mitwisser's twice-dyed eyes, dyed by some physiological thaumaturgy to the bluest depth of topaz, there fell, as I stood watching, a thin and horrible stream of tears.

The fright of it—the revered scholar, the severe paterfamilias, undone by a devilish contrivance fit for a junkyard—made me stammer. "To-tomorrow," I brought out, "I'll look for a, for a place where they sell these things. A ribbon, and paper, and some carbon sheets if you like." But I was certain that "carbon" came to him as no more pertinent to his purpose than if I had uttered "coal mine." He was a man used to service in all things large and small; he had already told me so, and I had observed it for myself.

He did not dismiss me. I ran. I ran to my bed; my tongue was a dry rag in my mouth. He had frightened me, I was in a chill of shock, my fear amazed me with its headlong insistence, it was beyond volition, it took me over, it pinched and shook me. He had opened—to me!—his violation, his rending. They had torn him—like wild beasts, they had torn him. They had thrown him out, he had escaped with his life, with all of their lives; and they had severed him from the Karaites, who were as dear to him as his children. For the sake of the Karaites—to repair the breach—he journeyed every day to the Reading Room, where they lay concealed in tomes kept under lock and key, untouched for generations perhaps, who could tell? When he returned in the evening his fingertips were black with old dust and, no doubt, new inferences. The Karaites—his mind's inhabitants—were as dear to him as Anneliese or Willi or Gert or Heinz or Waltraut; and surely dearer than his Elsa, whom he had banished from his sheets.

There she was, his Elsa, across the room, asleep, her secretive face to the wall, the wife who was no wife.

He had wept! And how was I to get some money? I had promised to buy a ribbon, paper, carbons—what else would that miserable fossil of a machine require? Well, finally the reason for my employment was exposed: I was to be the caretaker of a cast-off typewriter. I could not ask Professor Mitwisser for money; it was the shame of that dilapidated instrument, his dependence on it, his dependence on so unformed a creature as myself, that had crushed him. The machine had made him weep —him to whom the salons of Berlin had once bowed! My pockets were empty. I had spent my last dollar on chocolate bars. I was afraid to approach Anneliese, even on behalf of her father: she was adamant, it was forbidden, she was not to speak to me of money. And I was not to speak to her or anyone about my unpaid salary: I was to wait and wait, and I could not object, because they had taken me in when I had nowhere to go—a refugee of sorts.

In the meantime, I was hiddenly flush with money of my own, in twenty-dollar bills. Ribbon, carbon, paper; alcohol for cleaning the keys; a small can of oil. For a few dollars the fossil might be restored to life, and then my acquaintance with the Karaites, whatever they were, could begin; I knew only that Karaites were not Charismites. Cautiously, noiselessly, I pulled open the bottom drawer of my dresser. The Bear Boy, quiescent in his scalloped collar, lay there as silently as Mrs. Mitwisser in her bed. I pushed him aside to find Bertram's blue envelope.

It was not there. My fortune was gone.

11

IN THE MORNING I raised a hullabaloo.

I was eighteen, an unformed creature, and (as people say) ignorant of the world. I had endured my stringent childhood in Thrace, a backwater townlet where lives were turned away from the impress of events even as they were unfolding—a period of turbulence that had begun to shake the ground of Europe. For the denizens of Thrace—for Lena and her sons, and for every other native household—Europe was beyond reality, and for me it was nearly the same: the fanciful habitation of Pinocchio and Becky Sharp and Sidney Carton. (Only many decades later would I come to agree with Ninel about the useless delusions of literature.) Yet I question now why I did not question then, in that third-floor bedroom in the marshy reaches of the Bronx, what even I, in my unformed ignorance, could see was Professor Mitwisser's peculiar situation. Why, after his rescue by the conscientious if mistaken Board of the Hudson Valley Friends College, was he not instantly recruited by some eager university? It was an era—I have since understood—of foreign flooding: an influx of refugee scholars, injured, diminished, confused, streaming into the chaos of an alien haven and hoping for an academic berth of some kind; for a replica of the old life, the old reverence. A substantial flock settled in the New School in New York; a handful went to Chicago and Princeton; the rest, in their broken dignity, dragging their medals and degrees, drooped toward whatever uncertain welcome they might find in institutions north or west or south. Mitwisser was not among any of these.

At eighteen I was as uncomprehending of the times—of all that world-upheaval—as if I were still a raw weed in the hinterlands of Thrace; even so, I saw in Mitwisser something vengeful. He was off course; he was not what he had been; but the weeping that had terrorized me made me believe that everything was tainted for him, he had given up on retrieval. No waiter would bow to him ever again. What was a university to him now? Devils lurked in those honored halls; his own students, his own colleagues, had ended as devils. And all those others, the great foreign influx, the scholars, the refugees—they were only dwarves in this new place. Mann, Einstein, Arendt, yes, the grand explainers (I would one day pursue them myself), idols of the popular journals; but the rest were dwarves, rebuffed, humiliated, obscured, trampled on, *zwergenhaft*. Better to be a heretic! Better to be a Karaite! Better to separate oneself from the explainers! To set oneself against the explainers!

It was through glimmerings like these—primitive and unschooled though I was—that I took in Rudolf Mitwisser's discontents on the night the money in Bertram's blue envelope vanished. I knew nothing of world-upheaval, I knew nothing of that great scholarly flood. But in Mitwisser's tears as they fled down the rough channels of his scored skin, I caught the glitter of heresy—the resolution of a man who has turned his back on a received course.

And I did raise a hullabaloo. I thought it was my right. I lasted until morning and then I raised a hullabaloo—and in between, roiling on my pillow in that airless room through which drifted the silent inhalations and whispery expulsions of Mrs. Mitwisser's breathing, I schemed how I would compel Anneliese to speak of money. Now she would speak of it. I would force her. I would press her with the force of an iron press. There was a thief in that house, and except for me no one who was not one of *them*: no one who did not belong to Professor Mitwisser.

Mrs. Mitwisser, as usual, slept late. It was her habit to keep to her bed until the morning's tumult of ablution and tramping was over and the house had grown quiet. I dressed noiselessly and stayed where I was. I heard the front door open and close; from the window I could see Mitwisser stepping into the beginning heat of the day in his fedora and proper woolen suit. He had a rapid, concentrated stride, and the end of the street soon digested his giant's shape; it dematerialized around a corner, uninnocent of some recondite heterodoxy perhaps, but guiltless, I was certain, of theft. He never came near his wife's domain. He had never set foot on the third floor.

A boy stood on the threshold, a yard from Mrs. Mitwisser's shut-up eyelids: they resembled pale oyster shells. I had by now learned which boy was which. This was the middle-sized one.

"Anneliese wants you."

"Good," I told him; it was Gert, Anneliese's most frequently employed messenger. "Tell Anneliese I want *her*. Tell her I want her right away."

"You have to get papa's machine fixed. It has to be ready for when he needs it tonight."

"Tell Anneliese I want her upstairs, quick!"

Gert's glance went anxiously to his sleeping mother. "Is it mama? Is mama all right?"

"It has nothing to do with mama. Now will you go? I'm telling you to go!"

Mrs. Mitwisser's legs twitched under the blanket. Her eyes shot open. "*Ach, lass mich in Ruhe,*" she murmured, and lifted a shoulder for shade against the infiltrating sunlight. Her lids hopped up and down.

There was a drumming on the stairs: Anneliese with her troops, Waltraut in her arms, three excited boys stomping behind her like a round of popping ammunition.

"Is something the matter with mama? Gert says something's the matter—"

"*Was ist los?*" Mrs. Mitwisser sat up with the mindless jump of a marionette.

"I had money in my dresser," I said. "It's gone. Someone took it."

"*Da muss etwas los sein—*"

"See what you're doing to mama!"

"My money's been taken. I had it right in there," and I pointed a shaking finger at the open drawer next to my bed.

Anneliese picked out her coldest tone. "Is this what you wake up mama for?"

"My money's gone," I said again. "I had money put away and it's gone."

Heinz looked as interested as if a night moth had at that moment

60

unaccountably passed through the room. "Where'd it go?" he asked.

"Maybe into your pocket," I said.

"Don't you dare accuse that boy!" Anneliese cried.

"Not that boy? Then which other boy?"

Abruptly she set Waltraut down on her feet; I watched Anneliese's fist jut into a small boulder crowned with taut knuckles; but the other hand hung open. Her temples, exposed by the tightly drawn hair, reddened, then ebbed to a bloodless translucence. A shrewdness seeped into her whitening stare. "You haven't got any money at all. It's a story, isn't it? If you had money of your own, you wouldn't stay with us, isn't that so?"

"It was in an envelope, a present from my cousin—"

Gert broke in with plain relish: "How much was it?"

"Whoever took it knows how much."

"There was nothing to take," Anneliese said grimly. "It's just a story. To make a commotion about money—because you think you won't get paid. Paid for what? You haven't begun yet. Have you begun? What have you done for papa? Nothing. Papa wants you to put his machine in order, and you haven't done even that."

"I can't buy a new ribbon without money."

"You think of nothing but money," Anneliese said.

She was, I recognized, a marvel of cunning: she was reversing the charges; she was accusing the accuser. The hullabaloo was slipping away from me to become her own. And meanwhile there was a confusion of movement all around: Mrs. Mitwisser tearing at her nightgown, frantically ripping holes in its bosom with her fingernails, Willi darting from Anneliese's side as though her hot scorn would lick out and burn him, Waltraut dropping to the floor and crawling strangely, fearfully, as if in dread of a slap, toward her mother's bed, Heinz and Gert all at once snickering—alarmed elastic giggles that growled into muteness—because they had glimpsed, through a long rent in the fabric of her gown, Mrs. Mitwisser's sunken pink nipples.

"Heinrich, Gerhardt," Anneliese warned, "let mama rest. Leave her, please." To me she said, "You've made mama worse again. I'm going to tell papa to get rid of you.—Willi, downstairs, *schnell!*"

But Willi was peering into the space where I had hidden the blue envelope. "Look, she's got it, didn't I say so?" He held up the ragged Bear Boy. "She keeps it down in there, see?"

"Get away from my things," I told him lamely. I was defeated; I saw how Anneliese was swelled up with her bitter powers. To be sent away—the desolation of it, the peril. Where could I go? Where, and to whom? My money was stolen; my hullabaloo was stolen.

Willi fled. Like the others, he was all obedience. And Waltraut, on hands and knees like a tiny dog shrinking from a blow, went creeping, creeping toward the flailing figure in the bed across the room, the worried moon of her small face appealing for some motherly reflection. None came. Mrs. Mitwisser's quick eye preferred the wandering cracks in the ceiling. She was a mass of clutched banners—her sweated hands were bunched in streamers of torn cloth. She seemed to chew the air; those wretched German noises were wrenched out of a keening mouth.

Crouching on the floor, Waltraut put up a little wrist and pushed it under Mrs. Mitwisser's mattress. Out swept a flying fan of playing cards. Then she put up her little wrist again, as thin as a flute, and drew out Bertram's blue envelope.

She who would not agree to be a beggar had become a thief.

When the uproar of the morning lessened (I was the owner of that hullabaloo after all), what fell out from Anneliese's subdued account was this: Mrs. Mitwisser had merely intended to assure herself that when her only pair of shoes wore out she would have the wherewithal to pay for another pair.

My money was restored. I removed a bill from it and went out to reconnoiter a fresh typewriter ribbon for Professor Mitwisser's antediluvian machine.

Anneliese said, "When James comes, we'll have plenty of money again. He's going to come, you know." I did not know. I did not understand, and she had returned to the haughtiness that declined to expose the further history of her family.

12

I BEGAN MY NIGHTLY VISITS to Professor Mitwisser's study—a name it hardly merited, since he kept away from it more often than he inhabited it. It put me in mind anyhow of a monk's cell: the wall of books like mute stones set all around, the marital bed abandoned by conjugal twoness, immured and ascetic, the little wooden table toward which Mitwisser's lordly curl of a finger impatiently propelled me. I was an "assistant" with a simple duty: I was to record Mitwisser's words as he recited them from his notes. The crippled typewriter, it turned out, failed only intermittently, and I soon adapted to its several idiosyncrasies. The "w" was damaged, and the letters would sometimes skip, leaving wide spaces within a single syllable. The shift key had a habit of getting stuck, so that I would type a line all in capitals, as if the phrases were shouting back at me.

Mitwisser was oblivious to these difficulties. He was lost in his own intentness. At times he would stagger up like some large prehistoric form and claw at a volume in the wall; his eyes narrowed over the open pages as before a grassy veld concealing some living morsel of a creature about to be snapped up. These intervals of sudden prey may have hinted at a certain quickness of concentration, but the process as a whole was achingly slow. Often I sat languid with my hands uselessly dangling; I loathed these long waits. The silence was almost glutinous. It was August, in the heart of a heat wave that had lasted for days. In the mornings Professor Mitwisser would depart wearing his thick felt hat as usual, but with his jacket over his arm: the relentless early sun, already merciless, had the power to unbutton his formality. The nights were worse; the roof tiles had been absorbing torrid scorchings for hours, and there was not an electric fan in the house.

His notes were mainly in German. He spoke them aloud, translating into English as he went. It was not for my sake—what had I to do with any of it? And even if I had been able to respond to German dictation, he would, I saw, have chosen otherwise. He was disposing of his mother tongue; henceforward his work (no matter that he formulated it privately in the language of his birth) would venture forth publicly in this new, if somewhat overlavish, dress. His words, as I wonderingly transcribed them, were ornate, now and then boldly archaic; they had a lingering stately pace, logical, reasoned. On occasion they halted altogether, like a turn in a dance, or a rest in a march.

All that was a deception. It was a disguise. At first it seemed that the unbreathable sultriness of those summer nights was our influence, our muse—but it might have been the opposite. It might have been Mitwisser who was the muse of that stifling airlessness, that ovenlike seizure—or so I felt, as little by little his cause was revealed to me. Boiling rebellion was Mitwisser's subject. He was drawn to schismatics, fiery heretics, apostates—the lunatics of history. Below the scholar's skin a wild bellows panted, filling and emptying its burning pouch; a flaming furnace exhaled fevers. It was not August's torch that spilled the sweat from our necks. It was Mitwisser's own conflagration, invading, heaping up a pyre in that room with the shut door, out of which stuttered the unsteady nightly tapping of a typewriter.

There were libraries beyond his horizon: an archive in Cairo, another in Leningrad, destinations as remote and as unlikely for Rudolf Mitwisser in 1935 as the rings of Saturn. New York—the Reading Room—disgorged for him what it could: certain rarities, and secondary and tertiary chroniclings. Deficiencies. But—by now—Cairo, Leningrad, London, New York, the irretrievable Berlin, what did they matter? He had become his own archive. Babylonia, Persia, Byzantium teemed in the sockets of his eyes; choirs of esoteric names rang out against the ceiling. I grew used to hearing the twisted Egyptian music of al-Barqamani, al-Kirkisani, ibn Saghir, al-Maghribi, and the braided trio of Arabic and Aramaic and Hebrew, and, when contrariness overcame him, the exclamatory extrusions of German. He was that—an archive; a repository of centuries; a courier of alphabets and histories. At home, before they threw him out, they had esteemed him because no one knew what he knew. And here—now—he was scorned for the same reason: no one knew what he knew. He was scorned, he was in isolation, he was alone in his quest. (His quest? Is that what it finally was?) He was violated. He was friendless. He was, in a manner of speaking, wifeless.

One night visitors came. They came at ten o'clock, when Waltraut and the boys were asleep. I had already buttoned Mrs. Mitwisser into her nightgown; I had already forgiven her. Each night I was obliged to forgive her: it had grown into our mutual ritual, she begging my forgiveness, I patiently granting it. Each night she recited the narrative of her theft, how she had once spied me looking into an envelope filled with dollars, how she had been tempted, how she had considered only the matter of her shoes wearing out, and then what? The shame of it! The peril! She would not be a beggar, no! They might ingratiate themselves with that James, they might go on their knees to that James, they might James themselves inside out, she would have nothing to do with their scheming, no!

I left Mrs. Mitwisser in her bed. She was alert, breathless, bright-faced; she pulled at my blouse to keep me. But my duty was below: Anneliese had instructed me to stand at the green front door and guide the visitors into the narrow dining room.

Earlier I had set out teacups all around the scarred oak table, where the family, except for Mrs. Mitwisser and Waltraut, habitually had dinner. "Not like that," Anneliese scolded; she removed the cups and laid out a white tablecloth. The occasion was to be an elevated one. Six or eight men filed in; one wore a skullcap. They had arrived nearly simultaneously, in two cars, and appeared to be all of an age—between forty-five and sixty. It was the first time since I had entered the insular fortress of the Mitwisser household that strangers were being entertained. And still there was no air of welcome, or even of invitation; it was more a convention than a visit. The men exchanged small familiar grunts and settled into their chairs while Anneliese and I handed out plates of miniature frosted cakes. I marveled at these cakes: they were not our ordinary fare. I had never before seen such exquisite morsels, delicately layered, each crowned with its own sugar-whorl in the form of a tiny flower. Somehow, for the sake of this unusual company, money had been found for fancy cakes; but the cups were chipped, and mazy brown cracks meandered over them.

I poured the hot water directly from the kitchen kettle: Bertram's way.

Anneliese whispered, "The teapot! Use the china teapot, can't you?"—with such ferocity that I began to understand that some ceremony was under way. Was it to be a down-at-the-heels echo of those Berlin salons where Mitwisser had once been fêted? Was it a celebration, a commendation? The tea darkened in the pot. The little cakes gleamed. The visitors murmured, indifferent, detached, waiting.

"Go up and let papa know they're here," Anneliese said finally.

I knocked on the study door, though it was open. Professor Mitwisser was standing in the middle of the room with a brush; he was brushing the jacket of his suit.

"How many have come?" he asked.

"I think eight."

"Eight? Then four have declined."

So he had summoned them. This night was his own creation.

"Tell them I am just finishing a bit of writing. Tell them in ten minutes I join them."

He went on brushing. Whoever they were, he would be their master.

Anneliese had posted me just outside the dining room, with the teapot at the ready. I refilled the cups, and still Mitwisser did not come down. I had misjudged—there were seven visitors, not eight: a dozen had been summoned, and it was five who had declined. I took in that irregular row of drumming fingers and tightened shoulders fixed in a forward curve, and temples either bald or graying, lined with ridges. Even the youngest of them had darkly graven markings under the eyes. These were worn and creviced faces, accustomed to tedium, like a crew of salesmen biding their time before making their pitch. I was struck by the mildness of their patience. Only the man in the skullcap showed a vague irritability, rolling and unrolling the tip of his mahogany beard with a stiffened thumb. The beard, together with the skullcap, signaled an aspect of some practice or piety, and this set me to reflecting on how Mitwisser, a student of the history of religion, after all, was in his own life bare of any sign or vestige of belief. In that family there was no rite or observance, no Sabbathday or Passover or sacral new year. It had been the same—the same absence—for my father and me, and for Bertram; my father had declared himself an atheist, and Bertram relished Ninel's aloofness from such matters. But Professor Mitwisser's brain rocked and shuddered with the metaphysics of long-ago believers, men for whom God was an unalterable Creator and Ruler—and still God was nowhere in that house. Like the biologist who is obsessed by the study of the very disease to which he is immune, Mitwisser had raised a wall between belief and the examination of belief.

That was what it all came to, then: this wall, which the others doubted, or condemned, or assailed.

When at last he stepped into the light, they stood up with a formal cordiality, and he shook hands with each man, one by one. He was wearing his freshly brushed suit-coat, though the molten August heat was so intimately invasive that it crept into the ears and along the necks of the company: they had all torn open their collars, where the sweat pooled in the hollows of their clavicles. From the constraint of these unraveled visitors it seemed improbable, at first, that Mitwisser had met any of them in some former circumstance; or yet again perhaps he had, distantly, at one of those international congresses frequented by seminarians, or even on his home ground, at sessions of the Religionswissenschaftliche Vereinigung, in Berlin or Frankfurt or Heidelberg, before world-upheaval had thrust him into this unlikely place. Or he may have confronted them only through some cautious yet abrasive correspondence. It was anyhow clear that he was familiar with their views and positions, whatever they were, as they were familiar with his. A dangerous awareness glowed between Mitwisser and the visitors: it was his imperial force that had compelled them to await him in the steaming heaviness of this equatorial room, where damp elbow pressed against damp elbow and the tea misted their eyeglasses with its own hot breath, and a secret savagery, like an ember rekindling, longed to break out. The man in the skullcap, it developed, was a refugee Viennese. A white-nosed fellow with a deformed left hand was revealed to be a specialist on tenth-century Egypt; with his good hand he quietly plucked a cigar out of his moist shirt pocket and sucked at it with so much diligence that he soon had the ceiling befogged. This encouraged the cigarette smokers, and since there were no ashtrays to be had (these were as foreign to the house as electric fans), I ran around the table dealing out extra saucers to catch the burnt-out stubs.

The bearded Viennese had started off, diffidently enough, in German; Mitwisser nearly flogged him into English. It was a surly moment: a ukase. *I have disposed of that tongue*, it said, *and so must you.* In all that smoke and swelter I saw how this aroused them, though I could detect no plausible link between the ordinary plainness of these men (except for the yarmulke and the bad hand, it was pointless to try to distinguish one from the other) and the turbulence that was beginning to spiral out of their suddenly violent mouths. These mouths, which had seemed so flat and contained, like the mouths of shrewdly affable grocers, were now wildly twisting and spewing, a gathering tornado of virulence. Or they were like the mouths of those sideshow magicians who draw out strings of colored cloth flags from their throats, an infinitude of flags, endlessly, endlessly. But these were not innocent flags; they were brutally pelting philosophies.

They were fighting him. They had come to fight him. They had come because he had summoned them to fight, and they felt the old vestigial power of his call; or because they were led by the dark curiosity that trawls minds to the grotesque, or the superseded, or the discarded, or the openly perverse; or because he was in merciless and deadly eclipse; or because it was they—their side of it, the party of victory—who had tossed him into eclipse; or because of their own volcanic anger. They raged against his will, his obsession, his desire—his thought. He was a violator (but he believed himself violated by world-upheaval, by their accusations, by their doubting enmity); his purpose, they said, was to subvert, to overthrow. He had deserted the green and fertile furrow, he had turned passionate, he had left disinterestedness behind, he had ruptured the Olympian surface of the scholar's detachment, he had submerged the distinction between the investigator and the investigated, the hunter and the hunted, he was no longer a historian after quarry, he had become the quarry, he had flung himself into the hearts of his prey. He had broken through the wall, the wall he had professed—the wall between belief and the examination of belief. A false profession. He had the smell of a renegade.

The white-nosed man with the bad hand dropped his cigar. A cry— high-pitched and sharp, a treble upstairs shock—was shooting through the smoke.

"Waltraut," Anneliese whispered, "all this noise, it woke her—"

But I kept my place under the dining room lintel. "Leave her be, she'll fall back—"

"Go and see!" Anneliese commanded.

I kept my place. It was Mitwisser I wanted to see. He stood—he had never taken a chair—under the spell of a resignation concentrated and embattled but strangely tranquil: a ship captain who is unsurprised by a squall. He looked satisfied; I thought he was satisfied. If you court the sea there will likely be a storm, and he had courted the sea, he had brought the sea into his own house, he had *made* the storm, he was the god of the storm, he was satisfied!

Again that cry: now it was descending the stair, now it had thinned to tiny breathless phantom moans enveloping a barefoot figure. Like a bird in a rush of wind, Mrs. Mitwisser flew into the room.

"Gentlemen, it's no good, it's no use"—she pulled and pulled at the torn breast of her nightgown—"no good at all—"

The visitors fell into a motionless silence.

"My dear Elsa," Mitwisser said.

"No good at all," she chanted, "no use, no good—"

"Mama," Anneliese pleaded.

"What is broken, gentlemen, you cannot put it again back, *nicht wahr?*"

The visitors rose in a body and mutely trickled out the door; only the man in the skullcap hesitated before Mrs. Mitwisser. "*Guten Abend*," he said.

"*Guten Abend*," she replied: a chatelaine presiding over farewells after an evening of delicacies and wine.

Anneliese took her mother's hand and began to lead her away. Mitwisser's enameled blue eye trailed after them; his face blazed. "Quite right," he said. I hardly knew what he meant by this; I was thinking what an oddity it was that he had ever lain beside the woman in the torn nightgown. He turned back to me with a little shrug of surprise, as if he had just discovered me there: "You see how it is," he said. "I have no peers in this matter. What lies beyond the usual is dismissed, it is regarded as wasteful and perverse. They judge it—my work—to be pointless. What was once valued there is not valued here. Here they lack the European mind, they are small."

"But isn't one of them from Vienna—"

"That one is no one at all. I will return now to my study. Please to shut off all these lights." He gestured toward the kitchen, where the kettle still steamed, and reached out himself to the dining room switch.

He left me in the dark, among empty cups and littered plates.

13

THE VISITORS never came again. The house resumed its isolation. The drawn-out heat wave ebbed. Mrs. Mitwisser no longer asked my forgiveness. Her playing cards remained under her pillow; a new pursuit lured her. She sat on the edge of her bed, with a little low chest drawn up beside it, sorting out the curlicued colored shapes of a vast jigsaw puzzle. The picture on the box was of a forest scene: masses of leaves, the trunks of trees casting dark columns of shadows, a foxtail glimpsed in a clump of bush—a confusion of chiaroscuro. I watched her assess the jumble of pieces, and saw how shrewdly she judged and matched and fitted together; she considered before she experimented. She was a scientist in a laboratory. If the experiment turned out to be successful, it was because she had considered. A square of noon sunlight fired the wild wisps of her hair; she yawned; then she continued the hunt, bathing her fingers in the mixed-up cardboard froth of yellow and orange and brown.

"There will after this be two more boxes," she informed me. She was prepared for a season of puzzles. This one belonged to Willi; he didn't care for such things. Neither did Gert or Heinz, who had given up their own boxes. The boys, all three of them, had no interest in puzzles or cards (they hated cards) or even books. They fled the house the instant they woke. They were bored with water and marsh, and nowadays were out exploring the neighborhood, where they happened on a meadow ideal for kite-flying. It lay behind a soldiers' monument—a tall cenotaph topped by a winged bronze Victory and dedicated to the fallen of the Great War. Every morning they ran to the meadow to fly their kites. Then they would lie on their backs in the grass, manufacturing whistles out of moist green blades and staring up at the sun-gilded angel. And afterward they would jump up to run with the kites again, in a flagging wind, so that the kites would swoop down and suddenly lift and finally crash, like fallen soldiers.

"He gives presents," Mrs. Mitwisser said. "Many presents. *Immer, immer!* Puzzles, kites. This James!" It came out "Chames," bitterly, in her resisting and clotted accent. With a wandering hand she sculpted an apparition out of the air: a puzzle-piece in the form of an invisible man, whose presence hung over the house.

I said, "He's kind to the boys then—"

"To my husband he is kind. So kind we become *Parasiten.*" Her attention flitted away. With quick precision she locked a scalloped bulge into its small harbor. A flowering twig materialized under her palm. "And you, Röslein, they don't pay you, hah?" Her tongue felt along her lower lip, navigating, as though she might find a word cruising on its surface. Then she found it: "Confess!"

"They don't pay me, no. I mean they haven't yet."

"They cannot pay until he permits. There is no money until he permits. He permits the puzzles and the kites. He permits the new shelves for my husband's books. He permits the pretty little cakes. He permits the flat in the city, and when that is not useful he permits this house. He does not permit you because he does not know you are here." Mrs. Mitwisser laughed. It was a laugh of perfect sanity. "We have no money because we are *Parasiten.* When he comes he will see you and they will tell him and he will know."

"When will that happen?"

"When he wishes, then he will come."

She held up a pair of unlikely shapes—each one a circle of fangs—and snapped them together, efficiently, like the jaws of a crocodile. Or like a navigator squeezing the legs of a caliper in order to shrink the world.

14

THE KARAITES.

I begin to see them, dimly, dimly, passing shadows, remote echoes, grayly trudging on the farthest rim of history, the other side of history, the underside. They are inked letters seeping through the backs of the pages of old chronicles: faint glyphs glimmering, just visible, an inside-out alphabet.

They come to me piecemeal, little by little, at Professor Mitwisser's whim. Or else he discharges them in a great cannon-blast of erudition, a whole colony shot out all at once in a single obscuring cloud.

They are dissidents; therefore they are haters. But they are also lovers, and what they love is purity, and what they hate is impurity. And what they consider to be impurity is the intellect's explorations; and yet they are themselves known for intellect.

Intellect engenders meaning: interpretation; commentary; parable; illumination; insight; dialogue; argument; corroboration; demurral; debate; irony; anecdote; analysis; analogy; classification; clarification. All these the Karaites repudiate as embroidery and fraudulence in the hands of their enemies (though not in their own hands). And all these are Talmud, the first layer of which is Mishna, containing commentary on Scripture, and the second layer of which is Gemara, containing commentary on Mishna. The exegetical voices calling to one another across the centuries grow more and more populous, denser and denser. A third-century sage will contradict a first-century sage; a fourth-century sage will disagree, and take the side of the first-century sage. A fifth-century sage will hold to a new idea altogether. If you were to stand on a mountain—Mount Tabor, say, or even Olympus—and turn your ear downward toward where the minds of the philosophers reside, you would hear the roar of impassioned colloquy below, like a wakening polyphonic thunder. And this would be Talmud, the fuguelike music of the rabbis conferring over the sense of a syllable out of Genesis.

All this the Karaites refuse and deny. In the ninth century they become the rabbis' foes. Scripture! they cry, Scripture alone! They will not tolerate rabbinic interpretation. They will not allow rabbinic commentary. They scorn metaphor and the poetry of inference. Only the utterance of Scripture itself is the heritage divine!

The rabbis (whom the Karaites call the Rabbanites, or the school of thought that clings to the rabbis) reject the Karaites as literalists. The Karaites, they say, see only the letters; they do not see the halo of meaning that glows around the letters.

The Karaites ridicule the Rabbanites. They ridicule them because the Rabbanites declare that the Talmud, which they name the Oral Torah, was received on Sinai by Moses together with Scripture, the Written Torah. The Rabbanites claim that the sacredness of the Oral Torah is equal to the sacredness of the Written Torah.

Literalists! retort the Rabbanites. Narrow hearts! At Sinai the minds of men were given the power to read the mind of God. Otherwise how would men know how to be civilized? How would we know how to understand a sentence—or a story—in Scripture?

You understand it twenty different ways! scoff the Karaites. One says one thing, another says another thing. And this clamor of contradiction you call equal to the Torah itself!

It is equal, the Rabbanites respond, because the radiance of Torah directs men's thoughts. Out of the soil of strenuous cogitation, which is the engine of holy inspiration, and which you Karaites demean as mere contradiction, burst the sweet buds of Conduct and Conscience. The Rational Mind is the Inspired Mind.

The Rational Mind, argue the Karaites (but they do not notice that they are arguing Talmudically, since Talmudic argument is what they disdain)—the Rational Mind will not accept that the so-called Oral Torah, codified by human hands recording human opinions, is equal to the Written Torah given by God to Moses at Sinai! You Rabbanites indulge yourselves in delusion. There is in you no law of logic. Hence we depart from you, we reject all ordinances and adornments, inferences and digressions, alleviations and mildnesses, that are not in the Written Torah. We sweep away your late-grown lyrics that have crept into your prayerbooks. Our liturgy draws purely from Scripture, not a jot or tittle of it man-made! Away with your late-grown poets, away with your late-grown jurists! Moses alone stood on Sinai!

Thus spake the Karaites. But the Jews until this day embrace the Rabbanites and their ocean of exegesis and disputation, of lore and parable, as fertile and limitless as the cosmos itself—while the Karaites are a speck, a dot, a desiccated rumor, on the underside of history. Sa'adia Gaon, in the tenth century, in his famous polemic against the Karaites, blew them with a puff of his lips into the darkness of schism.

This was how, dimly, dimly, and little by little, I derived the nature of the Karaites at my typewriter at night, to the chanting of Mitwisser's esoteric recitations.

And dimly, dimly, and little by little, like ink bleeding through paper, I came to believe that of all the creatures on earth, it was only Mitwisser, Mitwisser alone, who thought to resurrect these ancient dots and faded specks. Their living remnants might languish still, across from the Baltic Sea, or close to the Black and Caspian Seas, sequestered in queer European pockets; but they were shriveled, hidden, lost. Mitwisser's illuminations scarcely followed them there. Isfahan, Baghdad, Byzantium had seized his brain and driven it back, back—thirteen, fourteen, fifteen centuries back, into the muffled quarrels of sect after sect, doctrine upon doctrine. The Karaite laws of consanguinity and incest were more urgent to Mitwisser's gaze than the streets he walked on. These fevered and forgotten heretics and schismatics—their creeds and codes and calendars, their migrations and mutations, the long generations of their thinkers—these were his own.

Only his children mattered as much.

15

328 St. Peter's Street
The Bronx, Nevv York
September 5, 1935

Dear Bertram,

 The first thing you'll probably notice is hovv every double-you has a split all the vvay dovvn the middle, so that vvhen I vvant to type "vvindovv," say, or "vverevvolf," it comes out looking

like that!

 There are other problems too. VVatch out for those big blank skips that look like stutters in mid-sentence! Sometimes vvhen I'm using this machine I feel as if I'm piloting an aeroplane in a vvindstorm. I can never tell vvhat's about to happen, vvhether I'll be pitched up or dovvn or   sidevvays. (See?) It takes getting used to, though by novv I can pretty vvell control the rudder, or vvhatever you call the thing that keeps an aeroplane on course. I could ask Heinz—he knovvs all that sort of science thing. (I'll explain vvho Heinz is in a minute.)

 VVell, novv that you see vvhat I've been given to vvork vvith here, you'll understand hovv much I miss your typevvriter. (I had almost begun to feel it vvas <u>my</u> typevvriter.) Only I'm afraid you'll think vvhat I really mean is that I miss <u>you</u>. (I guess I

do.) I'm pretty sure Ninel
doesn't vvant me to bother you vvith letters, since you never told me vvhere you'd be. So I've tried hard not to vvrite, and for two vvhole months I haven't. Not that I'd exactly knovv

vvhere! And you haven't been able to vvrite to me, just in
case you ever vvanted to, because that address in Nevv York
City I sent you (I hope you got my postcard!) isn't vvhere
vve've ended up. There aren't any skyscrapers, it's definitely
not Manhattan! VVe're in a strange half-vvild place at the
edge of things, some little houses and plenty of empty lots,
and a svvamp nearby attached to a st   ony beach.

The family is strange, too—all tightly bound together,
vvhich you'd expect of refugees, only there's a sort of desperation in this house, they're still not feeling safe. The mother is
sick. The father is a kind of fanatic. It's the father I'm supposed to be vvorking for—I'm something like a secretary,
though actually I don't knovv vvhat I am. I do knovv that I'm
an outsider to these people—it's as if they've got a secret society of their ovvn. There are three young sons, and each one
has three sets of names. That Heinz I mentioned, he's Heinrich, and sometimes, vvhen they're in the mood, Hank. Right
novv he's interested in clocks. He takes them apart, so that
you can never tell vvhat ti   me it is. The chronology
seems all vvrong anyhovv. There's a daughter vvho's only
tvvo or three years younger than I am, but from the vvay she
is—very strict and solemn—you'd think she's a tired old
vvoman of forty. And there's a three-year-old, going on four,
vvho still sleeps in a crib like a baby. Her name is the ugliest
thing I've ever heard. The mother doesn't take care of her at all.

The house is mostly very quiet, especially novv that summer's over and the boys are in school. They go to the local
public school, vvhich the father thinks is useless but doesn't
oppose, since he's all for their forgetting they're Germans. The
older daughter and I vvatch over the little girl. That's the part
of the day I don't like, it's terribly boring, though it vvould be
considerably vvorse if she vvasn't still taking long afternoon
naps. The father stays avvay until evening, vvhich makes it
sound as if he has a job. He doesn't. The older daughter ought
to be in high school, but isn't. It's partly because the father
                              vvants her to look after

the mother and the little girl, but mostly it's because he vvants to supervise her education himself. She's the most studious one and his favorite. He's alvvays bringing home books for her to read, or else he finds something on his ovvn shelves, and then he quizzes her. Lately he vvon't allow any of the family to talk German. (He has the older daughter <u>read</u> it, though.) The mother speaks German some of the time anyhovv, you really can't tell her vvhat to do. Sometimes I think her sickness is a kind of vvar. She's like a revolutionary—she vvon't go along with the rest of them.

I've tried and tried to find out vvhere they get their income from. Not that they're anything like vvhat Ninel vvould call coupon-clippers! The mother lives mainly in her nightgovvn and the father in his one suit. The mother keeps hinting that they're dependents of some sort, but you can't rely on anything she says, vvhich is too bad, because she's the only one honest enough to vvant

Here I stopped. What did Mrs. Mitwisser want? And what was it I wanted from Bertram? The crack in the damaged key—so familiar by now that I scarcely knew it was there—all at once began to leak light, like an unexpectedly opening door. A clear split, a severance: Mrs. Mitwisser from her family, Mitwisser from his former elevation, the Karaites from the mainstream . . . Bertram from me. I thought of Bertram in his new life with Ninel. I imagined Ninel reading this letter; I imagined what she might say. I thought of the money in the blue envelope. The crack widened, the light shot through. A bribe! The money was a bribe. Bertram had bribed me to keep out of his future.

I took hold of a corner of the sheet and tore it from the platen. The paper came out ripped, jagged, with a zigzag scallop across its lower half.

And there stood Anneliese in the hallway, reddening like a sudden scar.

"What are you doing in papa's study in the middle of the day when he's away? You have no business in there now, get out!"

16

MY NIGHT SESSIONS with Mitwisser were growing sparser. Often when I appeared at the door of his study he sent me away and summoned Anneliese instead. Then the door was shut against me. I leaned my cheek on the wall and listened. There were nights when they read Carlyle and Schiller; at other times it was Spinoza. One week Mitwisser set Anneliese on a course of spherical trigonometry. The hum of their voices, seeping through, was unruffled. Anneliese was eager and quick.

"Papa puts off his night work for me, so you mustn't let mama interrupt," she warned me. "Papa wants you to keep her occupied while I'm having my lessons."

I knew what "occupied" signified: Mrs. Mitwisser was to be silenced. She had taken to singing again, German songs with pretty tunes. She had a loud coarse alto that seemed unnatural, as if what erupted from her throat was unable to reproduce the sound in her head, or as if she was punishing the music. Or else she was punishing Anneliese: the singing had begun when it was announced that Anneliese would not be going to the public high school.

"My husband makes her like himself," Mrs. Mitwisser grumbled. "She will become *eine Puppe*, he will give to her too many books, she will become *verrückt*."

She sang to blot out Anneliese's lessons. Gert and Willi slept through it all, but Waltraut habitually awoke and cried, and Heinz who was in the bed next to her crib awoke and complained, and the house that was so quiet all day was noisily chaotic at ten o'clock at night.

Mitwisser put an end to it. He called me into his study, where Anneliese was sitting at my little table—the typewriter had been cleared away. I looked all around for it, and there it was on the floor, pushed into a corner. It meant I was dismissed, displaced. Anneliese's notebooks lay open before her. I glimpsed her handwriting, as vertical and orderly as a row of chessmen—a European script not unlike her father's.

"My wife," Mitwisser began, "suffers from intellectual tribulation. She is perforce distant from her own affairs, deprived of her laboratory, of her true life. Her mind"—here he hesitated, while Anneliese opened her fist to play with her fingers, pressing the index finger of one hand against the index finger of the other—"I will say instead her *spirit:* her spirit looks back. You see it is the language—the language draws her back into the old places, the old life, so it is the language that must be deflected, defeated, evaporated—"

"Papa would like mama to improve her English," Anneliese said. It was the coldness of diplomacy, the father's anguish, or desperation—or was it merely his hope for relief?—translated into the daughter's briskness. And I, taking in the bossy lift of Anneliese's chin, the small suggestive tilt that signaled my obedience, translated further: no more intrusion, no more noise, no more German! Not in song, not in speech.

"You will read to her," Mitwisser finished.

"But if she won't—if Mrs. Mitwisser isn't willing—"

"She must be induced."

The rough artificial voice pitched itself higher and came fluting down on us in a flood of light-hearted mockery—an imitation, it almost seemed, of a madwoman's merry mockery:

> *Mein Hut der hat drei Ecke,*
> *drei Ecke hat mein Hut.*
> *und hätt' er nicht drei Ecke,*
> *dann wär er nicht mein Hut!*

I found Mrs. Mitwisser on the edge of her bed, as usual, bent over her puzzle pieces; but they were all undone, scattered. She was detaching shape from shape, restoring them to a scrambled mound, her quick wrists shuttling with the speed of a gleeful child pulling the legs off insect after insect.

"*So ein schöner Wald!*" she greeted me. "No more. You see? I break it."

"You can work it all over again," I assured her, "some other time."

Then I saw that she was taking pains to twist and crush each piece: the forest demolished.

"It is dead now. What is broken you cannot put it again back." She let the mutilated pieces sift through her fingers (fingers faster and nimbler in their movements than Anneliese's, and also smaller and more flexible), and looked up at me with a smile so obscurely at odds with the actions of her hands, and so unexpected and fresh and pleasant, that I felt I had for some reason won her approval. "Do you enjoy my funny song? A funny song, you know, for children."

"The children are sleeping, you wouldn't want to wake them—"

The smile receded. "Anneliese, she does not sleep!"

"Anneliese isn't a child, she's studying—"

"Down there, in his *Bücherei*, do you know what he teaches to her there?"

"History, I think. And literature and some math."

"He teaches to be *ein Bettler, ein Schmarotzertier! Ein Parasit!*"

And she sang:

> *Fünf Finger, aber keine Hand,*
> *Ein Schuh, doch ohne Sohle,*
> *Erst weiss wie eine Wand,*
> *Dann schwarz wie eine Kohle.*

"Please," I said. "It's not the time now, Mrs. Mitwisser."

"Such a funny song, *ja?*" The smile had resumed. "I explain it for you— *ein Handschuh!* What is clean you make dirty. You put in this glove the hand, it becomes puppet, you see? And if you teach to hold out the hand, it becomes beggar, dirty, *Parasit*, you see? It is because we have no more money. No money!" She threw out the kind of laughter that had long ago married itself to satire.

In her unpredictability, Mrs. Mitwisser had grown predictable; she specialized in refrains. Her broken mind, wherever it wandered, came back to money—though often enough, because of the needle-eye of taunting through which she threaded those refrains and obstinacies, I doubted that it was broken at all.

I missed my nights at the typewriter; I missed Mitwisser's Karaite recitations and emanations. I envied Anneliese, closeted with the conflagration of her father's furies. I even envied the three boys, who seemed wilder every day (they were gradually turning more and more American), departing in the morning with shouts and returning with shouts and punches, schoolboy style, their bookbags spilling loose sheets. School had solidified their names: they were now, incontrovertibly, Hank, Jerry, and Bill, though only with one another, and never for Anneliese. I envied them the liberated boisterousness of their lives outside our decorous and disciplined walls. Within these walls, only Elsa Mitwisser had chosen unrestraint.

It did not occur to me to envy Waltraut, still clinging to a motherless infancy she ought to have outgrown. Except for the two chocolate bars I remembered to give her, her fourth birthday had passed without notice. Her crib was her refuge—lately she was refusing to climb out of it, and lingered there all afternoon, dozing like an elderly dwarf. Or else she would sit on her pillow and dress and undress her doll, sometimes peering through the bars to see if anyone was happening by. The doll was an early possession, a refugee along with the Mitwisser family: it had a porcelain head, a red circle on each cheek, a tiny tongue protruding from partly open lips, and long legs stuffed with straw; also black fabric shoes frayed at the toes. It was a yellow-haired Bavarian doll in a dirndl. Now and then Waltraut dropped the doll and squeezed her knuckles against her ears; I had been witness to this oddness more than once, when Mrs. Mitwisser's singing drifted down the stairwell. I pitied Waltraut—I was her only playmate, and an unwilling one. In that house no one inflamed my thinking more than Professor Mitwisser.

"Have you started mama on her English?" Anneliese asked, a few days after her father's directive.

I said we had begun a novel.

"An American novel? Papa says it ought to be something that won't get her agitated."

"An English one."

Anneliese was satisfied; she trusted that what was not American would not shout or punch or agitate.

The novel we had begun was *Sense and Sensibility*. There were books all around—rows and rows of them, quantities and quantities—

but, as far as I could tell (so many were in recondite tongues and alphabets), no books of invention. The Karaites, to be sure, had invented themselves—not out of nothingness, but, as heretics will, out of an already existing splendor; yet they subtracted from imagination rather than added to it. Mitwisser's ten thousand volumes, with their bottomless excavations of Karaite heresy, could be thought of as fable, since history, in its own way, is fable, or at least parable. But what was wanted—what was wanted for Mrs. Mitwisser—was simply Story: a story about men and women free of history, except their own. "She must be induced," Mitwisser had decreed. Mrs. Mitwisser was not to be induced; she would slip away like a cloud altering the light, or she would thin her cheeks with the irritable vibrations of her little songs and lullabies. And since she was not to be induced, I reflected, she must be seduced.

This idea sent me to the middle drawer of the dresser next to my bed (the drawer just above the Bear Boy and Bertram's envelope—that blueness for which Mrs. Mitwisser had been forgiven a hundred times), where Ninel's scavenged presents lay among my underthings, the claylike smell of the Salvation Army's damp cellar still faintly in their pages. *Hard Times*, which had Ninel's tepid approval, I set aside at once—Mrs. Mitwisser had endured enough of hard times. It was Jane Austen I snatched up, and I knew exactly why. It was because of the money. Ninel had intended *Sense and Sensibility* as punishment or rebuke or sneer, to remind me that the novels I loved were steeped in the pre-Marxist capitalist darkness of their wickedly imperialist times; their domestic attractions eluded her.

I recited:

The family of Dashwood had been long settled in Sussex. Their estate was large, and their residence was at Norland Park, in the center of their property, where for many generations they had lived in so respectable a manner as to engage the good opinion of their surrounding acquaintance.

Mrs. Mitwisser understood all this very well; it glimmered with unfamiliar familiarity; none of it was beyond her comprehension. She understood it *pleasurably*—remembering when she had herself lived in so respectable a manner as to engage, etc.; and when the Dashwood fortunes fell—"Their mother had nothing, and their father only seven thousand pounds in his own disposal"—she warmed to the affinities she instantly felt: the loss of money, the necessity of money, the hope of money; standing, expectation, repute.

I read and read until my throat thickened and my voice blurred. I read aloud night after night, the Scheherazade of that half-barren spot in the distant reaches of the city. The squat wooden chest on which Mrs. Mitwisser had been working her puzzles was still in its old position. I placed a lamp on it and drew up a chair; Mrs. Mitwisser sank back into her pillow. Below, in Mitwisser's study, the cadenced iambic murmurs of father and daughter, question and answer, intermingled. The boys slept on. Waltraut, secure in her crib, never woke. The madwoman's songs were snuffed.

We had got as far as Chapter Thirty, with the faithless Willoughby betraying Marianne Dashwood, and Mrs. Jennings deploring the man who "has no business to fly off from his word only because he grows poor, and a richer girl is ready to have him," when Anneliese appeared at the door and whispered my name.

"Rosie! Come out here for a minute."

Mrs. Mitwisser's head, under the lamp, bucked like a small shaggy horse. Her quick hand took hold of my knee. "You must finish," she said.

"Anneliese wants me—"

"First you must finish."

Anneliese stepped toward us. The two brown braids that coiled around her ears had lost their pins; her hair flooded down past her shoulders and over her breasts. I had not known that her hair was so long. It was as if, with its release, the danger I had always been wary of, the danger of a restrained ferocity, was draining out of her: out of the ends of her spreading hair. One demon was dissolving; another was forming: it had begun by undoing her braids.

She caught up the book—her wild arm circled and made a wind—and threw it on Mrs. Mitwisser's bed.

"Come out, I want to tell you something!"

I followed her. We stood in the dark of the hall.

"Papa gave me the news just now. Just now, though he's known it all day—since this morning. There's a letter finally."

An impatient shifting in the bed. "Röslein, where do you go, *komm schnell zurück*—"

"If mama hears, she'll just carry *on*." Anneliese pushed me deeper into the dark. "It's James," she whispered. "James is coming! Papa kept it to himself—he waited till the boys were asleep, he doesn't want them to get all excited too soon. But we need to get ready right away. Heinz goes in with Gert and Willi, and I go in with Waltraut, and James goes across from papa, in my room, so we need to do the sheets and things."

"And your mother?"

"She stays just where she is. In with you."

"No, I mean about—this James."

"Well, she has to take it, she has to swallow it, that's all!"

I thought this over. Fear of Anneliese was dying in me: with her hair unbound and raining down, hiding those diminutive matronly alien earrings, she was, I saw, only a girl.

I said, "Will Professor Mitwisser have to swallow it too?"

"What a stupid thing to say," Anneliese spat out. "Papa and James, you don't know a thing about it. They're like one person. They're exactly the same." She whirled away from me so forcefully that the spray of her hair came whipping against my face. "I need you to help with the bedding early tomorrow morning, that's the point. Now go back to mama."

Half-sitting, sunk into her pillow, Mrs. Mitwisser had grown quiescent. I believed she had fallen into a doze in spite of herself. The lamp was pulled nearer; she was very still. The light whitened the visible bones of her wrist and her narrow fingers. But her eyes were unsealed, sleepless, rapt. The small white fingers were gripping the book that smelled of cellar. Mrs. Mitwisser was reading, in a seizure of concentrated intelligence, an English novel.

Her canny husband had accomplished the obliteration of German in every room of the house except his own.

17

THE MITWISSER BOYS had long bones and long feet. It was plain that they were destined to grow tall. Heinz was already showing signs of lengthening: his arms strained out of their sleeves. Willi, the smallest and the youngest, was the most beautiful. His eyes were as round as wheels, with almost no tapering at the corners, brown melting into a black so dense that one expected distant starlight to filter out of it, as out of a bottomless black firmament. The impatient skin of his temple pulsed; his was the sexless beauty of a young child. Waltraut had none of this. She was languishing, she had lost smiles and affection, she was becoming a tiny crone: the life of the house was aging her. She cared for nothing but her doll.

In that family of long bones—bone of forearm, bone of thigh— only Mrs. Mitwisser was different. She was a little woman with whom a giant had seen fit to couple. Mitwisser, the progenitor of all those long bones, stalked and circled like some great mobile statue quarried out of a mountainside; he was obliged to dip his head down when he entered a room, so as not to strike the lintel. And Anneliese, flying from one household task to another, seemed to rise and rise into loftiness, her elastic neck evolving out of the long level bone of her clavicle. Mitwisser and his daughter, a pair of colossi; and next to them—though she was rarely next to them, and was more often sequestered—Elsa Mitwisser, short-necked, narrow-shouldered, small-fingered. It was as if she had designed this narrowness, this smallness: all her children had been formed on some scientific plan within the confines of her littleness. She was a scientist and a naturalist, and both science and nature are in pursuit of efficacy and economy. Both science and nature rebel against disorder and fracture; and yet disorder and fracture had vanquished and desolated her. They had overturned the governance of her mind.

But I wondered still whether she was truly mad, or whether her madness had itself come into being on some scientific plan. World-up-heaval had capsized and stupefied her. Then she must answer! Answer disorder with disorder, fracture with fracture; she must refuse and refuse. Once or twice, having refused, she recanted. She had refused her shoes—but now she wore them. She had refused the language of exile —but now she was in thrall to a narrative wherein mind was governance, and a nation was stable, and disorder and fracture were tamely domesticated. She spoke of "Chane Osten" with an ardor that only anger had been able to ignite, and when she got to the end she began again, though she complained of the smell. She did not protest the language of exile; she was immersed in it, captivated. True madness, I thought, does not reverse itself. True madness will not recant. Was she Hamlet, for whom madness is ruse and defense and trap, or was she Ophelia, whom true madness submerges? And her smallness: she had schemed it to set herself apart from those Mitwisser giants—to escape them by curling into hidden corners. Now she curled with her book. Privy to magickings and delusions denied to others, she shrank herself at will. She was a little woman with unknowable powers. She had no love for her children. Waltraut longed for her and feared her.

Her idea of James was mad. I was sure of it as soon as he came through the green front door with a dirty wet knapsack on his back and a scarred suitcase, running with water, in one hand; the other was pulling off a dripping knit cap. It was raining, pelting, the drops heaving horizontally like bullets in a barrage, a lead curtain of waterfall blown sideways. It was the kind of rain that made me obscurely anxious, in the way of some remembered alarm, or warning, or turning point. We had left Albany in the rain—but that was an ordinary downpour, a thing of chance. Through the open door as he lumbered in, weighed down and soaked through, I smelled that half-metallic smell of earth and concrete, the mixture of contradictory elements that sometimes swelled in my nostrils when I saw, in my dreams, my father's car crumpled in the road, under a hammering screen of murderous rain. I feared those dreams. They swarmed like reenactments of something foretold.

He was not young; neither was he old. He was a ragged sort of fellow. If I had met him in the street I would have taken him for a vagrant and given him a wide berth; I would have dreaded the accidental touch of his sleeve. He wore rubbers over his shoes, but no socks. When his cap was off a heap of black hair went tumbling over the streaming lenses of his glasses: impossible to see his eyes behind all that water. A vagrant; a vagabond; a man with a knapsack and no socks. This was James, James the deliverer, the James who was to deliver my wages, the James who had supplied this house, and the pretty little cakes, and the puzzles and kites, and the lavish apartment in the city that had been relinquished on account of Mrs. Mitwisser's waywardness; this was the James who had made them *Parasiten*, the James whose messianic coming, Anneliese had predicted (was she as mad as her mother?), would shower them all with plenty of money.

The boys were all over him, an onslaught of boys, climbing and slapping and screeching and punching and squeezing; they were squeezing him dry, his feet spurted puddles, a geyser of laughter splashed up. Laughter! Mitwisser was in it, inside the laughter, afloat in the rowdiness, gurgling like the others, like his own unbridled boys. I had never before seen him laugh. It altered him. Hidden creases, bursting into folds, corrugated the long slab of his jowl, and there, behind the contorted lips, like secret things exposed, were his big ruined teeth. Folds and contortions: the twistings of his mouth were hideously recognizable. Mitwisser in his melancholic ambassadorial coat and vest, Mitwisser laughing, exactly resembled the Mitwisser I had witnessed in the great glut of his weeping.

He hurtled forward and embraced the vagrant and kissed his two cheeks. "Welcome, welcome," he cried.

"Whoa, I'm being throttled here. Hank, get off my neck, dammit! Bill! Hey! Unhand these primates, Rudi, can't you?" He was thrashing like a wild man, roaring; he had called Mitwisser Rudi, which was unimaginable. In this house of rules, he had no rules.

Only Anneliese stood back. She had restored the snail-like coils over her ears. Her tiny earrings glinted. She faced the wet wild man with his wild forelock and wild roar and said formally, "This"—her palm outward toward me—"is my brothers' tutor. From when we first came." But it was I, not James, who was being explained—he was as self-evident, for all of them, as the rain; so I did what was expected, and held out my hand, and said my name.

"Rosie," he repeated, and Anneliese said, "She types for papa." I watched her take the man's things—the knapsack, the suitcase, the knit cap, the jacket frayed at the collar, everything sodden and leaking rain— and saw how he handed them over, not troubling to look at her, crowing and beaming at the boys, his arm solidly around Mitwisser. She disappeared with his belongings, and in a jubilant parade he led the rest of them in; he was a Pied Piper, he was jolly with all of them. "Hey you! You Rosie!" he called. "Where's the little one? Fetch me that Wally, I've got to see that old Wally!"

At the head of the stairs I came on Mrs. Mitwisser, barefoot and again in her nightgown—an hour ago she had been fully dressed. The top step was littered with bits of paper.

"He is here," she said.

I picked up a handful of the paper fragments. "What's this?"

"He has come. Now he has come."

Jane Austen lay dismembered, page after page torn to pieces and strewn like confetti in a path that ended, or began, at the foot of Mrs. Mitwisser's bed. How Ninel would have been pleased!

18

THE NEW SLEEPING arrangements had to be gotten used to. The three boys were jammed together in a single room, the room that had been Gert and Willi's. But now Heinz was with them, an intruder mimicking Anneliese and ordering them to do this and that; they protested with shrieks and howls and flying missiles—pencil cases, pillows, hard thick balls of knotted socks. Anneliese's small store of possessions was heaped in a corner near Waltraut's crib. Cots were carried from floor to floor. All these displacements were for James's sake; for the sake of the immensity of his coming. He had come, he was here. Anneliese's bed was his bed, where Anneliese had slept he now slept, close to Mitwisser's lair. Only Professor Mitwisser was left undisturbed. And though I kept my place with Mrs. Mitwisser, the walls of our common cubicle, trembling from the boys' pummelings yards away, were electrified by a change larger than the refiguration of the rigid chessboard of our little house. We had been eight; or, rather, *they* had been seven, and I a hireling, never an intimate. Now we were nine, and the ninth was more than an intimate. He was a power. There was power in his laughter, and the laughter crept into the walls.

Mrs. Mitwisser could not be made to go downstairs; she ate from trays in her bed. It was like Albany again: the tray with its leftovers waiting to be taken away. But she was quiet. She returned to her cards, laying them out on the top of the wooden chest while noiseless wisps of angry breathing burst from her. Anneliese's nightly lessons had stopped; it was James who sat with Mitwisser. The door was wide open. It was as if an eyelid had lifted. Talk swarmed out, talk and the rusted vibrations of Mitwisser's estranged hilarity, sudden high bleats erupting out of his heavy dark bass. James's voice was thin and light. His eyes behind their lenses were small inspecting devices; his glasses flashed, and the flashes swept into crannies, searching. He was a kind of detective. How long would he stay? There was no hint of his leaving. In the mornings, when Mitwisser departed for the Library and the boys were off to school (reluctantly now, crowding around James, teasing and pushing), he plucked up Waltraut and swung her between his legs and told her she was a little mouse and he a big lion, and then he told her she was the lion and he the mouse, and she ran circling and hiding, screaming with pleasure. But there were times when Mitwisser did not put on his hat and pick up his briefcase and walk with that rapid giant's gait into the street and toward the train. Instead he would take James by the arm and lead him into his study. They murmured together in the sunlight that came shooting through the high window. Even the light seemed new; I had never before noticed how it stamped a white rectangle on the carpet. No one summoned me. Anneliese gave me few instructions. She brought her mother's meals to her and came down again. The blue veins in her translucent temples faintly beat; for the first time I saw how she resembled Willi. The days were different now. The nights were different.

Boxes began to arrive. They were large and heavy. One was brown and very large, carried in on the shoulders of two men: a bed for Waltraut. Another box held half a dozen dolls, each in native costume—a Spanish doll, a Polish doll, a Swedish doll, a Tyrolean doll, all petticoats and colored headdresses and silk boleros, and a Scottish boy doll in tartan and kilt, with tiny bagpipes sewed on, and another boy doll with a painted face, dressed like a clown in a white ruff. And after that, though I never knew how it happened, Waltraut's crib disappeared. There was a box for Heinz: an Erector set and a square electric clock without hands —big numbers dropped out of nowhere and clicked into place. And for Gert a scooter with blue handlebars and a harmonica and a fleet of three biplanes with rubberband engines. And for Willi roller skates and a balsawood birdcage with a yellow canary inside, made out of calico, which sang when its beak was twisted.

There was nothing for Anneliese.

When Mitwisser was away James sat in his study—that sacrosanct cavern no one dared enter. Sometimes, on one of their chases, Waltraut pursued him there, the two of them whirling from corner to corner, Waltraut half wild with hilarity, and James shouting "Mouse! Mouse!" And then Anneliese would come and lure Waltraut away. Waltraut had turned lively. It was as if she had awakened from melancholia to become a normal child again.

But the house was not normal. The door to Mitwisser's study was always open. Passing by, I saw James in Mitwisser's chair, handling Mitwisser's mysterious volumes. He held them doglike, inquisitive yet uncomprehending. "You, Rosie," he called. "I need you to tell me something."

It was eleven o'clock in the morning. The boys were at school, and Anneliese had taken Waltraut with her. They walked out to the dusky shops under the train trestle, Waltraut's little hand in Anneliese's. This too was new. Waltraut had abandoned her old Berlin doll with its straw-stuffed legs. It had vanished together with her crib; she never looked for it. She forgot her deep infantile afternoon sleep. The smells of autumn were all around, the smell of reddening and browning leaves; the heat ebbed out of the sidewalks. Our summer walks seemed distant and unreal.

Mrs. Mitwisser was aware of everything below—even two flights below. She cocked her head, listening. I was certain she was cocking it this minute. Her hearing was keen. Her ears were avid and angry.

"All this stuff is Greek to me," James said. "Can't figure if I've got the alphabet upside down or sideways."

"I think some of it really is Greek," I said.

"I suppose you can't get into it either."

"No," I said, "I can't."

"How about this?" He put his thumb on the page to show me.

I had lately learned the look of those marks. "I guess it's Hebrew, though it might be Aramaic. So far Professor Mitwisser won't let me touch those books, he says I'm not ready. Anneliese's the only one."

"Why poke your nose in something if you don't know what you're poking it in, is that the idea?" Under the glint of his glasses he gave out a thin satiric whistle. "Myself, I don't hold with that. How about the German? Can you read the German? There's a whole lot of German in here. What's this, Arabic?—Arabic, sure, I can tell Arabic, I lived out there."

"I can't read any of it."

He had made himself at home in this room. He had brought his teacup in.

"So what do you do for Rudi? Annie says you type things up—"

"Professor Mitwisser dictates and I type."

"On that derelict thing over there? That pile of old bones?"

There it lay, pushed aside: the typewriter with the split in the double-u. I was nervous standing in the square of morning sunlight. The glare was in my eyes. I thought of Mrs. Mitwisser upstairs, fingering her grimy playing cards; I thought of money.

"Professor Mitwisser hired me back in Albany," I said.

"He hired you? You were hired?"

"He put an ad in an Albany paper and I answered it."

"He hired you?" he said again. "That means a salary, doesn't it? All right. Fifteen—no, eighteen dollars a week. Will that do?" The sly whistle. "You must be worth something to Rudi, or you wouldn't be here."

"I help out a little," I said.

"I hear you're trying to get the Frau Doktor to start talking the king's English. Rudi would like that. You'd do him a service if you accomplished that. Some people need to change their lives if they want to live at all. But not Rudi, Rudi's got to keep at it. Rudi's a great man, Rudi's tremendous—I hope you understand that." He took a sip of his tea, looked hard at me over the crescent of the cup, and swallowed the rest down. "What were you doing up in Albany?"

"I was at the teachers' college."

"Annie tells me you quit."

Why did he ask what he already knew? I said, "The cousin I was living with got married, so I had to leave." For a reason I hardly fathomed, I added, "His wife is a Communist."

This made him fall into a long laugh. I recognized it; it had passed like a wave through the children, it had passed through Mitwisser. I had heard it at night, mingled with the shock of Mitwisser's broken crowing.

"A Communist? No fooling, if your cousin ever takes over, my goose is cooked. She'd do me in. I'm a goddamn genuine plutocrat, that's why."

Plutocrat was one of Ninel's words. I wanted to explain that Ninel was not really my cousin, that Ninel and Bertram were not really married, but just then, over our heads, like some monumental coin flung down, a gonglike crash shook the ceiling.

"Mrs. Mitwisser!" I said, and ran upstairs to see.

She had hurled her breakfast tray into the hall beyond the bedroom —the little narrow hall where Anneliese had whispered to me of James's coming.

"He pulls you, he pulls you to his side! He buys you, he gives money! With this money let him go to live in the El Dorado, not here!"

Some days after that, late in the afternoon, another box, compact and weighty, was delivered to the green front door. The boys gathered in a circle around Anneliese as she opened it. Inside was a shining black Royal typewriter, redolent of new metal and fresh oil. The old machine, the fossil, was gone.

"Look how good James is to you," Anneliese told me. "A stranger like yourself. When papa comes home it will be such a surprise."

"No it won't," Gert and Heinz and Willi all called out together.

"No it won't," Waltraut said. These were her first English words.

Not long afterward I learned that the El Dorado was the name of Berlin's most luxurious hotel.

19

THE NEW TYPEWRITER was lodged in a closet. Professor Mitwisser had no use for it now; he had no use for me. Each night he took tea with James in his study. Anneliese carried in the tea things on a tray—it was different from the dented tin platters that went upstairs to Mrs. Mitwisser. This one was made of china, with a pattern of yellow roses all over it, and matching cups and saucers, and a creamer and a sugar bowl and a fat round pot. The cups were rimmed with gold. Like the new typewriter and the toys and Waltraut's bed, the tea things had just been introduced into the house. The "tea things"—this was James's name for them. "My mother was fond of tea things," he said, "she owned dozens"—and because of that "dozens," I suspected him of parody.

He poured the tea for Mitwisser. Into his own cup he spilled something else; I saw a tall amber bottle standing near his foot. And it occurred to me that when he lingered here in the mornings with his teacup, there was whiskey in it.

"That one and his schnapps," Mrs. Mitwisser threw out at me from her pillow. "He sits with my husband and makes the ha-ha-ha, *dieser Säufer!*"

The language project was abandoned. Neither inducement nor seduction could draw Mrs. Mitwisser. "Chane Osten," rent, was dismissed and abolished. Mrs. Mitwisser kept to her bed and fidgeted with her cards. She would not look at a book in English. She would not look at any book. She gave a small scream—a scream more than a whimper—when I attempted to read aloud to her. Instead I began to read to Waltraut (a carton of picture books had suddenly materialized), but often enough Anneliese would snatch her from me: James, she explained, had requested a romp with old Wally, and the three of them, Anneliese and Waltraut and James, would set out for one of the weedy meadows, hay-like and autumnal now, that ringed the neighborhood. One morning a taxi appeared. "It's off to the Bronx Zoo with old Wally," James announced. Anneliese said, "Take care of mama," and then she and James lifted Waltraut onto the seat between them and shut the door, and the taxi rumbled away.

There was nothing I could do for Mrs. Mitwisser. I was no longer permitted to bring her food. She would not accept it from me—I stood accused of having James's money in my pocket. Once again I had no duties; yet two weeks after my conversation with James, Anneliese silently put into my hands a twenty-dollar bill, a ten-dollar bill, a five-dollar bill, and four silver quarters. All but the ten and the coins I hid away together with Bertram's blue envelope—not in the dresser drawer under the Bear Boy, as before, but in a new hiding place. In the back yard I had stumbled over one of Willi's discarded sneakers, torn and drenched and half covered with mud. It seemed an impregnable cache, immune to theft. I let it dry and cleaned it as well as I could, and stuffed into it Bertram's money and much of the money Anneliese had given me. The sneaker lay locked in my suitcase, and the suitcase itself was safely stored under Mrs. Mitwisser's bed.

I was idle; I was free. There were whole days when James would summon Anneliese out for still another excursion. "The kid needs to get out," he said. "You can't keep a little thing caged up like that." Taxis came and went, while I wandered through the empty house, myself caged, listening to Mrs. Mitwisser's steady sighs and groans. Private mutterings and garbles had replaced the coarse singing; she was invoking secret spells and maledictions. I took to looking out the windows, this one and that one, but there was little to see, only the gray curbs, the row of small houses with their low evergreen shrubs, the patch of muddy yard where, under the single tree, I had found Willi's sodden sneaker. Here and there a triangle of sky. From the window of the boys' room the sky was largest of all, and against it, in the distance, a dark horizontal blur: the high trestle, several streets away, on which lay the streaming tracks that led to the true city, and to the great Library where Mitwisser toiled day after day.

When the boys clattered in after school, it was Heinz who carried up Mrs. Mitwisser's afternoon tray. Early that morning the taxi had swept away Waltraut and her pair of escorts. This time it was a puppet show that lured them; it seemed there were more puppet shows in the world than anyone knew, and more toy shops and carousels, and more unexplored far-away playgrounds. Mrs. Mitwisser in her nightgown sat upright with a red glare that swelled her eyelids; she chewed her toast with angry lethargy. Nearby, in the little hall outside her door, sprawled on their bellies, her sons were howling over a game of Monopoly. A present from James, a prize brought back from Waltraut's last outing. The dice rattled, there were shrieks of hilarity. A gambler's game; I heard Mrs. Mitwisser's mumbled *"Er soll zum El Dorado gehen"* (the El Dorado had turned into one of her spells), and thought of my father throwing dice for shoes at Croft Hall, and put on my coat and left the house.

The ride into the city was long. The train began in the air, at first level with roofs and treetops, and then increasingly shadowed by the upper stories of lofts and factories, until it shook with the shock of the blink through the tunnel's blackness. When I came up from the subway at Forty-second Street, it was into a flowing gully of striders, gray fedoras like a field of dandelions gone to seed, hurrying women stuttering on Chinese heels. A denatured autumn wind smelled of trolley ozone. Under the dusty towers of Manhattan dusk was quickening.

At the corner of Fifth Avenue, turning south in that human river, I saw through the falling dark a pair of lions—stoic flanks, steady manes—and behind them the Library's broad stone steps, where hoboes squatted with their bundles. Past the doors, marble—marble up and marble down: a kingly hall, polished corridors hung with manuscripts and old prints, a lofty marble stair, and then the cavernous Reading Room, elongated, measureless, its far ceiling carved and painted gold, its walls running with oaken catalogues (their thousand drawers, their million cards), the immense tables wide and gleaming, spotted with green-shaded lamps, the hundred men and women hunched or half-reclining, books lying open like flocks of dormant wings, the whir of pages fingered. A misty veil-like absence stirred in the spacious emptiness above all those bent necks, as if ghosts were playing in the nowhere: invisibles humming the noise of noiselessness.

In a nook protruding from a wall and framed by shelves standing at right angles to each other—a small secret chamber in that vastness—I discovered the Hotel El Dorado. It was listed, together with photographs, in a brittle old manual called *Grand Inns of Europe: The Modern Tourist's Guide.* I pulled it out from where it was wedged, among tall bound maps (nations that were no longer nations) and crumbling city directories (Turin, Munich, Glasgow, Rheims, Aarhus, those brightly named Old World settlements with their hidden storied streets), and read: *Berlin's most illustrious hotel. 55 suites, with parlor and bath. Three resplendent dining rooms, vintage wines, celebrated orchestras, evening parties welcome, uniforms permitted.* A photograph showed a fringed canopy, a doorman in operatic epaulets, a pretty young woman with bobbed hair smiling under a cloche. Uniforms permitted; the Kaiser's officers; an obsolete regime. Was this one of the hotels into which the Mitwisser family had grimly paraded, wearing their best clothes, pretending to own the rights of legitimate guests, in order to use the toilet in the lobby? On the next page, two more photos, the first displaying the El Dorado's façade: it resembled a cathedral, with gargoyles and spires. The other was of a huge bed heaped with ruffled satin cushions, captioned REST PEACEFULLY IN GERMANY'S MOST WELCOMING CITY.

I shoved the *Modern Tourist's Guide* back into its niche; with a tiny rasp the fragile canvas binding tore. A gash. On either side fragments of maps trickled down.

All the bent necks. Notebooks and fountain pens. Pyramids of reference volumes. Histories. Lost languages. Men in shirtsleeves and vests, their pens zigzagging; here a woman ferociously recording numbers under a magnifying glass. Restless slidings of feet, a hand stretched up against the light from a bronze-based green-shaded lamp. The movements of elbows. Bent necks; more stretches; yawns.

Far away, across the length of the Reading Room, an infinity away, Professor Mitwisser sat. I saw his giant's back, with its monumental shoulders; I saw a hump on the table before him: his hat. All around, the rustling of gathered papers, chairs scraping, books slapping shut like so many gunshots. It was half past five; the great hall was thinning out. I looped my way through emptying aisles until I was as close to Mitwisser as I dared. His briefcase was propped, limp and unopened, on the seat next to him. The limitless plain of that enormous table spread itself perfectly bare from end to end; its lamps went suddenly dark. "Closing, we're closing," a voice warned: a distant tiny female voice, vibrating out of a void. Mitwisser was motionless. His head, a heavy fallen thing. His long arms in their well-used woolen sleeves. His eyes, terrifying blue starers. This was the man whose nights were newly given over to laughter; to the comedy of James. He looked to me now like a mummy exposed—a mummy whose wrappings had been stolen away.

20

I SAW HIM THERE the next day, and some days after that. It was easy for me to leave the house. No one minded, no one noticed. I chose only those times when Anneliese had gone off with James and Waltraut on some daylong excursion; there were more and more of these excursions. At first I made sure to wait until the boys came home from school, at half past three, when Heinz would take up Mrs. Mitwisser's tray—the meal that either Anneliese or I had prepared that morning. But after a while it seemed useless to wait. Mrs. Mitwisser was anyhow asleep. It was her habit to fall into an early afternoon doze—she woke only when her sons flooded the hall with their clamor.

At one o'clock I was already on the train into the deep city. Was it wicked to abandon Mrs. Mitwisser to an empty house? I was on my way to a greater wickedness: I meant to spy on Professor Mitwisser yet again. That had not been my first intention. My plan had been to accost him— how he would be startled!—and to explain that I was eager to assist him: hadn't I been hired for that? I was ready to fetch books, even to transcribe pages, as long as they were in a familiar alphabet that, however laboriously, I could copy. My plan was to offer myself for work. But there was no work. He was punctual; he believed in regularity. He was driven by a scholar's obligation. He came every day with his hat and his briefcase.

I found a seat at a table somewhat to the side and behind him and watched him. He was not always idle. Sometimes he drew out a paper from a pocket and a pen from his vest and set one beside the other. Then he would pick up the pen, scratch out a word or two, and drop it again. Or he would push back his chair and wander toward the great central desk to collect a thick volume he had ordered. Under that immense ceiling his shoulders were drained of power, his big frame was dwarfed. The daily journey, the punctuality, the regularity—all pretense. As long as James was in the house the Royal would remain shut up and mute. He was a man without a place in the world. I felt I was spying on disgrace. There was excitement in it: would he look up and around, would he recognize me in such unexpected surroundings? And if he did, what would I say, what would happen? To tempt the possibility, I moved to the table directly in front of his, squarely in his line of sight. But his eyes were fixed on his hat.

It was past three o'clock. Now his head had fallen. I saw the creases in his neck, and thought of Mrs. Mitwisser marooned in a trance of desolation. The late autumn sun, masked by granite, was bringing charcoal shadows to the feet of the Lions. As I came down the terraced stone steps toward Fifth Avenue, a rhythmic shouting, like the repeated barks of dozens of coxswains, flew up in ragged spurts from the street. A straggle of marchers carrying banners and placards was beginning to disband. The fringe of onlookers was already dissolved into chaos; all that remained were a few remnant disputants. A bearded man in a gypsy bandanna darted up to one of the Lions with a dripping paintbrush, splashed a red streak across its paw, and ran up the stairs. A policeman on horseback let out a yell and clattered away. A woman with a cropped head wearing men's trousers sank onto the bottom step, smacked down the stick of her placard, and looked up at me.

"Well, well, well," she said—her voice was hoarse, she was one of the coxswains—"if it isn't the little bookworm herself, the one Bert threw out, right where you'd expect her to be—"

"Bertram didn't throw me out," I said.

"—right in front of the robber baron's monument, look at that—"

I said again, "Bertram didn't throw me out. You did."

"You can't say you're not better off. You can thank me for getting you out of Albany—I heard you got out," Ninel said. "Albany's a dead end. I *told* Bert I wasn't going to get buried there." She held up the stick of her sign: it read, in large purple letters, NCDPP, and below that, in smaller black letters, NATIONAL COMMITTEE FOR THE DEFENSE OF POLITICAL PRISONERS. "I'm down in the Village now. There's plenty activity in the Village."

It struck me that she had said "I," not "we," so I asked where Bertram was.

"Back there where I left him. He moved out of my old place, so who knows. A faker, he wasn't serious. It was all sentiment for him—as if there's a difference between sentiment and slobber. Slobber doesn't get anything *done*."

Over her head the Lion's paw was bleeding paint.

"See that? That's how things get done." She nodded her stick upward toward the Library's great doors. "Know who built this thing?"

"It's free," I said, "anybody can use it—"

"Sure, and the poor broken backs who hauled the stones, it was free for *them*, wasn't it? That's right, go ahead, love your benefactor—"

It was the same as it had been: Ninel bewildered and frightened me. Her talk was no different from the sign on her stick.

"My benefactor," I said, "was Bertram."

"I'll bet. He gave you money."

"How do you know that—"

"That Little Orphan Annie look you used to put on? I wormed it out of him. He gave you money that should've gone to the movement. The last straw."

"Ninel!" someone yelled.

"Hey, Charlie—Charlie!" She stood up and waved: the bearded man in the bandanna was bounding down the Library steps.

"Took a leak in John Jacob Astor's very own latrine," he said. "Improved it a bit, too. Swabbed a big bloody A right in front of where it said MEN. Ran out of paint, shoved the brush down the toilet.—Who's this?"

"Some parasite down from Albany. Her papa rubbed noses with the swells. Here," Ninel said, handing me the long pole of her placard, "stick this up your benefactor," and walked off with the man in the red bandanna.

Parasite. Mrs. Mitwisser's very word.

21

328 St. Peter's Street
The Bronx, New York
October 26, 1935

Dear Bertram,

   I tried to write you once before, on a sick old typewriter, but I
didn't know where to send a letter, and I still don't. As you can see,
this is a nice fresh ribbon, and the machine is brand-new. I'm the
first to use it, though it isn't mine. I pulled it out of the closet where
it's been stored—it was bought for my employer, Professor Rudolf
Mitwisser, who

October 26, 1935

Dear Bertram,

   How I wish I knew where you were, so I could send you this letter! I suppose I could write care of Albany General, if you're still
working in the pharmacy, but somehow I feel it isn't somehow I feel
it wouldn't

October 26, 1935

Dear Bertram,

   You will be amazed to hear that I've seen Ninel! She came out of
a march just as it was breaking up. She had a banner and her hair
was shorter than I remembered but otherwise she looked just the
same. It was some sort of protest, and she was with a man who was
throwing paint. This was in New York, on Fifth Avenue

This was in New York, where I am liv

I am not living exactly in New Yo

There were crowds all around, and police, and noise and yelling. I was at the Forty-second Street Library in my capacity as assistant to

I had gone to be of assistance to

October 26, 1935

Dear Bertram,

I've heard that Ninel has deserted you

I've heard that Ninel's left you, so it's a good thing, after all, that you never did actually marry

I've heard that you and Ninel have parted, and I don't know whether she and you are still in touch, despite everything, but if you are, you probably know that she

October 26, 1935

Dear Bertram,

I continue to think of you with affection. Only yesterday I referred to you as my benef

October 26, 1935

Dear Bertram,

If you are still in touch with Ninel (I understand that she is no longer with you), you may have heard that she and I met, briefly, on a New York street. But that wasn't the day's only surprise. I'm sure you remember some of the things that were in that box they sent from Croft Hall after the accident. Those shoes, for instance, practically new. You gave them to someone at the hospital. And you probably remember that children's book, one of the Bear Boy series, not in very good condition. You thought my father may have kept it out of some sentimental feeling he had about it, and I was almost tempted to think the same. But no, Bertram, no! He saw value in it, he saw the point of it. I mean he gambled on a chance one day to get a good return on it. I found all this out because of Willi, the youngest son of Professor Rudolf Mitwisser, whom I'm assisting at who hired me to no use no use no use at all my god I sound like Frau Doktor M

22

I COULD NOT WRITE to Bertram. I thought it was because I resented and disliked the new typewriter. It belonged, like the tea things and the toys, to James's regime, under which all steady rituals were discarded, and everything usual was made to seem obsolete. James had introduced both health and sickness into the house. Waltraut's whole face, even to the triangle of her chin, had grown ruddy. Her mouth was eager, showing tiny teeth. She was speaking English and forgetting German. And Anneliese: she was serene, she had lapsed into a pose of uncaring, she was almost languid. She moved with liquid slow steps. She gave up scolding the boys. They were as untamed now as a herd of ponies.

But Mrs. Mitwisser was again barefoot and in her nightgown, and would not come downstairs; and Professor Mitwisser took on his nightly mirth like a disease.

Ninel's shorn head and wide trousers. Her mockery and her stick: I felt she had beaten me with it. It was Bertram who had sent me away; he was not serious, it was all sentiment. He had kissed me on the mouth and sent me away. He had given me money and sent me away.

When I came into the house, I found them all in a kind of hush, circled around the big table in the dining room—circled there as Professor Mitwisser's enemies had been, months back, on that airless August night. A small rush of dry leaves clung to my feet and floated past me through the open door. Waltraut was in a corner, singing to herself, absorbed in twirling and somersaulting one of the new dolls: it was the Spanish doll, with its high black hair held by a comb, a flounced scarlet gown and flamenco dancer's heels. Waltraut murmured and hummed; she was rosy and happy, and her little teeth gleamed.

Around the table sat James and Anneliese and Gert and Heinz and Willi. The boys were almost ceremoniously quiet, as if in the spent aftermath of some nameless rite. When Willi saw me come in, he jumped up and ran out of the room.

Gert said, "Bill's robbed you, he's a dirty robber."

"I just wanted to show James. I didn't *take* it, she can have it back—"

"You went in there and got it out."

"Come back here, Willi," Anneliese called. "Didn't mama see you? Mama saw you, didn't she?" She slid her brown eyes from James to me. "If you had been in the house—"

"I went to the city. I met someone."

"What does it matter where you went," Anneliese said, and stopped there.

Heinz said, "You don't know anybody, so how could you meet somebody?"

What should I tell this unkind long-limbed boy? That I had met Mitwisser gazing at his hat? That I had met Ninel's mockery and her stick?

"I ran into a sorceress on Fifth Avenue," I said. There was a contagion of grimness; there was grimness all around.

James looked at me, not casually; a new way of looking.

"Where did this thing come from?" he said.

Then I saw the Bear Boy with its torn flyleaf lying open on the table.

"It was in my father's things when he died."

"Your father," he said. "Is this a joke, your father?"

"I don't know why he had it."

"But you know what it's worth, don't you."

The Bear Boy was sitting in a tree. He had long loose brown bangs. His legs were dangling from a branch. He was wearing blue socks and brown shoes with two sets of buckles, and a white blouse with a ruffled round lace collar. The collar was edged with blue piping; a bird with an orange worm in its beak was embroidered on a pocket. On the ground below—the grass was very green—stood an outsized green hat, high and broad and grand, as green as the grass. The hat might have passed for a green hillock, except for a tall peacock's tail of green feathers sticking up from it.

Underneath was this rhyme:

I don't like me
partic'larly,
but when I see
the other boys,
ruffians in their filth and noise,
oh! I—like—me!

"That hat," James said, "was bought in 1911 by J. P. Morgan for sixty thousand dollars."

"But it's only a picture," Gert said.

"A picture copied from a real hat."

"Why would anyone pay so much for a silly hat?"

"Because of the Bear Boy. Anything the Bear Boy touched turned into money. His shirts, his eyeglasses. The Bear Boy," James said, "was the King Midas of his day."

"I know that story," Willi said. "Whatever King Midas touched stopped being alive."

"It's a baby story," Gert said. "And this whole Bear Boy's a baby story. We used to have it at home, only it was called *Bärknabe*—"

"*I* know that," Willi said.

"You don't remember, you were too little."

"Yes I do. I do so remember, I even told *her*." Like an accuser, he pointed a finger at me. And as if I had been rightly accused, I felt a flare of guilt, though I could not tell for what.

"And this thing," James said, "is worth piles more than that hat."

"But the front of it's ripped and it's got spots all over—"

"The Bear Boy's spots. His spots are worth plenty. His butter, his jam. The book his father gave him when he was five, he wore it out until he hated it. . . . What a joke."

Anneliese stiffened. "You should see about mama," she broke in. "To go off that way and leave her alone—"

"She was asleep. She was perfectly safe," I protested, "and the boys would be coming home—"

"She sleeps too much." She turned to Heinz: "When you brought up mama's tray, was she still sleeping?"

"They were playing handball after school, and Gert wanted to stay, so we sent Willi home to do it."

"I made the toast and got the milk," Willi said; but his neck had begun to redden. I had seen Anneliese's neck redden in just that way. "Mama wasn't in her bed, so that's when I went and got the Bear Boy. Because no one was watching, but it was just to show James—"

"Mama wasn't in her bed?" Anneliese said.

"No."

"Where was she?"

The redness spread to his forehead; his ears flamed, his head flamed. "I looked all over the house —"

"Tell where mama was," Anneliese said.

"In James's bed. With a scissors, cutting up his pillow."

To me Anneliese muttered, "And this is what we pay you for?" There was more rote than fervor in it; she was grim and dry.

But I thought: it's James who pays me, not you!

"What a joke," James said again. He slapped the Bear Boy shut, and I understood my guilt. It was not because I had deserted Mrs. Mitwisser. It was, as always, on account of my father's vice.

23

THE NEXT MORNING, after the boys had left for school, Professor Mitwisser took up his briefcase as usual, put on his hat, and called me to him. He looked vaguely unkempt, and I saw that he had not troubled to shave. A thin white frost misted his chin.

"You must never again do such a thing. You must never again go out from the house in that way. My sons are only children, they are not responsible, you must rely on them for nothing. You must never again leave my poor wife by herself. Is this understood?"

His head was low, his shoulders high; his shoulders were a cave. He made his way into the street too cautiously, like a man in hiding.

"You'll be in charge of Waltraut today," Anneliese told me. "James needs me to go with him."

"You're not taking her with you?"

"Your job is to look after Waltraut and mama. Please remember that."

"My job is to assist Professor Mitwisser."

It was easy now to be defiant; Anneliese no longer had influence over me. She had grown lenient. It was as if she no longer had influence over herself.

"Papa has to be away all day for his work, you know that. And his nights belong to James." An egg was boiling in a pot. She was preparing Mrs. Mitwisser's morning tray—but her look flickered upward, to Mitwisser's study, where James sat with his teacup in Mitwisser's chair. "You shouldn't mind about Willi. Now go and get Waltraut."

"Mrs. Mitwisser won't let me come near her," I complained.

"Oh, just do your job, won't you?" An unfamiliar idleness purred in her throat. "I told you, papa and James are exactly the same, nothing else counts."

Waltraut lay in James's lap, playing with a string.

"Teaching old Wally cat's cradle," James said.

I said, "That's not tea you've got in there—"

"The real stuff, right. Braces a man for the day. Saves his soul from yesterday." He gave a small push; Waltraut, fists entangled in webs, slid off his knees. "I suppose you've got an inkling about your dad liking his dice," he said.

Now I felt his power: the power that clutched at the house, the power of health and sickness, the power that drew Mrs. Mitwisser to her scissors. A tramp, a vagabond, an idler, an invader! *Dieser Säufer.* But he divined things; he knew things.

"He won it off me," James said. "I would've given it to him, I'm always looking to get rid of all that sort of trash. Those goddamn fancy *shirts* ended up in London, in some museum over there." The stretched-out laugh. "But that fella wanted to play the odds. He was hard up, and still he wanted the odds."

Then, in the whirligig of incoherence I already suspected the world to be, it was confirmed that the Bear Boy had gambled with my father, and my father had won, or had slyly been permitted to win, the Bear Boy's own relic, spotted with the Bear Boy's own jam. The relic could be turned into gold, and I was its heir.

Anneliese was standing in the doorway. "Here's mama's breakfast. No cereal, she's tired of cereal, she leaves it in the dish. Take it up, please, I don't have time." To James she said, "I'm ready."

"I want to come too," Waltraut squealed in her high lamblike voice. She looked up at James with her round stare—the Mitwisser eye, but with this difference: it had grown used to a cornucopia of puppet shows and carousels.

"No, you don't," James whispered. "Today the mouse doesn't want to come out of the house"—and I caught, vibrating under the cajoling words, an electric burr that seemed to say: you have served your purpose.

24

MRS. MITWISSER was again begging my forgiveness. She confessed to a crude offense, an insult, she was all contrition, she had done me an injustice, an injury, not once but twice: first she had taken my money, and then she had blamed me for taking James's money. The first was theft, the second was . . . she did not know what to call the second. I was a servant in the house—wasn't that what I was, a kind of servant? and as such I deserved to be paid, and since *they* ("we," she said, with the loftiness of an empress) were incapable of paying me themselves . . . At home the servants—the maid, the cook—were always promptly paid, every Friday morning, except for the governess, Mademoiselle De Bonrepos, who received her salary on the first of the month in a little silken drawstring sack, along with some small gift, so that it should appear the gift was what was being handed over, rather than money, it would not do to be too overt, too bald, a governess is not a maid . . .

I forgave her many times. I watched her take a deep bite out of her boiled egg. Her teeth were as orderly and unspoiled as Waltraut's. "You see?" she said, and displayed the bitten egg: the crescent left by its absent crown. "My first papers, they are from this bite." She copied its curve with her finger in the air. "I go with Herr Doktor Schrödinger to Switzerland, to Arosa, the bite is not there, but anyhow we can know where goes the shape, you see? . . ." They called it, she explained, Schrödinger's equation, a wave function that extended throughout space, just as the missing outline of the bitten egg extended in principle beyond the existing body of the egg. They had spent the December holidays of 1925 in Arosa, she and Erwin, at a fine hotel. Anneliese, a child of six, was at home in the care of Mademoiselle De Bonrepos, and of course it was in those days not proper, but her husband knew nothing of it, nothing, he was the whole time in Spain, in an archive there, searching after one of his beloved Egyptians, ibn Saghir was it? They were not lovers, she and Erwin, never, in fact they were competitors, rivals, they slept in separate rooms but worked much of the night in his, and it was in his room, past midnight, when they had ordered some refreshment to carry them through, that she had bitten into the boiled egg, and there it was, the explosion of *seeing*, the possibility that had until that instant eluded them, the idea that the object of their passion, like a wave of the sea, was after all not guaranteed to linger in one place, it was a force not a thing, their wild-hearted wandering fickle electron!—oh, they were elated, and the laughter, the comedy, the absurdity, the thrill of that egg! Together they struggled to formulate the equation, it occupied many nights, by day they walked, arguing, along the mountain paths, the lobby had a great Tannenbaum hung with colored-glass globes sheltering candles, yes, they were suspected of being lovers, the Swiss are eternally suspicious. . . . Schrödinger, that arrogant tall young Austrian with his tall forehead and his eyelids moistly quivering, like wet lips, with the excitement of it, and she his designated assistant, a married woman and a mother. . . . At the Institute they accepted her reluctantly, she was fully a colleague yet they took her to be Schrödinger's subordinate, they could see no woman as their equal, but her papers could not be resisted, they could not be denied, she was there on the strength of her papers, they were as much hers as Schrödinger's, and it was *she* who had bitten the egg. . . . What times those were! Pauli, Heisenberg, they were all in their twenties, Fermi was just twenty-three, herself twenty-eight, only Erwin Schrödinger was older a little, they all had different theories, they were like a band of mystics pursuing imagined angels: waves and particles!

"And after," she finished—after what? after Switzerland?—"I become pregnant with Heinz."

She was abruptly silent.

In the little hallway outside the bedroom door—just where Anneliese had whispered to me about James—Waltraut loitered, pushing a toy car through a tunnel in a tower built of blocks. The car struck the tower and it clattered down, scattering blue and yellow cubes. Mrs.

Mitwisser blinked at the noise, looked out, and turned away. Waltraut did not look in.

"The little one speaks now all the time English," Mrs. Mitwisser resumed.

"Children learn quickly," I said. But what Waltraut had learned—it had come quickly—was to keep her distance from her mother.

"And the boys, they become hooligans—"

"They're like all boys."

"Willi, he is thief."

"It doesn't matter," I said, though it did.

She was conscious of everything. Even when she slept, she was awake. She lived at the top of the house, an all-knowing goddess in a cloud: she listened, she heard. She contemplated thieves and thievery. Schrödinger, for instance: he was and was not a thief. They had worked side by side, but it was she who had bitten the egg. Yet they called it Schrödinger's equation, and in the end she was driven out! Expelled from the history of the electron. Expelled, she said (like Willi, like Anneliese, she had a neck that reddened), and said it again, in the idiom of truth, so that I should take it in: *Vertrieben! Vertrieben aus der Geschichte der Physik.*

History had wronged her—not Schrödinger, not the history of the electron (this was her strange phrase, enveloped in a cascade of those unruly names, Born, Bohr, Dirac, Jordan, Verschaffelt, Kramers, Ehrenfest, Lorentz, and more, and more!). It was world-upheaval that had wronged her. She had run away from world-upheaval, and her mind, her mind, was at all costs not guaranteed to linger in one place, it was a force not a thing, a function that extended throughout space . . . and therefore, even if not wholly understood, it could be, after a fashion, trusted.

I told her then that my father had killed a boy.

Only Bertram knew this; and Ninel.

Mrs. Mitwisser was indifferent to the killing of a boy. It wasn't one of her boys, and anyhow she was indifferent to her own boys too. She was indifferent to my having had a father—had she ever cared whether Mademoiselle De Bonrepos had a father, or whether the cook or the maid had a father? She pushed away her tray. There lay the jagged remains of the half-eaten egg, ridged by her pretty teeth. A gray fatigue—

an interior fog—settled over her. The fevered fanatical nights of Switzerland were slipping away; they had been her glory; the memory of them agitated her even now, and wore her out. Or perhaps she was again submerged in that black limousine circling round and round Berlin.

"He crashed up a car," I persisted, "and killed a boy, and he told lies and he gambled. He gambled with James."

She was not indifferent to James. "You tell me this why?"

"It's what Willi did, he took what belonged to my father—but you heard it, you heard! You were just upstairs, and you heard—"

She said serenely, "I cut with the scissors where he puts his head."

I said, "My father *knew* James, at least he met him once—"

"Then also your father is *Parasit!*" A cry of triumph, or of sympathy.

It was as if she had made a gash in my breath. From under her blanket she drew out a tiny scissors with rounded tips: a child's scissors. I recognized it from a doll's toiletry set that lay in the tumble of Waltraut's new toys. The little scissors was, I saw, the natural corollary of Schrödinger's equation, the logical ghost that follows science—if Jane Austen can be shredded and scattered, if James's bedding can be snipped into snowflakes, it is to formulate a proof: that the lightning electrons are everywhere at once, that the particles are both cause and effect, that nothing has shape or stasis, that thought itself is merely flux, that history seeps and seeps and never sleeps; and that James, even James, can be driven out.

I marveled at how placid she had become, and how her eyes stood out like oil-darkened knots in wood. She leaned across the ruined breakfast and touched my face; it was a kind of experiment, an investigation. It was the first touch I had ever had from her. Was it because she supposed my father too was an enemy of James? But she was mistaken: my father had gambled with James and won. On the other hand, if he had been permitted to win . . .

"Now I will say to you," she pressed, "two beliefs. One is for silence, the other not. My husband believes that Heinz is not his son. Consequently he loves him. And this James, *dieser Säufer!* He believes he is Karaite. Consequently he loves my husband. Now you will understand, *nicht wahr?*"

I asked which belief was for silence.

"Ach," she said, "my husband's darlings, the fireflies."

The fireflies were the Karaites. They glittered for their little hour, and then they vanished. This she told me with so much obsessive intelligence that it was confirmed she was purely a scientist. The electrons were imagined, yet they were efficacious and plausible. The Karaites were not, so why speak of them, why give one's lifeblood to them, why depend on them? Why not drive them out?

25

AT FIRST the Bear Boy loved the pictures his father made. He stood behind his father's drawing board, and saw how the watercolors, pale and magical, flooded the sinews of the drawings. He watched himself slowly bloom into being: it was himself, a furry-haired boy, posed as his father had had him pose, sitting on a branch, say, or poking a stick into a puddle, or painting a face on an onion, all those curious ideas his father had about what he liked to do. He really did like to do some of them, he really did like painting a nose and a mouth on an onion with its funny topknot, and he didn't much mind the blouses his mother sewed, and he didn't care about the long bangs, he could push them away. . . . At first he loved the pictures, and he was interested in the strange way the stories grew out of his father's seeming to study him, though he didn't like feeling studied, and he didn't like the double buckles on his shoes, and he didn't like it that his mother rouged his knees to please his father's eye when he was sketching. His father was always sketching and always fiddling with the stories, inventing rhymes and words he would never say, never *could* say, and pretending that his mother's big old green hat could *talk*, when everyone knows a hat can't talk, even if you fold it, as his father did, into the shape of giant green lips. He didn't like being studied, and he didn't like having his knees rouged, and sometimes even his cheeks, but still something exciting was happening, that was clear, and one morning—his mother was *very* excited—his father put into his hands a pretty little book with a picture of the green hat on the cover, and himself curled inside it. "Well!" his father said. "There you are!" It wasn't an ordinary book, it was like no other book in the house or in the world, his mother explained, because it had Arrived From The Publisher and his father had Written and Illustrated it.

After that there was much more excitement, with the doorbell clanging, and people gathering at the gate and looking in the windows to see if anyone was inside, to see if *he* was inside, and new grownups everywhere, strangers, someone to Answer The Letters and someone else to Take Care Of him, though he wanted only his mother, who smelled thrillingly of cigarette, he never wanted his father, who needed him to stand still and pose, with his bangs all the way down in front of his eyes and making a blur, and suddenly there was a Gardener, and his mother said how nice it was that they now had Means, his father was Famous and he was Famous too, but what was Famous?

He was five then, and when he was six two bad things crept in: he stopped being Jimmy because all the people who were reading the stories to their children (there were thousands of them, his mother said) had begun to think of him as the A'Bair Boy, which got to be the Bear Boy, and the second bad thing was he had to go to school and learn to read, and in school everyone called him the Bear Boy, as if he was a stuffed animal you took to bed, or as if he was exactly the same as the pictures his father made, and not a real boy. Also there was a third bad thing: he did learn to read, and when he was seven—by then half a dozen of his father's storybooks had Arrived From The Publisher—he could read them himself; and he hated them, because his father *in the books* was naming him the Bear Boy, and he felt (and he was right) that he would never be Jimmy again, he would have to be the Bear Boy in buckled shoes and long bangs and flounced collars all the rest of his life, like a Raggedy Andy doll that never changed its clothes. Toys were nothing to him now, he had heaps of toys, he had trains and a dozen large and small Raggedy Andys, and trucks and cars and a wooden milk wagon with a wooden horse to pull it and a fort filled with lead soldiers in different uniforms and an Indian tent. For a little while he even had a doll house; it was the only toy he truly cared for. And he was ashamed of his knees.

But he knew he was Important; that is what Famous means. His father, who made up the stories and painted the pictures, was the Famous One really—his mother told him this—and the woman who Took Care Of him told him the same, the woman whose neck hung down all on its own and was all wrinkly, like an empty cloth bag; still, it wasn't his father they came to photograph, it was the Bear Boy. They picked out three or four of his toys (his toys were becoming public things, like swings in the park) and sat him down in the middle of these and called him the Bear Boy and tried to get him to laugh. He never laughed for them, and that seemed to increase his Importance. "A small grave face under blinding bangs," someone described him (it was in the rotogravure section of a newspaper), which was how his father now began to draw him, so that the later books showed him to be Solemn, and Solemn looked Preternaturally Wise, and Preternaturally Wise was Delightfully Whimsical. And they had to take him out of school, he was too Famous for school, he was in danger of being kidnapped (though this was kept from him), so he had to be Educated At Home, which is how *The Bear Boy from Apiary to Zedoary* arose, the eleventh of the series and the most colorful, with flower and animal decorations framing each page, and the silly green hat singing:

> Apiary's bees.
> Aviary's birds.
> Zedoary's petals.
> Those are words
> To make you sneeze
> Among the golden kettles,

and here was the Bear Boy kneeling beside the green hat on his rosy knees, with a miniature golden kettle nearby, and another one dangling from a tree. An owl perched on his left shoulder, while overhead a big orange sun, petals all around its face, was being showered with bees. The Bear Boy knew that the kettles had been inspired by teapots (altered to kettles for the rhyme), because the Bear Boy's mother—now that they had Means—had acquired several lavish tea sets, china with gold rims, and sugar bowls and creamers and fat round gold-rimmed pots for tea leaves. Oh, they had Means!

It was all right until he was ten, and endurable when he was eleven, but at twelve he had glimmers of a certain oddness, not the usual oddness, he recognized (how could he not?) that his life was different from the lives of other boys, that only he was Important, the others plainly weren't, and he knew that he was bound to be stared at, though the photographers had gone away and his wrist bones were beginning to stretch the sleeves of his blouses. At fourteen he grew an Adam's apple, and the glimmer of oddness darkened into a dread. It was a dread of everything; it was a dread of living. He understood that there would be no escape, he would always carry the mark of the Bear Boy, he would have to carry it into old age; when he was forty they would say of him, "Look at that fellow, he's the Bear Boy all grown up," and when he was seventy they would say, "*That* was the Bear Boy, can you imagine?"

In January of the year he was sixteen, his mother went out of doors with her cigarette and caught cold, and the cold invaded her lungs; she coughed wildly for a month and of course began to get better, she seemed well enough, but then all at once succumbed. He was alone with his father and his father's drawing board. He was no use to his father, he was too tall, his father sketched from photographs, the stories were coaxed out of the air, they were woven of air, they turned more and more Whimsical, and the boy in the pictures was still five years old, and meanwhile the Bear Boy was enameled, he was immortal, though his author was not—so that one day, three years after his mother's death, the Boston *Herald* ran a half-page notice with this headline:

JAMES PHILIP A'BAIR, SR., 68,
AUTHOR-ARTIST,
CREATOR OF TALES BELOVED
BY CHILDREN WORLD-WIDE

But the Bear Boy did not go under the earth with his creator. The Bear Boy could not perish, he had voyaged into too many languages, he went on and on, furry-haired and solemn-eyed, Preternaturally Wise and Whimsical, equipped with his Jellydrop spell and his bouncing multisyllabic verses. In Germany he was second in sales only to *Emil und die Detektive*, in Great Britain and all its colonies he vied with Beatrix Potter. He turned up in Italy and France and the Low Countries, and even (clandestinely) in the newly founded Soviet Union, where his dress was vilified and he was denounced as an idle aristocrat.

The Bear Boy wrote bitterly in the margin of the notice in the *Herald*:

APIARY

AVIARY

ZEDOARY

MORTUARY!

—or else he did not actually write this in the margin, though he had intended to, instead he sang it meanly to himself in the green hat's voice, meanly, because now all the Means, the plentiful horns of plenty, were spilling over him, the Bear Boy had become an Estate (royalties unending, royalties into the far, far future!), and he was its Inheritor. He was the possessor of everything he loathed; he was the possessor of what his father had made of him. Whatever he had been in the purity-time of his birth, whatever he was meant to become, his father had overlaid with embellishment: with lie and impurity. He did not speak in verses. The games his father devised were not his games. The Jellydrop spell was a fabrication. Even his clothing, the blouses, the socks as high as his knees, the double-buckled shoes, the *rouge*—all a romantic imagining. Even his hair! And when it developed that he was somewhat shortsighted and in need of eyeglasses (the woman who Took Care Of him had discovered this), he was certainly supplied with the glasses, but denied the relief of wearing them too often: the pale oval of the Bear Boy's small face, as innocent as an empty plate, was not to be cluttered; so he lived with blur, the blur of the long bangs tickling his eyelids, and the blur of mild myopia. He knew himself to be an appurtenance: the offspring of the impostor who animated his father's books. He was not a normal boy, he was his father's drawing, his father's discourse, his father's exegesis of a boy. His father had created a parallel boy; his father had interpreted him for the world. The Bear Boy was never himself. He was his father's commentary on his body and brain.

26

SNOW FELL; and a letter came from Bertram. The snow, beginning stealthily in the middle of the night, blew down hour after hour, as if some bloated invisible sky-bound stomach was spewing it out: a cold white vomit. It wrapped itself around the feet of the telephone poles and tufted and weighted their wires until they drooped. The snow was a surprise; it was early December, and autumn's traces had not departed: there were still dry leaves, shaped like crumpled conches, along the curbs. A torrent of dense flakes noiselessly covered roofs and bushes and sidewalks. The train trestle was clogged with snow. The trains ran sluggishly or not at all; ice coated the tracks. Professor Mitwisser opened the door, looked out, saw the struggling letter-carrier slanted against the wind, took the letters from him, and put away his hat.

"Today, then," he told me, "I must work in my study."

He handed me Bertram's letter and picked his way around Waltraut, who had turned the stairs into a stadium for her dolls. Each doll was propped on a step: six steps, six costumed figurines. The boys, relieved of school, were chattering over Chinese checkers in their room, breaking out now and then into shrieks; there was the irregular crash overhead of some heaved missile. The dazzle at the windows seemed to dim the house into a cavelike dusk. Anneliese and James had not returned.

Mrs. Mitwisser was putting on her shoes. "I go downstairs," she said.

"I'm just about to bring up your breakfast—"

She found a shawl and threw it over her nightgown. "I go downstairs," she insisted.

She sat at the dining room table and allowed me to serve her. Her shawled back was regal. She kept her eyes on her toast. Only yesterday the toaster had been useless; one of its panels was twisted sideways off its hinge. Heinz had fixed it.

"My husband," Mrs. Mitwisser said, "*er ist doch zu Hause.*"

I had seen him shut his study door as his wife descended past it.

"And this James, he is not in the house."

"The storm—"

"He will not come back. That one, no." She took my hand with conspiratorial warmth. "So we are free, *ja?*"

Bertram's letter was in the pocket of my dress; Bertram's voice was in my pocket, against my thigh. How I wanted to be quit of Mrs. Mitwisser's portents—if only she would go to her bed again and sleep her perpetual sleepless sleep!

But she bent and plucked a scrap of white triangle out of her shoe and unfolded it.

"*Schau mal!*"

Inside the little paper boat was an inch of dark hair.

"That one! I see, I find—" She waited for me to comprehend. "My Anneliese, she puts under that one's pillow."

"Anneliese's hair? Under James's pillow?"

She displayed it. An oval cutting of deep brown. Unmistakably the color of Anneliese's. But it was, I saw, no different from Mrs. Mitwisser's own brown hair, straying and wild.

"If my husband will know," she confided, "*wie tragisch* . . . ach, how unhappy he becomes."

She smiled a little—a lament—and moved to the bottom of the stairs to survey Waltraut and the tiers of dolls; it was plain she wanted her husband to know what lay in her shoe.

She spoke to the child in German. Waltraut did not reply—she was diligently poking at the clown doll's celluloid lids, opening and closing them. Up-click, down-click, up-click.

"*Komm, die Mutter ist da—*"

Waltraut did not reply.

The mournful vague smile ebbed. "That one takes my children. That one steals my children. I have no children—"

"You have five," I said, pointlessly; Bertram's letter was secretly heating my side, my thigh, my hip.

A dark whisper. "Four." She held up her fingers, hiding the thumb. "My husband, *nein!* That one is thief!" she cried.

Mitwisser called down, "Please to come immediately." A thunderclap of urgency.

I left Mrs. Mitwisser standing forlornly in her shoes and shawl, and pulled out the new typewriter and set it up on the table in Mitwisser's study. James had abandoned his teacup there. I removed it; a redolence of schnapps meandered out of it. Mitwisser was gripping a packet of notes in his big fist. He was strong and ready: the ghostly hunched shape of the Library was transfigured. Ambition reared up in him like an animal awakened.

"Al-Kirkisani!" he announced. He gestured at the keys almost violently, and despite their recent familiarity spelled these syllables out for me; then let loose a volcanic flood of recitation. I was already well acquainted with this name: Jacob al-Kirkisani, the peerless Karaite thinker of the early tenth century, born in Circesium, in upper Mesopotamia. Principal works extant: *The Book of Gardens and Parks*, and *The Book of Lights and Watchtowers*. Numerous as-yet-undiscovered treatises. Traveled to China and India; recorded certain Hindu social customs of the time. A believer in reason, in *rational proofs built upon the knowledge based on sense perception* (Mitwisser dictating), in *the perfection of the whole of Scripture in the way of account, address, statement, and question, relating to fact, metaphor, generalization, advancement, postponement, abridgment, profusion, separation, combination* (Mitwisser dictating, all this from the "Principles of Biblical Exegesis"). His grandest assertion: *Scripture as a whole is to be taken literally. If it was permissible for us to take a given biblical passage out of its literal meaning, without a valid reason for doing so, we would be justified in doing likewise with the whole of Scripture, and this would lead to the nullification of all the accounts therein, including all commandments, prohibitions, and so forth, which would be the acme of wickedness* (Mitwisser dictating).

The acme of wickedness! I was shocked by these words. They were dear to Mitwisser; they were all at once a vestibule to memory. In the middle of the night, he said, he had been startled by glare; there was too much light, falling sheets of a white brilliance that played eerily over the ceiling. The house was still. Across the hall James's room, the room that had lately been his daughter's, the room she had surrendered to James, was empty. James was gone, he had not come back; his daughter was gone. Because of the storm they had not come back. The snow, the undulating heaps of snow; the midnight veil of light. Long ago, snow in Berlin, everywhere a multitude of Christmas lights; but he was far to the south, in sunlit Spain, researching an archive, where he found nothing. In the north the trains were stopped, the trains were frozen to the tracks, snow and ice all the way up to the Baltic Sea! Berlin ringed by mountains of snow. He could not get back—because of the storm he could not get back. He sent a telegram, extended his stay, returned to the archive (an obscure Islamic library), and discovered the Egyptian he was looking for. The weather grew milder, and he was restored to Berlin in a state of satisfaction: the Egyptian was in his hands. Yes, yes, it was long ago, and his wife . . . never mind his poor wife. Today a letter had come! A triumph of a letter! Only today! An hour ago!

(Today! An hour ago! A letter! It burned against my hip.)

Some weeks past, idle in the alien city, in the Library, his head down, dreaming perhaps, troubled, ah, call it wretched, he was after all a miserable fellow with his poor wife and despite his dear children, his dear Heinrich, his splendid Heinz, he thought of that long week in Spain, those crumbling documents, sanctified writings, sanctified by age and reverence, precious old scrolls in their fluent Arabic calligraphy, the beauty of ancient things, how they rejoiced his eyes, and yes, he had found his Egyptian, but he remembered now—he lifted his head and stretched the muscles of his seeing upward to the Library's embossed gilt sky as if the labor of it could carry him away, away from New York to the life before—how he had happened on a certain slot, a niche, a cache, crusted with grime, the place was neglected, the curator was pleasant but lazy, a dark dirty hole in fact, where it might be possible . . . His fingers scurried into the filth of that cavity, drew something out, something on India, an insufficient glance, he wasn't looking for India, he was after his Egyptian, he shoved it back. That was a decade ago. It had turned to dust in his thoughts. But under the gold of the Library, his head down and dreaming, dozing, wandering . . . The upshot was this: he had written to that obscure Spanish archive, never imagining anything might come of it in the chaos and commotion of that torn country, always there are divisions and hatreds, elections overturned, the threat of tyranny. The old curator, a gentle Moroccan, was dead. The new one, an Arabist from Cádiz, a Fascist—he was now termed Director—was a dervish of organization, and had cleared out grit and disorder, and could put his hand precisely on any document that was desired. The fee for hiring a copyist, however, was tremendous, and also the fee for the service itself (which he suspected meant, in plain language, a gratuity for the director); but here was James, right here in the house, and James understood the need. . . .

Seven barren weeks, and today! Today the letter from Spain! Here, right here in the house, a thin letter, two thin sheets, in al-Kirkisani's own densely graceful style, signature of that unparalleled scholar's mind! A fragment—ah, well, a copy, to be sure, yet see, a fragment of a lost work on Hinduism, far richer in its brevity than the meager notes in *The Book of Lights and Watchtowers*, belonging apparently to a separate and much longer tractate based on an Arabic translation of the Bhagavad-Gita. The Bhagavad-Gita! Inconceivable, amazing find! That a Karaite thinker, indeed a genius, had once touched on the Bhagavad-Gita, oh immense, immense! Inconceivable, amazing, immense! It opens before us a fathomless well of speculation, of unsuspected new leanings, of unknown marvels! And the *mystery* of it—consider that where Karaism contracts, Hinduism teems. Therefore! Can it be that al-Kirkisani, King-Jewel of the Karaites, looms forth as a heretic among heretics?

On Professor Mitwisser's vast open palm lay a battered envelope with many foreign stamps. He looked down at it with the ravenous eye of a conqueror. Then he tapped the typewriter with his thumbnail; there was a faint ringing sound, as of water spilled into a narrow glass. "It is because of James that I have it," he said.

From the foot of the stairs came a repetitious thump. Bump-bump. Bump. Bump-bump. Someone was jogging the dolls up the steps and down again. "See, see!"—Mrs. Mitwisser's imploring whisper.

Because of James (because of money), Krishna and Prince Arjuna were coming to lodge among us. And al-Kirkisani, ferocious fence-builder against the extraneous, ferocious claimant and defender of the scripturally pure — Mitwisser's treasure, Mrs. Mitwisser's firefly! — was letting them in.

Meanwhile I was certain (I believed absolutely) that Mrs. Mitwisser had clipped those shreds of curl from her own head. A head that insinuated; a head that incriminated. A head that spiraled equations. She was a woman of schemes and hypotheses. Thievery germinates, pullulates: a boy is a thief, a man is a thief, a continent is a thief! And if James's bed conceals a secret intimacy, if he means to steal Anneliese for himself, if he is seducer, violator, thief, then will not her husband send him away? And will they not then be free?

27

14½ S.E. State Street
Albany, New York
December 2, 1935

Rosie, hello, you needle in a haystack!

What a time I've had tracking you down! That swanky Madison Avenue address you sent just before you departed our fair city? Nice picture postcard of designated destination that was: a thicket of skyscrapers. Wrote to said swanky address amid said thicket. Letter came back.

I admit I never returned the favor—never let you know where I was headed. Your card came and Ninel saw it too. Then we moved over to Ninel's place. No point now letting you know where—she isn't there anymore, and neither am I. More's the pity. You can see from the above where I've landed—in someone's attic. A tiny attic in a big old brown-shingled house. I like it well enough. The owners are a nice Neapolitan family. I've got two windows and one medium-size flowerpot containing four geraniums, courtesy of Mrs. Capolino.

How did I find you? (*If* I've found you.) The truth is I owe it to Ninel. She put me in mind of how to get to you. If something collides with her principles, she can be pretty passionate—you used to see this for yourself. She was never against the Quakers, though, since she's a bit of a pacifist anyhow. Who knows if that'll last, the way things are heating up in Spain these days. A bunch of the comrades, Ninel's gang, are thinking about going over there to join the Loyalists and fight the Fascists. It wouldn't surprise me if Ninel went, pacifist or no pacifist, if there's actually a war.

We were having an argument about it—we were having lots of arguments around that time. I said, You can't be anti-Fascist and still be a pacifist, and Ninel said, What about the Quakers? It's part of their religion and they're anti-Fascist, they save people from the Fascists. I said, What's this sudden esteem for religion? You don't give a damn about religion. And just then, out of the blue, I remembered your telling me, maybe it was in the postcard with the skyscrapers, that the fellow you went to work for used to be involved with some Quaker college around here. So I looked it up, and hied myself over there, and sure enough, it's how I got on your trail. Seems they've been requested to forward any letters for Herr So-and-So to some unlikely boondocks in the outer Bronx. Well, if you're still with Herr Whatsisname, then I've found you.

The big sad news is that Ninel walked out on me. Too many arguments, I guess. Not that I didn't enjoy watching her blow up! She's got a demon's tongue, and I admire that, even if she did break my heart. She walked out on me, and did it behind my back no less. I got home one night from the hospital with a chicken I'd picked up from the butcher's, and no Ninel. So I threw out the neck and the legs—Ninel usually made soup—and cooked the thing myself and ate it alone. Didn't much like it.

Let me know if you get this. Tell you why. A piece of mail came for you via Croft Hall, and I've been holding it for months, since even before I moved in with Ninel. (Mentioned it in the letter that got returned.) I'd enclose it here, but it might turn out you aren't really *found*. I'm coming down to New York one of these days and if you're there can deliver it by hand.

Yours,
Bertram

The letter disappointed. It angered—it did not satisfy, it wounded. Bertram spoke only of Ninel; Ninel and Ninel and Ninel. He was after

Ninel; it was on her account that he was coming. He intended to woo her back: he longed for the slash of her demon's tongue. I was barely a side-thought, and Bertram, what was Bertram? He was no better than a postman: "A piece of mail." What was Croft Hall to me? Ninel had thrown me out; Bertram had bribed me to go; Ninel had run away; Bertram was running to get her back. How I wished that Ninel would go and fight Fascism at the other end of the world!

I answered Bertram. He wrote again. We agreed to meet, but where? I could not think where. The Library, I said finally. The Library is all I know of the city.

I imagined him appealing to Ninel: I had to come down to give the poor kid her mail. Something to do with that rotten dead dad, she might need someone to hold her hand.

And Ninel, spitting back: Tell it to the Marines!

I was Bertram's alibi, his pretext. I was saving his face. Because of me—because of a stray piece of mail from Croft Hall, and what was Croft Hall to me?—he would never have to acknowledge, even to himself, that he was running after Ninel.

28

MRS. MITWISSER was a failed prophet. James came back the next day, and Anneliese with him. As Mitwisser had surmised, it was the storm that had kept them, transportation was impossible, lines were down, etc. Anneliese murmured these things, they were quietly accepted, and the house appeared to resume its rhythms—the boys to school, Waltraut to her solitary play.

Yet if Mrs. Mitwisser had failed as a prophet—here was James, the fog of his breath rising in the doorway, his glasses clouded, his knit cap pulled down over his ears—she was not altogether a false one. Something had altered: it was as if an odorless odor, a fume drifting aslant, was misting the walls. James was here; he had come back. Anneliese had not. Her simulacrum roamed from room to room, from task to task—but whatever she did, she did carelessly. She wore a carapace of remoteness. She was becoming neglectful. Mrs. Mitwisser no longer received her tray. Every day she put on her shoes.

She had begun to court Waltraut in earnest.

In the mornings Professor Mitwisser beckoned me into his study and shut the door; he swept up a huge arm and ordered me to my place at the typewriter. The daily journeys into the city were abandoned. His head was erect, drawn forward, a beast sniffing prey on the wind. Adoration of the renegade al-Kirkisani had strengthened him. His voice leaped and fell back, leaped and fell back. He was Vasco da Gama, he was Magellan, he was Marco Polo, he was Columbus! He had found his India—not the illusory land of error and miscalculation, but the real and true India. He saw how logic begets logic, the distant logic inflaming the nearer one. And sometimes he tossed up the lesser Karaites —Salmon ben Jeroham, for instance, that Salmon who followed al-

Kirkisani and sang in prosaic verses his rage at the Rabbanites. Mitwisser bellowed, and I beat out on the keys:

> Their words have become void
> and meaningless
> and out of their own mouths
> have they testified
> that they have drawn God's wrath
> upon themselves.

God's wrath! The acme of wickedness! Mitwisser and I were alone, circling in a lake of marvels and shudders. A daredevil glittering vertigo shimmered around us. No one was permitted to enter—not even James. Or: we were not alone—phantom renegades flew from corner to corner, brushing Mitwisser's heavy skull like imaginary bats. Sweat glistened in the creases of his neck. Al-Kirkisani, ben Jeroham, ben Elijah, al-Maghribi, Basyatchi—ah, Basyatchi of Constantinople, mathematician, astronomer, poet, author of a vanished work on the stars! And Moses of Damascus, the emir's reluctant secretary, forced convert to Islam compelled to go on a pilgrimage to Mecca, composer of cantos of thanksgiving when the Almighty restored him to his rightful faith! And the others, jurists, philosophers, grammarians, polemicists! Sahl ben Mesliah of Jerusalem, who called Sa'adia the Rabbanite a scoundrel, the very Sa'adia whom the Rabbanites revere as their Sage and Gaon, accusing him bitterly *in words straight as nails*. David al-Kumisi, who denied the existence of angels despite their presence in Scripture, defining them merely as *fire, cloud, wind*. And that earliest of the Karaites, their founder, Anan ben David, whom the Rabbanites charged with *building up a hill of heresy, seducing Israel from the tradition of the Sages, inventing books and laws out of his own heart, setting up his own disciples!* (Mitwisser bellowing, dictating; and I, the emir's secretary, beating on the keys.)

I collected the morning's work and handed it to Mitwisser. His look, as he took the sheets from me—I felt the excitation of his fingertips—was animated, reckless. The blue eyes released their lightnings. I knew him to be a climber on the hill of heresy.

He was ready to dismiss me. He turned his back and went to contemplate the window's white brilliance. Threads hung from the cuffs of his sleeves.

I said, "Your wife seems better today."

Now he faced me. Elation deserted him. He had forgotten his wife.

"She comes downstairs to eat."

He was silent.

"She's even looking after Waltraut a little—"

"My wife's nature is reclusive. It is her nature," he said.

I wondered if I would dare. And then I did dare. "Why does your wife call James a Karaite?"

"She is unwell," he said quietly.

"She hates him."

"My wife hates no one. James is our family's good friend. It is our"—he was momentarily frozen—"our situation that makes her unhappy."

"She wants him to go away."

"He is very welcome here. My wife is well aware of our affinities." His rough hand was on the doorknob. "The work this morning is finished, Fräulein. Please not again to affront me by exceeding your duties here."

29

MRS. MITWISSER did not return to her bed. An abrupt energy inhabited her: she dressed herself, she laced her shoes. She took up the small domestic obligations that Anneliese had abandoned. Waltraut no longer shrank from her.

Unexpectedly I had become her confidante. Twice she had been unjust; twice I had forgiven her. And more: I too knew what it was to be a *Parasit*—wasn't I the daughter of my father, yet another dupe of James, yet another *Parasit?* She was prepared now to alter her tactics. What good had it done to shut herself away, to hide? He had gone off—she trusted they would be free—but he had come back. He had come back! Despite the evidence of that dark curl of hair. Anneliese had brought him back, that was why, and look how subdued she is: she defied him, she denied him, she would not allow him to carry her away, she brought him back, together they came back—how fatigued she is, a sleepwalker, see how quiet, her hair hangs over her face. Now it is Anneliese who hides from him! But the right way is not to hide, not to shut oneself away, not to let the particles fly—a scissors is not a sword. The right way is war. From here on I am a warrior, I will meet him on the battlefield!

She was electrified; once again she had bitten into the egg.

"He will go," she told me.

At night the laughter: James and Mitwisser closeted in Mitwisser's study.

"You hear? You hear? My husband, he is that one's *Sklave*." She circled her neck with an imaginary chain.

I listened. The laughter scraped and gargled. The house vibrated. The boys and Waltraut were asleep; it was eleven o'clock. Anneliese was invisible—she had taken to sitting in a corner of the kitchen, a pencil in her mouth, staring into a smudged notebook: she appeared to be in charge of her own education. But there was no ambition in it. Was she hiding from James? I believed she was waiting for him.

Mrs. Mitwisser stood in the little hallway, her head tilted, her short fingers braided, her fine teeth clutching her cold lip. "It will stop," she said. "Tomorrow it will stop. Down there," she said, "in my husband's place. It will stop." Her distraught clever eyes challenged me. "You see I am his wife!"

The next evening, as early as nine o'clock, and wearing a fresh nightgown, Mrs. Mitwisser restored herself to the conjugal sheets. She lay in her husband's bed in her husband's study, and the nightly laughter was banished.

30

A FEW CARS had grooved trenches in the middle of our small street, but the aging snow, graying, hung on feebly, mostly in dirty heaps against the curbs. The milk-driver passed through, still with his horse in that period of Model A Fords, and round lumps of yellowish turds, laced with bits of undigested straw, fell steaming onto the icy road. By now the trees had shaken off their white piping, though an occasional twig clung shiveringly to its thin rim of snow. The rickrack roofs of the neighbors' houses pricked at a vacant sky—a sky that seemed never to have harbored the sun since the beginning of the world. Not one of these neighbors was known to us. We were hardly aware of their comings and goings; there was no theater but our own ingrown proscenium. From the window of my room on the third floor—it had become altogether mine since Mrs. Mitwisser had deserted her bed and lamp—I could see the blue-green wintry fuzz on the bronze Victory that lived at the top of the memorial shaft in our Bronx meadow.

Mrs. Mitwisser had won her night battle against James. Her uneven nipples, peering mutely through her gown, barred him. The foreign spines on the raw shelves across from Mitwisser's bed took on a marital smell—or, if not that, then the smell of a woman usurping her husband's place. She was there so that James should not be there. When Mitwisser called me in to him in the morning, the bed was sometimes made, and sometimes not. I could not tell whether the wilderness of it embarrassed him—his wife's shed nightgown sprawling over the sheets, the blanket left open in the shape of arched petals, out of which a thick body-warmth rose. It was not unpleasant—it had displaced the dim unwelcome waftings of James's teacups—but it affected Mitwisser like an extra presence. He was no longer alone with his cunning old heretics.

He felt that his wife had come to poke her finger in al-Kirkisani's eye. She had slept beside him. In her sleep she had thrown her silky arm over his back; a restless leg struck his naked thigh. Had she returned to his nights so that James should keep away, or because she had become normal?

"Now it is enough," Mitwisser said finally. He was, as always, agitated by the peculiar rapture of his exertions. His breath was perilously quick. "Please to shut the door as you go." I had endured the typing for three hours. My shoulders ached. The tender balls of my fingers tingled, as if sparks had shot up from the keys; their glass shields had captured the light, and sent violet streaks into my pupils. My last glimpse backward was of Mitwisser bowed like a courtier, immersed in the worship of his ghostly papers.

James stood on the landing.

"You," he said.

I passed him by: the man who had gambled with my father.

"You're the one, you're behind it, you're the one who runs that woman. No one else knows how, so it's you. You told her to sleep in there." He flashed a ribald thumb toward Mitwisser's study. The backs of his hands were stippled with short rust-colored hairs: he held them up like semaphores. The amber odor of teacups drifted from him.

"Mrs. Mitwisser does as she pleases—"

"Somebody runs her."

"Her mind runs her," I said.

She had begun to rule the house; she seemed normal enough. She had once been accustomed to speaking to servants: her instructions were unanswerable ("Waltraut must be fed," "My husband must have his button there"), and I took them as I had taken Anneliese's. Anneliese was in retreat. The twist of her neck under her loosened hair was desultory. She riffled the sheets of her notebook; I caught sight of tidy numbers and diagrams. Her father had forgotten his pupil. But Mrs. Mitwisser was fashioning herself into a semblance of motherhood. In galloping German she pressed on Waltraut a dozen endearments: *Spatzi, Schatzi*, my little sparrow, my treasure, my prize, my birdlet . . . for Waltraut these were only noises. She pulled away at the sound of a German syllable. Mrs.

Mitwisser was unperturbed. She had laced up her shoes for a purpose. She had laced up her shoes, she had tidied her dress, she had remembered her servants, she had placated her child—she had thrust herself into the middle of things, the little one's supper, her husband's missing buttons, the dust on the floor. For a purpose! Her vigilant eye turned a furious maroon; inside her head (she had combed the outside to a decent smoothness) an engine pumped darkened blood, and her warring look went trailing after James.

In the city it was different—not a hint of snow anywhere. It was as if there had never been a storm at all. The manholes breathed fitful steam. The pavements were dry and clear. Cars and pedestrians hurtled by. No one wore galoshes. On Forty-second Street an icy wind fractured the air like a tuning fork, vibrating with every step and sigh. In front of the Library the steadfast Lions squatted; the paw of one of them still carried a faded red stain.

I found Bertram in his overcoat, leaning against the marble balustrade of a marble staircase. There was old grime between the balusters, and little light overhead.

"Not much traffic, great spot for a lovers' tryst."

I sat down next to him. "Bertram," I said. "Oh Bertram!"

"Oh Rosie." He gave me his sidewise grin. I saw three crinkly white hairs, new to me, snaking over his ears. "Well, how's life with Herr Krautenheimer?"

"They've mostly stopped speaking German. They don't want to be German."

"They? How many are there?"

"A whole family. I tried to write you about them once, only . . . I didn't."

"Couldn't. Well, that's Ninel. Likes to cut the umbilical cord." He stood up and stretched. I had forgotten that Bertram was a short man; I had been living with giants. "I was down in the Village this morning," he said. "Over on Ninth and Broadway. She's got a little flat down there."

"When I met her she was with someone—"

"You met her? Ninel, you saw Ninel?"

So Ninel had said nothing to him. What was I to Ninel?

"Didn't she tell you? A march was breaking up."

Bertram laughed. "What have I wrought? I should never have handed you that piece of liturgy. What were you doing in a Bolshie march?"

"I wasn't in it. I was . . . here. With Professor Mitwisser. There was a man throwing paint out there, and Ninel had a sign—" Here I stopped. I wanted to tell Bertram about Professor Mitwisser; I wanted to tell him about the Karaites, and about the Bear Boy. But he would speak only of Ninel. "I still have it," I said. "That pamphlet you gave me, with the pink cover? I kept it because you gave it to me."

"Hey, kid," Bertram said.

"Are you getting back together with Ninel?"

"God, she's a force!" He moved up a step and down again; he was restless. "Forget pacifism, pacifism's down the drain, and damn it, she means it. There's a civil war brewing over there, and she means it. She's collecting for it. Money. Uniforms. I think even guns." He almost howled. "She wants me to go with her. And then the next thing she tells me, I'm too soft."

"Maybe she's too hard."

"Let's walk around," Bertram said.

We went up a marble flight, turned down a marble corridor, and entered a small overheated room paneled in polished dark wood. In the middle of the floor stood glass-covered cases holding manuscripts. A librarian's table was in a corner, with an empty chair behind it.

Bertram peered into one of the cases. "Elizabeth Barrett Browning," he said.

I looked into another. "Robert Browning. Three letters to Elizabeth Barrett."

"As good a place as any," Bertram said, and from the deep inside pocket of his overcoat took out the envelope from Croft Hall.

It contained two handwritten letters: one headed by a gilt crest, the other only a folded sheet of lined school paper.

To Whom It May Concern, the first read. *The enclosed was lately discovered in a Fourth Form teacher's desk, one used by Jacob Meadows during the unfortunate period of his employment here, hence it failed to be shipped with other effects some time ago. We desire to withhold nothing, and herewith return it to his survivor or survivors.* It was signed by the headmaster.

"They want to get shut of all of it," Bertram said. "Bits and pieces included."

I unfolded the second letter and spread it out across Robert Browning.

Dear Rose, my father began, *This is to let you know that the Tricolor's been after me for $750 he claims he lent me. I wouldn't ask that rich bastard for a potato. I won it off him on a bet, I said my class would beat his class. You're my witness that I had all females at the time. He hasn't the foggiest I'm out here, so if he comes looking for me just keep quiet. Say hello to the Cousin. Your Dad.*

That was all there was.

"Don't cry," Bertram said.

"He never answered when I wrote him. Not once. And he never mailed this one. It's horrible anyhow."

Bertram asked, "What's this Tricolor?"

"A man who taught with him in Thrace. His name was Doherty. My father was pretty sure he was the one who got him fired."

"Was he?"

"I don't know and it doesn't matter." I laid my head on the case. "That headmaster. He sent it for spite. Because of that boy."

Bertram pulled out a handkerchief. I thought he was going to wipe my face with it, but instead he blotted up the tears that had dripped onto Robert Browning's glass. I remembered the tidiness of his kitchen.

"I shouldn't have brought the damn thing down to you," he said.

"You wanted to see Ninel."

"Well, anything that came from Croft Hall—"

"Like this lovely keepsake, thank you." I was suddenly angry. My chin was streaming; I had my own handkerchief, and dabbed at it. "I'm not sentimental about my father, you know that. You're the one who's sentimental. That's what Ninel said, that it's all slobber."

"Slobber?" He blinked. The word struck him across the eyes. "She said that?"

"She said you aren't serious."

"The last of that insurance money, the furniture, the lease, the devil knows what else. I've been serious enough to let her clean me out. Believe me, I'm cleaned out. And then she tells me I'm soft."

This made me relent. "I'm glad you're soft. If you weren't soft you wouldn't have let me stay with you."

A diminutive gray-haired woman materialized out of a door behind the librarian's table and took her place at it with the authority of a potentate.

"Please don't lean on the cases, it's not allowed," she ordered, and expelled us from her hot realm.

We lingered before the Lions. The wind invaded the hollows of our coat sleeves. "Are you going back downtown?" I said, shivering.

"I'd like to take another crack at her. I'm not giving up. There's something *in* her, even if it's thunder and lightning."

"She'll never come back to Albany."

"No."

"She's going to Spain."

"Looks like it. Maybe not."

"Professor Mitwisser just heard from over there. One of his Karaites got mixed up with the Bhagavad-Gita."

Bertram whistled. "Is that what you're about these days?"

"I'm not about anything."

"Poor kid. Listen, don't worry about that scribble from your pa. He's out of everyone's reach."

I saw he had no curiosity about my life. He cared only for thunder and lightning. We shook hands. Then he put his arms around my waist and kissed me as he had last kissed me in Albany. His mouth was warm, and I imagined he was thinking of Ninel.

At the Forty-second Street subway station I spotted a trash bin at the end of the platform and tossed in the envelope from Croft Hall. The Number Six local came grinding in, and I returned to the remnant snows of the Bronx.

31

At nineteen the Bear Boy fell into the hands of lawyers. It was an ambush he had not foreseen. He had already chopped off his bangs (he did this on the day his father's obituary appeared in the *Herald*) and attempted a bonfire of the very first blouse his mother had sewn for him, which she had so carefully stored away in tissue paper. He opened a drawer and discovered it, and crushed it, together with the tissue paper, into the largest of his mother's china pots, and threw in a match and watched it ignite. The paper flamed and quickly ebbed, but the cloth only charred and gave off a bad smell.

Then the lawyers arrived, it seemed in herds, though they were only three: Mr. Brooks, Mr. Winberry, and Mr. Fullerton. He did not understand their language, no matter that they explained and explained; he wondered that they were never exasperated and never lost patience and never accused him of obstinacy. His father would certainly have been exasperated; his father had growled at him for so much as squinting, when he was only trying to see across the room. The lawyers spoke of "trusts," "instruments," "indentures," until he was as immobilized by tedium as when he was obliged to pose for his father, standing stock-still and forbidden to squint. They told him, very respectfully, that he was free to do whatever they in their counsel thought wise, now that he had so much money. It was money they meant, though they never said the word; he was learning how many ways there are to speak of riches, if you happen to be very rich, without once mentioning money, and it came to him one afternoon, when he was caught in the manacles of their language, that it was only his riches (those trusts and instruments and indentures, all the names his money went by) that inspired their forbearance and their deference. Under the caressing weight of so much respectfulness he felt their contempt: how unripe he was, how raw, he was no better than a child, he was *that* child, the Bear Boy, and look, look at the unreasoning foolishness of that bonfire, childish, gone up in smoke! He had no inkling of the value of his things; he had no inkling of the value of the estate; he had no inkling of the value of Messrs. Brooks, Winberry, and Fullerton.

In the end he dismissed them with an "arrangement": everything they termed "inventory" would be his to dispose of as he pleased, and the money, under whatever names they gave it, was to be placed in a very large teakettle, which he could pick up and pour out whenever he liked. It wouldn't be a real teakettle, of course; it would be a legal thingamajig, the sort of contraption he declined to understand. He was scornful of contraptions; he feared them. He had lived nineteen years as his father's contraption, and that was enough. But it did not escape him that, whatever shape such a legal kettle might finally take, there would be teacups aplenty for Mr. Brooks, Mr. Winberry, and Mr. Fullerton.

Very patiently, very respectfully, Mr. Winberry asked him how he would begin.

"Begin what?" he said.

"Your new life," Mr. Brooks said.

"Your independence," Mr. Fullerton said.

"Oh, I know what I want. I've always wanted one of those, the kind with pockets all over, only my father would never let me have one, because he said it would spoil my . . ." He tried to remember what his father said it would spoil: something to do with his back, the fall of his blouse over his back. "I think it was my posture," he said.

He let the lawyers sell the house that the Bear Boy had grown up in and made famous, and went out and bought a knapsack and a steamship ticket, and sailed for Cairo.

32

JAMES HAD COME to believe that my foremost obligation in that household was to control the madwoman; all the rest—my service to Professor Mitwisser—was pretext. He concluded this partly from observation, but mostly, I surmised, because Anneliese had told him so. She may have suspected it; it may even have been true. James blamed me for Mrs. Mitwisser's confidences. He saw them as conspiracies. He blamed me especially for the little paper packet in Mrs. Mitwisser's shoe.

"You put her up to it," James said, "that trashy stunt."

"She told me she found it under your pillow."

"It's all stupidity. She cut a piece of her own damn hair—"

He had pulled me aside; in that narrow house it was a feat to talk without witnesses. But it was morning; the snow had receded, the boys were back at school, and Mitwisser, already closeted in his study, had not yet summoned me. On the third floor Mrs. Mitwisser and Anneliese were bathing Waltraut. I could hear splashing and angry cries. Waltraut disliked baths; she fought them.

"She wants you out," I acknowledged.

"Well, Rudi doesn't. He handed me that stupidity and laughed."

"You always make him laugh."

"He laughs when he's embarrassed."

"In that case," I said, "you must embarrass him a whole lot."

"That clinches it. You're aiding and abetting—"

"Mrs. Mitwisser follows her instincts. I told you she has a mind of her own."

"A mind that's shot. He laughed when she cut up my pillow, what else could he do? And that bit of hair . . . what else could he do? The kids like me, I like the kids—"

I thought of Bertram's kiss. "Anneliese's not a kid," I said.

"You ought to just do what you're asked to do and keep your nose out of things. And remind the Frau Doktor that without James they'd all be out in the street."

"She knows that. She scratches at it all the time."

"I could have you out in the street too," he said, "in half a minute."

"No you couldn't. Professor Mitwisser wouldn't let you, he needs me."

"You? There's a joke. It's me he needs."

I could not dispute this: he was paying for the running of Mitwisser's household; for the running of Mitwisser's brain. He had paid for the retrieval of that fragment of al-Kirkisani. He was paying for everything. He was paying for me.

"You've made me rich," I said.

"Eighteen a week's not bad for nowadays."

"I mean when you gambled with my father."

"That was upstate and a while ago. Anyhow it was his dice."

"You let him win, isn't that what you said?"

In James's look a small distracted smile flickered. I believed it was satisfaction. He had run into a fellow who was no one in particular, who supposed *he* was no one in particular, and in no time at all had rid himself of a thing that had once belonged to the Bear Boy: he had foisted it on some ne'er-do-well who would put his hopes in it.

"Could be he figured I'd burgled it. Bum dice maybe, not that I cared. I told him hold on to the thing, all those crazy collectors, they're bound to cough up a pretty bundle."

I imagined my father waiting, year after year, for someone suitable to sell the Bear Boy to. In Thrace? In Troy? The boys of Croft Hall? My poor wayward father, compelled to embrace a treasure—a treasure taken on faith—until the day of his death: what did he know of collectors? Where would he find one?

"And I'll be damned, the damn thing pops up again down here. Like some goddamn voodoo you can't shake off. Listen," he said roughly, "just keep that thing out of my sight."

I saw that he had chosen me for an enemy. And in the way one puts a question to an enemy I asked, "Why did you stop Anneliese's lessons?"

"What?"

"You got in the way of them. Before you came she was in there every night with her father."

"That's just the point. Rudi keeps her shut up. She ought to see more of the world."

"She's seen a lot of it," I said.

"The old one. I'm talking about the new one."

"Professor Mitwisser lives for what's old. It's all he thinks about."

A grin. "He thinks about me."

"Because of the money."

"He likes the money, sure, I don't deny that—" He stopped and looked around, like a man suspecting spies. But there was only the watery clamor upstairs. "It's not old that counts for Rudi, it's throwing things over. He's got appetite, he's out to upset the apple cart. He works at it."

"You don't know anything about his work."

He took off his glasses, blew a speck off one of the lenses, and restored them. "I hear things, I pick things up. I tutored his boys, didn't I? Even Annie, for a while. Rudi knows I do him good."

From the top of the stairs came a slippery padding noise: Waltraut, naked and shining, escaped from the bath, a fugitive river-nymph spilling downward.

"Here's old Wally!" James said, and caught up the gleaming little body.

"I'm a mouse!" the child cried.

"A very wet mouse. And I'm the cat that's got you!"

To me James said, "Tell the Frau Doktor I'm here to stay until I decide to go."

33

ON CERTAIN DAYS —there was no pattern to them—James and Anneliese left the house together and did not return until evening. Mrs. Mitwisser had become resigned: she no longer hoped that James would vanish on one of these outings. If James should vanish, so might Anneliese, and then what? Her husband had dismissed the curl of hair—if it was a stratagem it meant nothing to him, and if it was not a stratagem it also meant nothing. It was no more than commotion. He resented and despised commotion. Since his wife had come back to his bed commotion had increased. His children were safe, there was no one to harm them, why all this commotion? She was in his bed; that was commotion enough. No conjugal heat warmed that bed. I knew this—wasn't I witness to Mitwisser's true coupling? His ardor was for the fever fuming out of the fragment that had been sent from Spain, those two thin sheets, purchased (by now this was hardly a mystery) with James's money. But the miraculous fragment was only a copy. He lusted after the original, a scribe's hand on rolled and pitted parchment; it was plain that the archive's new director was susceptible. A large enough offer— a superior bribe—might secure it, supposing James was generous, and when was James not generous? All that was needed for James to be generous, Mrs. Mitwisser confided, was for Mitwisser to cosset him, to work up that awful mirthful howling; to laugh and laugh and laugh. Thank God she had at least put an end to the laughter. And what did the terrible laughter signify? Ah, the fireflies. This James and her husband, they adore the fireflies, the fireflies blind them, her husband is blinded by this James!

No bribe, not all the money in the world, could now loosen the rough thing Professor Mitwisser had felt with his fingers in that filthy slot the old Moroccan had overlooked. And who, after all, will credit a fresh copy, so patently subject to fraud, who will dare to put his trust in it? Nevertheless here it was: the worldly al-Kirkisani, author of "A Survey of Jewish Sects," scornful of the Mishawites yet entranced by Hindu thought! No one had ever dreamed it. Erudition was against such a finding; intuition was against it. But Spain was in turmoil, and when Mitwisser inquired again, this time by telegram, the director replied that he was fortunate to be alive. The archive had been burned to the ground. The director was a Falangist; the arsonists, he said, were a criminal gang of Loyalists. The copy was all there was. Mitwisser's grand discovery—if anyone cared!—was doomed. They would say he had invented it; they would call him a forger. They were ready to accuse him of anything. Still, his children were safe, his Anneliese, his boys, his beloved tall Heinz, who was so ingenious with his hands.

Mrs. Mitwisser said, "Erwin Schrödinger, he also was tall. Tall like my husband."

And she said, "This James, he takes away my daughter."

"He always brings her back," I said.

"One day he will perhaps not."

She opened her narrow nostrils. She was afraid for Anneliese. She feared the illicit, she smelled the illicit. My husband, she said, he cannot so much as wind his watch to set the time, he is clumsy at such things, his big fingers, how clumsy and thick they are—*so gross und dick!*—whereas Heinz . . . *dieser verdammte Mann und seine verdammten Geschenke, er gibt, er gibt!* The boy Heinz, twice he pulls to pieces the funny clock James gives to him, and twice he fits the pieces together again. . . .

Her nostrils opened, she was exerting tiny rapid sniffs. Did she want me to think that Heinz was not her husband's child? She had shown her husband the curl of hair; he had turned away. And when, after childbirth, she had shown him Heinz, did he turn away? The curl of hair was her own; Heinz was her husband's own son. So I believed. But she was a purveyor of hypothesis, of possibility. She was a theorist. She had made me suspect Heinz. I often stared at him. He had the long bones of the other boys, and eyes as brown as theirs.

The weather was milder now, and still the Library did not draw

Mitwisser into the city. Under that gilt ceiling he had hidden his futility; or else the Library had itself withered to futility. His intellect—his desire—was a greater repository than any other; was there any archive extant in the world that knew of a Karaite link to India? Not New York, not Cairo, not Istanbul! Only he possessed this potent, this seductive, fragment—or if, elsewhere, someone had got hold of the rest of it, what difference, how could it matter? What greater master of Karaism was there? Al-Kirkisani had condemned the rival Mishawites: *There is not a single man skilled in knowledge and speculation among them,* al-Kirkisani wrote (and I had transcribed). And wasn't this precisely Professor Mitwisser's opinion of those other scholars of Karaism—if in fact there were any worthy of his esteem remaining in our century?

He kept me close to him at the little typewriter table while he paced before his shelves, seizing one volume after another, and tossing them on the bed behind us, where Mrs. Mitwisser's hairpins coiled like insects in the folds of her nightgown. The bed was unmade. The door was shut. There was nothing for me to do.

"Do you want me to go? I can come back later if you like—"

"You are not to go," he said.

But I saw that he was hardly prepared for our usual session. He had in hand nothing to dictate. I sat idly at the typewriter. The books he had removed were all in Arabic and Greek.

"Here is a man," he said, "a mind comprehending vastness, a luminary, a majesty, and history obscures him, buries him, suffocates him! Ejects him! Erases him from the future, suppresses him, names him dissident, subversive, heterodox, transgressive—"

Mitwisser's eyes flung out their electric blue.

"Transgressive, the key, the key! Dissident from the normative, then dissident from the dissidents . . . here, find my notes on *Lights and Watchtowers*—"

A ziggurat of typed sheets, my own handiwork, ascended jaggedly out of a carton at the foot of the bed. Mitwisser himself had classified them; they were in an esoteric order I had learned to understand.

"How slow you are," he complained. "There, just below *that* one, don't you see? Good. There, you have it. Please to read it."

It was a haphazard list. I read:

knowledge and reason
witchery
sleep and dreams
interpretation of dreams
the value of the shekel
suicide
medicine
astronomy
natural science
philology, Arabic
philology, Hebrew
commentary on Genesis
commentary on Job
commentary on Ecclesiastes
Mohammed and prophecy
Jesus and prophecy
art of textual interpretation
art of translation
solar calendar
nationalism
angel intermediaries
consensus and transmission
unclean animals
jubilee
dietary laws
Sabbath
the morrow after the Sabbath
kinship
the Nature of God

"Only a little finger's worth, it is not finished. One cannot make an encyclopedia on a single paper. And so much lost. Please to look! Is there Hindu thought on this paper?"

"No," I said.

"Then we shall put it there."

He picked up the two thin sheets from Spain, and recited (in darkened cadences, searching English out of foreign hooks and curves), *"Not by austerities, nor by alms, nor by offerings can I be known, but by devotion to Me Alone may I be perceived and known. He whose supreme good I am, without hatred of any being, he cometh unto Me.* Words from the Bhagavad-Gita, translated by al-Kirkisani into his own Arabic. He praises these words! And he writes—extraordinary!—he writes . . . he writes . . ."

The frightening electric eyes, blue tears seeping, and I again their witness.

" 'I, Jacob, am become Arjuna.' Extraordinary! And yes, yes, more and more! *Demoniacal men know neither right energy, nor purity, nor even propriety. Truth is not in them. The universe, they say, is without truth, without basis, without God. So say demoniacal men.* What, what is this? Truth is not in them, and do not the Karaites say exactly this of the Rabbanites? Here it is, I have discovered it, this knowledge, this new thing, mine!"

I felt very far from him then. I thought him the loneliest creature on earth. The path of tears was brilliant on his cheeks, even as it stumbled through low bristle—more and more he was neglecting to shave. Or was deliberately cultivating a brambly beard. A beard would exaggerate him—was that what he wished? His concentration was already exaggerated, and in a beard he would resemble a pietist. He had plummeted centuries backward, he was abandoned on the cold planet of the past, and all for the sake of a rejected schismatic, a rebel Jew, a man who had left no mark on the tree of history. A forgotten sectarian who mattered to no one. No one on any continent. No one distant, no one intimate. No one in this house. Not Mrs. Mitwisser, not Anneliese, not Heinz, or Gert, or Willi. Not James, no!

James was not in the house. A taxi had come, he had gone away with Anneliese.

I said, "What will you do now?"

"I shall record what I have found. Proof will be arduous. Provenance and context may require many months. Are you prepared to remain here?"

The question startled me. It was my own question: where was I to go? Only five days before, I had quietly—stealthily, it seemed—turned nineteen. "Nineteen years since my Jenny left me," my father might have said. I recalled his emotion—his only emotion that I knew of—with ebbing bitterness. I had no reason to be bitter. It was plain that Professor Mitwisser regarded me as alien but useful. I was compliant, I was quick, I was most often silent. My silence concealed watchfulness, but there was no answering notice. I had a kind of practical invisibility: beyond my usefulness at the typewriter I was extinguished. I was his typist, nothing more. But I gave him freedom to surrender to whatever moved him: he could stand before me weeping—for the second time!—because I was without substance.

And for the second time I asked, "Your wife calls James a Karaite, why is that?"

"My wife?"

"Is it that he's sympathetic to what you do?"

"Sympathetic? What language is this? Sympathetic how? To have feeling for my work one must have conquered the writings, the period—" He stopped; he would not waste breath on a catalogue of what he had conquered. He had conquered empires, continents, histories. He had conquered millennia. "I will require your presence here without interruption, do you understand this? I intend to prepare . . . to reveal . . . to lay an indisputable track—a track, not a mere trail—from al-Kirkisani to—" Again he stopped. I was the half-seen figure at the typewriter; he would not waste breath on what he intended. He dragged the humpveined back of his big hand across his eyelids.

"My wife," he said. "She cannot relinquish. For that reason she cannot discern. For myself, exile becomes relinquishment. I speak of exile. I ought to speak of escape. Naturally one must read German, but I will not employ that tongue, neither in speech nor in writing, however flawed or foreign my English may be."

"But sometimes you call me Fräulein—"

"What else would you wish?"

"I don't know. Rose. My cousin in Albany used to call me Rosie."

"I have no interest in familiarity. I have no interest in your cousin. My wife is not your concern. James is not your concern."

"He's yours, isn't he?" The tremor of my boldness.

"He attends to my children. He is fond of them. My children are fond of him."

I felt myself imprisoned in that room by a clever man with a hard heart. He cared for his children, he cared for James, he cared for al-Kirkisani, a thousand years dead. How I envied Anneliese! I was ready to believe Mrs. Mitwisser: Anneliese, not yet seventeen, had left the house with her lover.

They were returning now. It was early evening, they must be returning. Voices. A disturbance at the door. A disturbance on the stairs. Mrs. Mitwisser distraught, wailing. A tearing, a scraping.

Heinz: "I didn't *let* him in, he pushed me —"

Mrs. Mitwisser: "You cannot do this!"

Gert: "He's going up to papa's study —"

Willi: "It's not allowed —"

Mrs. Mitwisser: "*Lieber Gott, nein, nein!*"

The study door was wrenched open.

"I got it out of him, he told me you were out in the sticks somewhere, but I got it out of him. It wasn't easy getting here either, longest subway ride on earth, they tried to keep me out —"

Mitwisser stood frozen; the giant had become suddenly small. Ninel did not look at him. She was fixed on me. She was wearing a creased leather jacket and a workman's cap. She had on the same trousers she had worn when I had last seen her, but now they were clipped to a pair of suspenders. I recognized the suspenders. They were Bertram's.

"Bert had no right to give you that money," she said: the raucous call of the coxswain.

"But he did, he gave it to me."

"Fine. Now you can give it to me. I've got a use for it, and Bert said you'd hand it over."

"He didn't say that."

"What do you know about it? He said you'd give it to me."

"Are you back with him?"

"That depends on you."

I did not know how to answer.

"I told him," Ninel said, "if you gave me the money I'd run up to Albany now and then."

"Then you *are* back with him—"

"Maybe sometime. Right now I need the cash, I'm going to Spain."

Mitwisser's breathing grew shallow; the vibration of his throat had diminished. The ruined archive. The disappointing telegram. Falangists; Loyalists; the refugee fragment . . .

"Did Bertram really say—"

"Well, it wasn't *all* my idea, was it? He's broke himself, and you're in good shape here, you've got some sort of job—" She took in the disordered bed against the wall, Mrs. Mitwisser's nightgown, the errant hairpins, the typewriter. "At least you're not in cahoots with the gentry, like your old man." The white mist of Mitwisser's beginning beard had crept to his brow and neck. He was white all over. "The kid's got a job with you, right? I'll say one thing for her, she types like a demon." She threw herself down on the floor. I saw the soles of her boots. "Go get the dough, will you? Believe me, I'm sticking around until I can feel it in my pants pocket." She grinned up at Mitwisser. "Ever hear of a sitdown strike?"

I raced up to the third floor and pulled my suitcase out from under what had been Mrs. Mitwisser's bed. From Willi's old sneaker I drew out Bertram's blue envelope. The money was not whole. The ribbon and the rest of what I had bought for the old machine had depleted it by a small sum. I made up the difference with five dollars taken from my salary.

Into Ninel's open palm I counted out Bertram's money.

"Good. Five hundred. This goes to the cause."

"And what is that?" Mitwisser said in his new thin voice.

"Against the Fascists. For the people."

"You've tricked Bertram. He thinks he's getting you back," I said.

"He'll get over it."

The front door blasted like a gunshot: she was gone. I had obeyed her, I had been craven, Ninel in battle array had bullied me into submission. The money was snatched away, surrendered. I had raised no hullabaloo.

Then it hung before me that it was Bertram, not Ninel, I had obeyed.

Mrs. Mitwisser sat on the bottom step. Her shoes were in her hands; she was staring into their dark caverns.

"My poor Elsa," Mitwisser murmured.

Heinz said, "The man kept on yelling Rose. He wanted you."

"It wasn't a man. It's someone my cousin knows—"

The pants, the cropped head, the cap. They had thought Ninel in her cap and pants was a man. A man invading the house. A man storming in, a roughneck, howling, demanding, ordering! As before. As before. Round and round in the black car, the El Dorado, the tunnels of her shoes, the blocked tunnels. Blocked. Blackened.

Mitwisser loomed and swelled; he thickened to a roar. "See what you have done to my wife!"

That night Mrs. Mitwisser did not return to her husband's sheets; once again she was deposited in the bed opposite mine. And again I was dependent on the household's good will. Without Bertram's money, what was I? Even with it, I had nowhere to turn; but Bertram's blue envelope had supplied the illusion that my fate was my own, that liberty lay open before me, that I could depart when I wished, that I was the prisoner of no one's hard heart . . . and that Bertram had spread over me the wings of his affection. Bertram had no wings. He had given them to Ninel. His kiss was ash. My fear was that Mitwisser would send me away: I had brought into the house the most perilous commotion of all—it had undone his wife. His fragile wife, crushed. Foundering. She would not eat, she would not put on her shoes, she would not come downstairs. As before, as before. And how blooming she had been in her nice dress, how beautifully restored, how tenderly and coaxingly she had won back her littlest child!

I had lost Bertram's money, and without his affection what did it matter? James had anyhow assured me that I was an heiress. The Bear Boy in the green hat. Worth, James had implied, thousands. Thousands? A treasure taken on faith. Like my father, what did I know of collectors? Where would I find one?

In a day or so it became clear that Professor Mitwisser was not going to send me away. I could type like a demon; and besides, I was familiar with his undulating accent, his ellipses, his silences, the formal vagaries of his English; and when he requested it I could put my finger on any volume on his shelves, whatever its language. I knew the controversy over the conversion of Rabbanites to Karaites according to the testimony of Tobias ben Moses of Constantinople. And I knew the refutations of Karaite rationalism, in favor of poetry, by the Rabbanite Tobias ben Eliezer of Thessalonica. I knew all those curious conflicts and feuds, and those even more curious names and towns and regions.

He would not send me away. He could not.

James, passing in the hallway, whispered, "She's out, I'm back in, how about that?"

"No," I said, "it's going to be Anneliese's lessons."

But it was neither. Mrs. Mitwisser had vacated her husband's bed. The late hours in his study were released for Mitwisser's disposal. Spherical trigonometry and Molière with Anneliese, or shrieks and teacups with James. He chose the fragment from Spain; he chose the Nature of God; he chose al-Kirkisani. Each night I entered his study promptly at ten, shut the door, and typed against Mitwisser's ecstasy far into the sleeping stillness.

34

He hardly knew why he'd picked Cairo. Probably it was because of the Pyramids. Or because there were rumors that war was about to break out in Europe. He didn't care anything about it, but he guessed that if it was going to be England against the Kaiser, he was for the Kaiser, he couldn't be for England: his mother had dressed him like a little English boy, and his father had drawn him that way, he had been turned into a caricature of Englishness, and some people had even gone so far as to compare him to Christopher Robin. So of course he hated everything English, and was indifferent to Europe — but if there was going to be a war, he didn't want to be anywhere near it or in it. He did what all tourists in Egypt do, hired a guide, rode on a camel, sailed down the Nile in a dhow, gaped at the endless sands, the ancient stones, the crumbling paws of the Sphinx — and, in a decaying museum whose walls were cracked and patched, met the eerie stretched-leather face of a mummy. The mummy was in a glass case; a living fly had somehow got in and was standing on a horrible cracked yellow tooth, rubbing its front legs together. There were flies everywhere.

Jerusalem wasn't far; he went to Jerusalem, where there were just as many flies, and idling squads of Turkish soldiers, and monks in long brown robes and Arabs in dusty white djellabas and Jews in dusty black caftans. The soldiers and the Jews and the Arabs mostly wore proper shoes; the monks wore sandals, exposing their dusty toenails. It was as hot as it had been in Cairo, unendurably hot, but at dusk, which came on suddenly, a delicate coolness drifted from hill to hill.

He took a room at the YMCA, and every day walked over rocky fields sprouting sparse scrub — sheep nibbling at it under the weary eye of some elderly shepherd — to the Old City. He wandered into the souk to watch the cobblers and bloody butchers in their dim cavelike shops, and men in kaffiyehs smoking waterpipes in dirty doorways under medieval arches. In another part of town (to his surprise, fabled Jerusalem was no bigger than a small town) he bought a hat with a great brim from a Jewish shop, to keep the sun off. He avoided the Wailing Wall, but once he stumbled into what he thought was one of the smaller churches —the place was rife with sects—and though he never knew it, it was an old Karaite synagogue. Now and then there were riots: Arabs, Jews, soldiers. Knives, shots, screams. He ignored these events as well as he could; they weren't his affair. In late June he learned about the assassination in Sarajevo. He read it in the *Palestine Post*, went up to Jaffa, found an Italian freighter, and headed for Algiers.

It wasn't easy to get passage, even on a freighter, but in Egypt he had discovered the law of the Levantine bribe, which could procure anything one liked and satisfy any whim. All he had were whims, why not? He could buy whatever he pleased. The ship clung to the African coast, as if, like himself, it feared Europe's bellicose touch. In Algiers they spoke Arabic and French. By now he was used to the sound of Arabic, which he preferred to the sound of French, though both were only discord. France was in the war, and France was in Algiers, but it was also far away. He picked up a little French, enough to buy his dinner in a restaurant. Now he experimented with living well: a suite in the Hotel Promenade. He claimed he was an American businessman. He was almost twenty-one and no one believed him, but the value of his money was never in doubt. He bought a couple of bespoke suits and a Panama hat with a ribbon and a little blue feather; he bought a heap of silk ties, and flirted with the lipsticked blonde waitress in what had become his favorite restaurant. Sometimes she came late at night to his suite. He had been warned to keep away from Arab girls. Their brothers would take revenge.

But he disliked living well. He disliked his expensive clothes and gave them away, all in a bundle, to a beggar on the street, who kissed him on both cheeks and showered him with Allah's blessings. The silk ties and the bespoke suits felt like a costume. The Bear Boy had had enough of costumes: those humiliating scalloped round collars, that lace and trimming! He put an end to Jim and Jimmy, and began to call himself James. All around him they were attending to the war. The French were heatedly loyal; the young men enlisted and joined the fighting. He had more in common with the Arabs, who were inclined toward the Kaiser; they hated the French and wished them ill and wished them gone.

He tried to ignore the war. It wasn't only England and France (and the city was filling up with uniforms), it was Russia, Belgium, Serbia, Italy, Japan! America belatedly, thanks to that fool Wilson. And on the Kaiser's side, Turkey, Bulgaria, the whole Hapsburg empire; such uneasy bedfellows. Half the world shooting at the other half, what sense did it make? He was glad he could not read the newspapers, but the war was a nuisance anyhow, his money was repeatedly held up, and Mr. Fullerton wrote that Mr. Winberry was now in Officers' Training, and what a pity that James was stuck in such a godforsaken corner of the globe. He did feel a bit stuck; he had hoped to get a look at Scandinavia, mists and fjords and northern lights, but there was no possibility of ordinary travel now. So instead he strolled at night into certain alleys he had discovered, and shooed away the little boys who were selling themselves, and found the shadowy wall where kif could be bought from a man in Western dress who, in daylight, could pass for a local *avocat*.

The kif gave him dreams. He was always awake and could manipulate the dreams, though they came of themselves—and yet he could turn them, he could swell them up or narrow them down, he could lighten or darken them. It seemed he was in control of the plots of stories that were imposed on him. Once he dreamed he was a king, and at the same time he was the king's footman, and he could choose which he preferred to remain, king or footman; but it was imperative to choose, so he chose to be king, and the self that was footman dissipated into vapor, a perfumed vapor that wafted away into folds, like draped silk. And another time the dream had the shape of a window, through which he could see red storms and whirlwind-tossed gardens. Mostly the dreams were peaceful, the kif was friendly, and got him through the war, so that finally he was not obliged to take much notice of it. And when he visited the shadowy wall in daylight, the sun glared sharply against it; a shawled old woman sat with her back to it, cutting open melons for sale.

The kif was friendly, and under its tutelage he attained this knowledge: he did not want to be or to become.

In the daylight alley there was a creature with a hairless yellowed face who played a flutelike instrument, a short pipe pocked by triangular holes. He could not tell from the rags around its head whether the creature was male or female. A rusted pot on the cobblestones was there for the coins. He threw in, for the sake of the tune, the equivalent of ten American dollars, and the creature crowed with jubilation, and piped its single wavering tune again and again, lifting its knees, hopping and marching. The tune was thin, unclear, strange, derived from some unrecognizable set of scales; there was no orderliness in it, it wound and wound, a wire spiraling into an abyss, and he thought: That is what I wish, to be formless like this tune, and wayward: no one will predict me, no one will form me.

The blonde waitress (she wasn't at all pretty, but her legs were pleasingly long) who had come to his suite in the Promenade, now that he had given it up would no longer come. He had a room in a lodging house—bed only, no board. He did not like his French landlady, who (he assumed) suspected he was a mobster or a thief lying low; but he liked his little room, with its conscientious doily on this or that surface, to prevent water marks. He liked it because it did nothing to constrict or confine him, and the doilies, which had that intention, were only comedy. Algiers was comedy: the haughty French, the angry Arabs, the stupid war. The sexless creature, tootling on its pipe; the tune that emptied meaning out of Creation. His kif-dreams were senseless, formless, aimless. Under the tutelage of the kif he laughed. Crowing and laughing over the void.

The war ended. His ship docked in New York—a Swedish ship, the closest he would ever come to Norse imaginings. Mr. Winberry was dead, buried in France. But Mr. Fullerton and Mr. Brooks were where he had left them. "I'm back," he giggled into the telephone. They told him that because of the Bear Boy's continuing vitality, and despite the tumult of the recent conflagration, his assets—they never said money—were more vigorous than ever. He laughed again, straight into the telephone. Comedy, he said to himself (but his language was simple and loose, his language was down-to-earth, his father's elevated whimsy was banned from his mouth), is that which cannot define me. It was portentous to think this, it was arrogant, it was shallow—or so Mr. Fullerton and Mr. Brooks would have privately judged—but he believed it.

35

Heinz said, "It was a man, whatever you say—"

"It wasn't."

"I saw him, I was the one who went to the door, wasn't I? He said his name was Nino, and that he wanted you, and then mama looked right at him and yelled for me to shut the door, so I started to, but he shoved it in and ran up the stairs. It *was* a man."

He was carrying up Mrs. Mitwisser's tray: squares of toast, butter, jam, tea. An invalid's meal.

I said, "It was just someone who came to get money she thought I owed her, that's all there was to it." And added: "Her name is Miriam."

His neck reddened, the distinctive Mitwisser way; this seemed to me significant. "A lady wouldn't scare mama so much."

"She's a lady who dresses like a man."

"Why?"

"She wants to be a soldier."

"Ladies can't be soldiers."

"Sometimes they can."

He poked a finger into the jam and sucked on it. "Was that the money mama took? That other time she was sick?"

"Your mother's waiting for her food," I said.

"She won't eat it anyhow.—If you owed that money to the man . . . to that lady, why didn't you pay it before?"

"I didn't really owe it."

"*We* always owe lots of money," Heinz said. "Mostly we can't pay it until James comes."

I had no answer for this.

"Mama doesn't like James," he said.

"But your father does."

"Papa doesn't like strangers."

"Is James a stranger?"

"Anyone who isn't in our family is." His narrow brown eyes, so unlike Mitwisser's, sentenced me: "You're one too."

I remembered how Anneliese had once insisted on just this.

"Look at mama's tray," Heinz urged. "See? There's only a spoon. Anneliese said to cut the toast into little pieces, so mama won't have to use a knife. Mama isn't allowed to have a knife on her tray from now on. And you know what? Anneliese threw out Waltraut's little doll-scissors, the one mama messed up James's pillow with. And you know what else?"

"What?" I said.

"James is getting me a handbook that tells how to build a crystal set, and he's even getting me all the parts. I'm going to make my own radio, that's what!"

The house had no radio at all. Professor Mitwisser had barred it; he would not permit the presence of an instrument that vibrated with trivia and inferior caterwauling all day long. But Anneliese had told me that Mitwisser did not wish his wife to hear the news from Germany. Hitler had already dissolved the Reichstag, and a proudly Aryan people was about to cast their ballots for him in a jubilant national election.

"A proudly Aryan people": these were Mitwisser's words. Anneliese, repeating them, spoke them in the same tone Mrs. Mitwisser had used in pronouncing the El Dorado.

36

MRS. MITWISSER had lost interest in her playing cards. She handed them to me with a single angry syllable: "No." And again: "No." And because I continued to demur (what was I to do with them?): "*Nein!*" And when I failed to take them from her quickly enough, she tossed them to the floor, where they fanned out in confusion.

She had gone back to dozing in the afternoon. But at night she was horribly awake, watchful, suspicious of every sound. She flicked her eyes from side to side; in the half-light they were dim marbles rolling. She sat up in bed, listening.

"What is that?"

"It's Waltraut. A little night cough."

The child was bewildered. Her nose chafed and leaked; she had caught cold, as if from grief. So recently befriended, so seriously coddled, the dolls on the stairs, her mother's closeness, her mother's look . . . all abruptly withdrawn. She could not puzzle it out, and even Anneliese, and even James . . . Gert shook her off, Willi shook her off. But Heinz took her by the hand and showed her the long wire that was to be the aerial, the short wire that connected to the crystal, the copper wire that had to be wound around the coil, the capacitor with its interleaved wings, the funny earphones that turned him into a sort of animal. All these strange things were scattered on the big table in the dining room. Mitwisser never troubled to look.

"What is that? Who comes?"

The front door opened and closed: Anneliese and James, returning past midnight. Their outings—how else to name those recurring eclipses?—were growing longer and later.

But Mrs. Mitwisser, tremulous, let out a terrified croak: "*Der Mann!*"

And another time, when a passing car with an injured muffler roared by on our ordinarily silent street: "This boy, this boy!"

This boy? The house was full of boys. Willi, the beautiful one, and Gert, and Heinz. And the aftermath, the material residue, of the Bear Boy.

"Your father," she threw out, "this boy—"

He was alive in her mind. The boy whose body was broken up, together with my father's, on the rainy road to Saratoga. The boy she had taken no notice of when I dropped the rough stone of my father's crime into the roiling stream of her errant desires. But it had struck deep, it had lodged itself, she had swallowed it down. The stone lay in her belly.

"This boy your father kills, who is he?"

"I never found out his name. A schoolboy. My father was his teacher. It was an accident," I said, "it was night, and wet—"

"He teaches what, your father?"

"Mathematics. But my father's dead."

"To this boy who has no name he teaches death."

Her voice had the bitterness of words incised in blood.

"My Heinz," she said, "he wears my husband's name but he is not my husband's boy." And wrathfully: "I tell you before!"

But she had told me the boy was loved.

"My husband will do like your father, he will kill this boy. One day he kills him."

She had reverted to nightmare; she had usurped my father's nightmare. I saw, in the conflagration of her seeing, the critical logic of what hardly deserved the name of madness. Nothing was obscured, reality burned and burned. She knew and she knew. In the shadowed seclusions of our little house on a forgotten street in a nondescript cranny that turned its back on everything urban, hidden in cattails along the lip of a bay where the tide, going out, left behind the odors of seaweed and bird-lust—here in her nightgown, alert to the subterranean calamities of the world, sat the sibyl. All masks fell; or else all wore masks, in a teeming of reminders and representations: the past was the present, the present was the past, the meaning of one thing was the meaning of another, all meanings were one. Into this cauldron of all-ness a familiar evil had burst, wearing the mask of Ninel, and behind it a procession of up-heavals unmasked, the black car circling, the dead boy, the son who was and was not a son, and James, always James, invader, usurper, thief. All one.

The house was in disorder. Gert and Willi had become enemies. They fought with fists and lungs and teeth. They fought over property —who owned what, whether James had given the kaleidoscope to Gert or the mechanical frog to Willi, or vice versa. Heinz let go of Waltraut's hand, retreating beastlike behind his earphones, tapping the wire onto the crystal, catching invisible whirrings out of the air, while Waltraut ran wailing from boy to boy, crying for breakfast, crying for supper, and Anneliese drifted through the maelstrom, powerless, detached. Her notebooks lay unopened. Her eyes were furry. She kept them on James, sidewise, with a slyness new to her. And here was James, jumping into the cacophony, egging it on, promising new frogs, new kaleidoscopes, promising property heaped on property—a friend to anarchy and greed. His teacup dallied on the sideboard. It gave out its familiar fume, and he visited it often, sometimes scooping up Waltraut, who wriggled wildly, or deflected en route by an excited boy's pummeling. Wild, wild Waltraut, wild Willi, wild Gert! Heinz in communion with the ether, deaf to bedlam. Anneliese in trance: earrings glinting like bits of shattered glass.

Professor Mitwisser's door was a wall against this chaos. The work in the study had doubled; he had begun to call on me in the mornings. In these hours his recitations were rapid and decisive. Sporadic mutters of "*Rote Indianer*," strewn without heat, were drowned by wave after wave of his thickening phrases, dictating, parsing, rushing, flooding. Nights were different, sunk in the silences of ten o'clock. The silences were bottomless. Patient at the typewriter, my arms uselessly dangling, waiting for the coarsening voice to resume, I was, I knew, a blank mote in that blank muteness—the white pool out of which he drew, hesitating and straining, the phantom eels of his thought. He lifted his large ugly knuckles and clawed at nothingness. The grooves in his forehead darkened. And then a single volcanic word would spit from his whole face, a rage of gluttonous spite would overcome him, and his lips would rattle and babble those alien names, Yehudah Hadassi, An-Nahawendi, and old lost towns on obsolete maps, Castoria, Zagora, Mastaura, faster than I could keep up with them.

During one of the swollen silences that surrounded these nightly storms, I fell asleep over the keys.

"Sluggard!" Mitwisser's breath. The hairs of his nostrils. "Negligence! Delinquency!"

I said weakly, out of my shame, "Mrs. Mitwisser . . . she doesn't rest, she talks all night—"

"It is not my wife who is delinquent. It is not my wife who is negligent."

He released me then. It was meaningless, he said, to attempt to continue with a sluggard: I should return tomorrow in fitter circumstance. But his accusations reverberated—a delinquent wife, a negligent mother, a woman in bed. A sluggard.

My eyelids were heavy with sleeplessness. The previous night had worn me out—Mrs. Mitwisser chattering, clattering, clutching. She was clutching an object. It shone in the window's mild glimmer.

"Make the light," she commanded.

I switched on the lamp. She was crushing a silver rectangle against her breasts. The corners were sharp and left wedgelike marks in her flesh. I remembered the photograph in the ornamental frame—I had last seen it in the house in Albany: the black-haired young woman overshadowed by a tall wide-leafed plant; the stone urn; the cherub.

"*Die Mutter*," she said, as if speaking of a relic, or an icon. She pressed it harder into her body: under her nightgown the nipples pouted. It seemed to me that the madwoman in her sanity was suckling her own mother, and why not? For the whirling electrons there is neither before nor after, up nor down, and consequence can precede cause, why not? The lesson of the bitten egg.

Willi, I learned later, had found the photograph secreted among Anneliese's things.

37

He kept his old knapsack, a little ragged now (but the leather straps held), and wondered if he ought to get himself a motorcycle. In the end he took buses. He had no destination. To have a destination one needs an education: how else to be a pilgrim? He went, for instance, by happenstance—because the bus was headed there—to Walden Pond; it was no different from any other water. He contemplated enrolling in a university, but the thought of studying made him tired, and besides, what would be the point of it? He recoiled from books: he was a book himself, he was fifteen books, his bangs and his knees had been turned into a sort of scripture. The buses led him all over New England, and New England was boring, so he rode back to New York, telephoned Mr. Fullerton and Mr. Brooks (he declined to visit their offices), had a loud argument over what they called "numerous valuable items in storage," and found his way to certain clandestine bars. He missed the kif and tried a greenish powder recommended as "almost as good"—it wasn't—by a silly fellow he met in a bus station. These days it was necessary to drink in secret cellars, speakeasies that seemed jolly enough to their denizens, who smoked and flirted and snarled arms and legs around the nearest body of whatever sex (he did the same), and laughed about raids as if they were as random and likely as rain. He was in a raid himself once, and spent a few hours in the lockup, until he handed out hundred-dollar bills, which made his jailers suspect him of robbery, from the look of him—but they pocketed the bills and let him go. The next day, a Friday, he got on a train at Grand Central—on a whim he treated himself to a sleeper—and in the dining car sat down opposite a middle-aged man in a clerical collar and cassock. The man was not a priest. He was an actor traveling in costume. His name was Arnold Partridge, and he was getting off at

Altoona, where he hoped to join the rest of the cast just before the curtain went up. He was, he said, wearing a bald wig, which took a terribly long time to put on. Yesterday he had been obliged to attend the funeral of an aunt, his mother's sister, in Yonkers; the director could not prevent his going, but insisted (there was no understudy) that he return for the Friday night performance—hence his arriving fully garbed and accoutered, ready to set foot on the stage. He didn't mind running around impersonating a priest, he said. People treated him respectfully, as they never did without the collar, and anyhow impersonation was his business. It wasn't much of a business: he belonged to a small itinerant repertory company that lived from hand to mouth, playing only on the weekends.

"Playing what?"

"Rubbish," Arnold Partridge said. "Murder in the monastery."

"Are you the murderer?"

"I'm the one that gets his throat slit in the third act. Come and see."

His ticket was stamped straight through for Chicago. He tore it up (it hardly mattered, he could see Chicago another time) and alighted at Altoona together with the fake priest, who was, as he confidently announced, just in time for his entrance in Scene Two. At one dollar and eighty cents a ticket the Little Glory Theatre's sixty-eight seats were all filled, mainly with white-haired ladies in white shoes holding hand fans with the company's name printed on them under a picture of a Japanese bridge over a stream. The men wore unbuttoned vests over shirtsleeves and no jackets, and docilely kept their straw boaters in their laps. The plot was both intricate and ludicrous, but the audience was grateful, and clapped at intermission, and even more vigorously when the actors took their bows. The ingenue, who played (in pigtails) the priest's unacknowledged daughter, looked to be close to fifty. A ten-year-old boy had a walk-on part, and stood wordlessly, his eyes deadened by tedium. This same boy mounted a stool behind a table at the back of the auditorium during intermission and sold five-cent candy bars and bags of saltwater taffy marked "Genuine Atlantic City Boardwalk" for twenty cents each. He was the ingenue's son. He traveled with the company and never went to school.

Arnold Partridge found a place for his train companion in the rooming house where the actors were boarding, and by the end of the next week's performances the Bear Boy was moving scenery and sweeping up, with a promise of a part in Johnstown, where they would all have to polish their lines for the new play. Johnstown was smaller than Altoona, and the theater more decrepit, but the rooming house there, with its musty overused damp smell, was nearly identical. This didn't trouble him; he was used to feeling at home with the provisional; he was used to rooming houses. The Johnstown play had a heroic theme: Lincoln, from boyhood to martyrdom. The ingenue's son played Lincoln as a child. He was shown before a painted hearth with its painted fire, reading book after book, but he did not speak. The Bear Boy too had no lines. They gave him a long black coat spotted with moth holes, and an old-fashioned thick-barreled rubber revolver; he was John Wilkes Booth. His job in the penultimate scene was to shoot Arnold Partridge and flee into the wings. Backstage he discovered that the ingenue's son could not read the books he put his face into as he lay on his belly warming himself at the painted fire. They had tried to get him to memorize a few lines, but he balked. Everyone else had a script, he didn't. If he wanted a script like the rest of them, his mother said, he'd have to learn to read. He refused, and ran off to hide in the company truck, burrowing into the pile of stained and mended costumes. His mother wasn't married to his father. His father had gone away a long time ago; he couldn't remember him at all. He was useful enough when they needed bodies to people a stage. Sometimes they wrote him in; once he played a dwarf, and once a king's page. And always he was the child Lincoln, buried in books.

The company went from town to town, three cars in procession behind the truck carting big flats of scenery and crates of jumbled wardrobe. The truck was decorated with the company's name in tall red, blue, and orange letters, and stopped at street corners to sound its carillon and hand out round cardboard fans on sticks. Often there was no theater in these places, so they rented the local American Legion hall, and put up posters in store windows and on telephone poles. The Bear Boy, meanwhile, advanced from silent action—a servant, a deaf uncle—to speaking roles. He was no better or worse at it than anyone else; he had been an actor all his life, a fabricator compelled to wear the Bear Boy's skin. In these little central-Pennsylvania hamlets—Bellefonte, Pleasant Gap, Port Matilda, Tyrone—he declaimed, he loudly whispered, he falsely wept; he was mocking his old self. Everything here was fake: the fake priest, the fake ingenue, the fake young Lincoln in front of the fake fire, faking reading.

Arnold Partridge and the ingenue—her name was Bridget—were lovers. When the director disappeared (this happened in Chambersburg), taking with him three weekends' receipts, Arnold Partridge became the new director, by default, and Bridget fell into the Bear Boy's bed. She was too old—she was forty-seven—but she gave him nothing to complain of, and Arnold Partridge, now in charge of an impoverished company, was scarcely in a position to complain: the Bear Boy had instantly made up for the missing receipts, and then some. No one had imagined him as having any money, there was never a sign of it, it was a kind of miracle, it was the improbable third-act reversal. They had taken him for a species of roustabout, one of those hangers-on who attach themselves to theater folk on the road and are rewarded with bit parts in return for pushing the scenery. And wasn't he exactly that?

Yet he was not. They began to look up to him; Bridget was enraptured. He liked her tongue in his mouth, but preferred it curling on his member, a decent distance from his nostrils. She did whatever he told her to, so he sent her to a dentist in Harrisburg, to improve her teeth and her breath. He gave his part away and sat in the audience, as he had that first night, right off the train. Then he asked Arnold Partridge what he would think of hiring stagehands to push the scenery and load the truck, and whether he'd mind junking the old moth-eaten wardrobe and replacing it with everything new. "You're the boss," Arnold Partridge said. It was clear that the price of the stagehands and the new wardrobe was Bridget.

He told Bridget that her son ought to learn to read.

"He won't," she said.

"He will. I'll make him."

"Then you'd be a magician."

But he was already a magician. He had the power of surprise;

money could surprise, it could bewilder. It was delectable to withhold it and delectable to let it fly out, like a jack-in-the-box on a spring.

They had arrived in Lemonville, and were performing in the school auditorium. It was a rundown town with a single gas station and a sleepy general store smelling of cloves and camphor, where half-bald aging cats lay stretched on patches of burlap. On one end of town farmland began; on the other a yellow wood rose, circling a pond veiled by a greenish shimmer. He had discovered this place, a sort of glen fringed by a stone wall, on a morning walk with Bridget.

"Meet me at the wall near the water right after the Saturday matinée," he told Bridget's son, "and I'll give you this." He held up a ten-dollar bill.

The matinée ran from noon to nearly three. Browning leaves speckled the dirt at the foot of the wall; it was early autumn. As the boy approached, horse-chestnut shells crackled under his tread and a mass of sparrows pecking in low weeds went rioting, escaping into the trees. He had chosen this spot for its isolation.

"Take this right now," he said to Bridget's son, "and you can have some more later."

"Why?" the boy said. He put the money in his pocket. A sullen confusion roamed in his eyes.

"I want to give you lots of presents, that's why."

"Only because you like my mother—"

"Your mother likes me. But she'd like me more if I got her to like you more."

"You can't make me go to the dentist. I won't go, no matter what, even if you give me"—he thought a moment—"fifty dollars."

"I'll give you fifty dollars right now, and not for the dentist."

"You're crazy," Bridget's son said.

"They've got a good script for David Copperfield, and no one to play the lead."

"That's all *you* know. We did David Copperfield year before last—"

"Was there another boy in the company then?"

"Sure. My mother."

He threw his laughter against the wall: Bridget as David Copperfield! Bridget, with her fleshy hips, in short pants! And was that any different from himself, with his rouged knees? A ferocity seized him: he would cause this boy to renounce fakery. He stuffed four more ten-dollar bills in Bridget's son's pocket, and showed him the primer he had shoved into his own pocket.

"If I pay you to do it," he said, "if I pay you and pay you, will you learn?"

"You're crazy," the boy said.

"Will you do it?"

"Sure," the boy said.

The lessons began, there against the stone wall, and continued in Clearville, and then in Pearstown, and then in Mansfield. It was achieved: the boy was bright and quick and angry and avaricious. It did not occur to the tutor to ask the pupil what he would do with the money he had accumulated; it wasn't his affair. He didn't suppose the boy would give it to his mother, not that he would care. It was a revelation, an intoxication — getting that boy to read. A little miracle of sorts. The miracle wasn't witnessing the dawning of comprehension; what was Bridget's son to him? The closer he came to the boy — the two of them in studious seclusion — the more he was repelled by him. Dirty straw hair, monkey-flat small ears, teeth green at the gums and as crooked as his mother's; sweat dribbling down the sides of a fat pubescent nose. Worse, the sulking greed; ambition fueled by greed. No miracle in that. Never mind the boy, the miracle was what he felt in himself. He hardly knew what to name it; he scarcely understood it, but it was something remembered, a long-ago sensation returned, a kind of piercing behind the eyes. A burning. A transcendence. A mastery. The doll house, with its miniature cubicles and tiny figurines; his father's anger. The presents, endless presents, boxes from far away, sent by what his mother called the Reading Public and his father called My Fans. They sent him toy bears, mostly — brown bears, panda bears, polar bears, and bears more human than bear-like. They sent him knitted socks and scarves, and wind-up cars and paint sets and cushions cross-stitched with replicas of himself. From Sweden (where, his father told him repeatedly, the Bear Boy outsold Selma Lagerlöf) came the doll house. It was a countrified cottage with a peaked roof and scalloped eaves, and tiny chairs and tables, and four tiny beds for the four tiny wooden children who lived in it. The children, like the house, were hand-carved; they had yellow hair painted on, and red circles on their cheeks, and even on their knees. On their knees! No grownups inhabited this house. He moved the children from room to room; they were his to command. Wherever he ordered them to go, they went—he had only to grip their yellow heads with his fingers. And sometimes he told them not to move at all, to stand very still in such and such a position. They always obliged him, and then an electric feeling ran through him, a strange warm tickle rushed down the whole length of his spine, and if at that moment his father called to him, he would never answer, because it was so delectable to squeeze his fingers on the yellow heads of the little doll house people, to be in command, to be the master of the doll house. But one day the doll house disappeared. His mother explained that it had been given away to the poor children who had no toys, just as the knitted socks and scarves were given away, and the bears, and all the things he had too much of and didn't need. He knew, though, that it was his father who had removed the doll house. His father blamed him for obsession, for freakishness, for unseemliness, for wasting time and not doing his duty, which was to come when called and then to stand very still while his father, looking up and then looking down again, made sketch after sketch of the Bear Boy.

He left the company, left Bridget whimpering, tried Chicago for a week, didn't like it, and got on the first interstate vehicle that grumbled into the grimy bus station, an elongated old tin lizzie, burning oil, with a battered blue snout. It rocked him to sleep, and he woke up in Elmira, a town like other towns, no different from the towns of central Pennsylvania, but self-conscious over the bones of Mark Twain, whose grave lured tourist cash. A town proud of dead bones! He spent a night there for the sake of a shave and a haircut (he had let his hair grow to his chin, in proper thespian fashion), and went on to Endicott, Johnson City, and big Binghamton, and then north to Syracuse, Rome, and Utica. On the roads in between (the bus was now a rusty brown) he smelled apples. These places might all be called New York, but they were as remote from the offices of Mr. Brooks and Mr. Fullerton as the winey scent of fallen apples. He rode eastward, passed through Amsterdam and Rotterdam and Schenectady (too big), and ended in Clarksville, not far from Albany, where he settled into a rooming house almost too respectable for his taste. A sign on the porch read TOURISTS, but it was occupied by a bevy of elderly women, widows and spinsters, all retired schoolteachers. Sweet powdery odors came out of them. They thought him a pleasant novelty, a faintly enigmatic young man with freshly cut hair and large strong teeth and flashing lenses. He had never before been among old women. They struck him as exceptionally ugly, their bobbing dewlaps and the accordion folds that dented their upper lips, but he liked their inquisitive attentiveness. They fluttered around him and asked what he "did," and he teased them and said he was an entomologist specializing in the anthills of upstate New York, which had layered tunnels and traffic patterns endemic to the region—but he knew these chattering ladies, with their white hair identically coiled, were too shrewd to believe him. Finally he told them he was a failed actor on the lookout for a more sensible line of work; he had done a bit of tutoring, and wouldn't mind doing some more. The ladies were quick to find him leads. They were all too familiar with reading problems in children, and admired him for choosing so useful a vocation.

But when, on the advice of his ladies, the local mothers began summoning him to prop up their faltering offspring, he strolled out to a flower shop and ordered masses of roses wrapped in tissue paper, and piled them on the porch under the TOURISTS sign, and caught the bus to Saratoga and gambled away as many dollars as he had paid out to Bridget's son. That same evening he landed in Thrace, where he hoped to find a rooming house that could never be mistaken for respectable.

His knapsack held—it had always held, for spite, for repudiation, for vengeance, for some precipitate opportunity (only God, in whom he had no belief, knew the reason he kept it there)—the very first copy of *The Boy Who Lived in a Hat*, the one his father had placed in his small son's hands. A million and a half copies in print one week after publication! His father said, "You see what a wonderful thing can come of listening to me when I tell you not to move and to stay perfectly still?" In the beginning it *was* a wonderful thing—look, it was himself in the pictures, imagine! He turned the pages, and turned the pages, and ate his bread and jelly, and turned the pages some more.

But in Thrace he gambled the wonderful thing away—he gave it away, he threw it away. It had turned into an atrocity, evidence of a secret murder, a cadaver in his knapsack that stank and stank, a stink he was compelled, until he ran into that fellow in the schoolyard, to carry on his back wherever he went. He never forgot the date he got rid of it, the fifteenth of February, a date that seemed to agitate the fellow—or anyhow he made much of it, it wasn't clear why. The fellow was sly, not stupid, and his dice were worn to a shine. So were his eyes, blinking shiny bulges set too far apart under wary lids. He said he was a teacher, which was plausible (the schoolyard being proof, after all, a cement patch adjoining red brick), and that he had a child, which wasn't—he was so obviously a man alone, and angry. He might or might not credit the value of that old kid book, he said, but he was glad to try for it, just on the chance, he was a man who trusted in luck, even though he hadn't been lucky yet; he was willing to wait; you could never tell, and if the thing was the real McCoy . . .

"What would you get for a thing like that?" he said.

"It depends on who wants it. I'd say a couple of thousand now. More later."

"You would say that, wouldn't you. I've been conned before. If it's the real McCoy, how'd *you* get hold of it?"

"The author gave it to me. Years ago."

"Then why would you stand the chance of losing it?"

"I hated that man. You don't want to keep what you hate."

"Bravo. Here's five bucks on it. If you want, I'll throw in my kid for free." The fellow didn't talk like anyone's father. He didn't act like anyone's father. He said, "Why not? It's the goddamn fifteenth."

It was night; the schoolyard was deserted. He was just off the bus from Clarksville, where he had heaped up the roses for his ladies, and was on his way to look for a place. The usual kind, without the smell of face powder. He had a bottle in his pocket, and wandered into the schoolyard to get his bearings and have a smoke. The cigarette was unsatisfactory, so he tossed it away. Then he saw that angry fellow walking across the yard, his head down, his neck showing yellow in the murky light of a helmeted bulb clamped to brick. He had stayed late to mark exams, the fellow said. If he went home there was the kid. A neighbor woman was watching the kid, he said. He had no wife, he said. He was probably a liar: if he had no wife he had no child. He was a liar, and angry; his anger had something to do with the fifteenth of February.

"I'm stuck," the fellow said. "I've always been stuck." Him with a doctorate from Yale, he said, and here he was teaching elementary algebra in no man's land. "Now wait a minute, how do I know it's the real McCoy?" he said again. "I'll put five on it anyhow." He kneeled on the pavement. With a nicely turned wrist he rolled the dice — his lucky dice, he said.

In less than a minute the cadaver in the knapsack was expelled into Thrace.

The Bear Boy knew he had never before spoken those words aloud: that he hated the author of the Bear Boy.

38

"TONIGHT," Professor Mitwisser said, "there will be a visitor. Consequently I will not require your usual assistance, and since Dr. Tandoori will perforce arrive quite late, I will ask you to bring him to my study straightway. He has an auto and comes from a distance. Doubtless he will be chilled from the drive. Please to serve the tea immediately."

Not a single visitor (Ninel was hardly that) had appeared since the summer before, when Mitwisser's antagonists had muffled the dining room ceiling in the languid mists of their cigarettes—but then it was Anneliese who had directed the motions of hospitality. I had ascended; or perhaps Anneliese had descended into the smoke of absence.

There had been, it seemed, an exchange of letters. Dr. Gopal Tandoori, formerly a scholar of Indian philosophies at a college in Bombay, was invited to confirm not merely the quality of al-Kirkisani's rendering of the fragment from Spain—Mitwisser had himself confirmed this— but the nature of a particular strain of Hindu thought in relation to the thought of al-Kirkisani. At ten-thirty I stood at the green front door, waiting. A bitter wind blew in under the threshold. There were few automobiles at this hour; now and then I stepped into the cold and watched as the occasional pair of headlights approached and then passed by. Icy ovals gleamed in the road. The cars grew fewer and fewer. I went in and started the kettle. At ten past eleven, as I was setting out the tea things (James's things, on James's gilded tray), I heard the squall of a struggling engine and resisting gears: Dr. Tandoori had bumped the whole right half of his car over the curb and onto the pavement, just missing the streetlight.

A small man wearing a brown fedora and large red earmuffs emerged from the car, assessed its position, and left it as it was. I was disappointed. I had expected an Indian to be wrapped in white homespun, with his knees exposed, like Mahatma Gandhi in the newsreels. Dr. Tandoori was dressed in no extraordinary way. He headed into the house with a kind of bounce, handing me his coat and shoving the earmuffs into a sleeve. They promptly fell out. He bounced down to retrieve them. "Gravesend," he said, "and as I am an immigrant, I am often puzzled in the way of immigrants. Brooklyn, my dear, Brooklyn! The conditions of the roads, very bad, ice here, ice there! I confess I lost my way during several attempts to find it. When I first heard this name, Gravesend"—he was following me up the stairs—"I thought how the end of mankind is the grave, and yet, and yet! The name may refer to the afterlife! No doubt there are omens in the names of things, though I myself do not adhere to this belief. Ah, sir! Sir! We meet in this inconstant flesh, and shall we speak of universals and eternals? Truth to tell, I am myself something of a materialist, a position that has determined my fate, though the notion of fate is hardly becoming to one professing materialism—"

When I returned with the tea, Dr. Tandoori was seated in Mitwisser's chair, and Mitwisser had taken my customary place, facing the typewriter. "My, my, what a pleasant beginning. This fine hot tea," Dr. Tandoori said, "I am grateful for it. As I am an immigrant without a family, I am compelled to live a restricted life. I must boil my own tea! Put it that I am compelled"—a bounce, and the tea overflowed a little into the saucer—"to abandon text for textiles. My small joke, if you please. In my shop I must keep late hours, as you are kind enough to tolerate even now. May I assume that this young person is your daughter?"

"She is not," Mitwisser bit off. "She is my amanuensis." I had never before heard him use this odd word; it was briny with anger and, I thought, mockery. I was nothing so elevated as an amanuensis; it had lately become my morning's task to make up Mitwisser's bed. "You may leave now," he ordered.

"Please don't go—a young face is such a pleasure in the world. A young lady is so much a refreshment when two elderly gentlemen such as ourselves converse. It is like the presence of a bird at dawn."

I went to sit on the edge of Mitwisser's bed. I knew it to be a defiance and a violation, yet Mitwisser did not remonstrate—whether it was the restraint of his distaste that silenced him, or deference to his guest, I could not tell. There was nowhere else for me in that strange space—all at once strange to me then, seeing it through the visitor's eyes: the old books all around, the heaps of papers, the crates of files, the cramped odors of obsession, the intimate intrusion of the massive bed (it occupied nearly half the room) with its bodily reminders. Mitwisser was a man who had procreated; he had lain with his Elsa, he had gripped her body with his. He was not elderly, he was only worn. Dr. Tandoori was not elderly either; he was if anything too lively. He had taken up tailoring, he said, in place of philosophy. He reiterated that he was at heart a materialist. "I left my place in my college not quite voluntarily, a circumstance that obliged me to deal, as tailors do—pardon again my small joke—with *material*. With the fabric of unalloyed realism! It was said that I leaned too heavily in my lectures—indeed, perhaps too exclusively—on the school of Brihaspati and Brihaspati's followers, the Charvakas. Collectively they are known as the Nastiks, the materialists, the skeptics, the deniers—"

So Dr. Tandoori too had been thrown out, though he could not be called a refugee. He had merely been sacked: for championing a sect that sneered at the Vedas, the Upanishads, the Bhagavad-Gita. He did not seem humiliated—getting thrown out was something to relish.

"It was claimed," he said, "that I jollied my students. I jollied them, true, it is my nature, but it was claimed that I overjollied them. Nowadays I jolly my customers, and it is entirely—um—fitting. No one wants a grave tailor, surely not in Gravesend, declaring as it does the end of gravity—"

I was astonished to see a minute crescent of a smile grow itself on Mitwisser's lip. He had the look of an admirer.

"You speak of skeptics and deniers," he said.

"Oh yes, they disrespect the priests. You will find even in the Upanishads how the priests in procession are compared to white dogs in a line, each dog holding in its mouth the tail of the dog in front of it. Skeptics become mockers."

"The Karaites also mock."

"The Nastiks repudiate."

"The Karaites also repudiate. They separate from the mainstream. They ridicule the mainstream."

"The Nastiks are not merely separatists. They are nihilists. They repudiate mystical devotion, they repudiate faith. Faith for them is illusion." He burst out, "I like them awfully much!"

The crescent that was almost a smile widened. Mitwisser was pleased. I had never seen him so pleased. "Then are your Nastiks," he pressed, "the 'demoniacal men' whom al-Kirkisani—"

"—turned up in that bit of the Gita? More than possible, more than possible. But sir, your man . . . all your Karaites, as you describe them, look to divinity. My Nastiks contend that God is a figment. A figment! The world is composed of atoms, man is ruled by instinct. Holiness is vapor."

"Then you are telling me that your interest has nothing in common with mine," Mitwisser said. But he said it lightly.

"Oh sir! Dear sir! On the contrary, the impulse you showed in posting to me your *most* engaging inquiry is entirely—*entirely*—justified. And in truth it is impulse—impulse!—that unites us. Surely you see how we are united, you with your Karaites, myself with my darling Nastiks? Brihaspati, you know, their founder, ridicules the sanctity of the Vedas—"

"The Karaites ridicule the sanctity of the Oral Law—"

"Quod erat demonstrandum!"

Dr. Tandoori gave one great bounce and catapulted himself out of his chair; I nearly expected him to seize Mitwisser by the hand and dance with him in a ring. "Oh sir, nothing, nothing signifies more than this! The hot drive to dissent, to subvert, to fly from what all men accept! To deny tedium, to deny what passes for usual wisdom! To deny the given, the received, the begotten, the whole benevolent common foolishness! I had rather be an outcast tailor—though I insist that my Singer is a *very* fine machine and I am *entirely* attached to it, it holds a high place in my affections—oh, rather an outcast among outcasts than to stand with officialdom! With those who reign over thought! Oh sir, dear sir, you and I, we are free men!"

Professor Mitwisser laughed. It was different from the laughter he had laughed with James. His visitor, I believed, had brought him an hour of clear happiness.

"And that one," Dr. Tandoori asked, "that one out there, is he yet another amanuensis?"

A pale boy had appeared in the unlit hallway, breathing hard. A pair of earphones hung from around his neck.

"Papa," the boy began, and stopped. He stared at Dr. Tandoori.

"Or perhaps he is your son?"

"What is it? What? Why are you at this hour not in your bed? You see I have a guest—"

Heinz said, "There's blood. Blood on mama. Coming out of mama—"

"And why should he not be my son!" Mitwisser roared, and fled to his wife.

39

Dr. tandoori carefully smothered his ears under his oversized muffs. "With family it is not possible to rule exclusively over oneself. I had a wife once—a wife absolutely. She was pleased to have me leave her where I found her. In Bombay she is happy in my long absence. Rule or be ruled, an ancient observation. Tell me, my dear," he said, "how many children has Professor Mitwisser? That boy with the red eyes, and are there others?"

"Five altogether," I said.

"How unfortunate. Then despite all he is not so free. And how many—forgive an Oriental's small witticism—how many wives?—Oh my, my, a calamity—"

The calamity was a tire. It had gone flat. Bare-armed, I had accompanied Dr. Tandoori out to his car; I stood clutching myself in the cold as he circled all around it, examining the wheels, two in the road and two on the sidewalk.

"How unfortunate," he said again. "A testimony to the dominion of chance. Rule or be ruled, yet chance is king and matter its viceroy. Who can rule matter? Here! The culprit!" He held up a fat rusted nail that lay at the foot of the streetlight.

I left him pumping a jack (the bright earmuffs bobbing up and down) and philosophizing about the world's materiality, interrupted by explosive imprecations in an unknown tongue.

The bloodletting was minor. There were two injuries, one over the right breast, the other vertically along the wrist. Both were minor. What great harm could a silver picture frame do? Its corners were sharp, but a picture frame is not a knife. A picture frame is not a weapon. Mitwisser washed his wife's wounds and tried clumsily to bandage them.

"Elsa, Elsa, *was hast du gemacht?*" Blood was smeared across the face of the woman in the photo and on the stone urn and its cherub. He looked wildly around the room. "Anneliese, why is Anneliese not in the house? You, Heinz! How did this come to be?"

The boy was sobbing. "I was listening to my crystal set—"

"Your what?"

"My radio . . . and I heard a sound from mama—"

"Radio? Radio is forbidden. No radio!"

"It's my own, I made it"—tugging at the earphones—"and nobody else can hear it anyhow—"

Mitwisser brandished the bloody frame. "Who gives mama this? Idiot! Look how she cuts herself—"

"Willi, he found it and showed it to mama and she wanted it, so he gave it to her—"

"You are to protect mama!"

The flat of Mitwisser's huge hand came down brutally on the boy's head. A soft mewl, like an animal's, spilled out of him. Blank shock dulled his eyes.

"You see now." Lazily, almost dreamily, Mrs. Mitwisser turned to me; her fingers were fidgeting with the gauze patch above her breast. "My husband," she said in a tired voice, "he has the wish to kill this boy."

"It was Willi," Heinz wailed.

I was witness then to something new under the sun of Mitwisser's universe: he had beaten a child, and out of more than local rage. Some demon had caught him. Was it his wife he wanted to thrash? Was it (I thought of Dr. Tandoori's parting judgment) that he was not free? Chained to his Elsa, to his children, to his Karaites? To world-upheaval, to this house in a wilderness of insignificance? An hour of pleasure, and with a tailor!

"Go back to bed," he told Heinz.

And to me: "Look how the gauze loosens. Perhaps you can . . . or when Anneliese—"

"I'll take care of it," I said.

He was uncertain, distracted. The blow had shot back through his own body. He shook; the skin whitened under the white tendrils of his progressing beard. The hand that had pounded the child's head blazed.

His wife in her fading voice said, "You will not kill him. This boy, you will not kill him."

"Calm, Elsa, calm. It is only a little cut, a little accident. Lie back. Here, I fix the pillow so nicely, *sei ruhig* —" He took a volcanic breath; there was violence in it. "Oh my poor Elsa," he said, "why do you make such an accident? Such a danger to yourself —"

I leaned over her to apply the new dressing. She nudged me aside with a weak push. But something secretive in her look held me.

"So much danger," she said drowsily, and unexpectedly called out her peculiar name for me: "Röslein, you see now? Elsa must kill Elsa, then he will not kill this boy, you see now?"

Mitwisser covered his face with his terrible fists.

40

MRS. MITWISSER slept. Professor Mitwisser had instructed me to stand guard over his wife for the remainder of the night: I was not to take my eyes from her, I was not to doze off. He said all this almost meekly, brokenly; it was more an appeal than a command.

The house in its muffled half-silence took on an underwater blur. Sounds lost their origins—was that Heinz whimpering in a dream, or Waltraut softly snoring, with a throb as steady as a metronome? Breathings all around, as elusive and slippery as the dartings of small fish fleeing the jaws of big ones. On the floor below, between the walls of his study, Mitwisser's footsteps padded forward and back, measuring out time, or trying to undo it. Finally they stopped. He had heaved himself into the vacant tract of his bed. Anneliese was not in the house; James was not. The smell of urine swelled in acrid waves.

I saw the dawn. Or it saw me, peering over the windowsill and seeping higher and higher, until it cast itself across the sky, a vertical violet light, like a risen watchtower.

Mrs. Mitwisser stirred. I put my hand on her upturned hip.

"Let me clean you."

I brought a basin and washed her body, feeling ashamed to see her naked; but she was not ashamed. A willing invalid, she rolled over obediently as I set down a clean sheet.

"*Durstig*," she said.

I gave her water and she drank and drank, and asked for more. Her face was luminous in the brightening morning light.

"They do not come," she said. Her voice was rapidly growing stronger. It was acquiring a low thick timbre; it rumbled out of her bandaged breast like an orchestral drumming. "You see now? They do not come," and though she pulled at my blouse, I wanted more than anything else to be allowed to fall into my own cold pillow. I was heavy with exhaustion and the sickening press of enclosure; I envied Dr. Tandoori's self-declared freedom. How simple it was for him to change a tire and be off! How simple for Anneliese to break through the bondage of this house and vanish! Dr. Tandoori had his philosophy—it bound him to no clear structure—and Anneliese . . . Anneliese had James.

"Already it is the sun," Mrs. Mitwisser said, "and they do not come."

A jubilation had overtaken her, a cascade of talk tumbled from her throat, or from somewhere deeper, a foam of domestic schemings, busy feints and cunning surges, breaking now and then into a helpless sputter of German. She had succeeded, she had bled out her shrewd victory. Her victory was Heinz. He was safe. She had choked off her husband's thoughts. Never again would her husband dare to contemplate whose son her clever boy was—just let him dare! Only let him *look* at the boy, only let him *wonder*; and blood, her own blood, the blood of her hand, the blood of her heart, would rush out and vanquish him! She would die to save Heinz, and now her husband was caught, now he comprehended, now he would not ever again disguise hate as love. That is what harlots do, and who then is the harlot?

She spoke to me as to an accomplice. It was I, after all, who had supplied the seed, the hint (*der Kern*, she put it in one of her lapses) of her success. At this word—success—she felt for the dressing at her wrist, proudly: a dueling scar on display. As for the seed, as for the hint, it was this: my father, that other boy, my father had killed that other boy long ago, it was too late for that boy. But no, not too late for Heinz! Her husband's wild blow to the child's poor head was the first, yes—and it was also the last. It was her intent (her tone turned sermonic) to clean house, to deliver them all from dishonesty. She had completed half. Heinz was safe, and that was half.

She was logical, methodical; empirical. The piercing, the silver frame, the bleeding—these were the furnishings of her laboratory. No wonder she touched the glory of her wounds!

"If they will come," she said, and stopped. It was odd to hear that "if," a musing over an unproved theory, a kind of reversal: it had the sound of hope, and what was it she hoped for? She raised herself a little, to see out the window. There were only the snaggletoothed rooftops of neighboring houses. But her mouth was open, and her fine teeth threw off glints from the early sun like a purposeful code signaling to some farther sun beyond our own.

During the next several days Professor Mitwisser did not ask for me. I was to care for his wife, the work at the typewriter was subordinate to his wife's well-being, I was to keep his wife calm, calm above all, his own presence would not do, when he went in to his wife it stimulated her in dreadful ways. And the children too must be barred. He rattled out all these things again and again, and then shut his door against the troubles of his house.

On the fourth day he called me to him.

"What do you know about my daughter?"

"She went with James."

"Yes, yes, with James. That is not my question. I do not inquire about James. I inquire about my daughter. Her mother is ill and she is not in the house. My sons fight, the small child is distraught, and where is my daughter?"

He was ignorant of the life around him. He observed little that was not to his convenience. The crystal set, the Spanish doll sprawled on the stair, the teapot with the golden spout — so many additions and transformations, and he was blind to all of them.

"She no longer studies. She becomes indifferent."

"If she were sent to school—"

"My daughter has the European outlook. An American school is not fit for her."

"You send the boys."

"My sons are children. My daughter is a young woman. She should be at her mother's side. My daughter, not a stranger."

A recklessness gripped me, a contagion of unrestraint: I felt infected by Mrs. Mitwisser's exultation. Her bloody victory.

"That bit of hair," I said, "in your wife's shoe, that she found in James's bed—"

"Do not speak to me of this!"

"If it was your daughter's—"

"My poor wife is stricken, she hallucinates, she has lost her reason, she accuses this one and that one, she accuses herself—" The long bones of his forearms, giantly black in their black sleeves, chopped at emptiness like a pair of hatchets.

I said slowly, "Mrs. Mitwisser doesn't hallucinate. I think she sees."

"Please to go now, I have no need of you."

The great hands fell. He stood helplessly.

"My daughter," he said, "has been absent from this house for three nights."

"With James."

"He is our good friend, there is nothing amiss."

I had lost all awe of him. "Your wife," I began, and left the rest to dissolve in the air.

"I have no wife, my wife is mad!"

His wife saw everything. He saw nothing.

41

WILLI BROUGHT ME two letters. He looked disappointed: the post had come, and there were no packages. James's gifts, his surprises, had begun to diminish. Of late there was nothing. But the house was already mobbed by toys and games and boxes of various shapes, some of them barely opened and pushed aside. A corner of the kitchen was blocked by a pyramid of these acquisitions. It seemed to me that the postman's ring, and the shrieks and excited unwrappings that followed, aroused rather than sated the household greed. Only Waltraut was content with her dolls in their coats of many colors. Or at least she did not hope for more.

Willi said, "Somebody wants to marry you."

He was panting a little. He had run up the stairs. His comely head, an unripe version of Anneliese's, was all abandoned hair. It stood over his eyes like a lattice covering darkness; for weeks Anneliese had neglected to trim it.

"It says so in here," he said.

"Is that letter for you?"

"It's for you," he admitted.

"Then why did you read it?"

"The envelope was open. It fell out."

I examined the envelope. The flap was partly unglued. But the rest of it had been torn free.

"It's wrong to read other people's letters. It's wrong to go through other people's things," I said.

"If you get married papa will have to find someone else to take care of mama, and what about Waltraut? Anneliese isn't back, and papa — papa —" It was difficult to tell about papa.

I saw he was afraid. We were sinking still more deeply into wilderness—the boys at war, underwear unwashed, pots boiling over, Mitwisser pacing behind a shut door, his wife finicky in her bed, Waltraut unbathed and growing dispirited. At times she fell into inconsolable howls. If I made order in one part, decay was already seeping into another part. I, the stranger, was all that kept us from the last stages of anarchy—I had become a hidden engine of survival. No one took any notice of this. In that family, Willi alone—this thievish child—showed any curiosity about who, or what, I might be.

"I'm not marrying anybody," I told him.

I recognized the handwriting instantly. But I was cold to it. A letter from Bertram no longer had the power to stir me. He had sent Ninel to take away what had been meant for me. Even his kiss was not meant for me. He was hardly a cousin anyhow.

In the Mitwisser fiefdom a letter was nevertheless an event. Besides being deprived of a radio (the unearthly grumbles in Heinz's earphones didn't count), the house had no telephone. In 1935 almost every American family owned a radio, but a telephone at home was still not a widespread convenience. It was odd that such a thing was not among James's household surprises—had Mitwisser, condemning intrusion, prohibited it? Or had James himself inscrutably withheld it? We ate and slept on an island; we were marooned. The boys were a nation unto themselves. They squabbled and fought, but their loyalty was inward, despite their lives at school. No chum or classmate ever crossed our threshold. The disruptive world had no access to us, except by letter. And letters were rare enough: the cataclysmic revelation from Spain; now and then, in reply to Mitwisser's inquiries (I had typed a handful of these), a contentious Karaite trickle from here or there. Anneliese and Mrs. Mitwisser received nothing. And I—well, here again was Bertram. But I was apprehensive: why was he writing this time? Was it another needling from Croft Hall, was it some further remnant of my father's ignominy?

I took up the envelope Willi had invaded (let Bertram wait, I thought), and drew out a letterhead embossed with a picture of a spool of green thread. The thread wound outward in a long coil; at its end appeared the head of a snake, and out of the snake's mouth these words:

Gopal V. Tandoori, M.A., Ph.D.
Avatar of the Serpent's Philosophy
Fine Custom Tailoring
118 Gravesend Neck Road
Gravesend, Brooklyn, New York

My dear Miss [I read], my dear Amanuensis!

I beg your patience with this missive. Shortly I shall explain. May I hope that Mrs. Professor Rudolf Mitwisser has recovered well from her unhappy injury? And that you yourself continue in good health?

You should know that I have published numerous articles in the International Journal of Historical Metaphysics, situated in New Delhi. I was formerly a consultant to this distinguished periodical, but since my removal to these shores, alas no more. Fortunately, however, copies are stored in the Public Library, through which circumstance Professor Rudolf Mitwisser, disengaging my person from its wonted obscurity, discovered them. Following which, his communication journeyed around the great world! From New York to New Delhi to Bombay and ultimately, may I say happily, to Brooklyn!

Hence my acquaintance with this delightful gentleman, made still more gratifying by the presence of his charming Amanuensis!

During the period of my most pleasing visit, she (my portrait, please note, courteously eschews the second person) remains silent. Nevertheless I observe that she observes. I myself am crucially ob- servant. I observe this silent yet very intelligent young lady. Her eyes are small but respectful. Her upper lip is short, a style most ad- mirable also in our Indian young ladies. Her silence augurs mod- esty. She neglects easy mirth, displaying a most becoming gravity of disposition. She listens with understanding. She is ripe in percep- tion, yet appears to be robed in melancholy.

Not all freedom is desirable (you may recall that I touched on the subject of freedom). Not all rule is undesirable. One can be ruled by the eye—unexpectedly! One can be ruled by the heart—unexpect- edly! It is not always possible to deny the immaterial inward coursings of one's material nature. Hence you deserve to be informed that my wife (who is no more my wife) became thus through family arrangement, according to custom, neither through eye nor heart.

Allow me to clarify. Diligence in my shop, combined with indefatigable hours, has made me not precisely prosperous; but I may say that I want for nothing. It is my plan to curtail my night labors in order to pursue further work on a study already well launched. Indeed, it was begun some years ago, and I am only now inspired (dare I confess?) to bring it to fruition. It extends, until this moment, to one hundred and five leafs, all in the hand you see before you!

In short, my dear Amanuensis, I too am in need of an Amanuensis! I invite you to my comfortable home.

My flat, on the first floor (in the American count, the second) of a five-story brown-brick building, tidily maintained, contains two rear rooms, a capacious parlor, a well-appointed cookery, and a w.c. (with bath).

Remuneration shall be equal to the remuneration you now obtain from Professor Rudolf Mitwisser, and if a time should come when remuneration is no longer pertinent—when remuneration is superfluous—a time when you are ready to receive the admiration of my eye and the devotion of my heart—then—then (dare I utter it?)—I hope you will accept to be my wife.

You may wish to learn the subject of my study. I have entitled it "Contra the Gods." Note that it is my intention, should you look upon me with favor, to acquire an Underwood. Note also that my tyre has been repaired.

I appeal to you to pardon my forwardness. I reflect on your small lips with rapture!!

Sincerely yours,
Gopal V. Tandoori

What could Willi have made of this?

Like a sharp-eyed bird seizing on a single grain in an expanse of gravel, he had plucked up "wife."

Bertram's letter:

Hi there, Rosie kid!

This is my last night at the Capolinos'. As of tomorrow I'm out. They say they need this place for a newly married niece, but the truth is lately I've been slow with the rent. I don't think this niece actually exists (not that there aren't plenty of nieces! but they all seem to be grandmothers), it's only something Mrs. Capolino says. She doesn't like to hurt my feelings. Up here it's a tight enough squeeze for one, never mind a pair of newlyweds. Ninel said it felt like spending the night in a coffee pot. Anyhow I'm headed out for unknown vistas.

Now for the good (ha ha!) news. Got a pink slip from the Administrator. Out with the strikers one time too many, disrupting hospital routine, calls me an agitator. Your own Cousin Bertram, an agitator! I did appeal to some of the bigwig Trustees, but it didn't do any good, and I'm out of a job. Unfair in a way, because it's been a while since last time. I'm not with that crowd nowadays—nobody around to inspire me. So that's how it is, kid. Hard times.

But I hear *you're* all right. Ninel figures they've got you as some sort of secretary, she saw a typewriter set up with Herr Katzenjammer in charge. A bunch of refugees, a whole howling herd, she said, but you're in tight with them, you're all right, at least you're not strapped for cash. I'm glad you didn't mind helping her out— Ninel told me you didn't mind at all. She's gone off with her crowd, she's over there now, something to do with ambulances, but I'm pretty sure it's guns.

That's about it. I have to get back on my feet somehow, I've pounded enough powders and filled enough capsules for one lifetime. Got any ideas?

Mrs. Capolino says the geraniums are mine to keep—a goodbye present.

Take care of yourself, kid.

Bertram

In the dimness of the hallway mirror I studied my face. Was my upper lip very short? Was my mouth very small? I could not decide. But it was as plain as could be that the amanuensis in the looking glass was robed in melancholy.

By now a whole week had passed since Anneliese and James had left the house.

42

UPSTATE SUITED HIM: upstate, half decayed, with its dilapidated farms, barns and silos rotting, and in the towns tired frame houses with warped porches pleading for paint, town after town sluggish in the dazing summer glare, the business district—three streets lined with sickly stores darkened by canvas awnings—surrendered to exhaustion. He thought of trampled and abandoned anthills—it was a picture that kept recurring. Months ago, in Clarksville, hadn't he ragged those fussing old ladies with talk of anthills? And that sly fellow in Thrace, an insect of a man, with the bulging eyes of a praying mantis, a fool who didn't have an inkling of the Bear Boy's worth. Drenched in money. Good! The Bear Boy hidden away, buried, maybe trashed. Thrace behind him, Clarksville behind him, all those hiding places—he had hidden himself, he had buried himself through a winter and a spring, and had done it without the kif (the kif was long ago), though with a bit of help from the bottle. Mostly he slept the days away, but now and then he cleaned up and took the bus to Albany. Albany had more of what a man's nature needs: certain small hotels with bad reputations.

At noon on a warm June day he woke up in one of these, groggy and vacant-eyed. The woman had been gone for hours, and the room smelled of what the two of them had been drinking. He had no bill to pay (you had to pay in advance), and walked out into unfamiliar streets. Walking seemed to mend him—his legs, anyhow; the torpor, the masculine self-incrimination that follows hurried sex, drained out of his calves and thighs and knees, and he discovered, almost without noticing it at first, that he was running. The more he ran, the more he felt anointed, partly by the sunlight, partly by sweat. The liquor flew off him like pasted-on feathers whooshed away by the wind he was raising in the pure speed of the run. Whatever last night had left him with—a mood, a sensation, a dread, but not unhappiness, because unhappiness was his habitat, he lived inside it, it was no different from having eyes to see out of—his muscles on the move could evaporate. He ran! The neighborhoods were altering now, turning from seedy to creditable. He hurtled past the white columns of a white building, a square lawn before it, a black fence with iron staves: it was a college of some kind. He slowed and went back to look: a Quaker college. And then ran on.

Three days later he came to Albany, if not to stay really, then to stay for a while. He was led there by surprise. Albany had surprised him. It had flattered him: it restored his esteem for his body; it was an antidote to lassitude. It had thrust on him fifteen minutes of exhilaration. A block from the Quaker college he found a modest little hotel—its reputation was pristine, though here too you paid in advance, a month at a time. The sun was hot on the windowsills, and put him in mind of Algiers. Not since the dandyism of Algiers had he risen to the status of a wide bed in a hotel, where the sheets were changed daily, and a maid piled up fresh towels. Except for this—the plain fact that a hotel was not a rooming house—the William Penn had nothing in common with the Promenade. He learned quickly enough that a lady of the night would not be welcome here, and neither was the smell of a bottle. The communal breakfast parlor was austerely furnished: three long tables and a sideboard whereon baskets of brown bread and thick china bowls were set up in a row. Simple furnishings, simple food: the William Penn was an annex of the Hudson Valley Friends College down the street.

In the mornings the early sun, piercing through curtainless panes, woke him. He passed through the breakfast parlor, seized a bun, and was on his way. Running! It was the thrilling heat that propelled him, summer at the boil, steaming off his skin; or else it was those curious worn-out neighborhoods veiled by ancient unknown histories, or the strangely cold runnels of sweat dribbling down his shins. He was a flying bath, he was a fish hugging the tide, he was a wave! Intoxicated by weightlessness, a hundred times lighter than before. It took him back to the night he'd gotten free of the Bear Boy, on an impulse palmed it off on a nobody in nowheresville. An old, old scheme of his, brought off in an instant. Unless, well, loaded dice; then who'd conned whom? Anyhow the fellow had no idea.

There was a public toilet in a bend in the lobby just outside the breakfast parlor. He washed up—a radiant odor, just short of a stink, fumed out of the damp small of his back and his armpits—and went to reconnoiter one of the long tables. An attendant had begun to clear off the sideboard. He was late, it was half past ten, the hours allotted for breakfast were ending. As he made his way to the coffee urn, the last guests were leaving. A pair of (he guessed) businessmen carrying leather briefcases. A white-haired, hump-backed woman with a pince-nez and a cane. A swarm of children—too many children all in a cluster, and all boys. No, there was a girl among them, taller than the rest. It annoyed him that the food was being carted off; everything in this orderly hotel was precise. Yet the brown liquid in his cup was nasty: the very bottom of the pot, bitter and gritty with grounds. He determined to start his run earlier. It had become the center of his concentration—because it relieved him of concentration. It was its own relief.

At eight o'clock the next day the breakfast parlor was bustling but hushed (everything here was hushed, earnest, churchlike). The coffee was fresh, the buns warm. Traces of cinnamon hung in the air. He came in gleaming, as if soaked from head to toe in olive oil. His face was pink, and he felt he was panting like the little dog who had galloped after him, a little nervous thing yipping at his heels, though only as far as the curb, where it halted with a kind of Quaker decorum. Decorum ruled the breakfast parlor, so at the sideboard he stepped back to allow a small dark bundle of a woman to ladle a spoonful of blueberries into a dish; but her hands shook, the dish shook, and the berries scattered. At once a man—very tall, and somehow grim—hurried over and drew her toward one of the long tables on the far side of the room. The mob of children he had noticed the day before were seated there: a family mob, though quiet, even the baby, not what you'd expect of kids. The girl got up (there was only the one girl, unless the baby was female—from this distance he couldn't tell), approached the sideboard, and filled another dish with berries. But when she returned to the family table, the father had risen (he supposed it was the father), and was persuading the mother (he supposed it was the mother) to go with him. He gathered this from the father's expression, troubled and imploring, but mainly because the father had grasped the mother by the arm, attempting to pull her up. The woman only peered down at the berries the girl had placed before her. Then she dug her knuckles into them and ground them round and round in the dish. The girl began to cry. The other children stared and said nothing. But the woman spoke, and the man spoke, and the woman spoke more loudly, and the man appealed to her with an impatient sound, and finally the man took the woman by the shoulders and maneuvered her out the door.

They were foreigners. Their speech was indistinct: Swedish or Norwegian or such. He would be interested if they were Swedish. They didn't look like Swedes: all the children were dark, and the mother could almost pass for a Jew—but what would Jews be doing here? He saw that the children were growing agitated, though their voices were still low. German. It was German he was hearing, and Germanic wails out of the baby, who wasn't actually a baby: it scampered away from the others. A tiny girl, panicking. The older girl snatched the child up and led them all away. They were dressed oddly, the boys in short pants and high socks, the tall girl womanlike, dark hair wound in braids over her ears. Jewels in the lobes: this shocked him, it was so foreign.

The next morning it rained. He lay back in his nice laundry-smelling bed, with its pair of thick soft pillows, and watched the rivulets collide on the panes, two or three wayward tributaries coalescing in one decisive stream. The sky was flat and chalky-gray, bitten into by zigzag lightnings, like a sudden showing of teeth. And then the guttural tardy thunder, miles away. It threw him into a doze. When he woke again, the velvety drumbeats of thunder were even fainter, but the rain was insistent, flowing in opaque sheets against the windows.

He was curious to see them again, the woman who had resisted the man, and the man especially—that huge Teuton. There was something not right about the woman. There was something not right about the whole crew. A hauntedness, a precariousness. He knew how to recognize precariousness. The girl when she picked up the small child. Ancient eyes in a young face. But the breakfast parlor was deserted. The food had already been removed, the coffee was dregs, he had slept away the time.

After rain the revived sun bursts out like a gong. The heat caught him with the force of a thrown net. He remembered a nook of a delicatessen on the street just past the Quaker college and headed there, hoping for a sandwich: by now he was hungry enough. On the pavement in front of the green plot and the white columns he saw the girl. She was standing with her back to him—a long back—holding the small child by the hand.

"Well, hello," he said.

She turned and moved half a yard away, toward the iron fence.

"I saw you at the hotel yesterday. Having breakfast, your whole family. Is your mother all right?" Then it occurred to him that she might not understand.

But she said politely, "Thank you. My mother is well."

She was aloof. She had a kind of adolescent hauteur. This startled him. It was as if it was she who was conscious of a foreignness—as if he was the foreigner. And he knew she lied, or was simply wary. Clearly there was something not right about the mother.

"Then you do speak English," he said.

"I was taught it in school. Also by my father. But now I must study more."

"What about all those other kids?"

"My brothers must learn from the beginning." She said this in the tone of a command. Her chin rose up; she lifted her tidy head. She was nearly as tall as himself. He supposed she was no more than thirteen or fourteen, but she had a woman's decisiveness, and a woman's long back.

The child had found a stick, and was rhythmically beating it against a metal plaque attached to the fence. A sign of some kind.

"Waltraut, *nein!*" the girl admonished. But the child went on noisily hitting the sign.

"What did you call her?"

"Waltraut."

"There's a funny name." He felt in his pockets and pulled out some coins. He chose two of the shiniest ones and held them out to the child. She dropped the stick and came to him eagerly. "Here's a penny, and that one's a dime."

"Please, no," the girl said. "In my family we do not—"

He broke in, "For God's sake, it's only a couple of cents."

This seemed to fluster her. "We are here a little time only, I do not know yet how one explains the money."

He spilled a cascade of coins onto the sidewalk. The child looked up in delight. "See, that one's a nickel, five cents, and that one's a quarter, that's twenty-five. Go ahead," he told the child, "jiggle 'em, pile 'em up." And to the older girl he said, "I could show you the paper bills if you want."

A redness flooded her neck. "Please, no. We go now—" She bent to scoop up the coins. "Here, take please."

It was—what to call it?—trained probity. It struck him as stupidity—stupid pride over a handful of change. The small child playing at his feet charmed him: his pennies were being washed in a rain puddle. "Let the kid have 'em, same as mud pies, what's the harm?"

"Please, no," she said again. It was a directive, not an appeal. "My mother does not permit." And then, with the air of an empress: "We do not receive money that is not our own."

"Say it's a loan then. Hey, little one," he said, making a clown face, "you be sure to give me back all that used United States currency when I see you over at the hotel, okay?"

The child giggled.

"We have left the hotel."

"You have?"

"In the morning. My mother and my brothers are already in our new house. And here is my father."

He was striding toward them from between the columns that enclosed the College entrance. A towering Teuton in a heavy suit. Wool in June! It was outlandish; but the girl was an oddity in herself: the gravity, the self-possession. She had inherited the father's height, but not the father's eyes. His eyes were as blue as a Swedish sailor's; yet no Swedish sailor's glare was so fierce as this. The father growled down at the child, in German; the child was sitting in the middle of the puddle, wet underpants and a wet dress, washing money.

"From the hotel," the girl was saying (English emerging from German), "he gave them to her. But mama said—"

The father cut her off with a German grunt and majestically extended his hand. "You are kind to amuse my little daughter. You have bestowed on us our first American treasure."

So what mama would not permit was overruled by foreign courtliness.

He walked on to his delicatessen, ate his corned beef sandwich, and thought: why run? Not on a full stomach anyhow, but why run at all? Why run ever again? He had no destination, there was no finish line. When he came to the end of the run he found only himself: the same, the same. The more he moved on, the more he arrived at himself. Intoxication was brief—a seduction, an illusion. It didn't last. A snap of the dice, the Bear Boy gone in a flash. The impromptu thrill, and he was back to himself. Knapsack a tad lighter. Himself a bit—what? Cleaner. Not that he could ever be shut of the Bear Boy's residue, it was in his liver and his lungs. Contamination. Live without premeditation, that's the way. On the fly. Kif, booze, roses for old ladies, the bug-eyed fellow in the schoolyard. Bridget. The impromptu thrill, the moment's mastery, how different it must be for people who get thrown out of their old lives and afterward can't recognize themselves. Himself, he hadn't been thrown out, he'd crawled out on his own. Those people—foreigners. They looked dumbfounded. In a different language the larynx grows dumb. He knew the feeling, he'd been a foreigner himself (no, a traveler, a wayfarer, a wanderer, he hadn't been thrown out). The girl wasn't dumb, she'd said a few words in English. The father, somehow formidable. Spiraled out that elaborate—what? Mockery? *You have bestowed on us our first American treasure*, my God, what was that? Treasure, bestowed, what was all that?

He bought himself a couple of new shirts, paid for two months ahead, and settled in at the William Penn.

The girl had called it their new house, but it was old, in a fallen neighborhood. An abandoned filling station on the corner. Rotted objects in a vacant lot. Still, nice old-fashioned touches on the housefronts —you see them in these time-worn American cities, pitted brass lamps hanging from porch ceilings, a stained-glass fanlight above a door. At first it was only the girl—the imperial woman-girl—who was worth watching. The snail-braids over the ears, the tiny ugly earrings, the knowingness. That sober secret look. But finally it was the father he came for, the Teuton who was no Teuton, installed there among bits of cast-off tables and beds, the charitable leavings of good-hearted Christians, departing in the morning for that white-columned College, the oversized loping gait, the wool suit, at night doggedly unpacking crates of books in alien alphabets, sorting them out as if his life hung on their proper sequence.

He was there as tutor to the girl, but not for long: she flew past him, sitting for hours with one of her father's dictionaries, diligently writing on the topics he set out for her. Sometimes she was docile, sometimes recalcitrant. She refused "The History of My Family" but lowered her brown braided head obediently over "Gardens and Parks I Have Loved." She had grown quickly fluent, no tutor was really needed (such as he was, an actor again, an impersonator, the Bear Boy in yet another outfit), and anyhow she had responsibilities. The small child, the mother. Away from the hotel the mother improved. In the hotel she had been fearful, lashing out at ghosts in the blueberries, lashing out at the father, the children turned to stone—was it that she recoiled from the provisional, the betwixt and between? The Board had arranged for them to be put up at the William Penn—a temporary stopover while the house was being readied. In the worn-out Albany house with the pretty fanlight above the door, half filled with other people's discarded furniture, the mother was almost peaceful. The creaky stairs, her husband's regular comings and goings, his familiar scratchings among his books, her young sons safe in the public school, what were they if not a normal family? But still the mother was nervous. He could see how nervous, especially when he was in the house. He was taking her boys in hand, those solemn-faced foreign children. In school they were embarrassed. They were as quiet as sticks. They did not understand when spoken to. Their ugly foreign names were a humiliation, names as ugly and foreign as that ugly foreign Waltraut. (To have saddled a little kid with that!) Their new classmates ridiculed their unsayable names and their high black socks and their awful foreign earnestness.

He began by finding them new names, the kind that blurted out everything they were not. Hank, Jerry, Bill. Names like these go fishing with live worms for bait. Names like these are rowdy and raucous and poke and pummel and knock each other down and talk ordinary Albany lingo and jump from the top of the wardrobe, shaking plaster fragments out of the ceiling below. The new names changed them. The frightened little foreign gentlemen were becoming recognizable boys. He rough-housed with them and wrestled them to the floor and suffocated them with multiplication drills (his nanny, the one with the drooping jowl who had insisted on getting him eyeglasses, had suffocated *him*), and made them learn lists of words, not all of them polite. He taught them the rules of baseball. It wasn't at all the same as with Bridget's son. He never gave any of them so much as a nickel.

At the start he believed it was because of the girl that he had located them in the house with the fanlight. Located them, that's the ticket, they were dislocated people, no ordinary tourists, they weren't visitors from abroad, they hadn't come equipped with guidebooks for Niagara and the Adirondacks. He had seen the father leaving that white building with the columns. In the front office he asked about the sign on the iron fence outside: FRIENDS OVERSEAS RELIEF. He was taken to another office and interviewed—what exactly was he in a position to offer?

—Furniture always helps, you know. They get here with nothing.

—I'm a tutor, he said, I have experience as a tutor.

—What do you teach?

—Well, I've taught reading.

—I see. Can you teach English to newcomers? We have two families, he was told, the Steiners and the Mitwissers. The Steiners have only one child, the Mitwissers have a slew. They've just been brought over, and we've placed the father here. Distinguished scholar of religious history, specializes in Charismites. The family well-known over there, the mother something or other in her own right. A little disoriented by the trip, you know. The kids, not a word of English in the whole pack, except the oldest one, the daughter. I'd take the Steiners, the Steiners have only the one. Nice people too, they didn't give us a bit of bother.

—No, no, he said, the other ones, the Whatchamacallits?

—Mitwisser. The father is Professor Rudolf Mitwisser, we have him lecturing here.

—What a mouthful, fine, I'll take the Mitwissers.

—If they'll take you, he was told. The father is very particular about the family, we've seen that ourselves. He rushed us into getting the house prepared, it was awkward enough. His wife was uncomfortable in the hotel. She doesn't like hotels. An odd brood. You understand, he was told, all this is charitable work, you won't be paid for your time.

—I understand, he said.

—Your name and address? Ah, the William Penn, then you've run into them already? How long will you be staying?

—I'm living there for the time being.

He was handed a slip of paper: 22 Westerley.

—We'll inform Professor Mitwisser. These people generally show gratitude for whatever you do for them, but this one's a hard case.

Ultimately he was there for the father. It all came down to the father; it was the father he kept his eye on. The girl was only a child, a mysterious child; she wore a kind of Delphic pride. That look of knowingness had taken him in. Knowingness like a sickness. Was it the tallness that made her seem so womanly? The gravity, the veil of melancholy. Not a speck of laughter in any of them. Well, no, the boys—the boys were lately a herd of cattle, bellowing with the best of them. Or the worst. They pulled their long socks down to their ankles and scuffed their shoes and aimlessly punched the air or each other. He had them chattering in English now, even among themselves—not that it was all his doing. The drive to be like the others. They were picking up some nasty street words, though they still had the viscous slide of German in their speech, the curled-up *l*'s and the gargled *r*'s. The oldest, Hank, would never get free of an accent. The younger ones maybe. Not the girl. He rarely saw her now—she was always with the mother or the small child.

It was more than a month since the father had agreed to let him approach his children. He was absorbed in their safekeeping. He ringed them round with barriers; the barriers were all in the father's heedful blue gaze. There was, to begin with, the question of credentials. The Friends had sent him, so that was all right, but—how must one put this? —there was also . . . how must one put this?

—My children, my family, Mitwisser said, we are accustomed to . . . certain expectations. European ways, perhaps. I regret that we cannot provide recompense, the College is very kind, everyone is so very kind, but my own recompense here is . . . let me say insufficient. Unfortunately we are not . . .

—I'm a volunteer, he said, and grinned. Didn't they tell you that? It means I can come and go. No obligation either way. You won't owe me a thing.

—My daughter, my sons, they must not be . . . how shall I say? They must not be diminished. Always there has been a governess, but when we . . . and here, as you see . . .

—I had a nanny myself, growing up.

—Ah.

—I had more toys than I knew what to do with.

—My poor children, Mitwisser said, it was necessary to leave everything behind.

The interview was all at once at an end. The huge Teuton who was no Teuton. Distinguished scholar of religious history. The man stood before him like a beaten child, blazing with shame. Or like a child who has been made to stand and stand and stand.

They were penniless refugees, sunk in distrust. And yet the father had trusted him too quickly. Credentials? He had none: Bridget's surly son, ha!—but look how the mighty have fallen, beggars can't be choosers, and all the rest. They took what they could get. He'd had a nanny himself, that counted somehow. Besides, it turned out that the Mitwisser boys liked him, they were crazy about him, he drilled them for half an hour and then let them run wild for two hours. Behind the father's back, so to speak—the father was out lecturing on Charismites. The girl and the mother and the small child were mostly invisible. The small child, when he glimpsed her, was clinging to a foreign-looking doll dressed in a dirndl: they hadn't left everything behind after all. And all those books Mitwisser was sorting, hundreds of them, maybe thousands. They hadn't left those behind.

After a while he learned it wasn't Charismites, whatever they were, that preoccupied Professor Mitwisser. It was Karaites, whatever they were. Jews, something to do with Jews. This ancient rabbi and that ancient rabbi. It was all as alien as the moon.

One day he asked. He was surprised by Mitwisser's half-scowling surprise. It was as if he was defending a fortress. A fortress under siege, filled with deadly weaponry.

"What is your interest in this?" Mitwisser said. He did not wait for an answer. "My own interest is in theological deviation. In what is called heresy. Have you an interest in this? I think not."

"Not much interest in rabbis and such," he said.

That was the first time. The second time he asked the girl. He was heading back to the William Penn—there was a bus stop across from the old gas pumps—and spotted her sitting on a rock in the vacant lot that, from the look of it, had once been a children's playground. Rusted chains, broken swings. Litter all around. The small child squatted nearby, fussing with that doll in the dirndl, pretending to feed it bits of dry grass.

"Is this where you like to come?"

"We don't go very far. Papa wishes Waltraut to be close to home. So we come here, even if it is not so very nice."

He noted that in speaking to him she no longer said "my father": it had become papa.

"He keeps you on a tight leash, doesn't he?"

She did not comprehend.

"He watches over you."

"Oh yes. We are very much cared for."

"But there's nothing to be afraid of. It's not like over there."

"There is danger everywhere," she said.

"Those people Professor Mitwisser's involved with," he said, "are they dangerous?"

"The people at the College?" she said in alarm. "No, no, they are so good to us, papa's work, and also the house—"

"Not the College people. The ones in those books he's got his nose in."

She flickered out a rapid little smile. It came and went. "Papa's people have been dead a thousand years."

A thousand years. That was as far as he could get with the girl. The small child sidled up to him, pulling at his pockets. "Hey, you Wally you," he said, and lifted her to his shoulder and bounced her up there until she shrieked with laughter.

Mitwisser never laughed. Apparently his people, this old rabbi and that, had declared against it.

It was Frau Mitwisser who finally explained about the Karaites. He found her on the threadbare sofa in the dimly lit sitting room. She was looking into a silver-framed mirror (something else they hadn't left behind?), studying herself in the half-dark. He understood that they fretted about the electric bill. They ate boiled rice because it was cheap. They wore clothes out of season; the soles of their shoes had thinned.

When he came near she set down the silver frame on the scarred little table next to her; it wasn't a mirror at all. A hand-tinted old photograph: a small woman, a large plant.

He knew she disliked him. She had disliked him from the start. Was it that he was nothing like her idea of a proper tutor, deferential in suit and tie, deferential especially to his young charges—surely they were of a station superior to his own? His station: she could not fathom it. He had no station, no standing, no place: he had been sent to them out of nowhere, like the sunken mattresses and the worn tables. He seemed a sort of clown—he cavorted with her sons, he turned them into panting dervishes. Their shouts rang out all day. She felt detached from her own children. She could hardly recognize them.

She had noticed him in the hotel—in what they called the breakfast parlor. It wasn't very impressive, that hotel. She had known grander hotels at home, so grand that they had caused her to shake and walk with her hand on her chest to hide her fright. The new hotel—the one they had been sent to—was very plain. The breakfast parlor had no servants; one was expected to serve oneself from a bureau, like a waitress in a public café. From the corner of her eye she saw him rooted beside her, shining all over, sweat trickling down his forearms, his face mottled with heat, as if he had been heaving a sledgehammer. He took a step away; now he was behind her. She poured some berries into a dish. He was fearfully close, just behind her, she could smell the mammal heat of his armpits, there was danger everywhere, what did he intend? She began to shake, the berries shot out of the bowl . . .

It was a mistake, but still she begged Rudi to prevail on the Board to get them out of the hotel. In this place there were many mistakes. Charismites are not Karaites—her poor Rudi. They would leave this place as soon as there was money, he said, they would go to New York, it was of course useful to his work to be near a great library. But they had no money, there would never be money, they were thrown out, Charismites are not Karaites, she could not recognize her own children! Danger everywhere. Oh, if her mother could know how they had all been brought low! Her mother, ten years dead, the tinted face in the silver frame saved by a tremulous lie: it's nothing but worthless plate, *nicht Silber, sondern nur eine dünne Silberauflage. Völlig wertlos!*

He had given her a fright. She did not trust him. He was teaching her sons strange things. He was asking her strange questions—Rudi's work, Rudi's people. Rudi's people were runaways. Why did he wish to pursue them, why did he come to her, why did he not go to Rudi? But Rudi would deny him. Rudi was cautious, he was wary, he guarded his people, they were the same to him as his children, and also—how strict he was! how arrogant! To seize Rudi's people one must first penetrate their languages, their writings, their beliefs, their history, their exclusions. They abjured all that was not Essence. They denounced every abuse of Essence, every addition, every embellishment. What has fallen from the hand of God must remain precisely as it was received. What is first is eternal. To add is to undermine. Rudi's people, she told him in her thwarted English—she, her quick brain and tongue hobbled by unnatural, unwanted, impositions!—Rudi's people, she said, care for nothing but God's own word and will.

There is no God. He didn't believe in God. God was nothing to him. His mother, long ago, had murmured to him about the Baby Jesus, and his nanny had spoken sternly of the Cross and the Resurrection as if they were no different from the times tables, and had to be learned by heart. Among the scores of presents heaped at his bedroom door each morning there was sometimes a pillow embroidered with a religious picture, mostly clouds and cherubs with fat dimpled elbows and tiny wings surrounding a bearded saint wearing a halo. The halo was like the golden rings on his mother's new teacups. He was indifferent to cherubs and saints. They weren't toys, and the only toy that mattered (it was more than a toy, it had a real roof and windows you could peer into and a door that opened and shut) was the one that disappeared, the one that was taken away, the one that was an unconscionable distraction (his father grumbled) from the business at hand.

Her tongue was hobbled, but she knew her Rudi, she knew his people, and it was rare that anyone came to *her* to tell who they were! Rudi's people are perfectly obscure, she said in her hobbled voice (making do with fragments of meaning, pressed by him into eruptions of meaning), and except for Rudi they are of interest only to a handful of others, three or four in all the world. There are also the enemies of Rudi's people, who become Rudi's own enemies, even if Rudi's people are merely specks on the face of the earth, hidden lost particles incapable of revivification, so who should fear them? And who should desire them? They are no more substantial than fireflies.

Rudi's enemies, particles and fireflies, she was roaming now, ruminating foreignly, slipping away from *what is first is eternal, to add is to undermine*, how it burned in him! *They denounce every abuse of Essence.*

He fell to his knees before the battered table that held the silver frame. What, what was he doing? He grasped her two wrists, she was shaking, he was making her shake, he was threatening her, what was he doing? A tutor, no! What hideous creature had Rudi let in? His hideous eyes behind their lenses! The yellow light of the lamp, the yellow glints spiking his lenses, what was he doing? Would he harm her, would he harm her sons, her little daughter?

She could not see into his mind, but he—he saw, it was clarified, it lay before him, there in the thorny nettles of her half-choked thoughts, the pocked fragments of her telling. The monstrous burning. He released her wrists; he kissed them. He was frightening her, he recognized how he frightened her, but it couldn't be helped, it was monstrous, a conflagration, *what is first is eternal, to add is to undermine!*

"*Verrückt!*" she cried.

Somewhere a door opened: Mitwisser returning from his afternoon's lectures—the wool vest, the felt hat with its ribbon band, the cheap new briefcase.

"Elsa," Mitwisser said. He turned to his sons' tutor. "How is it that my wife is disturbed? Get up, if you please."

He got up.

"Rudi, Rudi," Mrs. Mitwisser called out, as if her husband were far away, in a distant room. But he was right in front of her.

"*Dieser Mann,*" she called, "*er hat so viele Fragen, Fragen, Fragen, er frägt und frägt —*"

"Elsa," Mitwisser said, "you must quiet yourself—"

But she looked at the man who had kissed her wrists. Her wrists were still trembling. She saw into his mind. She knew of whose party he was.

"He is Karaite," she said.

And Mitwisser laughed.

43

An hour came when the first boy, the boy born Jim, despised the second boy, the make-believe boy. He despised him, he renounced him, he threw him away. The fiery coldness (it was bitterness, it was rage) released him; he was free. The Bear Boy was a shed skin, and if at the same time he was proliferating, if he was a Household Name from one continent to another—according to Mr. Brooks and Mr. Fullerton, he had recently made his mark in South Asia; "lively, winsome, and adorable," noted the *Times of India*—well, never mind. For him the Bear Boy was a dead thing. Though not entirely. Not quite dead. The money came pouring out of the Bear Boy's head, and whoever believes that money begets absolute freedom has never known money that pours from the Bear Boy's head.

The woman had named him Karaite. She saw into him; she was deeply shrewd. She saw a man who ran; a runaway. A fugitive, a deviant. A danger. She understood him exactly. The husband didn't. The husband saw a man on his knees, his son's tutor; he saw his wife's agitation. And that was nothing anomalous. His wife had dropped something perhaps. She was often in tremor; she often dropped things. When she shook she became agitated. "Get up," he told the tutor. He got up. It was nothing. And when, shaking and agitated, his wife named the tutor Karaite, what else could the husband do but laugh?

It was the beginning of the long, long money-laughter.

The tutor, the impostor (they had taken him for a tutor, beggars can't be choosers, how the mighty, etc.), was given to improvisation: he had this much self-knowledge, though he supposed it was only the itch of restlessness. Living high in Algiers; and then not. Carrying the Bear Boy like a hump on his back for years; and then suddenly not. Arnold

Partridge and Bridget. He felt tossed by an inner wind, sometimes a boiling khamsin, sometimes a numbing cold. And sometimes he could not tell whether the wind was a furnace or an ice storm, they were so much the same. Now and then he received a note from Mr. Brooks and Mr. Fullerton (he rented a post office box wherever he landed), tactfully chiding him for "incaution." He was not incautious. He was counterfeit.

The woman opened her nostrils to take him in, as if deciphering an odor. She judged him. The girl—he avoided the long German worm that was her name and called her Annie—the girl had told him that her father burned to be in New York. She told him that at home in Berlin her mother had belonged to the Kaiser Wilhelm Institute: a scientist of some sort. That seemed unlikely: she was a witch more than a scientist. She had cast a spell and changed him into a Karaite. The husband laughed then—he laughed as a scholar laughs, hearing absurdity. It was not absurd. How was he, the counterfeit tutor, different from the Karaites, who rejected graftings on the pristinely God-given? He too rejected graftings. He was born unencumbered, nakedly himself, without a lace collar. The author of the Bear Boy had grafted on the lace collar. The moment he was free he tore it off. From then on he was all impulse.

An hourglass filled with money: this was the thought that came to him. An idea of affinity.

—I can get you people out of here, he said.

Mitwisser asked the source of this unusual offer of philanthropy, so unexpectedly, so absurdly, from his sons' tutor. Like the lawyers, he would not utter "money."

—I can get you out of here, he said again. Wherever you want to go. Whatever you need.

—And why would you wish to do that? Mitwisser asked, hearing nonsense.

—Because of those people. The ones you work on. I could set you up, you know. I wouldn't mind, I've got the money.

So he confessed. He confessed to being the Bear Boy. *Der Bärknabe!* Mitwisser's sons roiled in a tumult of excitement: *der Bärknabe!* The Bear Boy all grown up! But *der Bärknabe* spoke German; their tutor didn't. He looked like an ordinary man. Was he really the one? How could this be?

The girl explained about artists' models; she stared and stared. He was a nonentity who had come to their door. A nobody who had been somebody and was nobody again: the preposterous future of a fabled child.

Mitwisser did not at once believe him. It was too bizarre a thing to profess. Had he made it up, was it a ludicrous lie? On the other hand, why not believe him? He was not claiming to be a prince of the House of Romanov. He was not claiming to be a prophet. A modest enough assertion: he had once had a life in rhyme and pictures, he had once been the subject of a children's book—albeit an internationally famous one; in this lay Mitwisser's suspicions. Was this unprepossessing creature, of whom his sons were so lavishly fond, the destiny of that rosy painted elf? Mitwisser's children, all but the youngest, were intimate with the elf and his doggerel, they knew all of it backward and forward—at home their nanny had read *Der grüne Hut* to them over and over again. The red-haired Madame Mercier had read it to them in French! And here was the Bear Boy, in all the mystery of his transformation, standing before them like a prince or a prophet—the glamour of it, the enchantment in his sons' eyes!

From her corner the woman began to tremble. She picked up the silver frame from the little side-table and pressed it to her bosom—it slipped from her hands and fell to the floor.

—I used to drag a copy of it around with me, he told them. No more.

—No more, the woman echoed pointlessly.

—But I can't say I'm done with it. I mean it's not done with me. I'm still getting royalties and such, there's no end to it.

Royalties. A plausible word. There was a tincture of plausibility in the man. But also an unconfined raffishness. He was somehow off center, of a piece with this new country and its wild schoolchildren, its disorderly streets—only consider that patch of filth some yards off, where his daughter brought the small child to play in the dirt: at home in Berlin you would not see such civic deleteriousness anywhere! He reflected on disease. He was diseased in this place of exile; his wife diseased, his children tainted. He remembered the watchtowers of ancient citadels, the golden light of distant libraries.

44

ALONE WITH MITWISSER, the Bear Boy settled it. He would come and go; it wasn't his habit to stay stuck in one spot. He would come and go, and when he came he would give them—he said it outright—money.

—A stipend? No, no, nothing like that, he said. I'm not the sort that thinks that way, I'm not a goddamn lawyer, I don't care to be tied to any goddamn calendar. The first thing is you want to get to New York, right?

—Not for two years, Mitwisser said. My contract with the College goes to 1935.

—Well, break it, why not? Just pick up and leave.

—Oh no, not possible. If not for the College . . .

—What? You'd've been stuck over there? They'd get you? Listen, if you didn't want to be stuck over there, why stay stuck over here?

He broke into a laugh at this, and Mitwisser—he felt diseased—laughed with him, hugely, hilariously, a joke, everything the same, throwing over a position for which he was indebted no different from the terror of a family uprooted and pursued, all things in this place of exile level, level, level!

They went on laughing together. The tutor—a tutor no more—wound his arm around Mitwisser's neck.

—I shall not give up my obligations here. I am obligated, Mitwisser said.

—Your choice, fine. Here, take this for now.

The money changed hands. The beggar chose; he chose to be a beggar.

The Bear Boy came and went. He went, by train, straight across the breast of the land to have a look at the Pacific, and found a yellow beach, and lay there in the sun, with a bottle in his knapsack. The waves frothed like lions' manes. One day, for the lark of it, he got a job as an extra in a Western—they dressed him in spurs and a ten-gallon hat: it was the bar brawl scene. He turned up at six on the first day and not at all on the second. There was a joke in that, too: he'd been too drunk to get up on time to play a drunk. In California everything started too early. He didn't mind getting drunk in California, on the beach with the high waves curling nearby.

Mitwisser wondered whether he would return; he hoped he would not. The money was a disease—yet it was ease. It was meat; they had not had meat for months. It was new clothes for his children, especially for his sons, who were growing like young trees—his splendid Heinz, now almost as tall as Anneliese! His sons in their new clothes were more boisterously American than ever. Only Anneliese kept her old dignity. His wife kept her old shoes, and he kept his old wool suit, because the unclean money (as he thought of it, separating it from the clean money his position at the College sparsely supplied) was beginning to trickle away. Would the tutor come back, and give them some more?

For a long time he did not; Mitwisser's children ate rice. Far away, the Bear Boy dozed on a California beach. The tide rose and ebbed. He knew they were waiting for him—he had them in his hands. A whole family of children in that house with the pretty fanlight. He could open and shut the door.

By the time he reappeared (a season had passed), the money did not seem so unclean. It startled Mitwisser—civic deleteriousness!—that the man who had been his sons' tutor now addressed him as Rudi.

—James, Mitwisser acceded.

—Much better. Why don't you people get some more light in here?

—More light, Mrs. Mitwisser said to herself. Goethe's last words on his deathbed.

He sat with Mitwisser and told, laughing, how those movie people had outfitted him in a cowboy getup.

—They never got it back either. I gave it to some hobo on the beach. My father, James said, had me dressed up sillier than that.

And laughed. Mitwisser laughed with him; it was the least he could do for his children.

He came and he went. The tide of money rose and ebbed. More the first year, less the second. At the start he would take a room in the neighborhood (the William Penn be damned), but after a while it seemed to the girl that it was only right to invite him in, and he obliged. The father did not object; he had the father in his grip. Annie. Half child, half woman. Those tiny glints in her ears. The mother, he saw, withdrew to another part of the house when he was there.

He went, by bus, to New York. The lawyers' offices were smaller than he remembered them; Mr. Brooks was smaller. Mr. Fullerton was in the hospital, but was expected to recover fully, and would soon return.

He instructed Mr. Brooks to facilitate the rental of a large apartment within walking distance of the Library on Forty-second Street.

—Is it for you? Mr. Brooks inquired.

—No. Not for me, why would I want that?

—You intend this apartment to be lived in—used—by others?

—That's the idea.

—If I may say so, that would be extremely incautious. It would require certain restrictions . . .

—Just get it done.

Some weeks later he telephoned, long distance, from a pay phone in a drugstore and canceled the instructions for the city apartment.

—I'm afraid that at this point, Mr. Brooks began.

—Just do it.

The new plan was to find and rent a house—yes, an entire house—in an outlying section of the city. Countrylike, if possible. Mr. Brooks replied that Mr. Fullerton, a born New Yorker who was better acquainted with these matters, was in a nursing home. Unfortunately he had been felled by a second stroke.

—I'll do what I can, Mr. Brooks said. I'm up in Greenwich myself, I don't know much about the outer boroughs.

—And get some carpenters for shelves. Plenty of 'em. There's more books than anybody would believe.

He saw that Mrs. Mitwisser was growing querulous. She did not like him there. She complained that he shut himself up with her husband. She complained that he smelled of schnapps.

After setting Mr. Brooks on the right path, he took a train up to Canada for the lark of it (it was true that he had been drinking a little, sitting there laughing with Rudi), and this time forgot to leave them money.

45

THERE HAD BEEN a time when the nights with Professor Mitwisser in his study were my only unspoiled pleasure. I looked forward to the curious tableau we made — years later, that is how I imagine it: a motionless scene, I with my fingers stilled on the light-stippled glass of the typewriter keys, a twisted tail of hair sucked in at the side of my lip, he standing giantly over me, submerged in his dream of forgotten heresies. I see it that way, in stasis, as a kind of trance, in order to isolate those phantasmagorical hours from the turbulence and frights of that unhappy house.

Some three weeks after Mrs. Mitwisser's injury ("my wife's accident," he called it, as if she had merely dropped and shattered a dish, which sometimes happened), Mitwisser announced that we were to return to the work on al-Kirkisani.

He seemed less concentrated than usual, almost desultory. I waited while he searched through a bundle of papers, murmuring some syllables I could by now identify as Arabic, and tapping the arm of my chair when he could not find what he wanted.

"The passage on ladders and bridges," he said, as if to no one; but he meant me.

I riffled through my old transcriptions, and discovered it there: *ladders and bridges toward the perception of revealed truth.* "It's number four in the 'Principles,'" I said.

Ladders and bridges, lights and watchtowers! All this threw me into a delirium of rapture. It was not only the intoxication of these magicking words (which anyhow were nearly meaningless for me), but the wash of knowledge that came flooding in their wake: that the world was infinitely old, and filled to the brim with schisms and divisions and furies and losses. Not yet out of my teens, historyless, I was confident that I had plumbed the revealed truth of history. And that I was in mystical confraternity with Professor Mitwisser, more so than he could ever conceive.

He fixed his sea-colored look directly on me with a self-consciousness that had never before been evident.

"My son Wilhelm informs me," he said, "that you are in correspondence with Dr. Tandoori. Please to clarify."

"It isn't a correspondence. I mean I haven't answered. He asked me to come and work for him."

"That is scarcely what Wilhelm conveyed."

Willi's a snoop, I did not say.

"Do you intend to leave here? My wife, particularly after her accident, would wish you to remain. Particularly in the absence," he said hoarsely, "of my daughter."

He almost never spoke of this. He would not speak of it now.

"My wife," he resumed, "has grown attached to you, and I myself continue to find you of use. May I suggest that you will not profit from a . . . a position, let us call it, with Dr. Tandoori."

I asked why not.

"The man is godless."

It was an odd remark. A signal, or a symptom.

"But you liked him," I said.

"A divertissement. An artful pantaloon." He shut his eyes against me, and it was clear that he was suffering. "Perhaps," he said, "if Dr. Tandoori had not been present—then perhaps I—or you—if you had not lingered, Fräulein, if you had gone where your duty lay, with my wife, the accident might never—"

He wheeled round to spew out his broken accusations in the direction of the big bed across the room. But it was not Dr. Tandoori he was accusing, or his own dereliction, or mine. I remembered how Dr. Tandoori had charmed him; it was not Dr. Tandoori who harrowed him now.

"Godless men destroy young women," he finished.

What his wife had seen into long before, he believed at last.

Anneliese and James had been gone a full month. What was customarily done when a girl of sixteen, of her own volition, went off with a man who was a familiar of the house? Was it or wasn't it a question for public scrutiny? I did not dare to broach these uncertain speculations with Professor Mitwisser. His silence was a moat. He could not say his daughter's name.

Mrs. Mitwisser in the privacy of our bedroom bleated it out again and again. That wistful experimental "if"—"If they will come"—had lately turned into a remnant of a wail: "Anneliese, Anneliese, she does not come . . ."

I said carefully, "The police—"

"No police!"

"They help with missing persons—"

"That one, he is thief. He takes."

"All the more reason—"

"No police, no!"

She shrank from the word; she shrank from uniforms. Uniforms are dangerous, one must not put one's trust in uniforms! No police, no, no, one must have scruples, one must protect one's child, if there is shame it must be hidden, there is danger in police, there is danger in shame!

Fear of uniforms had never occurred to me. Neither, to tell the truth, had shame.

46

c/o Capolino
14½ S.E. State Street
Albany, New York
PLEASE FORWARD

Dear Bertram,

I was so very sad to learn that you've lost your job at the hospital. But since it's weeks since your letter came, by now you've surely found something suitable.

You didn't say how to reach you (that's a habit of yours, or is it Ninel's idea again), so I'm sending this to your old address. Maybe your ex-landlady will know where you've gone to. You say you're relieved that I'm not "strapped for cash." The truth is that this entire household is right now nearly without funds. Hard times.

If you get this and you do want to write again, be sure to mark the envelope PERSONAL.

Rosie

P.S. You'll be impressed to hear that I've had a marriage proposal!

c/o Mr. Thomas R. Washington
2 Showcorner Blvd., 6B
Albany, New York

Hello Rosie!

I've written PERSONAL all over the outside, so any potential culprit is well warned. That must be some unwholesome bunch you're with, if that's what's required!

It didn't take very long for your (slightly sour) missive to wend its circuitous way. Mrs. Capolino, out of a guilty conscience I'm sure, brought it right over to the local Y, where I'd been staying (fact is, I ran out of money and had to get out), and the Y—last known address, so to speak—shipped it down here. But Mrs. Capolino says I can have my mail sent to her place from now on, she'll hold it for me. She's got a new tenant and she's feeling sorry for me. I didn't let on that her geranium's dead.

As for work, I haven't found a thing—not so far, anyhow, and not for want of trying. Turns out I've got a bigger—meaning worse—reputation than I knew. I'm blacklisted just about everywhere as a rabble-rouser and troublemaker, if you can believe it! Not one other hospital would touch me—I'm tainted with unionizing. I suppose I've had my name and photo in the papers more than I should, but Ninel thought it was a good thing, scares the bosses, etc. Well, I didn't realize I'd gotten famous all over town!

After the hospitals I tried the drug chains, and one of them, not a bad fellow running it, kept me on for two days, and then sacked me when he sniffed out my evil history. The doctors at my old job wouldn't give me the time of day either—I thought maybe Prescott could help out, Prescott's the one who got your father the job at Croft Hall—but your dad's troubles left a bad taste, I'm afraid. I was hoping I could get to teach chemistry or the like to the oligarchs, but no go. Last week things got so bad that I walked into a restaurant and washed dishes for cash. Twelve hours of hot steam and it doesn't add up to rent money. If not for Thomas I'd be out in the street with the other bums. Thomas is an angel—he's putting me up for a while. You may remember him, he's the orderly I gave your dad's fancy English shoes to. He can't have me here much longer, though—his wife and little girl are on a family visit to Georgia, and when they get back I'll need to move on.

Here's an embarrassment. Since you're gainfully employed and your poor old cousin Bertram isn't, I was thinking if you could spare five or ten bucks now and then? Just till something works out. But it seems you folks have troubles of your own.

Bertram

P.S. I hope you haven't said yes to whoever's asked for your hand. Hey kid, you're a kid!

Dear Rose,

I cannot write to papa, he will be so angry. James is taking care of me. He is taking care of all of us. In the little packet inside this letter you will find money for the house. It is a great deal of money, so you must be careful with it. There is also money for your wages. Please tell papa that I am all right. James is showing me many new sights. We never stay two nights in one place. It is very exciting!

Anneliese

c/o Mr. Thomas R. Washington
2 Showcorner Blvd., 6B
Albany, New York

Rosie, I don't know how to tell this.

I'm still here with Thomas. His wife's mother in Georgia took sick, so he expects she'll be down there another week or so.

I don't know how to tell this.

I've just come from Mrs. Capolino's. There was actually a check from Prescott—a surprise, considering. I'm a bit of a charity case these days. I probably look the part.

So.

Charlie wrote from Albacete, they have their headquarters there. Charlie's part of Ninel's New York gang—a bunch of them went over third class on the *Normandie*, to Le Havre. They got past the border, made it to Albacete to pick up some equipment—God knows what that means, Charlie doesn't say—and then got shipped off to Barcelona. Some sort of workers' games to protest the Olympics in Berlin. The whole crowd was under fire, the government was trying to break it up, there was fighting in the streets. They hadn't let Ninel go with the men—they put her in a truck with some nurses. Charlie was shot in the leg, not all that bad, he says, but Ninel got it in the shoulder and was losing blood, so they sent her to a military hospital somewhere. Can't decipher it—La Sabriñosa? They patched her up, but an infection set in, and then pneumonia, and she's dead.

Rosie, Ninel's dead.

I don't know what to do or where to go. I don't know anything.

Bertram

Dr. Gopal V. Tandoori
118 Gravesend Neck Road
Gravesend, Brooklyn, New York

Dear Dr. Tandoori:

Thank you for the kind compliment of your invitation.

I regret that I must decline. I am content to remain in Professor Mitwisser's employ.

Respectfully yours,
(Miss) Rose Meadows

Dear Bertram,

I've just gotten paid, so here's half. It's tragic about Ninel.

Rosie

47

MRS. MITWISSER'S WOUNDS were becoming thin red streaks. Scar tissue had grown up over ragged shallow trenches. She sat on a stool near the bedroom window, high above the street, and looked out. She watched her sons leave in the morning and return after school. She observed the bickerings of birds from roof to roof. I thought she was waiting for Anneliese.

I did not tell Professor Mitwisser about Anneliese's letter—at least not at first. The household money she had sent I put in its usual place: James's china creamer, with its yellow petals and gilt spout. The money that had been designated for my salary, I noticed, had been increased by five dollars. One of these dollars I changed into coins—three dimes, ten pennies, two quarters, one nickel with the head of an Indian on it, and one without—and gave them to Waltraut. I had often seen James empty his pockets into her small hands. He had taught her to build squat round towers of money, and laughed when, with a child's brutality, she scattered them. There were lost pennies under all the chairs.

I was now established as Mrs. Mitwisser's intimate. At times a lava of talk came rushing out of her, shreds of rage or reminiscence, in a jumble of German and English; she complained that she was a prisoner in this room, in this house, in this deprived land—*"dieses Land ohne Bildung"*—and that only Anneliese in her rashness, in her folly, had eluded imprisonment. But I had begun to reassess these outcries—they seemed more calculated than spontaneous. They were (I had suspected this long before) feints and trials. In reality they were the lamentations of exile. It was not that she missed old comforts; she missed old dignities. She spoke often of *Bildung*, a term that eluded me. I had discovered Anneliese's worn German-English dictionary abandoned on a kitchen shelf, among the teacups. Sitting with Mrs. Mitwisser, I sometimes stealthily consulted it. But when I looked up "*Bildung*," I found only "education." For Mrs. Mitwisser it meant elaborately more. She would say of her grandfather (I learned that he had founded a chain of newspapers at the close of the century), "*Er war ein sehr gebildeter Mann*," and she said the same of Erwin Schrödinger. Eventually I understood that a man in possession of *Bildung* was more than merely cultivated: he was ideally purified by humanism, an aristocrat of sensibility and wisdom.

Once, she told me, she had bought a mischievous painting; it had betrayed her. It was meant to divert her husband, yet only his fireflies had the power to engage him. It was the week after New Year's, in 1925; she had just returned from Switzerland, a difficult journey. The unheated train faltered, then halted, then toiled warily on. Her feet in her boots were numb. All of northern Europe was under snow. A telegram from Rudi was waiting: there was no point to setting out, he could get only as far as Pamplona. Beyond that the ice barrier loomed. All the trains heading north were stopped, it was impossible to predict how long he would be delayed—but all was well, his work had gone satisfactorily, the Spanish warmth was a marvel, and how was the dear little Anneliese? She must not catch cold, Elsa must see to it that Mademoiselle De Bonrepos keeps the child from chill.

Anneliese did not catch cold; she was perfectly healthy, and perfectly silent. Her mother had promised to bring her a Christmas present from far away, if *she* would promise not to tell papa how mama had gone to a secret place, the only place in the whole world where rocking horses were sold, and didn't Anneliese wish for a rocking horse more than anything else? The rocking horse place was a secret, a secret even from papa, so don't tell! Anneliese would not tell; Mademoiselle De Bonrepos testified that she was the most obedient child she had ever come upon. To Mademoiselle De Bonrepos Mrs. Mitwisser explained that she was inescapably obliged to leave for Switzerland on Institute business, but since the child's father—how besotted he was with this child!—would likely disapprove of her absence from Anneliese during the festive holiday time, Mademoiselle De Bonrepos was also not to tell. And to ensure that Mademoiselle De Bonrepos did not tell, she tucked a much-fattened Christmas bonus, together with the governess's wages, into a little silken sack tied with a satin drawstring.

There were no rocking horses in Arosa. Instead there was the great Tannenbaum with its hundred candles and its thousand tinkling crystals, and the delightfully argumentative walks with Erwin, and the working nights in Erwin's room, and the revelation of the bitten egg. . . . The rocking horse was right here at home, almost around the corner, on the Kurfürstendamm, in the window of an antiques shop; she had passed it often enough. The Kurfürstendamm and the streets that led to it glittered; the light that struck the snow was stupendously bright—a dazzling Berlin winter light, sharp and blinding. Underfoot an invisible membrane of ice crackled with the sound of popcorn over a fire. The shop windows gleamed, the rings and wristwatches and earrings and spectacles of passersby flashed lightning sparks. In the aftermath of the storm, though there were still intermittent gusts, the air smelled of a strange electricity, as if a dynamo at the core of the earth had burned out all vegetation. The scraping of shovels on pavements rang out like bells grown hoarse. She was elated: the cold, the brightness, the rapture of the bitten egg, Arosa! She wore the same alligator-skin boots that she had worn in Arosa—collared and lined with gray fur, buttoned up to the ankle; and also the same long maroon coat that fell nearly to her heels, and the same gray fur hat that hid all her hair, and kept it safe from the wind. On one of their walks Erwin, arguing a point, had snatched it off:

—There! The thing's as plain as the hair on your head!

Her tidy bun flew apart, and her hair tumbled down, dropping loosened pins onto the path.

—Now look what you've done, she scolded. But she saw how he stared. Her hair was a thick brown flood. It looked syrupy, like boiled honey, and its wildness shocked him—the wind tore it from her scalp and threw it across her mouth. They had been talking of gene mutations induced by X-rays, and of the heat wave caused by the intense oscillations of atoms: a violent explosion produced by ionization. Her hairpins lay like curled-up insects at their feet. He stooped to pick them up, and she plucked them, one by one, from his open palm.

The rocking horse was lifted out of the window. Its price was more than equal to the extravagant bonus she had given to Mademoiselle De Bonrepos (could this obsequious young woman be trusted?); nevertheless the rocking horse was purchased and ordered to be delivered. It had once belonged to the Gräfin von Brandenburg in her childhood. Only the leather reins were missing, the proprietor told her, but these could be easily replaced. Anneliese would not mind about the reins, or else red ribbons would do just as well. The truth was that Anneliese had never wished for a rocking horse—what sort of child is it who doesn't dream of owning a rocking horse? She was uncommonly docile, uncommonly quiet. What pleased her was to sit in her father's lap and play with the things on his big desk—the toylike curved blotter that tipped up and down, for instance, with its ivory handle in the shape of a horse. It was the blotter that had suggested the rocking horse, and there it was in the window on the Kurfürstendamm . . . but no, say it had come from the secret rocking horse place far away.

The proprietor stood at his counter, patiently watching her remove her gloves to write the check—they were gray, furred and lined at the collar, like her boots. Her hands were noticeably small, and had the habit of mildly quivering when she was excited. The painting excited her: it was of a god distributing planets. It hung on the wall behind the proprietor's head. A portrait of a juggler tossing eight shining spheres—but only seven were in the air, describing a kind of stuttering wreath. One, as white as the white of an eyeball, had plummeted onto an old creased bit of parchment discarded on a patch of grass. The bottom corner of the painting, on the right side, was charred. The juggler's face was elongated, melancholy, stricken. Still, it was frozen in a theatrical grin.

—Who made that? she asked.

—The painter is unknown.

—You have no idea?

—It came from someone's estate, the proprietor said. A fire. If it was ever signed, the signature is burned away. I believe, he said, it is an allegorical portrait.

A second check was written, this one for the juggler. An allegorical portrait? A notion of minor interest to her. The price of the painting was far less than that of the Gräfin's rocking horse. To begin with, the painting was damaged, which decreased whatever value it might have had originally; and then, given one's ignorance of the painter, what value could one place on it in any case? Probably it was no more than thirty or forty years old. A Surrealist parroting, a little too deliberate. After all, it was no more than a curiosity.

But the juggler had her husband's face. Rudi's furnace-eyes, the melting point of cobalt, fourteen hundred ninety-five degrees centigrade! And his mouth, yes, Rudi's mouth exactly as she knew it, divided between heaven and hell. Or—the check fluttered in the fingers holding it out to the proprietor—did the mouth resemble Erwin's mouth? His mouth as she had tasted it, at first fearfully, diffidently . . . but Erwin's eyes were as dark as her own. Erwin too was unusually tall, so shockingly tall beside her. She was a small woman with small hands. Only her ambitiousness was large. During certain hours in the laboratory she felt nearly crazed with ambition.

The rocking horse for Anneliese, the juggler for Rudi—holiday gifts quietly and quickly collected from a single shop. The Institute was shut for the holiday, and Rudi was safe in Spain—why wouldn't he suppose she had been hunting for these surprises over many days? (The blessèd days in Arosa, with Erwin!) He could not imagine that she would fly from home and desert the child. But she had not deserted the child—and here to testify to this was Mademoiselle De Bonrepos, extravagantly rewarded.

In the week following New Year's Day it began to rain. The rain opened craters in the snow and the ice slid away. Anneliese was preoccupied with studying the icicles that had grown down, like elephant tusks, from the eaves; the more she gazed, the faster the rhythmical drops seemed to fall, until the icicles were no bigger than cats' teeth. When the rocking horse arrived, she climbed onto it obediently, holding on to the wooden ears, and by the time her papa returned from his searches she had forgotten that riders need reins. But she remembered not to tell how her mother had gone away to the secret place where the rocking horses were, and she remembered not to tell that her mother had not come back until after New Year's.

Rudi judged it a fine enough painting—he was touched by his

wife's present, though he thought it somehow eccentric (her gifts were generally mufflers and gloves) and didn't quite see what Elsa claimed to see, an extraordinary similarity to himself. It was not impossible; human countenances are molded on only so many lasts. But did she mean to compare him to a kind of clown?

—Oh my dear! she said brightly. Only look at the face, the beautiful face, so full of *mind*. As soon as I found it I knew!

—But a juggler . . .

—is a philosopher of time.

—Of timing, he emended.

—No, she said, time. The instant the ball leaves the juggler's hand it descends into the past, and the next instant it's already on its way to his receiving it in the present. It's what *you* do, Rudi!

She was inventing an allegory, to please him. An allegorical portrait, why not?

—And that parchment down there, she went on, you see?

—An open scroll, yes.

—A Karaite treatise, she teased. And that white ball, like an eye let loose?

—A lost chance, he said, entering into the game.

—No! A lost history. The juggler retrieves it and restores it . . .

—Silly little Elsa, he said. The game was too elaborate; it was too eccentric; why was she flattering him?—Here, he told her, I've got something for you too.

He had brought her a necklace, a string of reddish stones, and for the child a magnifying glass with a pearl stem. The enforced stay in the south had allowed him the opportunity to look for such trifles. The child went peering at every small object on his desk; she was fonder of the magnifier than of the rocking horse.

The painting was not a success. His wife had hoped it would amuse him.

—We must give the governess something, he reminded her.

—I already have.

He kissed her then, with the hungry heat of their separation—he exploring a distant archive for his elusive Egyptian, she cozily at rest

with the child, once or twice venturing out in her pretty boots to reconnoiter shop after shop, seeking the very thing that would gratify him. It
was too odd for his taste, it was too "original," and it obliged him to interpret, as if a picture was the same as philology. His enchantingly brilliant wife and her perplexing ideas! He hung the reddish stones around
her neck. His hand on her neck, the heat of his kiss — they foretold the
night to come. He longed for a house filled with children; it was almost
six years since the birth of Anneliese, surely they must begin to build a
family? But she was reluctant. She wanted her laboratory; she wanted
her notebooks with their esoteric markings.

And she thought: The juggler is a failure. The rocking horse is a
failure.

And in the night she thought: Rudi's mouth is not like Erwin's
mouth.

Heinrich was born in the autumn, in November, when there occurred a falling-out with Mademoiselle De Bonrepos, a clandestine
quarrel that could not be repaired. Mademoiselle De Bonrepos had suffered a reprimand, and all at once a new governess for Anneliese appeared, a red-haired young widow named Madame Mercier, and a nanny
for the new baby. Anneliese asked why Mademoiselle De Bonrepos had
gone away; there was no explanation. Her papa looked to the side, and
her mother only said it was necessary, and that there are some things not
for a little girl to understand. But Anneliese understood this much:
Mademoiselle De Bonrepos must have done something bad, or she
would not have been sent away.

And in fact Mademoiselle De Bonrepos *had* done something bad;
she had transgressed in some grave and shadowy manner, the cause of
which was hidden and unrecoverable. Anneliese tried to imagine what
the bad thing might have been. Mademoiselle De Bonrepos had permitted Anneliese to catch an October chill (but it was Anneliese herself who
had refused to put on her coat). Mademoiselle De Bonrepos had advised
the new nanny to complain about her wages (Anneliese had overheard
this), and now the new nanny was petulant and discontent. Mademoiselle De Bonrepos had shouted an unacceptable word at the cook when
the cook had neglected to serve her the dessert of glacéed pears (and it

was the very word Mademoiselle De Bonrepos had cautioned Anneliese never to utter).

Perhaps it was one of these bad things, or all of them together, that had prompted the reprimand. Or perhaps it was something else. The reprimand was delivered by Anneliese's mother early one morning, when tiny Heinrich awoke with a raucous scream and the nanny was downstairs in the kitchen, interrogating the cook about the cook's wages. Mademoiselle De Bonrepos was stung and humiliated; she protested; the reprimand was repeated, this time more stringently, in German-accented French. And now Mademoiselle De Bonrepos was not merely stung and humiliated, she was furious. That same day she requested a private interview with Professor Mitwisser—"No, Anneliese, you may not go to your papa now, please wait outside, over there"—and whispered to him that last winter, during the holiday time, when the Institute was idle, his wife had crept away with her valise and had not crept back until after New Year's.

Anneliese stood at the door, listening.

—But she was here. With the child. Here, in this house.

—No, sir. She was not.

—If she went out at all, it was to shop for the holiday . . .

—She was away for ten days.

—Impossible. Ten days?

—Yes, sir. Ten.

—Where?

—Switzerland.

—Switzerland! Impossible! Alone?

—I can't say, sir. I wouldn't know.

And after that Mademoiselle De Bonrepos was made to vanish, just as suddenly as if a magician had thrown a magic cloak over her, and then the new nanny was made to vanish too, replaced by another new nanny, and Madame Mercier (whose hair was exactly the color of Anneliese's favorite red-orange fur muff) arrived, and Anneliese's papa stared at the papers on his desk, and Anneliese's mother left the house for her laboratory without speaking to anyone.

Somehow, she did not know why, Anneliese believed that the trouble between her papa and her mother—there *was* a kind of trouble—had come about because of Heinrich. Heinrich was behind all of it. Or if it wasn't Heinrich really, it might have been the painting of the juggler. How queer it was that her papa had such a distaste for the juggler! He liked all their other paintings well enough, why did he look the other way when he passed this one? It was on the wall alongside the others, why did he look away? On second thought (Anneliese decided), Heinrich couldn't be the reason for the trouble: her papa liked him too much. He liked Heinrich, he liked all the other paintings (not that he took any particular notice of any of them), and it was only the juggler that made him bend his head as if one of the flying spheres had been catapulted out of the painting to bloody him between the eyes. Her papa liked Heinrich. He liked Anneliese. He liked his children, and after a while the trouble went away, or hid itself, and Gerhardt was born, and then Wilhelm, and then Waltraut. Her papa liked all of them, but sometimes it seemed to Anneliese that he liked Heinrich best of all. Heinrich, when he got bigger, could fix almost anything on her papa's desk that her papa's thick clumsy hands happened to break. Once, too vigorously blotting his great splash of a signature on a document with the University seal at the top, her papa broke off the blotter's ivory handle (the horse-handle), and Heinrich mended it so artfully that the seam of the rupture couldn't be detected. And another time he found two discarded old luggage straps and out of them contrived a pair of reins for the Gräfin's rocking horse. By then it was Wilhelm who rode it.

But every so often—so Anneliese imagined—her papa would bend his head away from Heinrich as he bent his head from the juggler, almost as though Heinrich was wounding him in the same unsettling way.

"Anneliese, when she is a little child," Mrs. Mitwisser told me, "she knows. Already she knows."

Proudly she caressed the long scar on her breast, raised like a row of miniature berries.

I asked, "What became of the painting?"

Her heated look wheeled up to the ceiling.

"Fritz," she said finally. But her voice was flat. "He is thief," she said in this flat mindless voice. Swarms of thieves; she was engulfed. Her eyes turned muddy and glintless. Then, inexplicably, she let out a quick laugh. Who knew if Fritz had taken the juggler? This oafish Fritz, an oaf, a lout, he could not tell the difference between sterling and plate, she had fooled him about the picture frame, perhaps he had left the others hanging there, the landscapes, the portrait of her grandfather, a small Renoir, suppose he had left the precious Renoir and carried away the juggler, and what was the juggler if not some insignificant imitation Surrealist kitsch? She had bought it to please Rudi; to tease him a little, too, because he cared for nothing but his Karaites, these fireflies that winked out their little lights and were given over to the dark of the world. And after a while the juggler (whose painted irises were as fiercely blue as Rudi's) did not please her husband at all, thanks to Madame De Bonrepos's tale-telling—oh, good riddance to the woman! Rudi was indifferent to art anyhow, Rudi was narrow, narrow, it was always the fireflies, but Erwin was replete, Erwin was copious, he spilled over *(ein sehr gebildeter Mann!)*, he loved Goethe, as she did, and he loved botany, as she did (he had a habit of mooning over plants, reflecting on their phylogeny), he was hypnotized by art, yes, yes, Italian painting especially! And when they threw him out, when they threw out Erwin Schrödinger just a month after she herself was thrown out, after Rudi was thrown out of the University, where do you think Erwin ran to? To Italy! To the paintings!

Erwin was luckier than her poor Rudi. Rudi was saved—"saved," what was that?—by a Quaker college in provincial Albany in barren America, what sort of rescue was that? Now he is nothing, he is *Parasit*, her poor Rudi. But Erwin was summoned to Oxford.

"He is there in 1933 one week, and what comes? They give to him the Nobel! Together with Paul Dirac, the little Englishman with the crooked teeth!"

She was becoming excited. Waltraut, playing in the hallway just within sight—dressing and undressing the Spanish doll with the high comb in its black hair—felt the danger of it, and began to shriek.

On the floor below a door slapped open in wild anger. Professor Mitwisser called up: "You! Fräulein! What is this chaos you are making? Take care of my wife! Take care of the child!"

From under her pillow, with shaking fingers, Mrs. Mitwisser drew out a pencil (a dirty stub escaped from a boy's schoolbag) and a shred of paper. It was a corner of a page from the torn-up *Sense and Sensibility*. Weeks ago it had evaded my broom. On this scrap she wrote, slowly, patiently, gleefully, with all her fragile force pounding downward, as if carving on cold stone:

$$3 \cdot 2983.10^{-24} \text{ cal.}/°\text{C. log } D$$

I asked what it meant; what was "D"?

The formula for entropy, she told me; for disorder; for (and here she amazed me by enunciating these syllables in English, with unmistakable clarity) "thermodynamical equilibrium." The "D," she said, stood for Death—what else did I think it could be?

48

Dear Rose,

The postmark will say Batavia, but we are not in that place any-more. We have been to see Niagara Falls! James does everything for me, he takes me everywhere. In an auto! James bought it, it is a black Ford. Riding in the buses made me so tired. I wish papa did not mind so much. I know that papa minds. When I say to James, I wish papa did not mind so much, then he becomes quite sad. He cares so much for papa. He is sad so often.

If the boys are having holes in their socks, you must mend them. But also you may buy new socks from the dry goods shop. Waltraut likes to go there too. You may buy her a pink ribbon. I hope mama is well.

Anneliese

When this second letter arrived, many-stamped and heavy with its packet, I thought I could no longer delay informing Professor Mitwisser.

I began: "The money for the house is here."

His white face was a barricade. He said nothing.

"There was another letter a while ago, with more money. Though not as much as now."

I handed him both letters. He glanced at them too rapidly—but I knew he had taken them in—and returned them.

"An accident, her mother bleeds, and my daughter is not in the house."

"She couldn't know—"

"Exactly. Because she is not in the house."

I said dimly, helplessly, "But look how happy she seems—"

"What is this folly? Happy! The man buys my daughter, I myself sold the man my daughter! For the money!"

I had never before heard Professor Mitwisser speak of money. He held up two roughened fists, like a pugilist, but aimlessly. There was nothing to strike—only the soft ocean of his manuscripts.

"It wasn't for the money she went with him," I said.

"Ignorance! My daughter is ignorant and the man is godless."

I did not believe Anneliese was ignorant. What I believed was that she had set out for the secret place where the rocking horses were, like her mother long ago.

49

AT FIRST he could not tell what to make of her. She was a child like the others—a silent child, a child who had been trained to reticence. A hush wound itself around this family like a vapor, or like a floating veil. They *were* a family, unmistakably: in the breakfast parlor at the William Penn he had recognized it instantly—not so much a huddling as a separateness, even a hauteur. The father, the weak mother, the phalanx of children. The tall silent aloof girl. The boys, the small child—these in time might be weaned from the orderly silence of that foreign house. Refugees. A house under the spell of exile. Those minuscule glintings in the girl's ears—were they fake (he didn't think so), or had they escaped being torn from the tender flesh? Pale round ears, sweetly visible under the two coiled braids.

When he came to them—when Mitwisser let him in—the girl was just under fourteen, long-legged and watchful. She sat close to him, hugging her dictionary; her ears were secret labyrinths. Her eyes too were secretive: she knew what no child could know. She knew things, she had seen things. He imagined himself weightless, treading phantomlike on the velvety lobe lit by that tiny jewel, and leaping from this soft perch into the dusky corridor of her ear, tunneling deeper and deeper, until he sank into the darkness of her mind. She was watchful; she was suspicious. It seemed to him—modestly compliant though she was—that she perceived him to be a sham: not a teacher, not a tutor, not anything like that, and it was plain she didn't mind. Instead she took him for a kind of wizard—erupting out of the blue, transforming her brothers into suddenly untamed creatures, free as they never would have been at home, as her papa would never have permitted them to be at home—but here everything was different, looser, stranger. There was an uncanniness even in the Albany light, as if another sun could reign in another part of the world. She watched him with a cautious gladness, how he was so inquisitive about her papa, how he was drawn to her papa; what was it that drew him? Her papa's people belonged to her papa's domain; no one but her papa had studied so much about them; at home he was bowed to and fussed over for having studied so much about them. At home they compared him to the man who had uncovered the ruins of Troy: his name was Heinrich Schliemann, he was in her history book, and her papa had named *their* Heinrich after him. But here her papa was hardly noticed at all, no one had ever heard of Rudolf Mitwisser, or even of Heinrich Schliemann. Everything was different here: Troy was a place not far from Albany! She was certain that the tutor—he said to call him James—had never heard of the real Troy, or Heinrich Schliemann, or her papa's people. All she knew of her papa's people was that they believed in God. She wasn't sure if anyone in her family believed in God. Perhaps her papa did, but her mother scoffed and said that the universe was made of tiny atoms, tinier than the tiniest seeds, and that God had nothing to do with how they behaved. Her mother understood how they behaved. She kept notebooks about them, and went every day to the Kaiser Wilhelm to do experiments about them. Her papa didn't care so much about the atoms—her papa cared only for his long-ago people. It was impossible to think that James would care about papa's people, they were so old and long-ago; but one day he took off his glasses and rubbed the lenses with his thumb and said that sometimes he nearly felt like one of them.

She stared up over the top of her dictionary and asked whether he believed in God.

—Oh no, no, nothing like that.

—Then how can you feel like one of papa's people? All they ever talk about is God, papa told me that.

He didn't explain. He said she was too young to figure out what he meant, and he wasn't convinced of his meaning anyhow.

Except for that one time, she never asked him about himself. She accepted that he was drawn to her papa—but the truth was he was drawn to all of them. In this different part of the world it wasn't unnatural that he dressed badly—for a tutor!—and not quite respectably, and that he wore a knit cap like a stevedore (the stevedores at Hamburg had worn such caps), and that his hair was uncut and spilled over his glasses, and that he carried a grimy knapsack and whistled and laughed and schemed tricks with her brothers and teased her small sister. He was everything her family was not. And when she learned, along with the rest of them, that he had once been *der Bärknabe*, how magical, how ghostly —a grown man rising out of a storybook! The very storybook Madame Mercier had read aloud to her brothers at home; and before that, Mademoiselle De Bonrepos.

Only her mother was not impressed. Her mother was discontent, her mother would not speak English, her mother would not put on her shoes.

At fourteen and a half, Anneliese discerned that James was nearly as much in the grip of her papa's people as her papa was, no matter that he didn't believe in God. There was something about her papa's people, the thought of them, that caught him by the throat, he said; and anyhow her papa was so in love with his people, it was almost as if he became them. Her papa and James! They were exactly alike, even though her papa was scrupulous about his hat and his jacket, and James was not. And even though James went away and came back and went away again. Whenever he turned up (you could never tell when it would be) he brought a quickening—the house quickened, her breath quickened, the boys went amuck, Waltraut ran in circles like a maddened pup. And her papa, who rarely laughed, laughed, together with James—they were so alike!

At fifteen and a half, she saw how he rubbed his lenses with his thumb and looked at her with his naked eyes. Her face dissolved, as it does for the nearsighted, into a watercolor indistinctness. Her long arms in their sleeves had grown longer; she was now very tall. He restored his glasses and observed a metamorphosis: she was all at once not merely a hint of a young woman, but genuinely womanly, in manner, in form. The breathing curve of her breasts, agitated. The neck, slightly bent; he wasn't prepared for the vulnerability of that top vertebra, so exposed, so brutally skeletal. The pure sweep of the jawline. The hair bound up in those restraining coils—what would it resemble, if she let it go? A brown scroll unfurling. She was as sealed as a nun. Was it because she was being kept from school? It was abnormal to be kept from school. He was willing to go on surveying her, the thin neck, the mazy ears with their ornaments bright as pinheads—but the boys were distracting him, demanding him, challenging him to knock them about; and meanwhile old Wally was clawing at his pockets, searching for pennies.

When she was sixteen and a half he discovered a flaw, an implausible flaw, in her constraint. She was subordinate only to her father; otherwise she was unyielding; she ruled the family. Authority shone from her like a nimbus. She spoke little and was obeyed. But there was an interloper in the house now, a girl older than Anneliese, something like a servant, ill at ease; at home they were used to having servants. This new person was not a servant exactly; they were no longer in a position to have servants. A secretary to the father? (He heard the rapid typing, like rain beating on canvas.) A kind of helper to the mother? She was too close to the mother; the mother hid herself from him; he resented the mother, he resented this new person.

—But it's you who hold the reins, he said to Anneliese.

—What a funny thing to say, what does it mean?

She had not mastered idiom. It was likely she never would.

—They all depend on you. That's what it means.

—At home we had an old wooden horse. The reins were missing and Heinz made new ones.

She held out her long arms to him then, to show him the invisible reins. She was untouchable; he would not dare to touch her. She was enclosed in a carapace, in a snow-white eggshell. The implausible flaw— she could yield, after all; she intended to yield—took him by surprise. She was an infant bird tapping with her little beak against the shell. Or else, with her rounded small breasts, and her sleeves streaming toward him, she was pleading for escape.

The ruse was her own invention. It didn't begin as a ruse; she was possibly not even aware, or only half aware, that it was a ruse, since her intent was only, to start with, a bouquet of lollipops, each wrapped in a different colored paper, with a rubberband around their stems. An outing for Waltraut, she's too confined, you said so yourself, no child should be so confined. So they walked with the child, he and Anneliese (he called her Annie now), to the shadowed shops under the train trestle, where a little grocery run by a couple from Sicily sold Italian ices and penny candy. The procession to the street of shops was a sweet impersonation —of family (he was rid of his), of ordinary domestic life. It was noisier and busier here, the grocery, the dry goods shop, the pharmacy with its two globes, the overhead grinding of the trains setting out and returning, a curving trolley track and the yellow trolley cars with their wicker sides rattling round it, the perpetual dusk under the trestle, an occasional solitary taxi passing. The unassuming hum of village commerce — and Waltraut, her tongue dancing over a bright lollipop, chanting in her new English *purple, orange, red, green, purple, orange, red, green.* Sometimes they chose to turn away from the bustle, toward the war monument and past the big meadow and the marshy edge of the water, where, when the tide was low late in the day, the frogs grunted in the mud, and a smear of pink horizon reappeared in the still pools. They stepped from stone to stone among the cattails, careful to select the flatter ones. What an oddly countrified corner of the Bronx Mr. Brooks had dutifully stumbled on! A dense whorl of mites revolved around their heads, catching the light like a length of silk. He picked up Waltraut, and Anneliese put out her hand to him, to steady herself on the crest of a wobbly rock. The hand felt fire-hot, as if a furnace lived in the hollows of her finger-bones.

At home, she said, there was a Punch-and-Judy in the park, or a children's concert, and always a gaudy carousel. Here, in this low scrubby neighborhood, there was nothing; they must go farther afield. The taxi didn't always arrive when summoned, especially when it was Gert she sent out to the shops to scout for a driver, who, seeing a gesturing boy jumping in the road, suspected mischief and raced away. But when Heinz was sent, his straight sober silhouette looking more man than boy, the driver would allow himself to be directed to where the three of them waited just behind the green front door — the tall girl, the small one, and James. And then followed a deluge of puppet shows and carousels, carousels and puppet shows! — during which Anneliese would slyly search in his pockets for pennies to give to Waltraut. He took her hand; he was accustomed to it by now. The fingers had cooled. On a gray afternoon the taxi drove them to a county fair somewhere in Connecticut. There were pony rides for children, led by bored boys dressed like farmers in overalls and straw hats. Waltraut was placed in a tiny chair atop a saddle, while a boy in a straw hat paced round and round a circular path. The ride was guaranteed for ten minutes if anyone cared to pay as much as half a dollar.

—Come, Anneliese said, and pulled him into a copse of elms. Now you must kiss me, she said.

Her fingers under his cap, twining his hair.

And after that the child was left to Professor Mitwisser's typist. (What else could you call her, if not that?)

—My mother is afraid of hotels, Anneliese told him. Because of the danger.

—Are you afraid? There's no danger here.

She was not afraid of an unfamiliar bed in an unfamiliar room with stains in the carpet—she didn't mind. But there was danger for him, even in this unprepossessing place the taxi had taken them to. The danger was that she didn't mind, the danger was the flaw in her, the yieldingness that was growing more urgent, her fragile neck, the gem-sparks that shot from her ears when she lifted her chin, her pinned-up hair when she released it. The half-inch drawstring of concentration between her eyebrows. She had schemed the ruse—the excursions with the child. It had never been for the sake of the child, or perhaps only for a time; it was for the sake of her fingers twisting under his cap, it was for the sake of those kisses out of sight of the pony path, or, before that, in the dark of the puppet theater, in a deserted patch behind the carousel, where the music was the loudest. And finally the child was discarded, pretext was discarded, she was becoming bolder and bolder. What had seemed to be reticence was a kind of waiting.

He had foreseen that he would yield to her yieldingness. She belonged to an aberrant family. He had never imagined a family like this one. His own—it was so long ago, his mother dead of lung cancer, his father dead of a stroke, hardly a family to begin with, it had more in common with all these puppet shows (himself the puppet, Pinocchio or some other fabrication) than with a normal household, it was all commerce and dress-up and performance, he was alone on a stage. These foreigners, refugees, how they clung to one another, clumped together in that narrow house; they were afraid of the stranger. So many children, the mother unbalanced by loss, the father gluttonous for news of an elusive ancient schism. Looking backward, the two of them. The mother hated him. He didn't doubt that the father hated him too—or at least he suspected it: false cheer, false embraces, agonized false laughter. The father was greedy for the money. The daughter was greedy (slowly it came to him) for the stranger. He liked getting rid of the money: trash money, contaminated by the rouged knees and the lace collar. The money made him master wherever he landed. He didn't think of it—he would repudiate such a proposition had there been anyone alive to put it to him, and no one, living or dead, knew to say it, certainly not dry-hearted Mr. Brooks, who had unaccountably got hold of the narrow house in this lonesome marshy niche of the otherwise swarming Bronx, the house narrow from the first and high because of its latter-day third story, stucco-flanked but shaped like the wooden doll house with its peaked roof: he possessed it now, the doll house and the doll house people, whose heads he had once pinched, maneuvering them upstairs and downstairs, his will their will.

She didn't mind the smell of the bottle he kept by him. She didn't mind this used-up room and its blotted carpet. Tears? Urine? Blood? She pulled him close to her; she didn't mind the look of the sheets.

—Now I will tell a secret, she said. It was really mine. Mine really! I put it there. I didn't want you to know, even though I did want you to know.

—What are you saying? Your mother . . . she did it, one of those crazy tricks. To get me out.

—No, no . . .

—And that Rose in cahoots with her.

—No, no, myself, I did it!

—You?

—But I didn't think mama would find it. I wanted you to find it.

One night, in wild daring, she recounted, not three perilous yards from the shut door of her father's study, where he sat laughing with James, she slipped into what had been her own bed, and was now his, to deposit under the pillow a moist brown curl of her sweat-dampened hair.

When he took her away—or did she take him?—a bleakness seeped through him. Bridget or Annie or anyone, what difference? Her yieldingness drove him, he was not unwilling, but his susceptibilities were elsewhere. They rushed toward Mitwisser's mocking heretics, those old lost runaways, swallowed by oblivion like whiskey in the throat.

50

HEINZ CALLED breathlessly, "There's a man out there."

On an oblong concrete slab, an inadvertently benchlike perch at the side of the green front door of our house . . . but here I must stop, in order to attend to these last words. Our house: more and more I thought of it as that. I was not entitled to this thought—I had too frequently been declared an outsider. But everything was so familiar, every cranny of every room, the sounds of the house in the day and at night, and I was so accustomed to my labors with Professor Mitwisser, and to Mrs. Mitwisser's plaints and Willi's slynesses (I distrusted Willi), that I felt oddly settled, as I never had felt before. The years with my father had always been precarious. My sojourn with Bertram—it was only that, a visitor's brevity—had been too quickly cut off. I was as rooted in this house as if I had been living among Mitwissers under a timeless dome. There was no comfort in it, yet it had begun to take on the repetitive consolations of the ordinary. Even that other outsider, James, had come to seem merely another bruise in a house of bruises.

The man was sitting on the benchlike slab. He had a little suitcase with him. Heinz had opened the door and there he was, just sitting. He hadn't so much as rung the bell.

"He said he was working up his nerve. And then he asked if Rose lived here, and I said yes. This time," Heinz insisted, "it really is a man."

I imagined then that it might be Dr. Tandoori hesitating at the door —Dr. Tandoori returning to woo me, possibly preparing a speech of courtship (a more comprehensive description of his w.c. perhaps), or else a reprise of his employer's pitch.

But the man was already in the house. Heinz had escorted him into the dining room, where he was circling the big table, surveying the scattered detritus of the Mitwisser children's lives—spent balloons, a beheaded lead soldier, a doll's torn petticoat, checkers spilling out of a broken box.

"Go away now," I told Heinz. "Go see about your mother." My tone surprised me: it flew out in Anneliese's old imperious voice, the voice he had once been quick to obey.

"I have to talk to my cousin," I said, and again surprised myself; was I beginning to believe that Bertram was truly my cousin?

He looked shrunken; the sparse twist of his smile was a dry inchworm. His curly hair was dusted all over, I could hardly tell with what: it was as if a peculiar rime had grown over him, or out of him, like a coating of flour.

"Got off at the wrong stop and had to walk. I forgot Ninel said it's the end of the line."

He had come up from the Village by subway, he explained. "Charlie's back there now—he's got a bad limp. Lots of Ninel's crowd are back. She's the only one. The only one who didn't make it back."

His shirt was rimmed with dirt.

"I figured Ninel's old gang would give me a break. Help out a little. Nothing doing, you know why? Ninel told them I'm against the Party. She told them I'd turned. They kicked me out after three nights, Charlie's idea."

"Isn't he the one who threw paint down the toilet at the Library?" I asked.

"Ninel never said anything like that." His hoarse breath was all denial, as if it was Ninel herself I was accusing. "Sometimes I feel . . . I mean if I hadn't let her have that money—"

I was afraid he would burst into weeping; I remembered that when we were last together, it was I who had wept. But instead he only twisted up his mouth.

"She would've gone anyway," he said, "hook or crook, I realize that. They're a bunch of Johnny One Notes. Cranks. If you're not with them they'll slap you down. Only—with Ninel—it was something else, I knew it, it was something else . . ."

"Thunder and lightning," I put in.

"The old lady down in Georgia—Thomas's mother-in-law—well,

his wife and kid came back in mourning, and I had to get out. Prescott ponied up the train fare, he was decent enough for that. And there's what you sent, and even a bit of a handout from Mrs. Capolino . . . Albany's a dead end."

He threw himself into a chair, exhausted. His head dropped down; the coating of flour, I saw, was a crop of gray hairs.

"I had in mind Ninel's people could put me up awhile, at least for Ninel's sake . . . just until I found something. Believe me, I didn't intend to show up here. The way things are now—"

I was suddenly alarmed: did he mean for me to take him in? How could I? How was it possible? I may have fancied this stricken house to be "our" house, but it was Mitwisser's, not mine. Yet how could I refuse Bertram? Hadn't he taken *me* in? And paid my tuition, and cared for me, and kissed me . . .

"I didn't know where else to go. A dog on your doorstep," he said.

"Oh, Bertram, don't—"

"I'm down to my last dime, Rosie, that's how it is. Maybe just for tonight, what d'you say?"

Bertram pleading: it was horrible to see. It made me ashamed, but also angry. I had surrendered the blue envelope to Ninel; I had nothing to give him.

I left him there in the litter of discarded toys and went up the stairs and, without knocking, stepped into Mitwisser's study. He was bent over a flurry of manuscripts and a row of books faced upside down, with their backs exposed in A-shaped peaks, like tepees, to secure a page. It was an awkward habit: he objected to inserting strips of paper to mark the passages he might wish to return to—books, he said, were not foxes, and ought not to have protruding white tails. For an instant I stood watching him write—in German, I noticed, and lethargically, lifting his pen in the air and keeping it suspended before bringing it down again, almost unwillingly, to eke out the next words. Across the room the disheveled bedclothes made a frozen tumble, like wreckage recently washed up on a beach. Claimed by Mrs. Mitwisser, I hadn't tidied up that morning.

He said, without looking up, "I did not call for you, why are you here?"

The newly carpentered shelves all around were prematurely arced under the weight of his library, as if mimicking the wearied curve of his shoulders. Behind the scissors-sharp blue of Mitwisser's eyes a dread was lurking; a smoke of desolation hung over him. But those eyes, which could so easily cut, were turned away from me, fixed on the idling point of his pen. "It may in fact be in vain," he had murmured the night before. I heard in it the tainted germ of something wayward, some pale interrupting doubt. My hands were still on the typewriter. He removed them, one at a time. The touch of his skin on mine had been unpleasantly tentative, like a clump of shed fur—harmless, but reminiscent of claws.

"Well?" he said.

"My cousin's stopped by. He's waiting downstairs."

"Your cousin? You have a cousin?"

"I did mention him once. His name is Bertram. We're very close, and he needs a place to stay—"

"Is this house a public accommodation? I have nothing to do with your relations."

"It would only be for tonight, if you wouldn't mind, and we do have an empty bed—"

He slammed the table with his big fist, so that the queue of tepees rocked and collapsed. "If it is my daughter's bed you are contemplating, no stranger is welcome there."

"James was," I said meanly.

This seemed to defeat him. The moment's store of rage was used up. He drew his shoulders inward; the whole of his great frame contracted.

"You won't be disturbed at all," I pressed, "it's just for the one night, and he'll be gone in the morning."

"And will you also be gone? Is this why your cousin comes, a relation out of nowhere? All at once a cousin, and he takes you away, is this what I am to expect?"

He feared my leaving. He feared my being taken away: by Dr. Tandoori, by a relation out of nowhere, by the claims of time. It was a confession: he had no Elsa, he had no Anneliese, he had a small child and three barbarian sons . . . The house was already lawless; he feared the ambush of the vacuum that waits beyond commotion.

"I'm not going anywhere," I assured him, and my envy of Anneliese flickered into light. Gone with a lover, gone into velvet silence. Another packet had arrived, this time unaccompanied by any note—voiceless money, silent money.

"Then your cousin may stay," Mitwisser said, "for this one night."

So Bertram entered Anneliese's bed, which had been James's bed, which became Bertram's bed. He did not depart in the morning. Instead, he busied himself cooking omelets—none of the Mitwisser children had ever eaten an omelet—and after that began reorganizing the kitchen, which under my distracted rule had sunk into anarchy. He had rested wonderfully well during the night, he told me; in all the days before he had been suffering from a crazed fatigue. At Charlie's he lay awake, calculating what he might say to make his case against Ninel's charges. In the end it was futile. Nothing he could argue in his defense was persuasive—they dismissed him as too soft (this was particularly painful, Ninel's old nastiness, he suspected they were quoting her). They accused him of shirking, he had avoided Spain, he had sent Ninel as his surrogate. He had turned her into a mercenary. He was heartless, he had paid her to serve in his place. He was a coward, he was unfit, he was not a proper comrade. A shirker, a lowlife, no better than a scab; he ought to have fought with the rest of them.

By now—it was still the first afternoon—Bertram had dusted every corner in the dining room and made order of the children's things. The checkers were back in their box, the doll's petticoat was sewn and restored to its mistress (he showed me the miniature sewing kit he kept with him), the headless soldier had been given to Heinz to be glued whole. This was the tireless Bertram I remembered, the Bertram who would not let a dirty dish remain idle for five minutes, who would sprint to the sink to render it gleaming. He had washed his shirt, I scarcely knew when, and somehow he had discovered the half-lame washing machine, with its creaking wringer, that frightened Waltraut in the blackest region of our faintly sewer-smelling cellar. The rope Anneliese and I had long ago strung from end to end of the cellar was bannered by a row of boys' socks and shirts. Bertram had laundered them all. Clothespins stuck up along the crowded line like live cats' ears, mysteriously bobbing a little, though in that sooty cavern (the coalbin occupied a part of it, and a huge ogrelike furnace growled nearby) there was no wind.

In the evening we all met in the dining room—all but Mrs. Mitwisser. The boys were wary, stealthily subdued, and Waltraut hid under the table. Mitwisser ate nibblingly, sniffing at the food. He seemed to sniff at Bertram too, who was scurrying in and out of the kitchen like a chef in an obscure restaurant attempting to make its name.

When the boys had dispersed, I tried to account for Bertram's not having left.

"He wanted to make the dinner," I told Mitwisser. I stood up to carry her tray to his wife.

"Where are you taking that?" Bertram asked. He was following me, pink-faced and cheerful; yesterday's misery had been swept away, together with the dust.

"Mrs. Mitwisser's got to eat something, she doesn't leave her room."

"I'll bring it to her if you like—"

"No," I said quickly, "a man she doesn't know, she'll think . . ." But Mitwisser was near, and I did not say what his wife might think.

He thought it himself. "The gentleman is not to intrude on my wife!"

Bertram examined the toast, the cold boiled egg. "I don't frighten people, do I, Rosie? Look, I can do better than that," he said, and seized Mrs. Mitwisser's dry meal and disappeared with it.

After a time a warm fragrance drifted out of the kitchen.

"Bread pudding," Bertram announced: a heap of it lay steaming in a bowl. "Come out from under there, little girl," he called, "and you can have some."

Waltraut peered out. "I don't know what it is."

"Try it tonight and I'll tell you tomorrow."

Mitwisser said grimly, "The gentleman will not be here tomorrow, will he?"

"Then I'll have to tell you now," Bertram said. "It's a pudding bird.

Its wings are made of pudding. First you trap it, and after that you roll it in bread crumbs."

"Don't come up with me," I warned him.

I had expected to find Mrs. Mitwisser lying with her hand over her eyes, courting a doze. But she was erect and vigilant in her nightgown, as straight-backed as a caryatid.

"What is that? Who is there? Is it that one? That one?" She gripped my arm: her fingers were strong, but I felt the tremor that shivered through the deep pinch.

"It's only my cousin—on a visit. He made this for you."

I watched her eat. She ate as one emerging from a long fast. The bowl was rapidly emptied. She held it out to me. "More," she commanded, in the style she might once have used with her cook.

Bertram did not leave the next morning, or the next, or the next. It was understood that it was his intention to go, but he never spoke of it; I did not speak of it. Once or twice, at night, leaning over the typewriter, Mitwisser would rasp, "The gentleman abides," with a satiric clip to the words, or else he would say only, "Ah, the cousin," as if there was meaning enough in this. But an unexpected calm was settling over the house: things that had been helter-skelter fell unobtrusively into place. Mitwisser's bedclothes were meticulously smoothed each morning; an unseen hand kept his fountain pen filled. Holes in socks were instantly stitched. The kitchen rang with a clash of pans, and suddenly a row of boys and a small girl sat docilely munching cake.

"Let me," Bertram urged, seeing me ascend, day after day, with Mrs. Mitwisser's tray.

But I answered as I always answered. "She's too nervous, you'll only set her off—"

"I can handle it."

He came down smiling. "She sure likes that pudding bird. You know what's the matter with that woman? She's hungry, that's all."

He had yet to learn of Mrs. Mitwisser's cavernous hungers, I thought—hungers not of the flesh, which no sweetmeat could satisfy. But from then on it was Bertram who took up Mrs. Mitwisser's tray. Waltraut trailed behind him, carefully transporting a napkin and spoon.

One afternoon he went to inquire at the pharmacy under the trestle. "A nice change from Albany, I could've been Trotsky for all they cared. But no luck, they aren't hiring. So there it is," he said, "hard times."

Domesticity pleased Bertram. The fastidiousness I had noticed so long ago was, I fancied, a kind of obeisance to his being a short man: it brought his scrutiny so much closer to dirty floors and sticky table tops. He wanted to undo confusion, to placate *things*—to clear them up, to sort them out, to draw out a peaceable kingdom from hubbub and jumble. He wanted to appease. He made sure to avoid being found in Mitwisser's path, though his study ("the Professor's bedroom," Bertram called it) was no more than a few yards across the hall from Anneliese's old bed. They seldom met, except at dinner, when Bertram in his new capacity as self-appointed chef lingered in the kitchen, mostly out of sight. When they happened to pass, it was usually on the stairs, and Bertram would murmur respectfully, "Good morning, Professor," or "Good evening, Professor." Sometimes Mitwisser nodded; often he did not respond at all. But when our nightly session began, he would drum his fingers musingly on the back of my chair (faltering in his dictation, as he did more and more at this time), and grunt "The gentleman, your cousin," as if reporting on an apparition he was scarcely certain he had seen. Whenever I thought Bertram too exaggeratedly propitiatory, I remembered that he, like me, had nowhere to go.

Bertram's pacifications, his quickness to serve, were an embarrassment. I saw how the boys were muddled by all this self-effacement. He was not so tall as Heinz, and no taller than Gert; even so, he rattled them. Once, when a fight was storming around him—Willi had swiped Heinz's earphones and was running off to hide them—a rush of panic bloomed uncontrollably all over Bertram's curly head. "What bullies you kids are," he said; his breath came hard. It was not a rebuke; it was a plea, spoken in a voice of sorrowing humility. It shocked them—it may have shamed them—and after that they took their quarrels and their fisticuffs out of his hearing. It made no sense to them that Bertram was in the house; it made no sense that their father had permitted it. At home, no cook or maid or nanny had ever resembled Bertram; it made no sense that Bertram was cook and maid and nanny all at once. And anyhow the quarrels and the fisticuffs weren't really out of his hearing — he only pretended they were, and they knew he was pretending. It was Bertram's dogma that if you behaved as if there was peace, then peace would accommodate you by turning genuine. Occasionally this doctrine bore fruit: Gert or Heinz would catch in Bertram's face a wistful look of hope, and the slaps and punches stopped altogether.

During one of these bewildered truces Willi asked whether Bertram was going to be my husband someday.

"You don't marry cousins," I said.

"Was Dr. Tandoori your cousin too?"

"Of course not."

"But you weren't going to marry him either —"

This annoyed me; there was cunning in it, an unripe cleverness. "I told you," I said, "I'm not marrying anybody."

It was not only Willi who was unsettling me in those raw days when Bertram was occupying Anneliese's bed and taking my place (or so it felt) with Mrs. Mitwisser. It was easy for Bertram to make himself invisible to Professor Mitwisser — he was upstairs whole afternoons, tending the invalid. He had enlisted Waltraut in the rite of carrying up Mrs. Mitwisser's tray — Waltraut following as usual with napkin and spoon, and lately with a small cup of something sweet-smelling, Bertram bearing his own warmly redolent concoction, and also, I noted, a glass of wine — but this newly encumbered ceremony was becoming mysteriously prolonged. When the boys were at school, and Bertram and the child were hidden away with Mrs. Mitwisser, the house was uncommonly still. It felt uninhabited, abandoned. I had nothing to do but wait for the night and Mitwisser's sharp call.

Ninel, I began to recognize, had all along been right: Bertram was too soft. He could be turned this way and that way; he was too obliging. This obligingness had its underside; it robbed Peter to pay Paul. Out of goodness, and to oblige my father's rough importuning, he had taken me in; but to please Ninel he had expelled me. He had lavished on me the blue envelope with its fat fortune, and then he had allowed it to be usurped. Bertram's goodness was treacherous. His softness was treacherous: a soft compliance was his unresisting means of setting the world to rights. With maternal guile, he could persuade the lion to lie down with the lamb—only, when this was accomplished, it was the lion who prevailed.

Wine had never before entered the house. Yet here it was, the glass that went up to Mrs. Mitwisser, and the glass that was set down at Professor Mitwisser's plate, and at mine. I had never tasted wine, and knew nothing of its subtlety, if it had any—but when Mitwisser put his glass first to his nostrils and then to his lips with a distracted, almost dreaming, concentration, it was as if some familiar wind was passing over, or even through, him: a wind from a great distance, from the past, from the time before they had thrown him out, from that Europe I had come to think of as a dense volcanic mass concealed under a disintegrating black veil. I knew nothing of Europe, I knew nothing of wine; I dimly believed that it was somehow noble, "aristocratic," the elixir of priests and kings. But I did not like this wine that Bertram had brought us—it was too tart, and too dark, like venous blood, and it smelled of seduction, of ingratiation. Bertram had quickly seen whose hand held the household scepter. I was merely the sentry who had let him in. Professor Mitwisser was the majesty who might keep or eject him, and to gratify this inconstant sovereign it was needful to nurse the curious invalid on the uppermost floor. Bertram was an excellent nurse. In ten minutes he could supply a poultice for an itchy scar, or a savory dish for a slothful appetite. The wine gladdened both the sovereign and his wife. It honored the sovereign, it calmed the wife.

"In Albany," I reminded Bertram, "*we* never had wine." I rarely spoke to him of those sheltering months when he had been my rescuer and comforter. But now I felt sullen.

"Ninel put me onto it."

I said acidly, "I didn't think the Party approved of wine."

"Well, Ninel did, why not? Italian peasants, French workers, wine is what the masses quaff. You know, the masses." He half grinned, in the winning self-parody I remembered.

A moment later the grin undid itself; it folded into a hangdog mouth. Whenever Ninel's name erupted between us, Bertram lapsed into somberness. At times I would mention Ninel solely for the sake of watching the gloom creep over him—these flushed openings into Bertram's buried suffering revenged me. I wanted to undermine his softness. It was not because of Ninel; Ninel was dead. In this house Bertram was, at least for me, a bad angel: that all-around usefulness, that stringent plea for harmony, for pleasing everyone, for sweeping us all clean of blemish—he was too liquidly noble, like the wine. Only the thought of Ninel made him seem solid.

He had begun to do the marketing. This had been Anneliese's task, and afterward mine. Bertram liked to poke among the vegetables, and in the dusky crannies of the shops under the trestle: it gave him ideas, he said. Waltraut went with him, pushing a little wicker doll's pram. It had been rediscovered in a heap of twisted and neglected toys—there were so many toys, a jungle of toys! The wicker pram was vital: he stooped to fill it with grocery bags. The bottle of wine—two bottles, in fact—he stuffed into his pockets, to free his arms for the bigger bundles.

He did not ask where the money for these provisions came from. But when I doled out the bills he said, "Cash . . . I never see anybody write a check around here. Or go to the bank. All right, none of my business—"

It was a kind of bravado. This small tactile transaction, his palm flattened before me as I counted out dollars, stung him. It shamed him; it shamed me. We were standing close, Bertram's face too close to mine (we were nearly the same height), shrouded by the intimacy of money dropping from hand to hand—the naked smell of public paper, its weightless burdensome rustle, its worn creases, like the skin of an aged woman.

"You don't understand, Rosie," he lamented. "You never saw her fired up, she had the spite of justice in her, and if I'd done things differently, if I hadn't let her take that money—"

It was his old chant. "You wouldn't be you," I said. But this blandness—I meant it only as evasion—fell on him unkindly.

"Soft!" he cried. "She called me soft!"

The spite of justice. It seemed to me he was enshrining Ninel in a hard shell of sainthood.

There had been three sporadic packets since the last—the last that had arrived without a letter—and these also were bare of any word from Anneliese. They were bulging, crammed with more dollars than before, as if in compensation for their muteness. Each packet was stamped with a different postmark. I had given up informing Professor Mitwisser of their appearance: he did not welcome it. A silent ukase was in force: silence answering silence. His children sensed it; even Waltraut understood that one must not speak of Anneliese, one must not speak of James —not to papa, not to anyone, not to the new stranger in the house.

But Mrs. Mitwisser was bound by nothing.

At midnight, in my bed across from hers, I said, "What do you and my cousin talk about all afternoon?"

She did not reply. She was asleep. She slept deeply and long. The empty wine glass had been left behind. It lay on its side next to her hairbrush. She had taken to brushing her hair, which had grown, in her self-confinement, down to her breasts. In the mornings she arranged it in a round braid at the back of her neck, with a few hairpins to secure it. Her hair was as brown and thick as Anneliese's.

"When you're upstairs with mama and Bertram," I asked Waltraut the next day, "what do they talk about?"

Waltraut looked at me with her small Mitwisser eyes. She had none of Willi's beauty.

"Mama talks about Heinz," she said.

51

IT WAS FORGIVENESS they talked of: the bitter, bitter withholding of it. Professor Mitwisser had never forgiven his wife for the secret journey to Arosa. Bertram could not forgive himself for Ninel's journey to Spain. So they talked and talked, while Waltraut busied herself with a wooden puzzle in the shape of a line of goslings, or fed make-believe pudding bird to her dolls.

They talked of how they were not forgiven, how they would never be forgiven, how Mitwisser would not forgive his wife, how he would not forgive his daughter. They talked of spite.

Mrs. Mitwisser did not know that the woman who spited Bertram by dying in Spain was the man who had forced his way into the house and frightened her into her old black tunnel of fright.

She spoke of another man. He had commandeered her family and spited them all, her husband, her children—her daughter! She spoke of this man incessantly, her mouth with its orderly teeth and pleasant scent of wine breathing in and out too rapidly, too urgently—so that Bertram thought the insinuator, the invader, whom she called James, had stolen money. She spoke of thieves and beggars, of parasites and fireflies. Her cries and confidences, which had belonged to me, all went to Bertram. She felt in him what she had never felt in me: a pliant sympathy, a nurse's sympathy; a mother's. Bertram was motherly. He listened and shook his head. He listened with angry smiles. He mourned Ninel exactly as she mourned Anneliese, angrily, unforgivingly.

"If they will come," she said, plucking at her faded haunted rhythmic plaint.

"They?" he echoed.

"My daughter. And that one. That one! . . . if she will come—"

That one, he knew, was James. A glowering phantom.

"She *will* come. She will," he assured her. I had never assured Mrs. Mitwisser of anything—the Mitwisser kingdom was too fragile, too tentative, subject to earthquake. I could not hold out a belief I did not own. Observing Bertram, I saw what this meant: in this unforgiving house I had insufficient sympathy. Or else my truest sympathies were with Professor Mitwisser, who welcomed them least, who was estranged from sympathy. It was typical of Bertram to swim meltingly into the instant face of need. Hadn't he once told me that I should trust in that untrustworthy tendril of memory, my dying mother clutching a rag doll? And hadn't he once persuaded me that my father had unaccountably secreted a worn children's book in his most private hoard out of a sentimental affinity for a picture of a boy hiding in a hat? Bertram said these things to assuage the moment's exigency. The moment won him. If the way to terra firma lay through the cosseting of the wife of the man whose word was law, it no longer mattered. What had begun thinly as opportunity thickened into sympathy. He was growing into the sinews of the house. It was slowly educating him, as it had educated me. I had had Mrs. Mitwisser as my unsteady teacher of fragmented histories. Bertram had me.

"This James she carries on about," he said, "the one who took money—"

"He didn't take any money."

"She calls him thief—"

"He took Anneliese," I said.

"The daughter. The daughter who went away."

"She went with James." It was somehow necessary to say this outright: the very thing that was forbidden. "It's his money they live on."

Bertram stared. "They pay your wages. You get . . . a salary"—he brought out this word unhappily, guiltily—"and you sent me a piece of it—"

"They haven't got anything on their own. Everything's from James. All of it."

He sucked in a long reflective breath, as if he meant to inhale all the world's mysteries. "How about that. How *about* that. He isn't in business or anything, is he? Some company big shot?"

"Nothing like that. It's some sort of inheritance—"

"A moneybags. Daddy Warbucks."

A whiff of Ninel. Her ghost speaking through him.

"Bertram, it's not like that. . . . They live on it," I said again. "The money just . . . comes."

The familiar half-twist of Bertram's mouth. The little pillowy intimate swell of his lower lip. It made me resist Ninel. It made me long for his sympathy, for his old, old kiss, with his knee on my bed.

"But why?" he said.

I knew why. It was not new knowledge. I believed I had known it ever since I had first heard Professor Mitwisser laughing together with James, a laughter that had the sound of grief.

"He likes to do it," I told Bertram. "Out of hatred, I think."

But I had no inkling of what it was that James hated.

52

THERE WERE NIGHTS when Professor Mitwisser did not call for me at all. And on the nights he did, it appeared that he had no work for me: but it was clear that he expected me to stand at the ready. He looked down from that immensity of neck and torso to make certain I was attentive — to what? He had given up shaving altogether. The new beard was creeping imperceptibly, laggardly; yet it aged him too quickly. His shoulders had an old man's hunch. Out of a white face the hot blue eyes leaped like panting tigers.

A distance from where I loitered, the tepee-shapes of the volumes he had turned topsy-turvy to mark his place were undisturbed.

"It is perhaps not possible," he said finally. He said it to the ceiling globe, where one of a pair of light bulbs had gone out. The room was dimmer than usual. "Without corroboration it remains only . . . conviction."

I caught — if not his meaning — his imperative, that urge below thought that beat in his brain. It pulsed against me mothlike, and I snatched it out of the darkening air. More and more it seemed to me that I inhabited his mind. Or the reverse: his mind came to me. I pinched it between my finger and thumb.

"'I, Jacob, am become Arjuna,'" I recited. It was an offering, as on an altar.

"Yes, yes — the very words. *Those* words!" he cried. "And the uncanny knowledge of the Bhagavad-Gita . . . Jacob al-Kirkisani, a runaway from the whole history of religion, do you understand? You understand this, yes?"

He was addressing me; I felt addressed. He was not speaking above or around me, as when I rattled the typewriter keys in tune with his voice. It was the first time he had allowed me entrance (how I felt this!)

into the sanctum of his meditations. I had all along been typist, amanuensis, servant, convenience; animate tool—Aristotle's term (I had once read this) for a slave. I was not his slave, no; but I had become his tool. One does not address a tool.

"What I have uncovered," he said, "is the labyrinth of renunciation. I have uncovered it in the heart of Jacob al-Kirkisani. In his heart only. It is not conversion, it is not syncretism, though there are fools who will insist on this. He does not journey to India to become a Hindu. He is no more a Hindu than a Hindu is a Karaite. He accepts, he receives, in order to refuse. In a man of supreme feeling refusal gives birth to refusal —that is the essence of it. The Karaites—how deeply, deeply I know them, I am their child, they are my children, I have penetrated into their lungs, their angers, their prayers! They reject, they rebel. But al-Kirkisani reveals that he is apart from these things. Those who rebel do not regard themselves as heretics. Hardly so! They believe heresy lies in the very men they repudiate. For them, whatever is orthodox is heretical, so they depart from it.

"True heresy is neither rebellion nor rejection, and I tell you I have uncovered it in the heart of al-Kirkisani! It is refusal of every refusal but God's, a new thing, a true thing! It descends into the labyrinth of renunciation, from abyss to abyss, until in the bottommost depth of bottomlessness there is nothing to breathe, only the vacuum of the One God, the One true God, God the heretic, who disbelieves in man, who casts off this worshipful creature for the charlatan he is. This is Jacob al-Kirkisani's meaning, it is what he has written—that it is God who is the heretic! Karaite, Arjuna, one or the other, it is all lost in the labyrinth, the One true God of heresy renounces all."

He had been pacing here and there, as I had so often heard him do, from the wall of books to the smooth broad bed and back again.

"You understand this, yes?"

I did not understand, I could not; but my instinct was for what inflamed him. The fragment from Spain; the Karaites, whose child he was, who were his children; al-Kirkisani, fallen out of Karaite rebellion into trust in a heretical God.

"You see, you see," he said, "what is my conviction worth? How will it be judged? What am I to do with it? It cannot be proved, it cannot be corroborated. There is not a scrap of paper in the world to verify it. I have only this thin copy, a copyist's hand, it will be taken for counterfeit, they will suppose me to have been duped, it is all in vain, in vain, I blinded myself, I was too quick, too quick—"

He came to stand before me.

"My dear Rose," he said—I was astonished to hear him say my name—"I ask you, where, where is my daughter?"

53

Dear Rose,

We are staying in this place for a time. I think it will be a long time. Where we are is called Thrace. Papa read to me once about a man from Thrace who looked up to study the stars and fell into a ditch. People laughed, but papa said it is common for a man of learning to be laughed at, especially in this country. I think of papa very much. I am sure I have disappointed him, but perhaps after a while he will not be so angry. He was very angry when I would not go to school, but later on he stopped. I hope he will stop again.

James never wants to go out in the auto. In the auto we went everywhere to see things, all the little towns, and it was so interesting and strange. Sometimes I am sick in the auto, I thought it is because of this that James never wants to go out, but it is really because he is so sad in the little towns. That is why we have come back to Thrace. James says he can laugh in this place, I dont know why. Thrace is not so very different from all the other places, and even here James does not laugh so much, he is always sad. Perhaps the schnapps makes him sad, I dont know. We stay a great deal in our little room and hardly go out at all. Mama would not like it about the schnapps, but I dont mind. I think of mama very much. She is so very thin, you must make her eat more. You must make sure that Waltraut is not unhappy. She likes a pink ribbon to tie her hair.

Anneliese

There was no packet. There was no money.

54

THEY DROVE from town to town—Carthage, Rome, Ithaca, Oswego, Oneonta, Cortland. In Elmira he took her to see Mark Twain's grave; there were two or three other visitors there, all standing under umbrellas in the hard rain. She had asked to come to this place: she had read *Tom Sawyer* at home, she said. She remembered that Tom had cried at his own funeral, and that was comical, but she liked Erich Kästner so much more. And she liked *Der Bärknabe* still more—so often Mademoiselle De Bonrepos had read it aloud, singsonging the verses! And, later, Madame Mercier—but in French. She had forgotten the French, but she remembered Mademoiselle De Bonrepos's singsong, with her flat French accent overlaying the bouncing rhymes. She could recite some of those rhymes, she told him, this minute. When she was very young she had no idea that what she was hearing was a translation—*Bärknabe* seemed to have been born into her own language.

—Do people come to look at your house?

—What?

Her questions, the intensity of her confessions.

—Where you used to live. The way they come here.

—It's gone. It doesn't exist. Got turned into an old people's home.

Mr. Fullerton, Mr. Winberry, and Mr. Brooks had informed him of this long ago. "Sold for quite a fortune," Mr. Fullerton had crowed, as if he might care. What he cared about then was his new knapsack with all the pockets, and his steamship ticket.

—But the *house* is there, she prodded.

—I suppose.

—People could stand outside and look through the windows! Do they? Do they come from all over the world to look?

—Good luck to them, he said roughly, if they do.

—James! I want to go there! I want to see!

—No, he said. No.

—But I want to, she insisted.

This child. At such times she was more child than woman. It was as if, in fleeing her family, she had released herself from dutifulness to defiance. To willfulness.

—It's nowhere near here, he said.

—Where is it?

—Over the state line.

—But we have the auto, so . . .

A hiss of recognition flew from her.

—Oh! Passport! We have no passport, no papers . . .

—What's the matter with you? he said. Where do you think you are?

—But if it is a border . . .

The preposterous ignorance. A foreign child who did not grasp ordinary reality. They had kept her from school, from an American high school, where she belonged. Not meandering all over in a Ford, pointlessly.

—What's the matter with you? he said again. Passport, what are you talking about?

She knew he was impatient with her, and it was only a misunderstanding, like her papa with the Quakers, why was he so impatient? One could go from upstate—that was what he called all these little places, towns unlike any she had ever seen before in all her life—one could go from here to anywhere at all, he explained, and no papers, no border officials! He explained this—how angry he seemed—but the misunderstanding left a cold space between them. She could not make out how to warm this space. And anyhow he did not comprehend what it was to be without papers, to have no passport, to cower before a uniform, to pay for forged papers, to bribe to get genuine papers, to learn afterward that they were no longer valid, never to have good papers, valid papers, a genuine passport! Never! He could not comprehend any of this, how free he was, how simple, he was like an angry child. Her papa had said the Americans were like children.

—Without papers, she instructed him soberly, we could not have run to Sweden, and from Sweden . . .

He shut out the rest of it. Sweden. He did not tell her (why should he? his thoughts were his own) that he had once longed for Sweden, the farthest north it was possible to think of. A country encased in immaculate cold, as numb and immobile as ice. The doll house had come from Sweden, and the wooden doll house children with their yellow hair . . .

—At the William Penn, he said instead, when I first saw all of you, I thought it was Swedish you were speaking. But you all had such dark hair.

—Even Heinz, she put in.

Her hair was very dark. It was as dark as her mother's. She lifted a heavy handful of it and pressed it into his mouth, to stop up the misunderstanding. For a moment it made a kind of peace between them. But then he gave her a little shove: he didn't want her hair in his mouth. The rain had soaked it.

After that they drove to Thrace. It was a considerable distance away, and he pushed into the night without halting, except once, at a diner set all by itself, like a lost segment of train, on a truncated street edged by a field. It was close to midnight when they came into the neighborhood of the schoolyard, and the deserted tract of concrete looked nearly as he had remembered it—the lit bulb, helmeted by a metal grid, protruding from the building's brick flank, candy wrappers crumpled here and there. A basketball hoop clamped to a pole—that was new.

He had the girl by the elbow and led her across the yard.

—Right about here. The burial ground, he said.

The glare from the single bulb filled his lenses; she could not see his eyes.

—What place is this? she asked.

—You want to visit a shrine? This is it. Here!

He broke into his high thin stretched-out laugh, the same laugh that burbled out of her papa's study when he sat in there with her papa, the two of them convulsed by intimacy.

—The Bear Boy's tomb. Here's where I dumped the thing. Only, he said, it turned out to be a joke.

The high garbling laughter. She thought it had the sound of Niagara Falls from far away.

—It came alive again, he said. Voodoo! Up from the grave.

It was troubling that she could not see his eyes. He was laughing at some secret thing. Usually it was the schnapps that brought this on: an angry sadness that shattered into a vindictive snigger. But a whole day had passed without the schnapps, and still she heard it.

—Where are we? she demanded.

He put his thumb under her chin and lifted it. Across the top of the building, in the wan orange light, she read: THRACE CENTRAL HIGH.

—Where you ought to be. A place like this. Rudi sends the boys, why not you?

It was the same as having no papers, he could not feel it, he could not know!

—Papa teaches me. He teaches me so much. I know more than you! she burst out. No one can make me go to school.

—Rudi won't allow it, that's why.

—Papa?

—He keeps you home.

He could not feel it, he could not know! The Americans are like children!

She showed him the fist of her left hand: how it would not close all the way. It curled only partly, like a reluctant snail.

—When we came papa said I must go to an American school. He said I must, I must . . .

She showed him the fist of her right hand: the fingernails hurt her palm.

—Papa said in Rome do as the Romans do. There is a law, you must go to an American school . . . No one can make me go to school!

Frau Koch's desk was on a raised platform. A short metal bar lay in the drawer of this desk. The lesson was on Bismarck: name two achievements that can be attributed to Chancellor von Bismarck. Frau Koch broke the bones of the left hand. Not with a ruler. The ruler was for the others. The ruler would not have been so savage. With the short metal bar Frau Koch smashed two narrow bones. Because I gave the answer.

Because I forgot that I was forbidden to speak. Because by then it was forbidden to be in that school at all. Because I would soon be thrown out of that school. Because it was imperative to be silent. Because it was imperative to be invisible. Because I spoke aloud. Because I gave the answer.

—No one can make me go to school ever again. Not even papa. Look, she said, I can easily make a fist with my right hand, see?

They drove to Ilion, Cobleskill, Homer, Horseheads, Naples, and Odysseus, and then came back, for the second time, to Thrace. The room they found was small and dark, but it was cleaner than most, and the house had a garden behind it: some nameless stalks in an exhausted weedy plot. The landlady served an early breakfast and a late dinner. In between she went off to her job as a waitress. There were no other boarders; they were alone.

But more and more James would not go out. It was odd, and disappointing: he had wanted to return to Thrace, where there was nothing of note to see, only a monotonous stretch of scrubby abandoned farmland all around, dead barns, a soporific Main Street (how queer, all these towns had blocks of shops identically named), and no local lore that anyone cared about. Thrace was unsympathetic. It appealed to some streak of perversity in him: to seek out the very site that aroused in him a bitterness, an irony she could not fathom, no matter if he explained it.

—A farce. A comedy, he said.

It was in Thrace that he had buried the Bear Boy, and among Mitwissers that the ghost had risen. That was how he explained it, with that short high laugh that attached itself now more to Thrace than to her papa.

—But look how much you help papa!

He was lying on the bed, with his hands tucked under his neck. Her mouth was on his throat, idly licking. He raised a shoeless foot and circled the shadows with it.

—A lot of good I'm doing his daughter, he said.

—Oh James, James, she said, I want to be with you, that's all.

—You don't.

—I do. I do, she said.

But she felt the little space spring open between them. Sometimes, when he caressed her, and let her put her hair in his mouth—it was a game they had, that led hastily to lovemaking—there was no space at all. And at other times a coldness seeped in, inch by inch.

She left him in that small dark room, monkish with its single dresser and two brittle wicker chairs (these had suffered a previous life outdoors), and went walking. All the days in Thrace seemed gray: did the sun never sojourn here? She passed the muddy Ford, unused for nearly three weeks. She felt vaguely lonely, perhaps because of the gray streets; otherwise she was never lonely. But why did he speak of her as her papa's daughter? Did he think of her simply as immersed in her family? Yet when she heard his way of saying her name—Annie—she believed she was herself, only herself, and when he grew impatient, it was because he was seeing her as he must first have seen her, as her papa's daughter, merely that. A refugee girl, an outlander. She supposed he took her in flickeringly, like one of those optical illusions where an image metamorphoses into a different image, but you cannot hold both images in your mind simultaneously. When he became impatient with her, even distant, she was all at once Anneliese, this foreign thing; and when he caressed her, Annie appeared. Oh, why could she not be Annie for him day and night?

She walked all along Main Street. At the end of it she turned back, having spied not far ahead the red-brick building that was the high school. Thrace, it turned out, was a drab town like all the others—but the others had enchanted her. They drove, they stopped, they gawked— he at her, amused at first by her delight. They ate in tiny steamy cafés smelling of fried potatoes. In Medusa they stood in a patch of grass in front of the courthouse and gazed at the violet fuzz of mountains that blurred the horizon's edge. In Odysseus (having landed there by bus; it was before they had the auto) they discovered a small traveling circus, with half a dozen acrobats, a clown, monkeys, a Fat Lady and a Fire-Eater. There was also a Sword-Swallower, but he was sick with flu and could not perform. Wherever they found themselves, she was exhilarated by an eerie newness: what unsuspected villages these were, what browning landscapes, what vegetable odors! And the fumes of fallen apples, sweet in their rot. How peculiar people's voices were, vowels inimical to her own larynx, staccato grunts that declined courtliness. No one bowed; it was democracy. The language too was uncivil, it did not distinguish between high and low. In Parnassus they drifted by a prison with pink walls and a garden of cabbages, unfenced; it did not frighten her. A man in an orange cap who was tending the cabbages waved. The strangeness was elating. The buses with their long noses and hard seats might have hurtled down from a different planet. The soup they ordered in one of those little cafés tasted of pickles; a red electric sign in the window bluntly announced PIE, FIVE CENTS. These towns, these towns, it was another country; the creatures who lived in it were not like those at home. The dogs barked unfamiliar notes, the cats curled their tails like alien clefs.

Her papa and his old, old, lost Karaites. No one in this new country bothered about them, only her papa. Her broken mother. How heavy they were, how heavy it was to be who they were, how heavy it was to be Anneliese! And how good, how free, to be with James. He could not know what she knew, he could not feel it, he had not seen the bonfires in the streets at night, and the broad black leaves of charred books, like spread-out bats' wings, and the smoke. He knew so little, it puzzled her, it was an absence in his brain, but it was also a relief, an anodyne, why should she not be glad that the Americans are like children? And he was *that* child, eternally: the boy in the lace collar, with a twinkling squint and rosy knees, and garlands of rhymes all around.

Schau ich mir Bärknabe an,
hab ich wenig Freude dran.
Fallen mir die andern ein,
nur Bärknabe will ich sein.

He was still lying on the bed, with his shoes off. This disturbed her; lately he never wanted to go out, why would he not go out? It reminded her a little of her mother.

—Hey, he said. You've been gone two hours.

—I had to walk all over until I found it. In such a funny place. I didn't find it on Main Street . . .

—You wouldn't. It's a dry town, I told you.

—Here, she said, and handed him a rounded object, swaddled like an infant.

He took it from her, and she recognized from his resisting sigh, and from the tiny inscrutable whistle that followed it, what he would say next. If he said it, it would hurt her. If he said it, she would feel sick. Sometimes the sick feeling came even when he did not say it.

—Annie . . .

—No, no, I want to be with you!

—You don't belong here.

—I do!

—You belong with your father, not here. Not this way.

—You don't know where I belong! she cried. You don't know anything! You don't understand any of it, you're like a child!

The runaway child calling him a child. He wrested open the bottle she had brought him—what else was there to do in this godforsaken Thrace? He could no longer endure how she ministered to him, how she yielded, how her yielding had become importuning, why would she not leave him be? Even her willfulness was servile: to have pestered him about the Bear Boy's house, why would she not leave him be? She was seventeen. She had pretty teeth, like her mother. Otherwise how was she different from that Bridget, why would she not leave him be?

Then it came to him that he could make a present of the Ford to their mostly absent landlady.

55

ELSA MITWISSER, formerly of the Kaiser Wilhelm Institute, doctor of physics, colleague of Nobel laureate Erwin Schrödinger (yet it was she who had bitten the egg), was unexpectedly in possession of an extra pair of shoes. They were blue leather pumps, delicately soled, scarcely worn, with a tease of ribbon bow at each toe. Plainly they had been danced in once or twice; and now they were newly polished, like two moons reflecting blue light.

Bertram had found them in a Salvation Army bin. On the day he came to us, he reminded me, he had mistakenly left the train at the stop before, did I remember that? A long walk under the snaking trestle; but on the way, dejected, unclean, he was all at once put in mind of Ninel.

"You had a vision," I said.

"Oh come on, Rosie, be nice. It's only that I spotted this Salvation Army place, that's all, and it just somehow brought her back. She used to get all her clothes that way, she didn't believe in dressing according to . . . well, class. And she got you those goodbye presents, Dickens I think, and what was the other?"

"Jane Austen. All about class. But I don't have it anymore—Mrs. Mitwisser chopped it up."

"She hasn't chopped up anything lately." He said this proudly; his conquest of Mrs. Mitwisser gratified him. It noticeably gratified her husband.

So I supposed it was Ninel's ghost that inspired Bertram to return one morning to the Salvation Army's bins, half a mile off under the trestle. Mrs. Mitwisser had allowed him to measure her naked foot; a familiarity was passing between them. Ten cents bought the blue pumps. Another ten cents bought the renewing polish. I did not ask him if he had communed with Ninel's spirit among the castaway shoes.

The pumps were Mrs. Mitwisser's trophies. She kept them next to her hairbrush. They were the spoils of the war she had long waged against the terrors of the house—had she not always insisted that it was not reasonable to live in a place of danger with only a single pair of shoes? Consider if they wore out, consider if they grew tattered from use, then how could one flee? The shoes Bertram had brought her were for dancing, admittedly—but no matter, this surely augmented their value.

"Sometimes," she confided, "one must put on the shoes as if for a ball. Even if not."

"How is that?" Bertram asked. But he already knew. She had told him about the El Dorado. She had told him how they had ridden round and round, round and round, day after day. She had told him about the juggler, and how she had fooled Fritz into thinking her mother's silver frame was only plate, and how she hoped it was the juggler Fritz had stolen from their walls, so that he could be fooled again.

Her bright look pleaded with Bertram to ask; she was ready to tell a third time, a fourth.

The extra pair of shoes gave her courage. She put on her old shoes and tidied her hair. She buttoned on a dress and palely, unsteadily, came down the stairs and into the life of the lower house. Bertram led her into his kitchen—it was by now entirely his. He had propitiated her demons, or stilled them; he had won her.

"I've got her chopping again." His sidewise grin. "Carrots for the stew."

"She never did that sort of thing," I said, "at home."

Those Mitwisser syllables—*at home*—sprang from me easily; I had acquired the native language.

"She's my sous-chef. She likes it."

"At home they had servants."

"Had," he retorted. "Had isn't have. I had Ninel, didn't I?"

"Oh Bertram, can't you see that she left you?"

"It was my fault. If I'd joined up—"

"You could never have joined up with those people." I took a deliberate breath. "You're too soft."

"What a thing to say. What a nasty thing." He gave me a wounded look. "You know what? You're not such a kid anymore. And you've never said a word of . . . I don't know what to call it. Condolence. Commiseration. It isn't as if you never *knew* Ninel. You haven't got any pity in you, they've done something to you here."

What had been done to me? It was mainly Bertram who had made me useless. His sympathies had engulfed and calmed them all—Mrs. Mitwisser and her children. Mrs. Mitwisser was in his charge; Waltraut was willingly under his thumb. Bertram's pockets were empty, he was powerless, he was a stranger in this fiefdom. But his mildness could somehow tame the boys—they were hardly aware of how he directed their armistice—and he had put a spell on Waltraut, who trotted after him like a small convenience. By becoming a servant to all, he had made servants of all. I was displaced; once again I felt that Bertram had exiled me.

I tapped on Mitwisser's study door. It was more than a week since he had called for me—it was left to me to search him out. His silence was permission. Otherwise he would send me away with an abrupt "Go." I entered at the usual time—it was ten o'clock—and saw that he was pacing in the dark, back and forth from bed to wall. I switched on the lamp that stood over the typewriter; its uncertain light showed me a man like a ship—an ocean liner viewed from the dock below. He had never seemed so thickly huge: the breadth and length of him, the massive shoulders, the great grieving head. Like a ship he moved in that confining space, lifted and lowered on the waves of his rough exhalations.

"I have no need of you now," he said. But he had allowed me to come in.

"I'll come back tomorrow then—"

"It will be the same tomorrow."

I had no care for decorum; I was frightened; I was fearless.

"No, no," I protested. "There's so much—"

"There is nothing."

The room was mobbed and heaped with my transcriptions. Stacks of portfolios pressed against the foot of the bed, along the walls, behind the door. Yet it was not only these hillocks of paper that surrounded and penned him: it was his own unraveling voice secreting those antique sages as a spider secretes its intricate lines, and the glass-shod keys lancing my eyes, and the phantom heretics mocking. And al-Kirkisani, prancing in air, close to the ceiling, circling the mosquelike dome that sheltered Mitwisser's brain.

"Professor Mitwisser," I said, and halted.

"My wife is improved. My house is in order, is it not? Your cousin is clever, I have observed this." With a muted thunder he heaved himself into his chair. "But my work is at an end, and my daughter . . . my daughter . . ."

I made my way through tides of manuscript to the wrinkleless coverlet (tended to with geometric precision by Bertram that morning) and sat down on its rim. Our eyes were almost level; his mouth was a warped knot.

"The amusing Dr. Tandoori," he murmured, and I grasped that he had last seen me there, at the edge of his bed, tentative and noiseless, during Dr. Tandoori's visit. "Do you understand that no one in this excellent country has ever given a thought to my investigations? They lack necessity, they invite futility. Obscurity breeds comedy. How then do I differ from a godless tailor?"

"Those men who came that night, *they* knew—"

"They came to deride."

How far away all that seemed! The cries of the man with the bad hand, and the man in the skullcap, had grown dimmer and dimmer, as if Mitwisser's adversaries had diminished to voiceless stunted china figurines.

"I am conscious," he said, "that I am open to such mockery. It is conceivable that I mock myself." He unknotted his mouth into a parody of a smile. "I suffer now from the silence even of my negligent antagonists. And in my foolish search for an attentive colleague I uncovered only"—the self-whipping smile stretched wider—"a sewing machine. Perhaps I too should take up tailoring, is this not so?"

"Professor Mitwisser," I tried again, "you see how your work is all around you, you see how immense—"

"Yes yes, how remarkable they are, my so very learnèd admirers! A hireling like yourself, oh yes, think how I am complimented. And that other, the ignorant itinerant who claims to be possessed by what he is unequipped to know—" His bitter rebuking breath invaded the narrow air between us. "I permitted it. I permitted it! Out of pity I permitted it!"

I made myself ask the reason for it. It was James he was sorrowing over, his wife's chosen enemy, and mine; I could not console him. It cut me that he spoke of pity; Bertram had charged me with having none.

"And why not? The man had no place. No present. No purpose. Nothing. Can you understand what it is to have nothing?"

"I came to tell you," I said slowly, "there's nothing much left. It's stopped coming."

The blue eyes burned. They inspected me. They looked murderous.

"Stopped? What is it that stops? My purpose? My place on this earth? My life? The life of my family?"

"The money," I said.

"The only one! Him alone! Who else but this ignorant itinerant has ever staked his life on my Karaites? Who else other than myself? Why should I not have pitied him? He and I, we two, no one else, that is how I am mocked! And in the end, in the end, in the end," he howled, "I sold this man my daughter!"

I felt then a terrifying blow, like that of a boulder crashing into the very center of my body. Mitwisser had thrust his great head into my arms, sobbing. I held it there, the weighty dome of that mind, for a long time, until the hot wetness seeped into the fibers of my dress.

56

THIS TIME she knew the way, so she avoided Main Street and zigzagged through side alleys, past back yards where hints of growth sent out small sensual botanic odors. The world was turning yellow, yellow everywhere: a low fence of white pickets, mostly broken, was tinged yellow, the tin roofs of half-rotted sheds glowed with a yellow shine. It was a late-March sun, a cold sun still, but warmly colored, hiding a tropical secret. Thrace in this bright hour was beginning to resemble all those other towns that had so amazed her with their unfamiliarity and lit her with a curious happiness. Here it was the towns that were foreign, not she, and she was drawn to everything that had no likeness to what she had known before. It was as if these unkempt straggly places could wash her eyes clean. She didn't much mind her errand, and she minded it now even less. James had promised her it would be the last; he was thinking, he said, of getting out of Thrace.

She made her clandestine purchase—not so clandestine after all; there were half a dozen other customers in that makeshift shop in a damply fetid basement. The proprietors were an elderly farming couple, half deaf and as ramshackle as their creaking house (the shingles were falling off, the porch was sagging), yet as cheery and innocent as if they were selling baskets of apples and pears. Their bottles were of all different shapes, and since James had asked her to bring him not one but two (why not, he told her, since these would be the last), she left with a pair of wrapped packages, the first of which might have been a narrow lamp, and the second a rounded pitcher.

It was a long walk back through the shortcuts she had discovered. The route that led from Main Street was far more direct, but the sunlight was new, and the little lifts of pleasure she detected circulating from her throat to her groin—they seemed to shiver with each heart-beat—took her by surprise. It was her old gladness—she didn't belong with her papa, she belonged with James! It was plain that she had made him understand this finally: for days and days he had stopped saying the thing that sickened her. How pleased she was that he had stopped! She followed him into their landlady's garden, grateful that he was all at once willing to catch the light. In his dour moods their room was becoming more and more cell-like, and the garden had the shamed yet brazen look of all back yards in Thrace. But the air was sweetening, and green points were pushing up around a mud-caked hose that prowled across the gray-ish earth. A silky wind shook her hair—it was always unbound now. She widened her nostrils to take in the perplexing mix of smells, impetuous bursts of grass, aging rubber, the sour excitements of James's sweat. He kicked at the hose; he was sweating, why was that, was it the schnapps? But he had announced that the lamp and the pitcher were the last, there would be no more, he was ready to leave Thrace behind, and good rid-dance to it. She was jubilant—they would soon be off in the liberating Ford, and oh, oh, where would they go?

57

THE MONEY had stopped coming. The house was asleep; only Bertram and I were awake. I was by now hardly the confident chatelaine who spilled dollars into Bertram's humbly waiting palms. He had entered, perforce, into the intimacies of our straits and stratagems. We sat at the dining room table, together calculating how to make do with what remained.

"No more wine," I instructed.

"The Professor's fond of it. It does his wife good."

"Bread or wine, one or the other."

"In that case, the staff of life. Wine."

"Bertram—"

"You never can tell, you could get another batch any day now."

"No," I said, "there's nothing," and heard in these hollow words an echo of Mitwisser.

A wild scratching at the green front door. It was not unusual: raccoons sometimes scurried at night up from the weedy woodsy outskirts of our neighborhood to sniff after the scent of habitation and its rinds and castoffs, bold enough to invade the very thresholds of human sancta. A feral scratching, a clawing, a beating, a bleating. A desperate creature. The noises went on and on, now with concentrated ferocity, now weakly, falling back in exhaustion or resignation. And then a girl's midnight convulsions.

Bertram let her in. He knew at once who it must be, but Anneliese was bewildered—had she mistaken the house after so many months? This small man, standing shocked in the doorway, no, no, she could not be mistaken, it was only the dizziness, yet here was a stranger taking her two hands, murmuring her name. . . .

"I live here," she told him. She could not think what else to say. The dizziness troubled her sight. She had fumbled for the doorbell and could not find it.

"So do I," Bertram said. In her loose dress, wound all around her, her body curled into itself, she was no better than an abandoned bundle. There were traces of dried vomit on the front of her dress. He picked her up and carried her in.

"Put her in her own bed. Take your things out of there and put her in her room," I said.

Bertram set her down and covered her shoulders with a blanket. She was shivering. She had brought nothing with her. A few coins dropped out of the pocket of her dress; it was all she had left. She had eaten nothing since leaving Thrace. She had not slept at all. On the bus she was sick. She tried to clean herself in the lavatory of the bus depot in the city, but her coat was too badly soiled, so she discarded it there, and then went down into the subway, and when the train drummed up from underground and ran along the trestle it was already night, and she felt sick again, and after that the half-blind walk from the street of shops, the dizzy blur, the small man opening the door, small but strong enough to lift her. . . .

The ends of her hair were sticky with vomit.

"Rose," she said. But she turned from me.

"Lie back. Bertram will bring you some tea."

"Where is papa?"

"You can see him in the morning. Lie back now—"

She obeyed. Her look slid nervously from side to side, as if tracking the movements of an invisible Japanese fan.

"Who is that man?"

"The bearer of mug and muffins," Bertram answered. "These should fix you up pretty quick."

The spoon wobbled in her hand. Bertram fed her bits of warm muffin. One by one she accepted them; one by one she spit them out.

"I can't," she said.

"You can"—Bertram's most maternal tone.

"Papa will be so angry—"

"If you swallowed a few crumbs? That's sure to get his dander up, won't it?"

"Bertram, don't tease. Let her be."

"The poor kid." A burble of vomit trickled over the blanket. He wiped it away and bent over her. "You want to sleep now, all right?"

Her eyes kept up their rapid waverings. I thought she must be hallucinating—what did she see?

"He will be so angry," she said again. It fell from her faintly, hoarsely, imploringly—but it was Bertram she was invoking. Abruptly she seized his wrist. "Why are you here? Why do you live in this house?" She pulled him nearer. "Is it for papa? Do you give papa money for his work?"

Her last errand in Thrace was for her papa, she said. She said it excitedly, pressing against Bertram, appealing to him. James had sent her out, not for schnapps—the two bottles were finished, he wanted no more. She must take another packet to the post office, he told her: it had been too long, there was no time for a letter. She watched as he cautiously backed the Ford up a narrow trail, hidden from the street, that sidled along their landlady's shabby garden. The Ford had been languishing where they had left it so many weeks ago, and its glossy black paint had grown brown with dust and spatter. A film of dried mud crusted the running board. Then she saw him tugging at the tangle of hose, and knew that he meant to rinse the auto clean before they set out.

She disliked going to the post office. It brought her within sight of the high school, and she disliked the high school, she disliked it that James had led her there, she disliked the schoolyard where he had laughed so bitterly.

It was bright noon. She heard the treble din of girls' shrieks from the schoolyard, and the repetitive thuds of a basketball on concrete, and the bellowing of young males. The post office was antiquated and ill-lit, with grooved wooden counters and a wooden grill, behind which the clerk in his formal collar and vest scowled as he weighed her packet on his brass scale. It was fatter than it had ever been before. A wall of murals loomed over her, Indians tending bonfires and Pilgrims harvesting, and across from these a dim flat row of locked brass boxes. James had the key to one of them, and sometimes came to collect a message, or whatever it was, from an old acquaintance named Brooks. It was plain that he loathed this Brooks; yet there was a sort of communication between them, if only now and then. He had given her the key: he had never before entrusted it to her. She opened the box and peered into it: it was long and dark and empty. The key was useless now, James said, she could toss it away if she pleased — but instead she surrendered it to the clerk, who took it with a speckled hand. She was impatient to slough off this relentless Thrace, to be rid of that speckled hand, and the brutal thump of the canceling stamp, and the screeching schoolyard nearby, and their spectral landlady's indifferent meals simmering all day on a greasy stove, and that shadowy languorous room.

A ragged privet hedge obscured the Ford as she approached, but when she went round to the garden side of the house she saw it. It did not look very clean after all, and the sun struck the windshield with so sharp a twelve o'clock glare that it made a blue-black spot on her retinas. Behind the blue-black spot the windshield wiper was shifting left to right, right to left, back and forth, in a frenetic beat. Under the falling sea of sunlight the wiper made a little hopping song: *whish-whoosh*, *whoosh-whish*, with a tiny squeal when it changed direction. The motor was on, rumbling and hiccuping. James must have stepped into the house to fetch their things. Shoeprints marked the dust on the running board. The Ford was alive and ready.

James was not in the house. He was in the Ford. His head was heavy on his chest. His hair, uncut for weeks, drooped over his eyes. He seemed mesmerized by the sun's dazzle, and by the sweeping music of the windshield wiper, tolling like a clapper. The Ford's windows were shut, all but one, and this one open only enough to leave a gap for the snout of the hose to slip through. She followed the hose to its tail. The tail was plugged into the auto's exhaust pipe.

Bertram was still in her grip. She threw off the blanket; she would not relinquish him; he let her wail against him.

A softness on the stairs: Mrs. Mitwisser in her nightgown, restless and barefoot. Her daughter's voice, low though it was, had risen to her. I almost believed she had a dog's hearing, or else she was like the hapless man in the fairy tale whose ears are so sensitive that he must stuff them up, lest he be compelled to listen to all the stirrings of earth and cosmos; a gnat's wings are thunder for him.

"That one? That one?" She searched all around. But there was only Anneliese in her dirty dress, clinging to Bertram.

She pushed me aside and gaped. "*Mein Gott! Sie ist schwanger—*" She rounded a hand over her own belly.

"Papa will be so angry," Anneliese whispered.

But Mrs. Mitwisser had gathered herself up; her whole face shone, her teeth shone like armor; she was all at once a force. With the assurance of an empress she called out to Bertram, "You will marry my daughter, *nicht wahr?*"

Bertram produced his conciliatory smile. An ambassador's smile. An invader's, a colonizer's. "Not yet," he said, "not yet."

58

THE NEXT MORNING saw a perplexing scramble of sleeping arrangements—mattresses transported from here to there, sheets set flying. It was very like the day James had come into the house; only then Anneliese had presided over the turmoil. All night she dozed unquietly, startling into wakeful fright. Bertram kept up his vigil—the fitful clutching of her fist, her face pressed hiddenly into the pillow that yesterday had been his. Shaking with resolve, Mrs. Mitwisser ordered Waltraut's bed to be trundled out to take its turn opposite mine, while her own was carried into the boys' room; it was to be Bertram's. And what of Mrs. Mitwisser, alone left standing in this game of musical chairs—nine players, eight berths—where was she to lay her head?

"I go to my husband," she said.

He submitted to it wearily. My typewriter was out of sight, shoved behind raw heaps of manuscript. His table was unrecognizably bare. His study, which I had felt to be the furnace of a laboratory where revolutionary affinities raged into conflagrations, was now no more than a commonplace marital chamber. I had no place in it. He was a monarch who had abdicated. He had recovered his daughter, but in humiliation. He was weakened; only his wife was made strong. The Karaites were surrendered to their oblivion. Al-Kirkisani was silenced. Mitwisser's aimlessness became mine.

I was aimless, I had no place in this house. Bertram ruled it. "There is sickness," he told the boys: they must not distress Anneliese, they must not come near. The warning sobered Heinz, it sobered Gert; but Willi took to taunting me. "Papa doesn't want you anymore, mama doesn't want you," he sang. And when he was sure no one heard: "Mrs. Tandoori! Mrs. Tandoori!" I was reduced, Waltraut was now my bedroom companion, and what was I?

Together, Bertram and Mrs. Mitwisser deliberated over Anneliese. She must not get chilled. She must have proper nourishment. They bustled around her, tempting her with this dish and that. Bertram could seduce sparseness into delicacy: his ideas, as he called them, were growing more and more ingenious. The money was dwindling; he was careful to be frugal. He had begun to shop as I had when I was a child, cadging vegetable leavings from the greengrocer. There was no meat. There was no more wine.

I was shut out from all but Mitwisser. His melancholy lured me to whatever unlikely corner he might settle into, turning round and round, a large restless animal. His stricken shoulders were hunched like a bison's. In the kitchen Mrs. Mitwisser was cutting up celery for one of Bertram's magically long-lasting stews, while Waltraut stirred at her feet, or went trailing after Bertram: the three of them were a cadre of industry. When Mitwisser rose, heavy in his big bones, I went after him. He did not object. He moved up and down our unobtrusive street—an airier version of those indoor pacings—and surveyed the row of housefronts with their identical stoops and stumpy lone evergreens planted like sentinels. "Where am I?" he muttered. "Why am I here?" He wore his mourning like a corruption. I watched him. I divined him; I absorbed him. I saw how he was fallen.

"Come down to the water," I said.

His sons in their noisy wanderings had now and again gone hurtling to the miry edges of our neighborhood, where the cattails and sharp rocks skirted a trickle of inlet. But Mitwisser, self-confined, had kept aloof from this small geography. His soil was alphabet, his sky was parchment. He let me take his hand—how broad it was, and rough—to draw him to the water's lip. We entered a boggy softness. Seagulls trafficked overhead. Seaweed smells lifted around us, as tactile as a skein. And before us rippled this tiny tributary of the Atlantic, whose outer limbs touched the docks of Hamburg and Stockholm.

"My daughter," he said.

"Bertram's taking good care of her. So is your wife."

Heavily he mounted a high flat boulder, and stood there like some great extinct Viking at the helm of a wooden ship.

"My wife is without remorse. My daughter has redeemed her."

I knew his thought. He was hemmed in by willful transgressors. Rebels swarmed around him. His wife had betrayed him; his daughter; his nation. Among these weed-slimed stones the street lamps of Berlin, the cafés, the salons, the honors, were as remote as myth. And ah, ah, once he had been infatuated with transgression and rebellion! With the spurned and reckless exiles of the past!

"Tell more about James," I urged. "There must be more—"

"Why should you wish this?" A gargling sound escaped him. He spat out a viscid clot. "The wise man speaks of ideas, the middling man of actions, the fool of persons. This, my dear Rose, is an intelligent proverb of the Arabs." He stepped clumsily off the rock; it was nearly a plunge. "How poisonous it is to breathe in this wasteland. What is this stink the wind brings?"

There was no wind. The crowns of the cattails barely swayed. "Seaweed and dead fish," I said.

59

I ALSO WATCHED BERTRAM. He was preoccupied with Anneliese: Mrs. Mitwisser was his satellite. In the mornings, huddled under her mother's shawl, Anneliese was brought into the dining room to be enthroned and fed. The boys were afraid of her. She shut her eyes and turned from them. Motionless, swollen under her wrappings, she was as cryptic as an idol. Often she wept secretly. She spoke only to her mother and Bertram.

Bertram's Ninel-fevers were evaporating. I had supposed that the commodity he held in common with Anneliese — that operatic tragedy of a pair of dead lovers — would inflame his lamentations. Yet of late he rarely said Ninel's name, and then solely, he explained, when Anneliese probed.

"She wanted to hear how I lost her. It was a mistake to tell, it broke her up."

"Maybe they'll meet in heaven, those two — Ninel and James. James the ideal moneybags, he could've outfitted Ninel's whole brigade."

"Leave it alone, can't you? The poor kid's suffering."

"You're not. You're over it."

"Well, Ninel did walk away from the likes of me, I'll grant you that." He came close, frowning resolutely. It was a frown of earnest monition. "You ought to be thinking about getting out of here, you know? Look around, there's nothing for you. What have you got? The old man?"

He had begun to refer to Mitwisser in this way. For Bertram, Mitwisser no longer weighed in the household's scales.

"What this place needs," he went on, "is a good midwife." The frown was rapidly transmuted into Bertram's inconstant grin. "Can't you just see Ninel sticking with a midwife? It's the way the peasants do it, she'd like it. If I'd been a midwife from the start, she'd've married me."

"She didn't believe in marriage anyhow. You said so yourself."

"Meant to give her a ring once, in spite of it. Never told her. Put it away, just in case. I had my hopes."

"Ninel wouldn't dream of wearing a ring, you know that."

"I guess not. Just the sort of thing she loathed." But he said this dispassionately.

"Bertram," I pressed, "you aren't really intending to do that—"

"What? The delivery? Why not? It's not so hard. I've seen plenty. In the hospital we used to call them catchers. Not to mention that I've got two experienced assistants, Elsa and Mother Nature. Elsa's had five of 'em, and Mother Nature's had millions."

"It's not right, she's got to have a doctor, she ought to go to a hospital—"

"You're forgetting who these people are. The haute bourgeoisie. They don't admit to these things, they're not supposed to happen. If they happen they don't expose them. They're the ones that're keen on wedding rings. The old man especially."

"No one knows them here. There's no one to judge."

"They judge themselves," Bertram said.

Ninel had faded: Bertram was enlisted elsewhere. I marveled at this abrupt expulsion of Ninel's persistent ghost. Only days before she had been vivid enough—her penumbra could be made to brighten at a word; it could glimmer out of a heap of discarded shoes in a bin. But Bertram sided with the immediate. What was nearest at hand moved him—moved, pushed, repositioned. He was attracted to risk, not for himself—the hazards of life lured him. In his mild watercolor way he sniffed after causes, after crusades. Hadn't I once (how long ago it seemed) been one of his causes? Yet at heart I had no use for causes, and Bertram had no use for me; he was ready to exile me again. The spite of justice: what did this signify? Does spite bring justice, is justice always an act of spite? Whatever he meant by it, it had leached out of Ninel's ectoplasm into the living cells that were forming, by day and by night, in the secret recesses of Anneliese's flesh.

She had turned illicit. She believed she must be a criminal. Her crime was inscribed in her papa's melancholy—mutely he condemned, helplessly he mourned. Her mother—how strangely she glowed, how queerly she gloated: James was not in the house, he was routed, she had had her victory. But was her mother's victory over James, or was it over her papa? Or was it because of Heinz? A mysterious simulacrum of Heinz was budding inside Anneliese's own belly, a creature her papa would stare at sidewise, or else would glance too quickly away from, or else would praise and praise overmuch; a creature under perpetual, undying, triumphal suspicion. Oh, how jumbled it all was, they were trying to make her eat and drink inside the whirligig that dizzied and sickened her, her eyeballs were driven from side to side, and couldn't they see how her arms had become spinning knives whose points pierced whoever came near, and if one of the boys so much as looked at her she would slice him to pieces! She wanted none of them, not one, not Waltraut, never her papa; only Bertram, who had lifted her and carried her into her old bed and nursed her through the first night, and all the nights afterward. Sometimes she felt that Bertram too was growing a tiny curled worm inside his own body: how else could he know so purely, so deeply, her smallest sensations? She wanted his hand to keep close to her, and the soft translucent web-skin between his fingers to fondle; and when the engine that rotated her brain was at its fiercest, she drew his hand between her legs, like a kind-hearted cup.

The packet from Thrace arrived, shockingly thick, stuffed with hundred-dollar bills. It was bloodied by a long row of reddish stamps.

"I told you, didn't I?" Bertram crowed. "You see? We're in the money again." He licked his thumb and, one by one, counted out five bills. "Here," he said, "I guess I owe you this."

I protested, "It's not yours to give."

"Why not? Have a look, there's a fortune here. And plenty left over."

"I don't want it, Bertram, and you can't do this, the money's for the house. It isn't yours."

"This much is yours anyhow, so take it. You'll need it when you go."

"It's for the house," I insisted, and shoved the bills back into their packet.

He twisted up his mouth, half thoughtful, half beaming. "And aren't I the house nowadays?"

60

Fullerton, Brooks, & Winberry
One Wall Street
New York, N.Y.
March 19, 1937

Professor Rudolf Mitwisser
328 St. Peter's Street
The Bronx, N.Y.

Dear Professor Mitwisser:

This office has been belatedly notified, by Detective Martin Corrie of the Police Department of Thrace, N.Y., of the untimely death of my client, James Philip A'Bair. It is my duty to inform you that in a letter addressed here on June 12, 1936, my client has designated you as his sole heir. Pursuant to this matter, the relevant documentation will follow in due course. You should be aware that Mr. A'Bair's estate, denominated in part as "Bear Boy Royalties and Rights," is in possession of assets of considerable value.

Very truly yours,
George C. Brooks, Esq.

61

THE MONEY FROM Bear Boy Royalties and Rights was delayed by several months. There were, to begin with, certain obligatory inquiries and investigations; there were reports and many more letters; there was a whisper concerning Surrogate's Court; there were dozens of discussions and ruminations and speculations—how rattled the landlady must have been, coming home that night to find the dinner heating in the double boiler untouched, and the body of her tenant already cold in the Ford. The shrieks, the excitement, the police, the identification: a passing notoriety in dusty Thrace; the town boys swarmed round to stare. A drunkard, hardly ever out of that stuffy room, and the stuck-up girl with the ugly accent and the long hair, who could figure what those two were up to? At least they'd been good for the money.

And the Ford, was it rusting now in her garden, red-browning into a surreal sculpture, sparrows nesting in the seats, the windshield knocked out? She was not so wasteful. The weathered pair of old wicker chairs that had once been in the garden, where they were beginning to rot in the sun, had been hauled upstairs to furnish her room-to-let. She was eager to sell the Ford. It would make up for the rent that henceforth would always be missing: a suicide's ghost is restless, everyone knows it returns to its last habitation, who would pay to sleep in a suicide's bed? And since Bear Boy Royalties and Rights, in the person of Mr. Brooks, made no claim against her for the return of the Ford, or for the equivalent of its value (he thought it a worthless detail), she was free to enjoy the dead man's bounty. It was almost as if he had left it to her.

Inquiries, reports, speculations; and finally Mr. Brooks himself, who came to us on a warm Sunday afternoon toward the end of October. Though the air still smelled of summer—a drift of seaweed up from the bay—he wore a gray tweed vest under a camel's hair overcoat. He was a widower who had the dryness of a man who has been long married to his firm. His purpose, he told us, was to make the acquaintance of his late client's chosen legatee. His visit would be brief; he had instructed his chauffeur to return in an hour. Bertram led him into the dining room, where he placed his hat on the table and declined to take off his coat. He had a freckled bald head; the lobes of his ears were scarcely formed, and grew directly back into the sides of his neck, and the wings of his nose— the nostrils' lobes—did exactly the same: flat and only faintly indented, they retreated into the surrounding pink flesh. Power and plenitude lived in that flesh. The careful nostrils took us in like an extra pair of eyes. They warned that just below them lurked a cold moral force: a mouth accustomed to speechifying.

His business here, he began, had a personal aspect.

It was Bertram he was addressing. His look dismissed whatever struck him as unnecessary. Waltraut and the boys had been standing gawking in the doorway—with the arrow of his elbow Bertram pointed them away and out of sight, into the silence they were pledged to. He had explained the lawyer's arrival as a momentous thing: it would disclose their future; but their future depended on their decorum, and their decorum depended on their silence. He herded them into the kitchen, where he had set out a row of baked apples, as a bribe. The sweet autumnal fragrance eddied through the house. Mr. Brooks had been announced, awaited, prepared for. James's gold-rimmed teacups were out, and the china teapot, and the rosebud-frosted little cakes that had not been seen since that August night long ago, when Mitwisser's doubters had come to assail him. They had believed him to be godless, and I, a novice at his feet, had believed the same.

I was no longer at his feet. He was sunk into his chair. I hovered behind him, as if tending a child in a pram. His big hand crept upward to feel for mine; he gripped it and would not let go. The months since Anneliese's return had aged him horribly. It had become his habit to shut his eyes when we walked out together—there was nothing he wished to see. We often went on walks, he and I, and always he sought out my hand. By now I was used to the map of his broad coarse palm, and those great hard knuckles bulging. When he spoke—he spoke little—it was usually of his wife. "My wife," he said, "is well. I observe how very well she is." But his eyes were half shut, and he stepped cautiously beside me, like a blind man. "You see for yourself," he said, "how well she is. My wife has come back to her life, is this not so?"

Mrs. Mitwisser had put on her blue pumps, to please Mr. Brooks. Her teeth gleamed contentedly: her smile was meant to adorn the hour. I saw how robust she had become. The middle of her small frame had widened—her stomach had grown a mildly protruding hillock—and her breasts and arms were roundly thick. Bertram cooked; Mrs. Mitwisser ate, always with fresh appetite. She was fat and strong and glad. Her gladness appealed to Mr. Brooks to notice her importance; to attend to the new importance of the house.

He ignored her. She was secondary and therefore unnecessary. He hadn't had Felix drive him back-of-beyond into the Bronx sticks to trifle with the secondary. He hadn't expected to be maneuvered into a place with so many chairs, at a table set for a party, what was the matter with these people? There were too many of them pressing all around, he wasn't their guest; he had come on his own steam. And he wasn't a peddler out to display his wares. First that mob of ogling children—finally it had dawned on someone, evidently the beneficiary himself, to pack them off, though even now there was an annoying clatter of spoons behind the door. And this bold overeager woman with her foolish twinkling beribboned ball slippers! Did she imagine herself a middle-aged Cinderella, about to be carried off to the palace? And over there the old fellow, mentally out of it probably, hanging on to his caretaker, why did they bring that one into it, what was the point? It was the heir he had come to survey, not this gaggle of gapers.

"I will admit," he told Bertram, "that my late client took me by surprise, though not for the first time. He has been, what shall I say, difficult, difficult since his teens. That such a cherub of a child should turn ... but it's not for me to judge. He was very young when the father died. Gifted man. Worldwide reputation. The firm made every attempt to stand *in loco parentis*, and I can't say it's been easy. A young man of whims. A maverick all his life, you could never depend on him to settle down. I'll tell you frankly, sir, this legacy is merely the latest of innumerable whims—unfortunately there's no remedy for it."

"You mean it can't be undone," Bertram said. He too had dressed for the lawyer. He had borrowed Mitwisser's jacket and tie. Traces of a lost regnancy clung to the creases in those elongated sleeves; they swallowed up Bertram's short arms, encasing him in their worn authority.

"I regret to say no. We've been through probate, it's all in order. I believe if my partner Fullerton were alive he'd have found some way around it, he was good at that sort of thing. Mental incompetence, the boy was never stable. There's no responsibility in it, from start to finish. Sends a letter, does himself in. All these years the firm pleaded for a will, something respectable. He wouldn't hear of it, everything loose, he had to have his way. I thank the good Lord his mother and father didn't live to grieve over what became of him. A wild man. A savage."

"*Wahrheit!*" Mrs. Mitwisser burst out. "*Barbarisch!*"

The vestigial earlobes paled. "My dear woman, what I say of my client is not for you to say. Let me remind you that you people are being enriched by this savage. The assets he leaves are immense, and none of his doing. His father's labors created him, he was nothing in himself. To my mind, it all goes down in dishonor." He turned back to Bertram. "If you ask me, the letter was mad. I'm all for learning, I've got nothing against learning. A library, a museum, a university, normal philanthropy! Something public and understandable. I wouldn't have cared if he gave it to the church, not that he'd ever do the decent thing. But this foreign parochial rot no one's ever heard of, no point or purpose in the real world, a private hole-in-the-wall hobbyhorse, a uselessness, a foolishness . . . well, my hands are tied. I won't conceal from you that I regret it. I regret it deeply."

"Then why do you come here?" Mitwisser muttered from the depths of his chair; he kept me in the vise of his fist.

But Mr. Brooks's look was on Bertram. "What's done is done. The fool threw it all away. I came to see for myself where it landed. You, sir," he told Bertram, "are the beneficiary of a fool."

Bertram drew out the angle of his smile. "Not me. It's the old man you want. What I am," he said, "is the son-in-law."

How he loved to pronounce these words! *Son-in-law, son-in-law:* they were still new in his mouth, not three months old. They were newer than the crib, the mattress for the crib, the tiny baby things, the baby bottles, the diaper pins—and anyhow these were not strictly new.

Bertram had found them all at the Salvation Army store under the trestle, a train stop away. The birth itself had gone well, with Elsa knowledgeably at hand and Mother Nature, as Bertram liked to say, in charge of the rest. Mother Nature was now a vivid presence among us. It was Mother Nature who brought on Anneliese's pains, and Mother Nature who accounted for her frights. Mother Nature allowed Heinz and Gert to watch the baby's head pulse itself out, and to see the umbilical cord severed; but Mother Nature in her wisdom kept Willi and Waltraut away. Mitwisser had shut himself up in a corner of his study (no more a study), as if hoping to hide in some dark crevice. But it was three in the afternoon, and the window was awash in thick light. The light had become entangled in Mitwisser's beard, bleaching it whiter yet, when Mother Nature gave her final signal; and then the birth wail rang out.

The child was called Miriam. Mrs. Mitwisser was gratified. "My mother's name," she said. Her fingers rubbed the place under her blouse where the scars had begun to fade. It was nearly a year since she had left the house. She squeezed into her blue pumps: "We go now," she insisted happily. She had never before set eyes on the great city; though they had docked at New York, the Quakers had sent a van—it was a kind of autobus—to carry them straight from the ship to Albany. Such buildings, such a city! They rode (she, and Anneliese, and Bertram) on something like the S-bahn, at first up high, curtains dangling over windowsills, and then even higher, flat tenement rooftops, and then a narrow curving river, and then, suddenly, the blinking tunnel. When they came out on Chambers Street, it was not at all like Berlin (the dear Berlin that had been *theirs*, before those insect-leg flags infested the storefronts), but also not unlike it. The morning whirl, the young women hurrying to their offices, the busyness, the streetcars, the traffic—only here the policeman had no wooden platform to stand on, and the churches were merely copies of real churches: they pretended to be old. She almost thought the three of them would run into Hermannplatz around the corner, and the big Karstadt with its escalators and floorwalkers—and how was this square, and that patch of green, different from Königsplatz? The Municipal Building, a gray wall rising from shadowy elephantine arches, might just as well have been the Staatsoper! Her heartbeat was loud in her ears, her toes throbbed in the blue pumps. The

City Clerk's office was not very clean, chewing-gum wrappers in the seats, disinfectant in the air. Twenty-four hours between the license and the ceremony: they had all been here the morning before, the same hour's ride in the S-bahn, the same mock-cathedrals, the same half-vision of Hermannplatz and Königsplatz; and again these darkened elephantine portals. A voice summoned her forward: she must identify herself as the witness. She had no wedding ring of her own, Fritz had taken it from her, there was nothing to put on Anneliese's bridal finger—but look! Bertram was ready with a ring, it had come to him from his mother long ago, he had meant it for someone else, it was too large for Anneliese, but never mind, it would do for the little ceremony, which was no ceremony at all, only a fleeting transaction in a bureaucrat's tedious day. The dusty artificial flowers on the City Clerk's desk made their obeisance, and Bertram and Anneliese were man and wife.

Mr. Brooks was irritated. He had not come to be duped further. It was more than enough that James Philip A'Bair, Sr., a gentleman if there ever was one, world-renowned, an acclaimed virtuoso (insofar as Mr. Brooks understood these things, the main point being that after all these years the royalties never ceased, in fact they grew, they accelerated, it was almost too much for a single firm) . . . wasn't it deception enough that so industrious a father, call him an artist but never a bohemian, should have the fruit of a lifetime's toil fall into the hands of some crackpot refugee? Mr. Brooks was chagrined, resentful: why hadn't he recognized right away that this ingratiating little man wasn't the one, he spoke without an accent, and all the rest of them . . . not that he could tell anything about the old fellow's caretaker, that girl holding on to him as if he'd tumble out of his chair if she ever let go . . .

The lawyer said formally, "Then I take it you are not Rudolf Mitwisser?"

"The son-in-law," Bertram repeated, and Mr. Brooks, who knew how to read the fine print, heard in that defining "the" a certain calm proprietorship.

"As I say, we have here a fait accompli," Mr. Brooks resumed, "yet I doubt he'd think of it on his own. I have in mind that my client was influenced—"

"Not by me."

"But you reside in this household—"

"When I got here he was gone."

Mr. Brooks stared all around. His client was capricious, willful, with the easy susceptibility of the willful, attracted to this and that. That recurrent fixation on Sweden, for instance, how he'd tried to get up to Scandinavia from Algiers, of all places, and during the war! Would that have been the next round of nonsense? After this present mania? Mr. Brooks remembered the freakish theater interlude, the costly refurbishment of a marginal troupe. . . . Someone in this house had infected him. Not the woman in the silly shoes—not clever enough, or she wouldn't have made herself so obvious an antagonist. So this old fellow was the one who was named in the letter, but good Lord, debilitated, powerless! He couldn't influence a flea, and the mute girl behind his chair was there only for what? To catch the old man's drool?

This house! This whim! Narrow and tall, three stories high—it had the configuration of a doll house. Mr. Brooks had gone through three brokers to accommodate his client's obstinacy. A quiet neighborhood. Nearby greenery. Reasonable access to the Library on Forty-second Street, what a stipulation! Everything a whim, every whim a crisis. He was under a spell; he was influenced. And he drank—don't forget that. He drank, he was open to influence, he was nothing in himself, what a descent from the distinguished father, what a squandering of a fortune!

The woman in the Cinderella shoes pivoted her hot victorious eyes upward, attending to a scarcely audible harmony of squeals. A girl carrying a blanket was coming down the stairs. She appeared to be still in her teens. Earrings glimmering through a long cloak of very dark hair. Wedding ring on the appropriate finger, a loose bad fit. This girl, Mr. Brooks quickly saw, was anything but secondary; she was the lodestar of the house. Even the quiescent old fellow—Lord help us, the heir himself!—raised his sorrowful head. The kitchen door opened a crack, pouring out a path of light into the dimness at the base of the stairs, where the girl had paused to rearrange the blanket. The blanket squirmed, kicked, squealed: an infant was inside it. Standing in that suddenly bright alley, the girl shone from head to foot, as if her figure had been hammered out in bronze. She gazed into the infant's face, as round as a half-dollar. The forum at the set table in the nearby dining room hardly earned her glance. Mr. Brooks was conscious that he was being moved, in spite of himself, by this unaccountable apparition, this tall young madonna whose skin seemed coated in light. He was not here to have his feelings touched. He was here out of indignation, out of disgust for his client's stupidity. To have entangled himself with a swarm of penniless refugees! To have given everything away, all of it, for the sake of a forgotten Jewish sect! (This being the language of the letter: "a forgotten Jewish sect.")

The startling vision—the young madonna had struck him with an inexplicable tenderness—did not last. A deluge of yammering boys, dammed up until now, churned out of the kitchen and made for the blanket. The baby was abducted from its mother and passed, uncomplaining, from hand to hand; clearly it was used to being fondled by these ruffians. It ended in the lap of a small girl, who sat herself down on the bottom step and pulled at the tiny thing's socks, exposing the little naked toes. To Mr. Brooks the sight of these toes, as creaturely as some animal's paws, was all at once obscene.

But it was decided; he understood. Forgotten Jewish sect, my eye! Surely it was this refugee madonna who had finagled a fortune out of his client, it had to be . . . yet the instant Mr. Brooks was persuaded of this possibility, he discarded it. Too young; married anyhow, the baby and that ring. Lord only knows why the good-for-nothing did himself in. Crazed. The letter was crazed. Promote Rudolf Mitwisser's studies of, and so forth and so on. Was it the drink that did it? That going off to the Levant, did it turn his head? People get religious delusions of the brain in places like that, it wasn't a Cook's tour, after all. More's the pity, good New England stock twisted out of recognition. The father never dreamed of such an outcome.

His hat was surrounded by empty teacups. They had never been filled. He picked up the hat.

"Well," Mr. Brooks said, "so much for that."

Mrs. Mitwisser seized him by the sleeve of his coat. "Not to go!"

"I beg your pardon?"

"You must see first our baby! My daughter's child, black eyes!"

"Madam," he said coldly, "my driver is waiting."

"You don't look! You don't see!"

He looked. He saw. The tall young madonna, a tower of beauty.

"Bad, you do bad mistake!" The woman was accusing him; she was pleading with him. She importuned him not to misjudge them. He was in error, he was misjudging them all. His client had been a barbarian, he was not to assume that *they* were barbarians! Here was her proper son-in-law; here was her proper daughter. His client had brought them disorder, but now all was in order, only look, see, the pretty baby, the mother, the mother's husband, a proper family! His client's contaminations had been swept away at last.

What was the woman carrying on about? She held on to his sleeve.

"Elsa," Mitwisser called—a mumbling, a weakness—"why do you make this commotion?"

"This man, he will not see what we are!"

Mr. Brooks shook her off. "I see that well enough. Now if you please, I've got poor Felix circling out there."

Mitwisser unfolded his long bones inch by inch, laboring out of his chair. He went to stand between his wife and the lawyer.

"My daughter's child," he said, "is the child of James."

Mrs. Mitwisser instantly appealed to her son-in-law. "Ach, why must Rudi say this? Bertram, tell how everything is in order, he must not say this—"

But Bertram only gave her a little push. "Go away," he told the boys. "Get upstairs, scram! Heinz, take the baby from Waltraut. Waltraut, go with them. Willi, didn't I say not to poke your nose in here?"

Mr. Brooks took off his hat and again placed it on the table. Then he walked all around, cutting a furrow of silence behind him.

"Come here," he said finally.

The young madonna obliged him.

"Rudolf Mitwisser is your father?"

She nodded sleepily; her hands were absent-mindedly cupping her breasts. They were heavy with milk.

"And your child is the child of my late client? Will you swear to this?"

Anneliese nodded.

"No, no, my son-in-law, he is now the proper father," Mrs. Mitwisser broke in.

"Be quiet, Elsa," Bertram said.

"Then you must understand that Rudolf Mitwisser cannot be the legatee. In case of issue, issue inherits."

"So the old man can't get the money," Bertram said, "is that it?"

The lawyer scowled. "My client's child is my client's heir. What came before is abrogated. Null and void. There exists a child. The child takes legal precedence. The infant will require a guardian, customarily the mother—"

The colloquy continued. Bertram filled the gold-rimmed teacups and passed round the little frosted cakes; no one took any. But he himself bit into one of the cakes. In this instance, he explained, it was impractical for the infant's mother to assume the responsibility of guardianship. She was still too much an outsider, too untried. Too bewildered and unknowing. She lacked the necessary competence, she barely comprehended the custom of the country—imagine, only a little while ago she thought she needed a passport to cross from New York to Massachusetts! She was in crucial ways still a child herself.

"Your client had no scruples," Bertram said.

"*Barbarisch*," said Mrs. Mitwisser.

"Nevertheless," Mitwisser said into his beard, "he is the father of my grandchild."

Mr. Brooks retrieved his hat. "There we have it. It seems my client has been cheated of his wish, and I can't say that I mind. I don't suppose the infant'll go chasing after dead old sects, hah? Though you can never predict."

From somewhere overhead a pulsating howl began, growing wilder by the second. Anneliese looked frightened.

"Hungry!" she cried, and fled.

"Then who will be the guardian?" the lawyer asked.

"Now that you've seen the lay of the land out here," Bertram said, "isn't it obvious?"

62

A RIVER OF PAPERS: first, the waiver—Mitwisser must acknowledge and renounce his invalid status as beneficiary; the legacy will be ceded to the valid heir, a minor. Anneliese must attest to the identity of the natural father. Bertram must be appointed legal guardian to the heir until she should reach her majority.

After which, the house would be free of the lawyer—except if or when Bertram might wish to consult with the firm, for which there would be the usual fee.

"Well, Rosie," he said, "what d'you think of that? We're knee-deep in capitalism, the kid's a goddamn tycoon."

Bertram was now installed as administrator and conduit of Bear Boy Royalties and Rights.

"But you named her after Ninel."

"I didn't name the kid. Elsa did. Sentimental, that photo and all."

"She does whatever you want her to do."

"Look, her mother was called Miriam, she's stuck on her mother. All I said was why not honor the dead."

"Does Anneliese know that Ninel was really Miriam?"

"Now why would my wife want to know a thing like that? Why make a fuss over a pointless coincidence? Hundreds of girls are named Miriam."

"And Ninel was one of them. Anneliese's got her ring, the baby's got her name. What do you call that?"

"Exorcism," Bertram said, and I discovered that I believed him: for Bertram exorcism was the same as acquisition—one preceded the other.

Certain acquisitions, formerly unwelcome, entered the house. Bertram brought in a Victrola ("Elsa's stuck on Bach"), a telephone, a radio.

"Papa doesn't let mama have a radio," Heinz said.

"You've got one."

"It's mostly static on my set, and it's not a real radio anyhow."

The real radio was encased in a polished wooden cabinet shaped like a miniature Gothic vault.

"She'll hear bad things, papa says."

"There are always bad things," Bertram said cheerily. "You can't avoid them. Meanwhile I'm thinking we could use a car, but I'm afraid my wife thinks a car's one of the bad things."

Son-in-law. My wife. Bach came spinning out of the Victrola, over and over again.

Bertram disappeared for a whole day. When he returned, he revealed that he had gone to see Mr. Brooks about buying a house. The house was in Mr. Brooks's own neighborhood in Mr. Brooks's own county. It was a very large house. You could even call it a mansion if you wanted to be grandiloquent.

"In a few months we'll be out of this rabbit warren," Bertram informed me.

There were no more trips to the shops under the trestle. Mrs. Mitwisser was pleased to be put in charge of the household supplies. Her voice on the telephone, ordering groceries and seeing to the hour of their delivery, had the accustomed ring of a mistress interrogating a servant. Wine was restored to the table. The telephone seemed to have no other use, except for Bertram's infrequent conversations with Mr. Brooks. They were always brief. Whatever Bertram had to say appeared to satisfy Mr. Brooks.

It was understood that my task was to watch over Mitwisser. He clung to me uneasily, and became strangely anxious when for any reason I was called out of his sight. Bertram's sympathies, flowing everywhere (hadn't he quenched Elsa's thirst, confided to him alone, for Bach?), stopped before they reached Mitwisser; and anyhow Anneliese's child was the center of things, and engaged them all. The infant might just as well be infantry, Bertram joked, a whole military brigade—it crowded the house with scores of appurtenances and a range of precipitate noises not unlike gunfire. Waltraut declared the baby to be *hers*, and clumsily put on its bonnet and took it off again, while Anneliese warned her not to be rough. Life was turning on its hinge: they would soon leave this place, they would go where Bertram was taking them.

I sat with Mitwisser in the tiny back yard. He clutched my hand as usual. Or else we would walk, he with his eyes half shut, allowing me to guide him into the harmless familiarity of nearby streets. He had balked at revisiting the water's edge, even when the tide was high and the bay turned lionlike, heaping up its mane of foam and devouring the seaweed and its acrid smells. One day we went a little farther, in a new direction, and came to a rundown granite bench set in a rectangle of dry grass and a few reluctant tiger lilies. An old lilac bush, split down the middle and ailing, hung over the bench: several heads of purple florets, every head as big as a cabbage, sent their syrupy fumes rushing at us. A scarred metal plate sunk in the ground, partly covered by dirt, disclosed that the bench was a gift to the citizens of the Bronx in memory of Theobald Bartlett Vandergild, 1859–1913, Councilman and Promoter of Public Improvements. If this place was an improvement, it had no public but ourselves. It lured us; it led away from commotion. The house was all activity, all turbulence—it was like Albany before the move to New York; and yet it was not. At the heart of it stood the young madonna, her solemn face lit by serenity. Anneliese with her child; with her wedding ring. It dangled loose and large on the finger of her left hand; it was destined never to slip off. This was the hand that could not curl into a fist, these were the bones that Frau Koch had hammered. No ring would ever escape this invisibly misshapen finger. The ring was sympathy. The ring was rescue. The ring was her mother's dignity. Only her papa was sickened.

Under the lilac heads, in the autumnal thick of their jungly scent—they were untended and untamed and wildly sweet—I devoted myself to Mitwisser's gloom. Weakness was in his gait, his silences, his unwillingness to look up; but coiled in Mitwisser's brain was the force I knew. Deformed, displaced. He had invested his old powers in melancholia.

"They're starting the packing today," I said mildly. "Bertram's supervising, so your books won't get mixed up. Anneliese's helping—she's the one who can read the titles."

He made no reply.

"The new house has nine bedrooms, Bertram says. He says it'll fit the family exactly. A room for each of the boys, one for Waltraut, one'll be the baby's, and then two more"—I skipped over Bertram's designations for these: the marital chambers of Anneliese and her husband, of Mitwisser and his wife—"and one for your study."

"I have no need of a study."

I had lied twice. Bertram had not spoken of a study; and it was Anneliese alone who had made certain that the books should be properly categorized.

"There has to be a place for your work. All those boxes of papers, everything I've typed up over the months—"

"My dear Rose, haven't you understood?"

"I have. There's new life now."

"New life? For whom? Do you speak of James's child?"

"Anneliese's," I said.

"Your cousin's," he retorted; and now I heard his buried force.

"Bertram's not really my cousin—"

"What does it matter? The man has married my daughter. And my wife rejoices," he said sourly. "She who rejected manna now relishes it."

"It's not James's money anymore."

"Whose is it then? The child's? By which is meant my son-in-law. Manna in the hands of my son-in-law. Is it James's any the less?"

He was gripping my shoulders; his eyes were full of the sea when it turns purple at dusk. The lilacs had got into them.

"In the past it came and it went. And now it is to come and to come and to come."

"Isn't that what you wanted? To be free to think?"

He loosened me and fell back. "Does thought command what happens, or does what happens command thought? Can one put things right by thinking? What use are such conundrums?"

"Things *have* been put right," I said.

"By what means, by what means," he groaned. A panicked blue stare. "You will be leaving us soon, is this not so?"

I did not deny it.

And for the second time he flung the wilderness of his head into my arms.

"Oh my poor Rudi," I said, "my poor, poor Rudi."

63

THINGS HAD BEEN put right. Mrs. Mitwisser felt it. The boys felt it. Even Waltraut felt it, pulling on the limbs of the warm-blooded puppet that had come to stay. Anneliese surely felt it: the infant's smallest cry caused droplets to spring from her breasts; she hurried to snatch the child from Waltraut to save it from famishment. What could be righter than the round, round face of this tiny angel, its round eyes, the round red button of its mouth? The little fingers pressed tightly around Anneliese's finger, tighter than the ring Bertram had given her. She knew the ring had been intended for Ninel. She didn't mind; death was erasure. Ninel was dead, James was dead. But here was Bertram, more motherly than her own mother, and here was her living child, more beautiful than any child on earth—more beautiful than Willi, who was anyhow leaving beauty behind, turning from child to rugged boy. Heinz and Gert were nearly men—it was manly to have witnessed a birth almost without flinching. Bertram had made them brave. He had obliged them to gaze straight into Mother Nature's naked wisdom. And he had restored all three to their true names: Hank, Jerry, and Bill, he said, were signs of insincerity. Under Bertram's patronage they withered away. Bertram had put everything right.

I filled my two suitcases: my belongings had been few when I entered the Mitwisser household; they were fewer now. I quietly added *Hard Times* and *The Communist Manifesto* to one of the boxes of books being readied for the move to the new house. Willi saw.

"Those aren't papa's. You shouldn't put them in with papa's."

"I got them from Bertram and I'm giving them back. Bertram can sort them out later."

But I was almost certain the books would remain in their boxes. The new house was not friendly to books. Bertram, together with Mrs.

Mitwisser, had gone several times to look it over. Its last inhabitants (who had asked a pretty penny, he reported), owned horses and rode. There were so many windows that there was really no wall space to speak of, and without wall space it would hardly be possible to accommodate shelves. Besides, the old man was no longer inclined to bury himself in those unfathomable lucubrations. The abundance of windows was the most remarkable aspect of the house—all that light, those views!

"Views of what?" I asked.

"Big lawns. Houses even bigger. The neighborhood's swanky," Bertram supplied.

Willi had come to watch me pack.

"I'm going to have my own room," he announced, "the way it was at home." But he said this mechanically. It was a fading echo. Home— the life before—was vanishing for him, as it already had for Waltraut.

His hand went to the tattered Bear Boy. He picked it up. "James's thing," he said, and stopped. The name had slipped out. He had not meant to say it. Like Heinz and Gert, he would not or could not speak of James. It was a superstition about death; or else, to spare Anneliese, Bertram had cajoled them all into muteness. Was it Bertram, or was it superstition? One put things right, the other put them wrong. They came to nearly the same. James was being erased, already receding into the white light of myth that had swallowed Ninel.

"Give me that," I snapped, and folded a sweater around it and put it in the suitcase, close to the ruined sneaker that held the sum of my erstwhile salary. It was not very much; for many months the formality of payment had ceased. No one mentioned it; no one noticed. I did not expect it or miss it. Mitwissers were an organism, and I was part of its flesh.

Willi recovered his tongue. "Papa doesn't want to move, but Bertram says you'll get him to."

I hesitated. I had so far told no one; Rudi had breathed it out of the lilacs. Was I to begin by telling this wanton boy?

"I won't be coming with you. I'm going away."

He looked at me shrewdly. "Mrs. Tandoori! Mrs. Tandoori!" It was his old trick—jumping out of corners to stage-whisper *you're going to marry Dr. Tandoori*, and lately *you've got a baby in your belly, just like An-*

neliese. Willi too believed in Mother Nature, even when she was busy elsewhere; and in this domestic maelstrom of death and birth and a wedding ring, who could blame him?

The news reached Bertram instantly.

"You're doing the right thing," he beamed. "Here, this is yours really, I wanted you to have it long ago, only . . . well, there's no reason now not to take it." He tore a check out of his checkbook (another new acquisition), and placed it in my obediently open palm. Above his signature I read: *Five hundred dollars and no cents.* "That should last awhile," he said.

The turnabout made me self-conscious; my face heated up. The money that had spilled from my hand into Bertram's was now flowing in the opposite direction. Mother Nature herself had no power to change a river's course, but Bertram could convert downstream to upstream, Anneliese the fallen to Anneliese the wife, mad Mrs. Mitwisser to mundanely triumphant Elsa. And me he had released. I was freed. He wanted me out. I had no further responsibilities here. Like its ancestor in the blue envelope, the check was a bribe to chuck me from the scene.

"I've said it before, Rosie. You're not a kid anymore. It's time."

He kissed me, full force, crushing my lips against my teeth. Under the pressure of his mouth my teeth felt like shards of ice; his mouth pried mine. It was the kiss I had longed for in that old lost Albany flat: a man's kiss. There was nothing cousinly in its deep invasions. It was what Ninel had known. It was what Anneliese knew.

"My wife is pregnant," he said. And then: "Where will you go?"

My wife. His kiss was still wet on my lips.

"Oh, I don't know."

But I did know.

64

I WAS UNWILLING to leave so much as a trace. I resisted the possibility of being found someday, by Bertram or anyone. I was headed for the genuine New York of the skyscrapers. I saw myself as the counterpart of that hungry aspirant, the Young Man from the Provinces—modernity had granted the chance of untethered motion to my own sex. It was not my destiny to be planted in a single spot of the earth, like that other discarded amanuensis of another century, Dorothea Casaubon, deprived of the want ads in a New York newspaper by hard chronology. I had cut out several of these from the *Sun*, which nowadays lay beside Bertram's breakfast plate. The great city, whose high crenelations obscured the horizon, was all the same nothing but vista: innumerable offices were summoning innumerable typists. Here at the breakfast table Europe was distant and almost silenced. Armies were massing, but they were no more than the black ink of a headline or a stutter out of the radio. Though her quick ears were alert to the infant's slightest stir, Mrs. Mitwisser was growing deaf to the thunder of Europe. She was healthy and shining. Her body, in tune with Anneliese's body, was shutting out world-upheaval. She no longer fought it with madness, or with the formula for thermodynamical equilibrium. Anneliese's child was distracting her into normality; her son-in-law was distracting her; and the new house. Bertram had promised servants, a daily maid and a weekly gardener. She was drained of fury, and of fury's magnificence.

These were not my thoughts as I prepared to leave that cramped house in an inconspicuous region of the city; they came to me long afterward, when the Bear Boy, with its stained pages, was all I had left to remind me of my sojourn among Mitwissers. Like Anneliese's child, I too was the Bear Boy's heir. It had held my mother's death certificate.

My father, almost by instinct, had tossed for it. And if the Bear Boy had fancied himself a Karaite (so woven are past and future), it was all I had of the Karaites. Night after night the boy in the pictures insinuated his unspoken prophecies. They were old-fashioned, these pictures, and for the most part pastel-colored. They had the golden charm of nostalgia; but they could kill. The boy in the pictures—his bangs, his blue socks, his squint, the green hat, the dangling kettle—who, after all, would not pity him? He lay now in the troublesome grave Mr. Brooks had painfully contracted for: not every burial ground under the eye of heaven will welcome a suicide. Not far off, under the sanctified earth of Troy, my father lay in disgrace. Somewhere in Spain lay Ninel, in what I took to be a soldier's grave. And in a suburb of Baghdad, for a thousand years, lay al-Kirkisani, author of those forgotten Books of grandeur, *Gardens and Parks* and *Lights and Watchtowers*. He had seen the Ganges, he had defended Scripture against the false adornments of men, he had uncovered heresy in the Godhead itself. He had tunneled like a worm into Mitwisser's brain. His bones were Mesopotamian dust, yet they had permitted me to witness ecstasy.

On my last day, in its last hour, I found Mitwisser sitting alone on the bench below the lilac bush. The big purple heads were failing under the first autumn chill. He was wearing his hat. Bertram had given him a cane to walk with.

"I'm going now."

"Yes," he said.

A silence hung between us. I tried to think how to fill it.

"Anneliese's having another child. Bertram told me."

"It is what is natural."

"And Waltraut starts kindergarten—"

An irritable flick of the cane. "Please," he said.

He could not endure domestic talk, and now that the worm in his brain was withered, what else was I to say? I put my hand on his shoulder.

"I'll always think of you."

"Perhaps not. It is what is natural."

"Goodbye, Rudi."

"Yes," he said.

I moved a few steps away and turned.

"Will you walk back to the house with me?"

He lifted his cane. "I have here my new friend. He tells me to look sharp. He opens my eyes."

"Then goodbye. My Rudi, goodbye."

The boys were gathered before the green front door. Patches of the *Goldberg Variations* drifted out—masses of bees.

"Bertram telephoned for a taxi! Where were you?" Gert called.

"It came ten minutes ago," Heinz said, "and the meter's running."

There it was, a yellow hump in the street, its engine vibrating and giving off heat.

"Mama can't come down. She's helping Anneliese with the baby's bath, and Waltraut's up there too."

Bertram emerged, carrying my suitcases.

"You're all set now, Rosie. Off to the big world."

He pulled at the taxi door. Someone was crouched in there, hiding.

Out jumped Willi.

"Mrs. Tandoori! Mrs. Tandoori!"

Acknowledgments

Sources for the Karaites include *Karaite Anthology: Excerpts from the Early Literature*, edited by Leon Nemoy (Yale University Press, 1952), and *Karaites in Byzantium: The Formative Years, 970–1100*, by Zvi Ankori (Columbia University Press, 1957).

For assistance with German idiom I am grateful to Dr. Susanne Klingenstein.

Heir to the Glimmering World

by

CYNTHIA OZICK

"A cause for celebration in the world of literature. Here we have a heroine to love, a story we can't let go of, gorgeous sentences, and ideas to wrestle with. I didn't just read this book. I devoured it." —Ann Patchett, author of *Bel Canto*

About the Author

© MARION ETTLINGER

"[Cynthia Ozick] has magical gifts as a storyteller . . . A distinctive and utterly original voice." — *New York Times*

"One of the finest and most imaginative writers of our time." — *St. Louis Post-Dispatch*

CYNTHIA OZICK is one of America's most prominent women of letters, acclaimed for her many works of fiction and criticism. Ozick was a finalist for the National Book Award for her previous novel, *The Puttermesser Papers*, which was named one of the top ten books of the year by the *New York Times Book Review*, *Publishers Weekly*, and the *Los Angeles Times Book Review*. She received the National Book Critics Circle Award for her essay collection *Quarrel & Quandary*. Ozick's work has been translated into fifteen languages worldwide. Her classic novella *The Shawl* was produced for the stage in New York, directed by Sidney Lumet.

For Discussion

1. With the brisk pace of its plot, its plucky teenage heroine, and its tidy, satisfying conclusion, *Heir to the Glimmering World* may be read as an update of the nineteenth-century novel. How does Ozick employ this venerable literary style so it resonates with a twentieth-century story? What ironies are present in Ozick's novel that would be absent from a Victorian novel? *Heir to the Glimmering World* ends in 1937; how does your knowledge of world events of the next decade affect your perception of the ending?

2. How do Rosie's actions differ from the actions of, for instance, a character from her beloved Jane Austen or Charles Dickens, and how might Rosie behave if the story were to take place today?

3. Herr Rudolf Mitwisser cites an Arab proverb: "The wise man speaks of ideas, the middling man of actions, the fool of persons." In her novel, Ozick "speaks" of all three. How does she make *Heir to the Glimmering World* work on different levels — as pure entertainment driven by plot and character and also as a novel of ideas? What elements of the novel did you find most engaging?

4. While the novel hinges on some tragic turns of event, it is also bracingly funny. How would you describe the overall tone of the book?

5. The title *Heir to the Glimmering World* invokes the primary theme of inheritance. How is each character shaped by the legacy of the past he or she has inherited? How do their respective fortunes or misfortunes affect Rose, James, and the Mitwisser children? Who, in your opinion, is the ultimate, truest heir to the glimmering world?

6. When Rosie begins to work for the Mitwissers, she seems bewildered at being employed by such sophisticated intellectuals: a religious scholar and an experimental physicist. In the course of her employment with the Mitwissers, she comes to view them as the complex and imperfect people they are. Why and how does her attitude toward them change? What events or observations deepen her understanding of them?

7. *Heir to the Glimmering World* is filled with characters who are abandoned and dispossessed, characters who are running away or are made to run away. How are Ozick's characters refugees, in the literal and the figurative sense?

8. As a result of the changes in Hitler's Germany, Elsa Mitwisser has lost her appointment at the Kaiser Wilhelm Institute, her career, her home, and possibly her sanity. In response, she effectively removes herself from the world, yet she remains acutely aware of the activities of her family. Is her lunacy an act? What would she gain or lose from such an act?

9. Ozick writes of James A'Bair's childhood, "He was not a normal boy . . . he was his father's drawing, his father's discourse, his father's exegesis of a boy . . . His father had interpreted him for the world." James has unhappily tried his whole life to cast off an identity created by his father. Similarly, Rose is running away from her past, and Ninel tries to invent a new identity for herself. Are Ozick's characters ultimately successful in their pursuits? How are we burdened by others' perceptions of us? How do we all, in some ways, invent our own identities?

10. On the surface, James A'Bair appears to sweep whimsically through life; he drifts effortlessly into the lives of the Mitwissers, for instance. Yet he is a character with a deeply troubled soul. How does

Ozick reveal the two sides of James A'Bair? Do his troubles undermine his likability? Do you find yourself sympathizing with him? Why does Elsa offer only vehement disapproval of him? Do you think his fate is inevitable? Why or why not?

11. One key theme of the book is the power of interpretation: the validity of it, the necessity of it, and also the inaccuracy of it. How do Rudi's and James's lives revolve around the idea of interpretation? Do you believe the Karaites' rejection of all interpretation is defensible? How does this theme resonate in other ways in the novel?

12. Professor Mitwisser's professional studies center on religion, yet he does not seem to be a man of faith. Religion hardly plays a role in his family life. Do you find this odd? What does this say about Herr Mitwisser?

13. In his theater days, James offers money to bribe an indifferent child to learn to read. What does this action say about his complicated attitudes toward books and literature, toward his fortune, and toward children?

14. Ozick prefaces *Heir to the Glimmering World* with an epigraph from Wallace Stevens: "The absence of imagination had / Itself to be imagined." How does this thought relate to the novel?

15. Many details in the novel offer significant comment on the worth and power of books, from Rosie's fondness for nineteenth-century novels like *Emma, Middlemarch, Jane Eyre,* and *Hard Times,* to Elsa's reaction to Jane Austen, to Rudi's joy at receiving a rare text. What importance does literature have in the novel and in the world at large?

A Conversation with Cynthia Ozick

In Heir to the Glimmering World *there are several actual heirs, including the profligate James A'Bair—a character inspired by the son of A. A. Milne, creator of* Winnie-the-Pooh. *What was the source of this inspiration?*

Some time ago I happened on the obituary of Christopher Milne, A. A. Milne's grown son, whom we know mainly through Ernest Shepard's indelible illustrations of a small boy in short pants. At his death he was the owner of a bookshop hidden away in the north of England, having attempted all his life to slough off his identification with Pooh and Eeyore and all the rest. He wanted to flee from the artifice of his father's creation: he longed to become an autonomous adult, to be a *man,* not the object of nostalgic pilgrimages to a living shrine not of his making. Or so I thought, reading that obituary notice. In my novel the character inspired by Christopher Robin is named James A'Bair, eventually to be dubbed the Bear Boy. The Bear Boy struggles to climb out of what Thomas Mann called "the well of the past," the past that has immured him in an imaginary childhood. His single-minded aim is to escape being costumed forever in lace collar and rouged knees, forever five years old.

Professor Rudolf Mitwisser, beneficiary of the Bear Boy's profligate ways, studies an ancient Jewish sect of scriptural literalists—they rejected all interpretation. How does Mitwisser's obsession relate to the Bear Boy?

It would be grandiose to call my novel a novel of ideas, but I hope I may venture that it is a novel of at least *an* idea: the idea of the necessity of interpretation, but also the danger of interpretation. What makes a human being? Language first, and then imaginative interpretation—the human mind cannot live without it. Like all literalists, the Karaites stood against imagination and interpretation, and they vanished out of history's mainstream. The author of the Bear Boy books weighed down his son with so much ineradicable embellishment that the man could never free himself from the invented boy. Whether interpretation is too little or too much, a withering will follow.

Aside from the underpinning of ideas, your novel is a delight to read, with a delightful narrator, Rose Meadows. Does she see these thematic notions you've just described?

Hardly. She is only an untried motherless eighteen-year-old, carelessly abandoned by a feckless father. And anyhow, for the characters in any fiction, and above all for readers, theme is subterranean, implicit, unobtrusive, the invisible underside of the story. Rose, though, *feels* intelligently, and she is an acute observer: she takes things in while mostly standing apart. I compare her to the traditional Young Man from the Provinces, who enters, unprepared, into unsuspected complexities. She starts out as a witnessing eye, yet some of the complexities she encounters occur beyond her consciousness or view: the Spanish civil war, for instance, or incidents in Barcelona, Berlin, Cairo, Switzerland.

Is Heir to the Glimmering World *a comedy or a tragedy?*

The story ends with a wedding ring and a baby—the conventional requisites for comedy—so I suppose it can count as a comedy. Yet since world-upheaval is pervasive, and there are three deaths, some may regard it as an anatomy of melancholy. But novels are only chronicles of human lives (even if those lives are invented) and merely retell our confusions of light and dark, of loss and promise. What matters, I think, is the conviction that something significant is at stake.

You've published four collections of essays and eight books of fiction. Which kind of writing are you more attracted to?

Definitely fiction. Fiction is all risk, all discovery, all confidentiality — even secrecy. Essay writing verges on being a public act and is driven more by the intellectual faculty than by the imaginative. But fiction . . . when I say secrecy, I mean not only the long, long immersion in privacy and isolation, and the wooing of phantoms out of the air, but those bodiless concealments and disclosures of language that lurk in certain turns of dialogue, or the turn of an eye, or a hand, or a shaft of sky. A watchfulness, an almost perilous vigilance. A novel can be written, so to speak, out of "sociology," and it will still be a novel. But when a novel's sinews are bound up in the most fearful intimations of language, when setting down a phrase feels tantamount to ingesting the blood of demons . . . just *there* is the difference between the safety of prose and the lusts of art: think of the haying scene in *Anna Karenina,* or the Marabar caves in *A Passage to India.* Call it language, call it intuition, call it seduction, call it idea-as-emotion. It is a voluptuousness only the novel knows, and the elusive grail we poor scribblers helplessly chase.

MARINER BOOKS / HOUGHTON MIFFLIN COMPANY
For information about other Mariner Reader's Guides, please visit our Web site, www.marinerreadersguides.com.

Trust

"[Ozick writes] with the gusto of a virtuoso . . . Her
fluency is endless." — *New York Times*

Money and conscience are at the heart of Cynthia Ozick's masterly first novel, narrated by a nameless young woman and set in
the private world of wealthy New York, the dire landscape of
postwar Europe, and the mythical groves of a Shakespearean isle.
Trust is an epic tale of the narrator's quest for her elusive father, a
scandalous figure whom she has never known.

In a provocative afterword to the Mariner edition, Ozick re-
flects on how she came to write the novel and discusses the cul-
tural shift in the nature of literary ambition in the years since.

ISBN 0-618-47051-4

The Din
in the Head

"It is not unlike falling in love, reading the essays of
Cynthia Ozick. Here is a mind that is gentle and
fierce all at once." — *Los Angeles Times*

In her first essay collection since the National Book Critics Circle
Award–winning *Quarrel & Quandary,* Ozick revels in the sub-
lime, sensual, and undeniable power of literature — and what
she deems its ultimate manifestation, the novel.

Houghton Mifflin hardcover, available
in spring 2006, ISBN 0-618-47050-6

Visit our Web site: www.marinerbooks.com

"I didn't come here to fight. I've been watching ever since the calf wrestling, and I think you're helping Sammy," Morgan admitted.

Jolie blinked. Had she heard him right?

"I came to tell you that I'll do whatever I need to do to help you help him," Morgan continued. His amazing blue eyes softened— he was actually conceding.

"G-good," Jolie stammered. As she looked at him, she thought about trying to apologize again, telling him that she hadn't meant to hurt him. But she knew he would only deny that she'd hurt him in the first place. "That's the way it should be. Our past, what happened between us—"

"Is the past," he said, firmly.

"Yes. We should still be able to help these boys even though we once had feelings for each other and it didn't work out."

What else could she say? She'd just come up against one wall after the other with him; he'd made it clear there was no sense in rehashing old history that he had no desire to revisit. So she stopped trying.

For now.

Books by Debra Clopton

Love Inspired

*The Trouble with Lacy Brown
*And Baby Makes Five
*No Place Like Home
*Dream a Little Dream
*Meeting Her Match
*Operation:
   Married by Christmas
*Next Door Daddy
*Her Baby Dreams
*The Cowboy Takes a Bride
*Texas Ranger Dad
*Small-Town Brides
   "A Mule Hollow Match"
*Lone Star Cinderella
*His Cowgirl Bride
†Her Forever Cowboy
†Cowboy for Keeps
   Yukon Cowboy

†Yuletide Cowboy
*Small-Town Moms
   "A Mother for Mule Hollow"
**Her Rodeo Cowboy
**Her Lone Star Cowboy
**Her Homecoming Cowboy
††Her Unforgettable Cowboy

*Mule Hollow
†Men of Mule Hollow
**Mule Hollow Homecoming
††Cowboys of Sunrise Ranch

DEBRA CLOPTON

First published in 2005, Debra Clopton is an award-winning multipublished novelist who has won a Booksellers Best Award, an Inspirational Readers' Choice Award, a Golden Quill, a *Cataromance* Reviewers' Choice Award, *RT Book Reviews* Book of the Year and Harlequin.com's Readers' Choice Award. She was also a 2004 finalist in the prestigious RWA Golden Heart, a triple finalist in the American Christian Fiction Writers Carol Award and most recently a finalist in the 2011 Gayle Wilson Award for Excellence.

Married for twenty-two blessed years to her high school sweetheart, Debra was widowed in 2003. Happily, in 2008, a couple of friends played matchmaker and set her up on a blind date. Instantly hitting it off, they were married in 2010. They live in the country with her husband's two high-school-age sons. Debra has two adult sons, a lovely daughter-in-law and a beautiful granddaughter—life is good! Her greatest awards are her family and spending time with them. You can reach Debra at P.O. Box 1125, Madisonville, TX 77864 or at debraclopton.com.

Her Unforgettable Cowboy
Debra Clopton

HARLEQUIN® LOVE INSPIRED®

Recycling programs
for this product may
not exist in your area.

 LOVE INSPIRED BOOKS

ISBN-13: 978-0-373-18927-4

HER UNFORGETTABLE COWBOY

Copyright © 2013 by Debra Clopton

www.LoveInspiredBooks.com

Printed in U.S.A.

I will not leave you as orphans—
I will come for you.
                    —*John* 14:18

In memory of Ms. Jo,
Grandma Edith and Grandma Sylvia.
Thinking of each of you makes me smile.

Special thanks goes to Carolyn and Joyce for
the research trip to The Purple Cow—what a fun day
we had. I think you'll see the research paid off well.

Also a big thank-you to my editor, Melissa Endlich—
your insights and encouragement
in this new venture were spot on.

Chapter One

Sunrise Ranch, Dew Drop, Texas

"Calm down, son."

Morgan McDermott's father, Randolph, cut Morgan off at the pass with a rasp of exasperation—which in no way, shape or form even began to match the anger-fueled exasperation Morgan was struggling to contain.

An imposing figure at fifty-two, Randolph had hair as black as the Texas oil pumping from the herd of wells across the ten-thousand-acre McDermott family ranch. The only differences between the two men—who shared chiseled high

cheekbones and square-jawed features—
was the whisper of white at Randolph's
temples and twenty years. Randolph was
as physically fit and hard-headed as any
of his three sons.

"Calm down?" Morgan gave a harsh
laugh. "Are you kidding me? You go behind my back and hire my *ex*-fiancée, and
you expect me to calm down? For starters,
Dad, we're partners. I'm supposed to make
decisions like this *with* you. Second…"

Morgan was so shaken up by what he'd
just been told that he lost his train of
thought.

Jolie Sheridan, here.

Randolph pushed back from his desk
and rose, meeting Morgan eye to eye.
"You know as well as I do that we needed
a teacher and we needed one quick. Jolie
has graciously agreed to fill the position
for one semester—"

"I don't care if *she's* paying *you* to let her
teach the boys here at the ranch—I don't
want her here." Morgan would never use
this tone with his father under normal cir-

cumstances. But being blindsided by the knowledge that his dad had gone behind his back and hired the woman who had broken his heart was not normal circumstances. "We're supposed to discuss this kind of thing, Dad."

"I understand your feelings, but there was no time. Besides, Jolie is familiar with the school and will fit right in."

Logically it made sense, but that didn't ease the betrayal. Morgan remained silent, trying to grasp the reality of his situation.

"Your past is something I'd hoped you'd overcome by now. I hated that you got hurt when she left. We all did. That said, I've made a decision and it stands."

Morgan rammed a hand through his hair. "How do you expect me to—" He halted at the stern look his dad shot him.

"I expect you to act like a man, not a brokenhearted teenager nursing a grudge."

His dad's words stung. "I got over her a long time ago and you know it," he growled, not remembering the last time—

if ever—that he'd been this angry with his father.

"Did you?" Randolph studied him, unflinching, from across the wide oak desk.

"You know I did. That doesn't mean I want to be around her for the next four months."

"You're strong. You'll make it. Maybe God worked the details out so you can come to some kind of peace with the situation. You may have gotten over Jolie, but you haven't forgiven her. You can't have peace until you do that."

This was a no-win situation. Yanking a noose tight around his emotions Morgan snatched his hat from the hat rack. "I'm late," he said, turning to leave. He pushed open the door of the Sunrise Ranch offices, his father's words trailing him.

"Mind your manners, Morgan McDermott. And remember, those boys out there are watching every move you make and learning from you."

"Some partnership," Morgan growled as the blazing Texas heat hit him full force.

It didn't begin to compare to the sizzling heat of his fury.

His life had just turned into a train wreck.

Ramming his hat onto his head, Morgan battled to get a grip on his anger. Stalking across fifty yards of white-rock gravel separating the barns from the office and chow hall, he fought to rein in his emotions. He had a herd of boys enjoying a very special moment in the barn and he intended to be a part of it come baseball-size hail or high water. And he knew—without his dad reminding him—that they didn't need to see him furious.

Sunrise Ranch was a working cattle ranch and foster home for boys who needed stability in their lives. Morgan took his job as their protector and role model extremely seriously. If he didn't, he wouldn't still be on the ranch in the first place.

Despite the heat or Morgan's mood, excitement rang in the early-morning air hanging over the ranch compound. Quickening his stride, Morgan approached the sun-faded red stable, the birthplace of hundreds of foals over the years. The sturdy, low-slung building had been on the property since Morgan's great-great-grandfather built it back in the early 1900s. Through the years there had been new barns and buildings added, but this lovingly maintained stable and the other historic buildings that dotted the property carried the memories of those who'd been here before him. This was their legacy to him and his two brothers, Rowdy and Tucker. His family took to heart the responsibility of passing it on to future generations.

Morgan hauled in a deep breath the moment he stepped through the stable's double doors. Instantly the scent of grassy, sundried hay and feed mingled with the smell of leather and horses, filled his lungs. And his spirit.

The stables held lots of memories from years gone by, but it was the hushed whispers of the boys at the end of the building that filled his soul and gave his life purpose.

Before his mother's death when he was

eleven years old, Lydia McDermott had had a vision to share the beauty and blessing of their West Texas ranch with less fortunate boys who had no place to call home. She'd died before she could make her dream a reality, but Morgan's dad and grandmother worked tirelessly over the next two years, getting the ranch approved as a foster home.

For the last eighteen years, sixteen boys at a time had made Sunrise Ranch their home. And Morgan, who had become a full partner six months ago, intended to help carry the torch forward—no matter who his dad brought on as the boys' teacher.

Moving down the concrete alley, the clink of his spurs and scuff of his boots bounced off the stalls. The chatter halted from the huddle at the end where a new colt had just been born, and the boys who were new to the ranch turned, awe on their faces. There was nothing like watching the miracle of life.

Yup, that was the only reminder Morgan needed that the boys came first.

Striding to stand behind them, Morgan patted one of the newcomers on the back and looked at the foal.

"It's about time you dragged yourself out here to take a look at the new little filly," Walter Pepper, his horse foreman, teased from inside the stall where he'd been assisting the mother. One of the best horsemen around, Pepper—as he'd been tagged in his early years—had worked at the ranch since he was a teenager, hired on by Morgan's granddad forty-five years ago. A stocky cowboy with a white head of hair, a gruff voice and a heart of gold, he loved to tease.

Taking in the coal-black filly curled up in the soft hay beside his momma, Morgan gave a crooked smile. "Looks like y'all've got it under control."

"She's as black as *your* hair, Morgan," nine-year-old Caleb declared, his green eyes shining. A blond-headed creative thinker and doer, Caleb was a regular fixer-upper, always coming up with ideas and taking tools and machines apart in the shop to figure out how they worked. But right now, he was wide-eyed like the rest of them, watching the mother horse tend to her newborn baby.

"Yeah," B.J. said, a grin lifting the seven-year-old's plump cheeks. "She ain't got no streak a white in her black hair like Beauty or Mr. Randolph gots." He puffed out his chest, proud that he was the first to make the comparison between the jet-black horse with the white lightning bolt crossing her face, and Randolph and his white temples.

"You're right about that, son," Morgan agreed, tousling B.J.'s brown hair as he studied Beauty. She was the first of twenty-five mares on the ranch who were due to foal in the next two months and she was kicking off the season like a pro. When the baby unbuckled her long legs and tried to stand, Beauty began nudging her gently on the rump, encouraging her as she struggled to gain her wobbly legs.

"Look, fellas, she's helping her baby get

up," Joseph observed, extending a lean, muscular arm from where he hung halfway over the rail. The oldest boy on the ranch at eighteen, Joseph was long, lanky and a good-natured encourager of the younger boys. He had his heart set on being a large-animal vet and Morgan knew he would make a great one someday.

"It's 'cause she *loves* her," ten-year-old Sammy whispered reverently, a whole host of wistfulness in his words that cut into Morgan's heart. Sammy had been at the ranch for only two weeks and was struggling. The kid's parents had given him up recently and before he could blink twice he found himself at Sunrise Ranch. The foster care worker had known the ranch had one opening and wasted no time getting Randolph and Morgan to accept Sammy into the mix. But Morgan could tell the poor kid was still grieving and in denial about what had happened to him.

Pepper's compassionate old eyes met Morgan's. These boys knew what it was to have a mother and a father who didn't care. Over the years Morgan had had many boys come to talk to him about how seeing a horse taking such tender care of her baby stabbed at their hearts on a raw level.

The first group of boys came to live at the ranch when Morgan was thirteen. They'd lost their parents, and because Morgan had just lost his mom to cancer two years earlier, he thought he understood what they were going through. It wasn't until he was a high school senior that he finally realized he didn't know where these boys were coming from at all. His mother had loved him with all of her heart. Death had forced her to leave her children—she never would have neglected or abandoned them.

It wasn't until six years ago when his fiancée gave back her engagement ring and chose a life without him that he felt some semblance of what these guys felt. It was a hard lick to know you weren't wanted.

For a moment, he went back to that day, standing in the drive, his heart in the dirt at his feet, watching Jolie Sheridan drive off into the wide blue yonder. He was over it—had been for some time now—but it had been a long, hard crawl out of the pit he'd fallen into. He'd made some mistakes on the way and fueled plenty of gossip in Dew Drop. But he'd lived.

He'd moved on.

He'd always known his life and dreams were here on the ranch, and even though things hadn't turned out exactly like he'd envisioned them, he'd managed to take hold of what God had entrusted to him and he was content.

Even happy most of the time.

At last the filly got her legs beneath her and managed to take her first wobbly steps, bringing Morgan back to the stable.

"She did it!" Jeb yelled. His nine-year-old enthusiasm startled the filly—she jumped and fell flat on her face.

Horrified, Jeb clamped his hand to the top of his head as the boys around him scowled. In the sudden silence the filly gathered herself up and this time rose more easily, with just a single nudge from her momma. Jeb gave a big silent grin. The excitement the boys were containing over the filly's accomplishment could very easily have blown the roof off the building.

There was a lot to be learned from what they'd just witnessed. Getting up from a fall was a life lesson well worth paying attention to.

"Okay, boys," Pepper said, coming out of the stall, "let's give mother and baby some alone time. You fellas can come back this evening after you get your chores done. You just have to promise to be quiet."

"Will do," agreed Wes, a stocky seventeen-year-old with curly blond hair and a cocky attitude. The boys looked up to Wes and Joseph, and the two teens took their leadership roles seriously. Morgan liked that about them.

By the time they were leaving the stable, rowdy laughter and joking had ensued. Morgan followed the group, somewhat calmer than he'd been on entering but still not pleased. His dad had deliberately made the decision about Jolie without him because he knew there was no way Morgan would have agreed to it. But Morgan's anger wasn't just based on personal grounds—in his estimation the last thing the fellas needed was another teacher who wouldn't stick around. And Jolie was *exactly* that.

As fate would have it, Morgan and the boys walked into the sunlight as Jolie herself whipped her cranberry-colored Jeep into the ranch yard, sliding to a halt across the driveway from them in a plume of dust. The doors and top were off the Jeep, giving them a clear view of her, with wind-tossed cinnamon hair.

Morgan's gut twisted in a knot and he came up short as if he'd slammed face-first into a flag pole. He had a clear shot of her. Rocks lodged in his throat. She was beautiful.

She had the boys' attention instantly, looking vibrant and full of life, every inch the world-class competitive kayaker that she was, long legs and tanned skin in well-worn jeans and a sleeveless orange tank top. She jumped from the vehicle with a big Julia Roberts smile on her face—and a hundred watts of pure joy slammed into the group.

It felt more like a sucker punch to Morgan.

"*Who* is *that?*" Joseph whistled as long strides brought her closer. There was no mistaking his admiration of Jolie. The kid was seventeen after all.

Wes elbowed Joseph out of the way. "Hubba, hubba, come to papa," he said. Morgan bopped him on the back of the head.

"Watch your manners, hotshot," he warned. "Both of you," he added as Joseph glanced at him, too.

"I didn't mean any harm," Wes said, his blue eyes dreamy. "I'm just in *lovvve.*"

Joseph put his hand on his heart and patted it, then gave his full attention back to Jolie.

"She sure is pretty," Caleb gushed as she came nearer.

True on all counts—Morgan could not

deny it. Jolie still had the ability to take his breath away.

"What's up, fellas? How's it going?" She greeted the guys like she'd just seen them yesterday and knew them by name. Looking like a bright beam of sunlight, she seemed to sparkle. She hadn't looked at Morgan yet, focusing all her attention on the sixteen totally engrossed fellas whose lower lips were now sitting firmly on their boot tips.

"You fellas must be my new class. I'm Jolie Sheridan, your teacher."

"You *are?*" Sammy cooed. The rest of them had suddenly become speechless.

"You bet I am." Jolie chuckled. "I'm excited to start school." Those luminescent green eyes met Morgan's for the first time and he was fairly certain he looked as grim as he felt because her smile faltered.

"We don't have to start today, do we?" Sammy blurted. Jolie gave them another sucker-punch grin as she put her focus back on the boys.

"Don't worry, little dude, school's not

till Monday. You have freedom today and tomorrow…and then you're *all mine, all mine,*" she sang the last words and ended with a wink. "I'm just getting the classroom fixed up today."

The woman had skills when it came to winning over a crowd. Of course she'd had this fickle group at her first hello.

"I'd be glad to help you," Joseph offered, finally finding his voice.

Wes Grinned. "Count me in." His chest was so puffed out Morgan feared the teen would throw his back out of whack.

Their eagerness had Morgan rethinking some things…like maybe it was time to offer Joseph and Wes some guidance on relationships, and what was acceptable around a girl. Not that the boys were around girls very much because they went to school on the ranch. Still, there were local girls at church and around town. Morgan made a mental note.

Jolie's eyes widened at their offer. "I would *love* some help if you fellas want to. Only if Morgan doesn't have plans for you, though."

Every eye turned toward him.

"You don't, do you?" Joseph vocalized their question.

He wanted to say that yes, in fact, he sure did. He wanted nothing more than to tell the kids they had other things that required their attention besides Miss Jolie Sheridan. But any cowboy worth his salt knew when he was caught.

The right thing to do—the *courteous* thing to do—was help out the new teacher and offer assistance.

Him included.

If it had been any other person, he wouldn't have even hesitated.

"Nope," he heard himself saying. "No plans that can't wait. Helping Miss Sheridan get settled would be the gentlemanly thing to do, so we'll do that first and then we'll go build the fence."

"I don't want to disrupt any plans you've already made," she insisted.

The guys erupted like squawking geese,

assuring her it was *no* problem. No problem at all.

Morgan suddenly wanted to take the boys and get as far away from Jolie as possible. But instead, he said, "Like the guys are telling you, it's not a problem. We can build the fence Monday after school if we don't get it done this afternoon."

She smiled at him and it hit him in the gut like a two-by-four. He was in for a beating while she was around, whether he wanted to admit it or not.

"Well, okay. Thanks."

"You're welcome," he said, his breath jamming in his throat.

She hesitated, her eyes locking on his for a second before turning back to the boys. Only then could Morgan breathe.

"If that's the case then follow me, good men that you are," she directed with a laugh. "Let's go see what adventures await us."

Waving to the fellas to follow her, she headed for the three-room schoolhouse. The boys trotted behind her looking like a litter of puppies with their tongues hanging out.

Morgan watched them go. "Just call me Jolie," he heard her telling them, her voice drifting to him over the distance, like a long-forgotten song.

"I heard she was back." Pepper came out of the stable to stand beside him. "Your grandmother told me she stopped by the kitchen yesterday and said hello. She said they had a real nice visit. Said she was worried about you, though. Me, too. I figure from that scowl on your face you just found out this morning."

So even his grandmother knew.

"How many others knew about this?" he asked, not even trying to hide his anger.

"Don't get me to lying. I just happened to see her coming out of your dad's office yesterday when you and the boys were off working cattle with Rowdy. I asked your grandmother about it."

Morgan shook his head, watching Jolie in the distance. His stomach rolled like he'd just been thrown from a rough bronc.

What had he been thinking when he'd offered to help?

Staring from beneath bushy eyebrows with concern, Pepper clapped Morgan on the back. "You hold your ground, Morg. Dig your boots into that gravel and don't budge. I helped scrape your heart up off the sidewalk once, and I ain't lookin' forward to doing it again in this lifetime."

Morgan shot him a firm look. "You don't have to worry about me. I learned my lesson a long time ago. I'm just looking out for the boys today."

"Good. I haven't ever disagreed with your dad about much, but this time I have to admit that I did. He should have never let that girl come back. It just ain't right, accident or no accident."

Morgan knew about the accident. His grandmother had told him how Jolie had nearly drowned in competition on a river. It hit him hard then and still did now, even if he had gotten over his feelings for her the day she'd given him back his ring.

Tugging his hat down low, he gave Pepper a nod and headed off toward the school. Might as well get this over with.

Despite the anger that still lived inside him, his pulse picked up speed as he started after Jolie. And his boots followed suit, not dragging anywhere near as much as he thought they should, considering he was going to help the woman who'd left him high and dry with his heart—and his engagement ring—in his hand.

Chapter Two

Did I make the right choice coming home to the ranch?

Jolie's emotions had been tumbling around inside her like clothes in a dryer since the moment she'd spotted Morgan standing beside the stables. The cowboy had always turned her world upside down with his midnight-black hair and deep blue eyes. Six feet of lean Texas cowboy with an extra inch added on for good measure—like the guy needed any extra help.

He'd been thirteen when she moved to the ranch with her parents. Immediately she'd thought he hung the moon. He'd probably thought she was a ten-year-old pest but was too kind to let her know it, unlike his brother Rowdy. Instead he'd endured her childish adoration with a patience that she'd tested on a regular basis.

How could she not have fallen in love with the guy?

"Where should this go?" Joseph asked, looking at her desk.

"I think I'd like it over there by that wall." Jolie pointed to the opposite side of the room from where the heavy oak desk was sitting now. She smiled, determined not to let the rush of the past and the uncertainty of the present distract her from getting her classroom set up.

She was impressed with the way the boys were willing to help. And startled and a bit shaken by the fact that Morgan had offered his help, too. Especially because he'd not hidden the fact that he was unhappy about her being here—his eyes had told the tale. She'd hoped time had healed old wounds, but even if it hadn't, she'd had to come home to the ranch.

Needed to come home.

Needed desperately to find the person she'd been, the person she'd lost somewhere in the depths of West Virginia's Gauley River.

She had loved Sunrise Ranch from the moment she'd moved here when her folks had been hired as house parents for one of the two foster homes on the ranch. It had been a wonderful place to grow up. And she was praying it would now be a place where she could heal and find the funny, take-the-world-by-the-horns girl she'd lost beneath the dark water of the Gauley.

The girl she was faking right now for these boys.

Coming up out of that water, her world shaken to its very core, the one thing she'd known upon gasping that first lifesaving breath was it was time to face her past....

Time to apologize to Morgan McDermott.

As if God was in agreement, this opportunity dropped in her lap and here she was.

"Is this where you want it...Jolie?" Joseph asked.

She'd told them right off to call her Jolie. She was just too laid back for anything else, even if she was their teacher. Besides, the ranch was home to the boys. Informality made it all the more true.

"Perfect," she said to the earnest young man.

"You got it, then." Joseph grabbed the edge of the monstrous desk and she was pretty sure he was about to try and move it himself. Not to be outdone, Wes was eyeing the floor-to-ceiling bookcases with determination.

"Hold off over there, Wes," Morgan demanded, coming in the front door and taking charge. Jolie's insides jangled as his presence filled the large room.

So much hung between them. She'd hoped to talk to him yesterday when she'd arrived, but he'd been working cattle at the far edge of the ranch. And so here they were in a room full of bright-eyed students, unable to talk about the fact that today had been their first meeting since she'd given him back his engagement ring.

"We'll get the desk moved first and then the bookshelves, Wes," Morgan said as he grabbed the other side of her desk.

"Thanks." Joseph grinned at Morgan. "We're putting it over there." He nodded his brown head toward the windows.

With Morgan's strength, the two were able to move the mammoth desk with ease. Once that was done they attacked the ten-foot-tall bookshelves. It ended up taking Morgan and most of the boys to move them.

Everyone's eagerness touched Jolie's heart.

She was smiling so much that she was almost able to ignore the fact that being around Morgan was causing her some heavy-duty stress—she could suddenly feel his presence like a weight.

"Where's our desks gonna sit, Jolie?"

Jolie looked down into the big, brown eyes of a wisp of a boy. "Sammy, right?" she asked, and he nodded. Sammy seemed like a nervous little fella. Uncertain of himself.

"We'll need to turn them all to face my desk. That way the light from the windows will stream across your desks. I *love* light and want y'all to enjoy it while you work."

"Can my desk be this one?" His words were as timid as the light touch he laid on the desk closest to hers, almost as if he were certain she would say no.

"Sure. It's got Sammy written all over it. Matter of fact, everyone can pick their desk."

Unsmiling, Sammy nodded and slipped into the wooden seat. "Only till my dad comes and gets me," he added in a quiet voice barely audible over the noise of the chaos breaking out behind him as the other boys began slamming into desks two at a time.

Jolie hardly even glanced at what was happening around her as her heart latched on to Sammy, who was so clearly suffering. "Sure," she assured him. "You can have that desk as long as you're here."

She wasn't sure what else to say. There were times when kids were on the ranch short-term. But most boys were here for the long haul—Sunrise Ranch had always been geared toward boys who had been totally abandoned by their families. The ranch became their home; the people, their family.

The poor kid got a wistful look on his face, then patted the desk next to him. "You can have this desk, Joseph," he called to Joseph—obviously Sammy's hero—as Joseph watched the rodeo going on over who got which desk.

"I'm too big to sit on the front row." Joseph brushed his brown bangs out of his eyes. "One of the shorter kids can sit there, and I'll sit in the back so I can make sure all you goofballs behave. Hey, goofballs!" he yelled, drawing all eyes in his direction. "One of you to a desk."

"Yeah," Wes barked loudly, crossing his arms and stepping up beside Joseph. "What kind of *animals* are y'all anyway?"

It looked as if Wes and Joseph had decided they were going to make certain the boys behaved for her. Jolie hid a grin—

and then her gaze met Morgan's. Morgan's eyebrow hitched upward, his dark denim eyes cool.

He has no confidence in me, she suddenly thought. Jolie was fairly certain Morgan would think she needed help in that department—if, that is, he even remembered how she'd let her class get out of control on her first day of student teaching. It had been a long time ago, and he might have easily forgotten the laugh they'd shared over the little boys letting the mice out of their cage and the hysterics that had ensued. Meeting his sardonic gaze, she hiked a brow of her own. "It'll be okay, guys. They're just excited. We're going to be fine," she said to Wes and Joseph, assuring all of them, as well as herself.

"Can you ride a horse?" Sammy asked, drawing her attention. She was grateful for the change of subject.

"Yes, I can. Can you?" she asked.

He shook his head. "Never been on one."

"He helped us work cattle yesterday,

though." Morgan stepped up beside the boy, giving him a smile that sent an arrow straight to Jolie's heart. Morgan McDermott had a soft spot for these boys.

He placed a hand on Sammy's shoulder. "You did good, Sammy."

"It was scary. I almost got trampled, too." Sammy's eyes were huge.

"Aw, come on, kid, it wasn't that bad," Joseph called from the back of the room where he was trying out his new desk. "If you stick with us, you'll learn not to be scared."

Sammy didn't look too sure about that.

"I ride," yelped Tony, a skinny kid around fifteen or so who looked like a young Elvis Presley with his swath of black hair, blue eyes and a crooked smile that made his eyes twinkle. He skidded to a halt in front of Jolie.

This led each boy to reveal he could ride. Jolie caught the flicker of fear in Sammy's expression as he realized he was the only one who couldn't ride. She glanced at Morgan to find his guarded eyes staring back at her.

"We're gonna learn to mug steers tomorrow after church," Caleb said, his freckles crinkling with his smile. "You can come, too, Jolie."

Sammy slipped his hand into hers and looked up. "Would you come?"

Jolie melted right there in the middle of the room. Turned right into a pool of liquid. "Sure I will," she said. She was pretty sure she would have jumped from an airplane if he'd asked her. "I love to calf wrestle, and scramble, too. But muggin' is my favorite! I used to be one of the best here on the ranch, you know."

"Seriously?" Joseph jerked to his feet, gaping at her from across the room. He and Wes exchanged disbelieving looks. "*You* can take down a steer?"

Jolie nearly shook her head. *Males.*

"Hey, y'all look like you don't think I can do it!" she teased.

"We just aren't used to girls—I mean, *women*—wantin' to do something like that," Wes drawled, glancing at Joseph and Tony.

Jolie smiled at the cocky, young cowboys, with their worn jeans tucked into their rugged boots and their T-shirts with the arms cut out of them. It was obvious that they'd been working that morning, most likely hauling hay, an ongoing job she remembered quite well growing up on the ranch. A picture of Morgan in that same getup at that age raced through her head and she glanced his way. He looked about as happy as a grizzly bear that had been awakened in the middle of a really good nap.

"I'm a little insulted here! Girls do this sort of thing all the time." She laughed when they all swallowed and looked a bit meek. "You'll find for the most part that I look at life with a bring-it-on attitude." She looked directly at Morgan before shifting back to the boys. "I haven't done it in a long time, but it sounds too fun to pass up. I'll be there." She looked at Mr. Grizzly Bear again. "May I speak to you outside?"

"Sure," he growled, swiveling toward the back door. "You boys don't tear anything up while we're gone."

Jolie thought Morgan was teasing even though he seemed far from a teasing mood. Surely he wasn't thinking the boys were going to destroy all the work they'd just put in. But then again, there *was* the incident with the desks.

Looking back over her shoulder, she was struck by the group. The picture they made reminded her of an old John Wayne movie, *The Cowboys,* about a bunch of ragtag boys who'd needed a gruff old cowboy to teach them life lessons. Although Morgan was far from an old cowboy, it was plain to see that these boys respected and admired him. And needed him.

Smiling at them, she winked. "If y'all want to finish turning the desks and lining them up, that would be great."

They all chorused, "Yes, ma'am."

Smiling at their politeness, she followed Mr. Grizzly outside and then passed him, leading him out of earshot of the class.

There was a large, gnarled oak tree still bent over as it had been all those years ago. She didn't stop until she reached it, turning his way only after they were beneath the wide expanse of limbs.

Morgan crossed his arms and studied the tree. "I remember having to climb up this tree and talk you down after you scrambled up to the top and froze."

She hadn't expected him to bring up old memories—it caught her off guard. "I remember how mad you were at having to rescue the silly little new girl." Mad? Actually, furious was more accurate.

A hint of a smile teased his lips, fraying Jolie's nerves at the edges. It had been a long, long time since she'd seen that smile.

"I got used to it, though," he said, his voice warming.

She laughed, encouraged by his teasing. "You had no other choice! I guess if you hadn't rescued me I'd never have made it to my teen years." But she was grateful to Morgan for more than that. She'd grown into a teenager who could handle almost any situation, a girl confident in her own skin. She hadn't been afraid to try anything because she'd been so crazy adventurous—and free to learn from her mistakes, thanks to Morgan and his brothers, Rowdy and Tucker, who had always been there to help her through. She'd idolized them, but at the same time, wanted them to stop babying her.

Morgan especially.

Of course it was Morgan who'd made her the angriest, and Morgan whom she'd fallen for. Their relationship had never been an easy one. The push and pull of attraction had started when she'd demanded independence, and then changed when she'd found herself desperate for his approval. But it became something incredibly complicated when she'd realized she wanted his love.

And then the pull of competitive kayaking entered the equation when Morgan introduced her to it on a lazy summer afternoon and things grew more complicated. She'd been fifteen, and her instant infatuation with the sport had been too much to ignore. For a young woman who craved the adventure world-class competition offered, Sunrise Ranch suddenly seemed… small. When Morgan made it clear that he had no desire to leave the ranch, Jolie decided she had no choice but to walk away.

Looking at him now, she was overcome by the memory of the internal war she'd lived through when she'd made the decision to leave.

It had been six years, but it felt like twenty.

They were standing beneath the shade of the old oak tree, electricity humming between them. When the smile left Morgan's eyes, Jolie sucked in a wobbly breath, forcing herself to focus on the job she'd been hired to do. "I'm curious about Sammy. Has he been here long?"

"Just a couple of weeks. He's our newest rancher. He's still having trouble emotionally, after his abandonment. It's a tough situation."

"He seems fearful."

"He is, poor kid. He knows his dad has been gone from the picture for a long time. But his mother gave him up to the state and now he thinks his dad will find out and come for him. He'll stretch the truth from here to Alaska, so you might want to tread lightly with everything he says until you give it a reality check."

"He lies?" she asked, a little more frankly than she'd intended. But she needed to know the truth if she was going to help him.

Morgan grimaced. "Kinda. More like the boy who cried wolf."

"The stories don't ever seem to change, do they, Morgan? I just can't imagine how these boys handle their families not wanting them. Or not caring enough to make loving homes for them."

She'd been around kids like Sammy all the time growing up. Some handled the situation with anger, some with denial, but it was all about fear. She understood that on a personal level—three times this week she'd awakened in the middle of the night because of nightmares. She pushed the thoughts away, praying she was up for this job.

"Sammy's a good example of how bad these kids have been hurt. They need people around them who will care for them and stick with them." The hardness of Morgan's tone matched the accusation in his eyes. "What are you doing here, Jolie? Why aren't you taming rapids in some far-off place?"

"I…I'm—" She stumbled over her words, tongue-tied by his question. "I'm taking a leave from competition for a little while. I had a bad run in Virginia and I— It was bad." She couldn't bring herself to say that she'd almost died, that she was lucky to be standing there. "Anyway, your dad was kind enough to offer me this opportunity."

"I heard about the accident and I'm real sorry about that, Jolie. I really am. I wish you a speedy recovery so you can get back out there doing what you love. But why come here after all this time? We dropped off your radar a long time ago."

"This is my *home*. It has never been off my radar." Jolie saw anger in Morgan's eyes. Well, he had a right to it, and more than a right to point it straight at her. She'd just thought she was prepared for it.

She was wrong.

"Morgan," Jolie said, almost as a whisper. "I'd hoped we could forget the past and move forward."

Heart pounding, she reached across the space between them and placed her hand on his arm. It was just a touch, but the feeling of connecting with Morgan McDermott again after so much time rocked her straight to the core and suddenly she wasn't so sure coming home had been the right thing to do, after all.

A jolt from a live wire couldn't have burned Morgan more than the touch of Jolie's hand. Shock waves coursed through him with a vengeance, his mouth went dry. There had been a time when he'd have done anything for her touch. He gulped hard and hardened his heart against a walk down memory lane.

He wasn't some kid anymore, holding his heart in his hands. He was a thirty-two-year-old adult male with a good brain between his ears. Or at least he'd thought he had a good brain.

"I did forget the past. A long time ago," he assured her, his skin burning where her hand still lay. He wondered if she felt the way his pulse had started galloping at her touch. They stared at each other as seconds slipped by.

"Yes, of course you would have," Jolie said at last, her hand squeezing his arm slightly before it slipped away. "But I was hoping there would be no hard feelings."

His jaw jerked in reflex.

"I didn't mean to hurt you," she said. "It really wasn't personal."

"You broke our engagement, then headed off in search of *better* things. I think I had a right to take that personal."

"That is not fair."

Morgan was suddenly not at all comfortable with where this was heading.

"I wasn't searching for *better,*" she said.

"I couldn't stay. You know I would have regretted it for the rest of my life."

"Well," he drawled icily, "that makes me feel a whole heap better."

"I'm sorry," she said, her eyes shadowing. "Morgan, I'm so sorry for the way it ended that day. I'm sorry for letting us go so far. I never meant to hurt you. I never should have accepted the ring in the first place knowing my heart was torn."

"On that we agree." At least she hadn't waited until the night before they were to walk down the aisle like Celia, the next woman he'd been fool enough to ask to marry him. Two in a row had made Morgan hang up any thoughts of ever popping the question again. Not that he ever should have started dating Celia in the first place.

"Look, Jolie, that was a long time ago. It doesn't matter anymore. Right now my concern is for those boys. They got hung out to dry by their parents and then their teacher left them for something better at the last minute. They don't need another person leaving. They need someone they can count on to be here for them."

Slapping a hand on her hip, fire flashed in her eyes. "I intend to honor my contract for the semester, and I'm going to do my best to help each of the boys any way that I can."

Morgan met her gaze with fire of his own. "I don't like your being here, but it doesn't matter—you are. I'll just have to hope and pray it all turns out okay."

Turning away he strode back toward the schoolhouse, leaving Jolie standing beneath the old oak. He used the walk to rein in his temper so he could finish setting up the classroom. The last thing he needed was for the boys to pick up on the bad vibes between him and Jolie—and if he wasn't careful, they would, before he even made it in the door.

How, he wanted to know as the schoolhouse got closer and his temper just got worse, was he ever going to make this work?

Infuriating man, Jolie thought, stalking after Morgan. "Stop right where you are, bucko," she demanded, sounding as if she was calling him out to a gunfight at the O.K. Corral. He swung around at the entrance to the schoolhouse, clearly startled. She marched straight up to him.

"You might not have any faith in me." *And my faith in myself might be shaken to the core.* "But while I'm here, I'll give these kids everything I have to give. No holding back."

For the first time since the accident Jolie felt a familiar strength ease through her, and she liked it. She'd had moments since nearly drowning when she'd felt as weak as a newborn, but she still counted herself a strong woman. She prayed that throwing herself into helping the boys of Sunrise Ranch would be a win-win situation for all of them.

"Key words, Jolie—*while you are here.*"

"It doesn't matter to you if I can do a good job, does it, Morgan? This is personal on your part."

"You bet it's personal. These boys are my *personal* responsibility."

Stung by his words and breathless with fury, she glared up at him, trying to ignore the fact that the man smelled of pine and leather. His scent played havoc with her senses. Her eyes, traitors that they were, slid down to rest on his lips. She inhaled, but all the air in the world seemed to have gone missing.

Focus, Jolie. Focus.

"Think the worst of me, Morgan McDermott. However," she said, her conviction ringing true in her own ears, "I will give these boys everything I have to give them."

He stepped so close they were almost touching, and she had to tilt her head back to look him in the eye. "That's exactly what I expect," he said. "They deserve it." His gaze fell to her lips and lingered for only a brief instant before meeting hers. Jolie's heart skipped a beat, and Morgan's eyes were nearly black with dark emotion—yearning? Fury? Jolie was rendered speechless by his scowl. What was going on in that mind of his?

He left her then, continuing toward the school.

As she followed him toward the back door, she was sure of one thing and one thing only: for the first time in weeks she was filled with a great sense of purpose. What God had in store for her and Morgan, she didn't have a clue. But God had plans for her at the Sunrise Ranch school and she was determined to prove herself to Him.

It was probably going to be a lot easier than proving herself to Morgan.

Chapter Three

When Jolie reached the main classroom a few seconds after Morgan, she saw Joseph holding the front door open for Morgan's grandmother, Ruby Ann "Nana" McDermott. Nana was the backbone of the ranch, a former barrel racer who ran the chow hall like a well-greased wagon wheel. Her vision had been essential in making Lydia McDermott's dream come true, and her heart had been essential in making the place what it was today.

Jolie knew that since Lydia's death, Nana had been just as much a mother to Morgan as she had been to the countless young ranchers who'd needed her love. Jolie had loved and adored Nana and the feeling had been mutual. In her sixties, Nana had deep blue, wide-set eyes, high cheekbones and a square jaw, and there was no denying that her son Randolph and her three grandsons, Morgan, Rowdy and Tucker, were from her gene pool. Before her thick ponytail had turned the color of pale steel, it had been jet-black like Morgan's and Randolph's— a long-ago gift of the Cherokee blood of Nana's ancestors.

Yesterday Jolie had been welcomed by Nana with open arms—there was never any lack of hugs where Nana was concerned. Today Nana hustled into the room like a woman on a mission, her ponytail swinging as she brought cookies to her boys—and checked up on Morgan and "her girl," as she always called Jolie.

She set the large tray down on a worktable beside the computer as the tantalizing scent of chocolate and cinnamon filled the room. Nana's smile was just as warm and sweet as the cookies nestled on the tray.

"Y'all have sure been workin' hard today, so I whipped up some of your favorite cookies." The instant she stepped back, it was like a free-for-all—the boys dived for the chocolate chip cookies, attacking them as if they hadn't eaten all morning.

"Glad you came on out today, Jolie," she said as Jolie gave her a hug.

"I thought it would be best to come and, you know—" she faltered as she looked at Morgan, who frowned at her "—get acquainted, with the boys, I mean, and get prepared."

Morgan looked as if he'd just witnessed her robbing a bank or something, his eyes narrowing in distrust. Jolie gulped and looked back at Nana.

"Thank you for the snacks. These boys deserve it—as you said, they've been working hard."

Nana waved off the comment. "These bottomless pits always need cookies." She planted her fists on her hips, giving Jolie and Morgan the once-over. "When I was coming out of the chow hall I saw you two heading around the back of the building."

Nana looked at Morgan, and Jolie thought she saw worry in her eyes.

"Um, we had things to discuss," Jolie explained. What else could she say?

"Morgan, how's your day going?" Nana asked when it was obvious the boys were too engrossed in cookie devouring to eavesdrop on their conversation.

Exasperation flashed in Morgan's eyes. "How do you think, Nana? Started out with a real bang in Dad's office this morning."

Nana blushed—surprising Jolie, since she wasn't the blushing kind—and she leaned in close to Morgan. "If it makes you feel any better, I told Randolph he needed to warn you."

"And what about you?" he asked.

"I— Well," she said, patting his arm. "We'll talk about this later."

Jolie wasn't sure what was going on, but it sounded as if Morgan hadn't known she was coming. Was that possible? The thought practically made her gasp. If that was the case, then no wonder he was so hostile. His dad had not only made the decision to hire her on his own, but had also kept it a secret—until today.

"You didn't know?" she whispered.

His lips pressed into a tight line and his left eyebrow lifted ever so slightly.

Jolie gasped, looking from Morgan to Nana. It was true—Randolph hadn't told him!

Nana turned to where the boys were scarfing down the cookies as if there was no tomorrow. "Did you fellas know Jolie is a world-class champion kayaker? She gets paid by sponsors to travel all over the world and compete using their gear. Isn't that right, Jolie?"

"Get outta here. For real?" Wes said, stepping away from the cookie fray.

Jolie nodded and her stomach dropped to her feet as a sick feeling washed over her in a wave. *Please don't go there. I can't handle that right now on top of everything else.*

She'd known it was ridiculous to hope

no one would mention her kayaking, yet she'd hoped exactly that. She gave a weak smile. "I've won a few competitions."

"Ha!" Nana hooted. "She's top ten in the country."

Morgan crossed his arms, his expression stormy.

"Top in the country!" Wes gushed, suddenly looking a lot younger than seventeen.

"Really?" Tony joined in, his eyes lit with expectations.

Alarms clanged inside of Jolie.

"What's kayaking?" Caleb asked as he and the other smaller fellas looked up from their cookies.

"It's like a plastic canoe that holds one person, and they compete on riding the rapids and stuff." Joseph had come closer, as intent as Wes and Tony. "We have some rapids on the river at this place. Do you know that?"

She knew what was coming next. She knew it and she wasn't even sure she could speak. But she nodded and fought for words as acid churned in her stomach.

"I—I started on those rapids when I was a kid. Morgan showed them to me."

That was all the encouragement the boys needed. They instantly erupted in excitement.

"Cool! Can you teach us?" Joseph said over the others' exclamations. Jolie silently prayed for God to help her.

"I've always wanted to learn," Wes gushed again, grinning like he'd just won the lottery. "Can you teach us?" he echoed as the others chimed in.

Jolie's vision blurred—where had all the air gone? She suddenly felt unbearably hot as every eye in the room stared at her. Her pulse pounded in her head like the roar of the white river rapids she now feared. Black spots began to spatter her vision like paint drops. She swayed, woozy, and her gaze swung to Morgan—for what? To ask for help?

I can't teach these boys to kayak!

Breathe, she commanded herself, even as her knees turned to jelly....

"Jolie!"

Morgan's voice rumbled down a long tunnel as Jolie sank like a rock.

One minute she was standing and the next she was swooped up into strong arms. *His* strong arms. Morgan McDermott's arms.

The arms she'd longed for since she'd walked away from Sunrise Ranch...six long years ago....

Voices floated to Jolie through a dark fog.

"She fainted," Caleb gasped.

"Passed smooth out," Sammy said in a hushed voice.

"I ain't never in my whole long life seen nobody pass out," B.J. whispered.

Though lost in the fog, it registered loud and clear to Jolie that her head was resting against Morgan's chest. His heart beat against her temple so hard it was no wonder she'd come to so quickly.

"Good thang you gone and caught her,

Morgan," B.J. continued. Jolie was surprised how easily she could already identify the boys just by the sound of their voices.

"Yeah, or she might have died," Sammy said solemnly.

"Caleb and Sammy, how about y'all get me a glass of water and a cold rag?" Nana urged gently.

"Sure! I'll get the rag," Caleb volunteered.

"I'll get the water," Sammy said. Their voices were followed immediately by the trample of feet.

"Jolie, can you hear me?" Morgan asked gently.

Jolie lifted her eyes and forced herself to pull her head away from Morgan's heart. Embarrassment warmed her face. "Faint of heart" was not a description of the gal who'd looked down the throat of The Gorilla—the burliest rapids in the toughest of all the extreme kayaking competitions in the world—and felt only an adrenaline rush and excitement. She was not a wimp.

Fainting was *not* in her vocabulary…or at least it hadn't been until she'd almost drowned.

"Give her some air, boys," Nana said. Moving in, she fanned Jolie furiously with a booklet she must have snatched from the bookshelf. "Honey, you're whiter than Walter Pepper's hair!"

Jolie would have smiled at that if she could have.

"How are you doing?" Morgan asked, his voice gruff in a way that made her heart beat faster.

"I'm okay," Jolie assured them, looking at Morgan. His eyes were full of concern—and questions. She was thankful they were surrounded by the boys—boys who were silent and looked a little scared. She needed to stand up and show them she was fine.

Even if she was fast becoming a wimp, she certainly didn't have to broadcast it.

"Are you sure?" Morgan set her on her feet, keeping his arms around her. "Maybe you should sit down."

Maybe I need to stay in your arms—
Maybe I need to get a grip!

"No, I can stand," she said firmly, and forced herself to step away from Morgan.

The concern in his eyes almost undid her.

This was the man she'd fallen for when she was sixteen years old. This was a gentler man, not the hard man she'd been dealing with for the last couple of hours. Sadly, she knew she was partly to blame for some of the hard crust encasing Morgan.

Praying her witless knees wouldn't buckle, she was pleased when she stood firm. All she had to do now was come up with an answer as to why she wasn't going to teach the boys how to kayak.

Sammy and Caleb came bounding from the back of the building, Caleb waving a washcloth and Sammy sloshing water from the glass as he ran, the hand clamped tightly over the glass not keeping the water from escaping. His big eyes were huge with fear. She hated that she'd worried him when he already had so many things bothering him.

"Sit," Morgan demanded, pushing her into the nearest seat. B.J. immediately came to stand beside her.

"You're whiter than a marshmallow," Caleb declared, pushing the washcloth into her hands.

"I'm fine," she assured him and the others as they all began talking about how pale she was.

"You scared fifteen years off my life," Sammy said, sounding like an adult.

Jolie had to chuckle at his tone.

"Sammy, you don't have fifteen years to scare off," Joseph teased. "You're only ten."

Sammy frowned. "She scared it off me, though."

Caleb blinked hard. "You scared me, too."

Jolie's heart warmed at their worry. "I'll be honest with you, fellas. It freaked me out a little, too. I mean, really, I blacked

out and woke up in Mr. Morgan's arms—
that's a scary thing!"

She won a round of laughter from all the
boys, and keeping the momentum going,
she drove the topic away from her. The last
thing she wanted was for one of them to
ask about kayaking again.

She caught Morgan watching her and her
insides did a swan dive straight to her toes.
Forcing her chin upward, she gave him a
smile and kept her balance as she stood.

Joseph frowned, his lean face looking
a little strange without the smile that was
usually plastered across it. "You're as wobbly as the filly we just saw born."

"I'm okay." She forced any shakiness
from her voice. "Now, let's talk about this
calf wrestling I'll be winning tomorrow."

"Winning?" Joseph grinned dubiously,
looking more like himself. "I don't think
so. I'm wrestling, too."

"Me, too," Wes spoke up, challenge in
his eyes. "Which means y'all are lookin'
at the winner right here." He pulled his
thumbs toward his chest and grinned.

Jolie laughed, feeling some semblance of herself returning. "You boys need to remember to never underestimate your opponent." She let her gaze slide to Morgan. He crossed his arms and cocked his head to the side, his eyes holding steady, assessing her.

She knew she wasn't fooling him. She also knew it wouldn't be long before he asked her exactly what the fainting was all about.

She wondered if he would ask purely out of concern, as any decent person would do, or if he would ask because somewhere behind that shield he wore, he still cared for her. She was just going to have to wait and see.

But in the meantime, she should probably figure out what to do about the fact that she desperately wanted it to be the latter.

Chapter Four

A little unhinged by her afternoon, Jolie headed straight for the Spotted Cow Café to see her longtime friend Ms. Jo. The café was in its mid-afternoon lull when she walked through the lemon pie–yellow door. She was immediately greeted by the moo of the four-foot toy cow just inside the entrance. The cow's hide had bare spots on it from years of kids petting it, but it mooed like a newborn bawling after its mama.

Jolie had good memories in this diner.

The soft buttery walls were covered with all manner of spotted-cow gifts from customers: knickknacks, cattle horns and mooing cow clocks were everywhere. It was a unique place, to say the least. Even the buffed-concrete floor was painted with large, irregularly shaped brown spots. They were supposed to represent the hide of a spotted cow but had come out looking more like cow patties, which was why Chili Crump and Drewbaker Macintosh, a couple of the old-time locals, nicknamed the diner the Cow Patty Café. Needless to say, that made Ms. Jo furious.

Jolie headed for the old-fashioned soda fountain at the back and her mouth began to water the instant the glass case of frothy pies came into view. Her stomach growled, reminding her that she hadn't eaten all day.

Pie sounded like the perfect meal after the day she'd had.

"That'll make you fat," Edwina, the longtime waitress, warned, hustling out of the back carrying plates of hamburgers and fries. She paused to give Jolie a lop-sided grin. "But it's worth every calorie and more. You can tell by my hips that I partake of a bite every chance I can get."

Jolie chuckled. Edwina was a character who'd worked for Ms. Jo for years. Skin as tough as boot leather and a personality to match, Edwina loved to tell tall tales. Rough as she was, she was part of the atmosphere and as dependable as all the cow clocks put together.

"You here to see Ms. Jo?" she asked. "She's armpit-high in pie crust—okay, so her armpits aren't involved, but she *is* in the pie dough, if you want to find her."

Jolie grinned. "Thanks, Ed. You keeping the cowboys straight today?"

Edwina huffed and headed toward the two cowboys sitting at the window. "Crazy men, I done told them they weren't welcomed in here but they keep comin'. I know it's not the food or my winning personality, so it's got to be my beauty. It's a curse."

Chuckling, Jolie headed through the swinging doors. She'd made Ms. Jo mad when she'd first arrived in town and only taken time to get checked in at the Dew Drop Inn before heading out to see Randolph. She'd known Harvey, the front-desk clerk, would have it all over town that she was back. By the time Jolie had come in yesterday afternoon, Ms. Jo had been told and was not happy that Jolie hadn't come by to see her. She was probably still a little peeved about it today.

Walking through the curtain into the large, spotless kitchen, Jolie waved at T-Bone, their cook, as she passed the grill and went back to the baking area. Ms. Jo, a compact little gal with short brown hair curled around her ears, worked the dough with a pie roller. Her alert hazel eyes locked onto Jolie as she entered the room.

"I know that look," she quipped, rolling pin wagging at Jolie. "You met up with Morgan, didn't you?"

Jolie gave a weary nod as it all settled down on her again. Keeping her energy up for the kids had been tough, and she was emotionally drained.

"By the looks of you, it didn't go so well." Pointing the rolling pin at the stool by the workstation, she demanded, "Sit down and talk to me." Heading to the sink, she rinsed her hands under the faucet. "How did Morgan react to seeing you?"

Jolie made circles in a small pile of white flour that was on the counter. "He isn't happy. At all."

"What did you expect? Flowers? You *did* hand him back his ring before hitting the trail for parts unknown."

"Gee, thanks for the support."

"You know I love you, but I'm worryin' you're fixin' to get yourself in some hot water."

"I apologized and he didn't take it well." She didn't go into the fainting episode. The last thing she wanted to talk about was the reaction she'd had to being in his arms.

Shrewd eyes held Jolie's. "You hurt Morgan when you left. And then, on the rebound, that boy went and almost married Celia Simpson. And she left him right after the rehearsal." Ms. Jo clucked her tongue. "I'd hate to see you lead Morgan down the wrong road again."

"I would never do that. Besides, he can barely stand to look at me."

"You know he's one of my favorites, Jolie. Kind of reminds me a little of my Clovis. He's got feelings that run real deep and it'll take more than words to prove you're sorry. But maybe working with those boys he loves so much will help."

Jolie was glad Ms. Jo didn't tell her it would be easy—they both knew it wouldn't be. Ms. Jo pulled a pie out of the glass icebox. "How about you and me take a break and have us a piece of this lemon pie with some coffee?"

Jolie sat up at attention. "Do you even have to ask?" She wondered if pie would help erase the feel of Morgan's arms around her. Her heart went erratic just thinking about how she'd felt snuggled against his heart....

"I think this situation is gonna need a bunch of prayers, too. For those boys' sakes, we need you two on speaking terms. Y'all don't have to make up and kiss or anything—goodness knows that would only lead things in the wrong direction. Just bury the hatchet and get it over with."

"Easier said than done, I think."

"In all honesty, this could be the best thing for Morgan." Ms. Jo brightened. "Maybe it'll help him move forward, find someone who'll actually go through with marrying him. Seems such a waste for a cowboy of his caliber not to have someone to call his own."

Jolie put a huge bite of lemon pie on her fork, breathed in the tangy scent and stuffed it in her mouth so she wouldn't have to say anything.

Because even after all this time, the thought of Morgan and someone else made Jolie want to eat an entire case of pies.

"How you doing, Morg, my man?" Rowdy asked Sunday afternoon.

Rowdy, Morgan's younger brother, ran the ranch's cattle operation and they were sorting the steers for the mugging together. "My boots almost had blowouts when Dad told me what he'd done."

"You think *you* had a blowout," Morgan growled.

Rowdy, who always looked as if he was ready for a good time, with lips that turned up at the edges and eyes shot with mischief, looked as concerned as Morgan had ever seen him. "So how did it go? The boys about talked my ear off at lunch. They're impressed, just in case you didn't know that."

"Thanks, I picked up on that all by myself when their jaws started dragging in the dirt. And Wes and Joseph started showing off their muscles."

Rowdy's lips twitched. "Should make for a good show tonight. But how are you?"

Morgan rested a boot on the bottom rung of the arena and studied the steers closely. "How do you think? I don't have a choice but to deal with it."

"Maybe that's a good thing." Rowdy hiked a shoulder. "You don't date, Morg. You act like you're married to the school. You have unfinished business and it's time to finish it, one way or the other."

Morgan grunted and kept his mouth shut.

"Would you look at that?" Rowdy whistled over the bellowing of cattle. "Pest is lookin' good."

Morgan turned to see Jolie hopping from her Jeep.

"Yeah," he snapped. "Tell me something I don't already know."

Rowdy chuckled, crossed his arms and leaned back against the corral to watch Jolie. Morgan shot him a glare, not fond of that glint in his brother's eyes.

"I thought you said you were all right," Rowdy said.

"I'm not in the mood, Rowdy."

"Touché. Don't get me wrong, I'm on your side. You got a real raw deal, but maybe that was all she had to give you at the time. Like I said, this could be a good thing."

"Maybe I don't want to discuss this right now."

Rowdy chuckled. "Like I said, *touché*. Got to go get myself a hug." Pushing off the fence, he strode toward Jolie, who had stopped to talk to their dad. Tucker, the eldest of the McDermott boys, was the county sheriff. He'd been talking with Nana, and now they all headed Jolie's way.

Morgan scrubbed his scratchy jaw—it had been a long night delivering a new foal, he hadn't had much sleep and this morning he'd missed church. He was *not* in the mood for this.

"Hey, pest," Rowdy drawled, using his pet name for Jolie. "You're looking good, but a little on the thin side. You not eating out there, making all that money having your picture taken in that yellow banana of yours?"

"Rowdy!" Jolie exclaimed. Rowdy laid an arm across her shoulders and hugged her as if she was his long-lost friend.

"Jolie." Tucker greeted her with a hug, too.

Morgan almost got lockjaw, grinding his molars watching, his dad grinning as though he'd just reunited the family.

Ten thousand acres of West Texas ranch lands suddenly didn't feel big enough. This "reunion" was enough to make a man ride off into the sunset and never look back.

"Hey, Morgan." Chet, one of the top hands, called from the cattle pens on the far side of the barn. "Got a sec?"

A couple of years younger than he was, Chet had grown up on the ranch as a foster kid and had stayed on. Like the other fifteen cowboys who worked for the ranch, he knew Morgan's history with Jolie… and Celia. There had been no teasing so far, and that fact alone told him they all thought he was on shaky ground now that Jolie was back.

It was embarrassing.

"I hear you fainted yesterday," his dad said as Morgan hit the fast track across the corral toward Chet.

He'd had Jolie's fainting spell on his mind since it had happened. Something was up with her, and he figured the last place she needed to be was running up and down this arena trying to throw a yearling on its back with her bare hands. Of course she lived in a world where she took her life in her hands every time she got into that kayak of hers and plowed through raging white water *and* over ridiculous waterfalls that weren't meant for humans to fall over, much less charge over on purpose.

And to think he'd been the one to introduce her to it. Little had he known she would fall for it and become one of the best. When he'd taken her kayaking as a kid, it had been slow, easy river runs, nothing life-threatening—

He stopped his thoughts in their tracks.

Jolie wasn't his concern anymore—hadn't been since the day she'd walked away, choosing kayaking over him.

"What's up?" he growled, reaching Chet.

Nudging his Stetson off his forehead, Chet met Morgan's look with frank brown eyes. "Thought the love and admiration was about to start piling up knee-deep to a giraffe over there," he drawled sarcastically, then pointed at one of the steers. "This 'un here's got a bad leg. Thought you'd want to pull it from the event."

That was no-nonsense Chet. Said what

he wanted and moved on. Morgan almost grinned. Chet wasn't one to get in another person's business—giving him his support by saying what he just had meant a lot to Morgan.

Morgan studied the limping steer. "Yeah, take him out."

"Will do, boss." Chet nodded to one of the other cowboys working the gate to open it up. He and Morgan flanked the steer to send him through the gate, and one of the other cowboys herded him toward a separate pen.

"Time to get ready for some fun."

Chet nodded. "Sounds good to me."

Watching him head off to gather the men, Morgan knew Chet had his back. That was more than he could say about his own family. Although maybe his brothers' affection for Jolie could come in handy. She might not want to tell him about the fainting episode, but that didn't mean she wouldn't tell Rowdy or Tucker. Regardless, Morgan was determined to find out what was going on, whether Jolie wanted him to or not.

Chapter Five

The familiar scent of dirt and cattle filled the air as Jolie tried hard *not* to watch Morgan. It was an almost-impossible feat—the man had gotten only better-looking in the past six years. His black hair curled out from under his hat, just whispering against his blue button-down. The color made his eyes look darker than ever. And he was in his element as he strode back and forth inside the arena with Rowdy and the other cowboys getting everything set up for the mugging.

"I got trampled by a cow one time. That's why I'm afraid to go out there," Sammy was saying to Jolie. He'd been shadowing her since she'd arrived at the arena. Something about the kid spoke to her, and she wondered why he'd gravitated toward her. She couldn't help thinking that it was the fear eating him up that had drawn him to her. Maybe on a subconscious level he recognized a kindred spirit of sorts.

Because she had fear eating her up, too.

And it irritated the dickens out of her. So much so that despite almost no sleep, she'd dragged herself out of bed and made it to church on just one cup of coffee. Her night had been awful, to say the least— just plain terrible.

It had started with thoughts of Morgan— specifically, the feel of his arms around her and the beat of his heart in her ear. Those sensations kept her awake half the night. When she'd finally fallen asleep, the nightmares arrived. Why, oh, why had she thought coming home would help ease them?

They hadn't eased one iota.

Instead, they'd come as hard as ever, if not more so. Always the same, she was trapped in a raging vortex, upside down and fighting to make it to the surface. Always ensnared and struggling for her life.

Somewhere in the wee hours of the morning she'd given up trying to sleep and lay covered in sweat, tangled in sheets and worn-out. In the month since the accident, this had become the norm. Usually she turned to her Bible, searching for comfort and peace. Even though peace had been elusive, she knew God and only God had brought her up out of that watery grave.

A person would think that if she knew *God* had yanked her out of that murky water, there would be no reason to be full of fear from her toes to her roots—but she was. And she didn't know what to do about it.

"You're scared?" According to Morgan, Sammy was prone to exaggerations so she wasn't sure what to make of his remark about being trampled, but she certainly recognized fear when she saw it. And it was like a flashing red beacon in his eyes.

He nodded. "Scared bad."

"That's totally understandable. Did the cow hurt you very badly?"

His gaze slid left, then back toward the four-foot-tall steers. "Broke my leg. My dad, he took real good care of me, though. And my mom." He paused, gulping. "She cried, it scared her so bad." He sighed wistfully. "They loved me so much they hated to see it happen."

Heart *slam!*—Jolie was suddenly desperately grateful for her parents' love and affection. She wanted to hug the child close—and at the same time do bodily harm to his parents for giving him up.

"I'm sure they did." Jolie wondered if he even realized he'd said "loved" in the past tense. "You remember that anytime you need to talk about them, or anything that scares you, you can come to me. If you want to," she added.

A half smile appeared that was one day going to make female hearts stop.

What a cute kid. And what a tough road he'd traveled. As had most of these boys.

A steer broke from the pack at the end of

the arena and ran full tilt down the inside of the fence right in front of them.

Sammy's head swung fast as he followed the black blur. Then immediately he turned back to her. "Are you really going to get out there?" he asked, his brows bunched in concern.

Jolie bit back a laugh. After all she'd faced in her kayak, a few half-pint cows didn't scare her. Not that she'd dare tell Sammy that.

"You bet I'm getting out there!" she exclaimed. "It's fun. If you learn how to do it right, even small people can flip a steer." He didn't look convinced at all. "You can do it, Sammy. It's all in the technique."

"We're going in two groups," Morgan called. Joseph clamored over the rail and jumped from the top rung to the ground. Instantly five more boys bailed over the rails and sauntered to join Joseph.

Jolie sure hoped she still had it—she hadn't run around an arena after a steer in years. It hit her that if she hoped to get Sammy to participate at all today, she needed to go in the first group and lead by example. She climbed the fence and dropped to the ground on the other side.

"No!" Sammy yelped, grabbing hold of her shirt sleeve through the railing as if he feared he would never see her again. "Please don't go," he implored her.

"It's going to be all right, Sammy. I promise. You'll see, sugar," she urged.

Adrenaline was flowing through her, a feeling she relished. She gave Sammy's hand one last reassuring pat, then pulled away. She had never let fear hold her back—until the accident. But today, there was nothing inside the arena that remotely frightened her.

Matter of fact, she felt more alive than she had in a long time. Pure fun was what she called this.

It had been too long.

With big, goofy grins, the boys were whooping and waving her over. She jogged their way, smiling.

"Count me in on this one," she called to Morgan. She rubbed her hands together, joining the boys behind the line that had been drawn in the dirt. Mentally she went over the names of the boys in the group— Joseph, Wes, Tony, Caleb and Micah, who was sixteen with rusty-brown hair, a lean face and eyes the color of well-washed jeans. They were all grinning from ear to ear as they looked at her.

Jolie clapped Caleb, the youngest, on the shoulder. "Hey, aren't you Mr. Braveheart," she teased, and his grin widened to touch his ears.

She was just starting to enjoy herself when she looked at Morgan. The man's scowl told her he wasn't happy with her at all.

So what else is new?

"You sure you want to do this? It's been a long time, and yester—"

Jolie cut him off. "I'm fine, and I'm sure. Let's get this muggin' goin'!"

"If she can ride those rapids, I bet she can mug a puny five-hundred-pound steer." Joseph grinned and spat a sunflower seed husk to the ground.

"Why, thank ya, Joseph," she quipped, gloating a little at Morgan.

He frowned at the teen. "Maybe you need to tend to your own business."

Joseph chuckled. "You sure been ornery the last few days, Morg."

"Yeah," Wes agreed. "Real grumpy."

Morgan's scowl deepened. "May I have a word with you?" he asked through bared teeth. Wrapping his hand around her biceps, he started walking her away from the group.

Once they were a good distance away from everyone he let go of her arm, leaving her skin tingling from his touch. She felt a rush of disappointment but wasn't sure if she was disappointed that she'd felt a tingle or that he'd removed his hand.

"I can do this if I want to, Morgan McDermott." Here was one of the problems that had prompted her to pack her bags six years ago—the man was pushy.

"You passed out yesterday. That's not like you. I've thought about it all night and I've decided that there must be something wrong. You going to tell me what that something is?"

I've thought about it all night. He'd had her on his mind—the knowledge sent a shaft of joy straight to her heart. She continued to glare at him, though, because she'd never liked his bossing her around. It was all coming back to her now. Once he'd put his ring on her finger, he'd started trying to dictate her life—tried to wrap her up and keep her safe. It was out of concern, but she was not a china doll and refused to be treated as one.

Even if she felt broken right now.

"I did not pass out. I got a little faint is all."

"You would have hit the floor like a rock if I hadn't caught you."

"Maybe, but—"

"Jolie, I'm not kidding. You come back here after all this time, and you aren't kayaking. You nearly died—yeah, I know you didn't elaborate on that, but Nana is my grandmother, so I'm informed. I know what a close call you had. I'm not blind and I'm not stupid, Jolie. There is something wrong with you and I want to know what it is."

The man was impossible. "It's none of your business."

He loomed over her, his scent filling her senses. "I'm responsible for everyone out here and if you have some kind of condition, I need to know about it. You were hired on to this ranch without my say-so, but guess what? That makes you my business, especially if whatever's going on affects your job."

So his interest in what was wrong with her was because she *worked* for him. There was nothing personal about it. Nevertheless, she caved under that blue-eyed stare, blurting out, "I'm having trouble sleeping ever since the accident. I'm having a few nightmares."

"Nightmares," he repeated, clearly startled. Then his expression softened. "I guess that's understandable after what you went through."

Jolie suddenly wanted to tell him more,

but was aware that all eyes were watching them as they stood practically nose to nose. This wasn't the time or the place. And now that she thought about it, she didn't want sympathy from him.

"I'm dealing with it," she huffed, "which is why I'm taking some time off. Now, can we get this done?" she asked.

"Fine, do it," he snapped. "Only, and I mean *only,* if you're sure you won't be passing out and getting trampled."

"Such a sweet thought," she replied, syrup dripping from her words as she crossed her heart. "I promise."

She spun and jogged back to the boys. Energy surged through her—for now, she was alive and unafraid, and Morgan McDermott couldn't tell her what she could or couldn't do.

She gave high fives to the boys.

"Let's do this," she said before turning her attention to the midsize steers milling about in a huddle. She took them all in and zeroed in on her pick, a hefty black angus that had some challenge in his eyes. Sure, there were a few mild-mannered ones milling around, but she'd never taken the easy route.

"Just so y'all know, I'm in it to win it," she warned.

"Win it," Wes said in comical disbelief.

"Win it," she clarified. Their disbelief was all the challenge she needed. She'd always liked having something to prove.

"Here you go, hotshot. Be my guest," Morgan said, issuing his own challenge as he handed her a rope.

Jolie stuffed the tie rope in her back waistband and gave the guys a grin just to egg them on because they were looking at her as if she'd lost her mind.

"All right," Morgan commanded. "This is our version of a muggin' competition. All of you will go at the same time and first man—*person*—to get the steer by the horns and to the ground is the winner of this group. Once we have the winner established of this go-around, then one of you will tie its legs and be timed on that. We'll do the same with the second group, and the overall winner will be determined by time. Remember, we'll have a team roping in a couple of weeks and you'd better be practiced up on your roping and tying by then, because I'm bringing out the real steers." This information won huge grins and a ton of chatter.

"Everyone behind the line and we'll get this show started. Get set," Morgan called, "go!"

It was on. Dirt flying, steers running, cheers threatening to lift the roof off the building, Jolie and the five boys ran out into the arena. Jolie focused on her target—which was heading for Denver, by the looks of it. Anticipating his movements, she raced after him. When he spun, she dived for him—and landed face-first in the red dirt.

Sputtering the bitter, gritty dirt, she was on her feet in a flash. Hands out to either side, she waved the steer back when it would have broken left. Scrambling for traction, she broke right, then lunged again...and grabbed him.

"Gotcha, big boy," she grunted, locking her elbows around the steer's blunt-tipped horns. Instinct from years on the ranch kicked in. One arm locked around the horns, she grabbed the animal's jaw, dug her boots into the dirt and twisted the steer's head as she leaned back on her heels. Once she felt his weight shift she hung on, pulled harder and let herself fall back into the dirt. The steer came with her, landing on his side. Only then did the riotous yells and cheers begin to register.

Holding the angry steer's horns to her chest, she waited for someone to come tie its legs. A shadow blocked out the overhead light and Morgan grinned down at her.

"I reckon you haven't lost your touch after all," he drawled.

Looking up at him like this felt so familiar, like when they were teens and this was a normal part of their weekly routine. The steer squirmed, reminding her that she still had it by the horns. Thankfully Joseph raced up and had three legs tied in seconds.

Sliding from beneath its head, Jolie stood and dusted off her backside. "If you ask me," she said, her poker face in place as Rowdy joined the group, "that was kind of slow."

That got a grin from Morgan. She grinned right back at him, and for a moment the tension between them eased and she felt her heart pick up the pace.

Rowdy jogged up and nudged her arm. "Not too shabby, pest. For a girl."

"A girl who had her moments of glory beating you both a time or two."

"I'm impressed," Wes said, wiping sweat off his forehead with the back of his arm.

"You did it!" Sammy exclaimed, elbowing his way through the group and grabbing her around the waist, hugging her tight.

"Hey, I told you I would." She returned his hug. A warm feeling expanded in her chest like a hot air balloon, lifting her spirits. Beaming with gladness, Jolie met Morgan's hazardous indigo gaze…and *whoosh,* just like that, all coherent thought evaporated right there under the big lights.

Morgan was rocked by the attraction buzzing through him as he watched Jolie. It was as if they'd been swept back to the past and the world was right again.

He was also more than a little startled by the enthusiastic way Sammy had just latched on to her. His thoughts were stumbling all over themselves as her dancing green eyes locked onto his.

Clearing his throat, he tried to clear his brain and turned his gaze to the kid.

Sammy connected with Jolie on a level that he hadn't come close to doing with anyone else. Morgan could practically see the kid's heart on his sleeve. And it immediately reminded Morgan that—no matter what he'd been feeling toward Jolie just minutes before—her being here was a mistake.

Oh yeah, a big mistake—of gargantuan proportions.

The kid needed stability—he did not need to fall for Jolie, then have her exit his life in a few short months. But Morgan's hands were tied. Jolie was the kind of person who drew people to her—no doubt about it. What could he do now? It was clear that it was already too late—Sammy was attached with a capital *A*.

"Morgan, did you see Jolie?" Sammy yanked on his sleeve to get his attention, too young to realize that Morgan hadn't taken his eyes off Jolie for even a second while she was out there.

"I saw. She was born to be a cowgirl." His observation came out before he could stop it. Born to be a cowgirl riding a horse— and ended up riding river rapids. The thrill was clearly much more exciting out there taming white water in places he couldn't pronounce much less compete with.

"I learned everything I know from Morgan, so do as he tells you and you can't go wrong."

Her glowing eyes settled on him, drawing him like some poor moth to a flame.

After all that had happened, he could still get lost in those gorgeous eyes of hers.

"Ha!" Joseph exclaimed, blessedly drawing Morgan's attention. "Morg taught me and you *still* beat me."

Jolie's laugh tinkled like wind chimes. "The steer has to cooperate, too, you know. That handsome hunk of a hairy dude wanted to be caught by me, I think."

"Well, duh," Wes drawled. "Who wouldn't?" That brought hurrahs from all and big goofy grins that were becoming commonplace around Jolie.

Jolie laid a hand on her heart and smiled at the boy. "Aw, that is so sweet."

She was a born dazzler. Morgan realized that in all of her wordplay with the boys, she'd still somehow managed to make them feel good about themselves, even though she'd beat them fair and square. He liked that, and appreciated it.

But what he didn't like was that he felt the shield he'd built up around his emotions slipping a notch as his admiration for her returned full force—he was feeling pretty dazzled himself.

Nope, he didn't like that. Not at all.

She hadn't even been back three days and he was already starting to think she was great again. He scrubbed the back of his neck, catching the half-amused eye of Rowdy.

Shaking his head, Morgan turned and headed toward the exit. While they prepared for the next groups muggin', he needed to put some distance between him and Jolie.

Some poor sodbusters just never learned.

Chapter Six

You can't go home again.

The words echoed in Jolie's head all the way back into town after the steer mugging. She'd never expected to come back to the sleepy little town she'd grown up in on that day six years ago when she'd hit the gas and aimed for the horizon. She'd left in a haze of confusion and tears, torn between two worlds. Now, here she was, amazing as it seemed, about to start teaching at Sunrise Ranch.

The boys on the ranch had instantly won a spot in her heart—and school hadn't even started yet. It felt as if she'd known them longer than two days. She was as attached to them as they seemed to be to her, and she knew it made Morgan edgy.

Everything about her made Morgan edgy, it seemed. But it sure had been nice to get a genuine smile out of him after she took down that steer. She'd felt that smile clear down to her toes. It had been hard to concentrate after he'd stalked out of the arena, but she'd done it and tried her hardest to convince Sammy to try, even saying she would go and help him, but he'd refused. She hadn't tried to force the issue—hopefully time would help him.

Time would hopefully ease the tension between her and Morgan, too.

Jolie pulled into the vacant spot in front of the three-story Dew Drop Inn. The old redbrick structure had originally been a dance hall saloon back in the 1800s. It had had a whole host of other aliases through the years, too, including funeral parlor, boardinghouse and restaurant. It was said to have welcomed many famous folks—and just as many infamous folks—inside its doors at one time or another.

It had been boarded up for years and fallen into terrible disrepair before Mabel Tilsbee bought it and poured her soul into it. And for over thirty years now it had been the Dew Drop Inn. Black porch posts held a second-story balcony, and Mabel kept two pots overflowing with ferns on either side of the ornate double doors with leaded glass insets and heavy brass fixtures.

Inside, wooden floors were covered with rugs that had been worn down over the years but still held a lovely charm and gave the place a welcoming feeling. For Jolie, the inn was home until she found a place to rent or decided to take the small house at the ranch Randolph had told her went with the job.

The decision was complicated by Morgan's being at the ranch, of course. She wasn't sure it was a good idea to be out there—around him—all the time, especially because it was obvious he didn't want her there. But even so, there had been moments—breathless times—when electricity crackled between them.

"Whoo," she whispered, just thinking about it. Even though Morgan had shut it down almost as quickly as it had happened, there was no denying they'd both felt it. And as a result, she was pretty certain he wouldn't welcome her moving out there, encroaching on him all the more.

It was a dilemma.

Swinging her legs from the doorless Jeep, she paused to stretch her aching back—taking a steer down by yourself did tend to strain muscles—and take in the rest of the town she'd left behind.

It had just two main roads that intersected, and smaller tree-lined roads that led to old-fashioned homes with spacious yards. She remembered it as the Mayberry of her youth. The newspaper office was on the far end of town, along with the hardware store and the barber shop. A church bench sat on the sidewalk between the two businesses, where the older men of town gathered to fix all the world's problems.

Chili Crump and Drewbaker Macintosh, whom she'd hugged at church that morning, were occupying the bench at the moment. In their mid-seventies, they'd taken the place of Snoot Pickens and Sargent Hanes, two characters who'd both passed but whose legends lived on in the tall tales of many.

A slight breeze fluttered over Jolie like whispers from years gone by. Yep, she was sure she'd been the topic of conversation on that bench many times—she could just imagine how it had been after she gave Morgan back his ring and hit the trail.

Poor Morgan. She hadn't really thought about what he'd had to endure after she'd broken their engagement. She'd mostly been thinking about her own pain, and her frustration that he couldn't support her decision to pursue her dream.

She swallowed, the breeze still whispering in her ears. Regret for the pain she'd caused settled like a rock in her stomach.

It was payback time—she was certain she was once more the hot topic on that bench, and everywhere else in town. She'd prepared herself for that when she'd decided to come home. But giving them something to talk about was a small price to pay to make things right between her and Morgan, to apologize for hurting him—something she had to keep reminding herself she was here to do. Apologize and heal— that had been the plan, but the feel of his arms after she'd fainted had taken her off track and confused her reasoning.

She wondered how Morgan felt about being in the spotlight, which she was certain she'd put him in when she'd rolled into town. Folks meant no harm, but Morgan was a pretty private person who'd already had way more attention than he'd ever wanted, thanks to her...and Celia. If she had to guess, she'd say he was less than overjoyed that she'd come home and put him back in the hot seat.

Scanning the rest of the town, her eyes came to rest on the Spotted Cow Café. Vibrant red geraniums overflowed at the entrance, and the bright yellow door stood out like a welcoming beacon. She'd been the one who'd come up with the idea to paint the door lemon pie–yellow all those years ago. Jolie's stomach growled as she looked at it. Clearly, the door did its job, and did it well.

Behind her the string of bells on the Dew Drop Inn's door tinkled merrily. Jolie turned back toward the inn.

"Well, I'll be! If it ain't Jolie Sheridan! Hon, it's about time you came back home!" exclaimed Mabel Tilsbee, rushing from the building. The owner of the Dew Drop Inn engulfed Jolie and hiked her up in the air. Arms clamped to her sides and her feet dangling at Mabel's shins, Jolie felt her body shake in the breeze. Mabel had always had a soft spot for Jolie. She'd also been the one who'd told Jolie that she'd never be happy if she lived with regrets.

"I am so happy you're here!" Mabel cried as she squeezed the life out of Jolie. "Goodness gracious, this is the best surprise ever. When I got back into town a few hours ago and I found out you had checked in, I couldn't believe it!"

"It's good to see you, too," Jolie gasped, trying to move her arms. Mabel started jumping up and down—for a woman in her mid-sixties, she was as strong as a moose.

"Mabel, come on now, let the poor girl go," Ms. Jo barked from behind Jolie. Mabel obeyed her friend and released her. Feeling like a dishrag wrung dry, Jolie grabbed the porch post for support.

"Thanks," she wheezed. "I heard you were on a mission trip to Haiti."

"God was good to let me go. And good to let me come home." With her hands on her hips, Mabel stared at Jolie, grinning with her whole face. "Jo, ain't she a sight for sore eyes? I've been keepin' up with you," she said, not stopping long enough for Ms. Jo to answer her question. "And I saw that horrible accident. Just *terrible*. It was awful thinking of you trapped under that raging water. It's a miracle you're alive. A pure miracle, and don't you forget it. God's got plans for you, hon—that's what it is. Your shirt got caught under there on something, didn't it?"

Jolie nodded, her stomach turning over. It should have been a common roll maneuver that she'd made in the water thousands of times. But her shirt caught on a wayward limb beneath the water and everything went wrong.

Jolie's pulse grew shallow and she feared another fainting spell. It was maddening to feel so stinkin' weak. "I'm thankful to be alive." She smiled and tried to put a good face on it, hoping they wouldn't see through her.

"And here you are," Ms. Jo said, her knowing eyes catching everything. "Home to have Mabel do ya in right here on Main Street."

"Hush," Mabel scolded. "I was just excited to see her."

"That'd be a reason to squeeze the poor girl in half."

Mabel hiked her chin, gave her friend a warning look, then returned her attention to Jolie. "So how are you? Jo told me you were having some problems from it."

Of course Ms. Jo would have confided in Mabel. Maybe she'd said something to Nana, too. Well, there was nothing she could do about it now.

"Some." She cringed. "You know, it was scary, I'll admit, and I, well, I thought it was time to take a breather." She looked from one friend to the other. "And the truth is, I'd been missing the place, and everyone..." Her voice trailed off.

Mabel nodded, her expression empathetic. "Jo told me you're working at the ranch. Land's sakes, that was a shocker! How's that going, you bein' out there and Morgan, too?"

Mabel never had been one to dance around the elephant in the room. She just walked up to it and grabbed it by the trunk.

"He looks fine—good as ever." Boy, was that ever an understatement! "He's not too happy to see me, as you can imagine. So how have you been?" Jolie asked. Time to change the subject.

"As ornery as always," Ms. Jo grunted.

Jolie chuckled. "You still keeping Nana and Ms. Jo in line?"

"*Phassh*—me being the ornery one? Those two are the ones who can't be kept out of trouble."

"That's exactly what Nana said about you," Jolie teased, thinking of her visit with Nana. She was sure that Nana had kept her two friends in the loop about everything after that visit, probably because they were all worried that Jolie was going to break Morgan's heart again. Of course the man had shields of steel up—his heart was in no danger whatsoever.

"Where's the fun in staying out of trouble?" Mabel asked with a smile.

Jolie chuckled—it felt so good to see her old friends. It had been strange growing up and not really knowing girls her own age. She'd had the boys at the ranch, and all these ladies—her mother's friends— whom she'd thought of as grandmothers.

A big white ranch truck rumbled into town and slid into the slanted parking space just in front of them. Nana smiled and waved out the open window, her navy eyes luminous in the early evening sunlight. "Hey, there, gals. Y'all ready? Hey, Jolie girl."

"As we always are, Ruby Ann," Ms. Jo said.

"We're heading up to weed the flower beds at the church. Come with us," Mabel urged.

"Yes, come," Nana said, bobbing her hotpink straw cowgirl hat with a peacockfeather hatband that matched her eyes. "No sense spending the evening up in that room alone. And I brought snacks." Those were magic words, because even though her lean figure wouldn't show it, Nana was a master in the kitchen, rivaling Paula Deen with her mouthwatering concoctions.

"Did you bring that spice cake I love for my welcome-home gift?" Mabel asked, winking at Jolie.

Jolie's heart warmed at their inclusion, her mouth watering when Nana said that she had indeed brought the famed spice cake.

"Sounds like a plan to me," Jolie drawled, feeling happier than she had in a while. The only thing that would have made this moment better was if her mother were here, too. Her folks had moved closer to Houston a few years back, to take care of her grandmother, and she didn't see them very often anymore.

"No way am I passing on that cake and y'all's great company." She looked down at her dusty clothes. "I've already swum in the dirt today, so why not dig in it?"

"That's my gal." Ms. Jo took her arm. "Come on, then, let's get this horse to a gallop."

Clucking and yacking away, they piled into Nana's ranch truck and headed out. *Maybe you* can *go home again.* The thought jingled through Jolie like a catchy tune as she settled into the backseat with Mabel, who was eyeing the spice cake in the wicker basket on the seat between them, temptation dancing in her eyes.

They drove past Chili and Drewbaker sitting on their church pew, Nana tooted her horn.

"Honkin' at your boyfriend, Ruby Ann?" Ms. Jo teased, hiking a brow at Nana.

"Ha!" Nana declared, chuckling right along with the rest of them. "That Chili is barking up the wrong tree when it comes to this ol' gal. But I do love to tease him."

They broke into more chatter after that, and Jolie felt good realizing that after everything she'd been through and all the ways she'd changed, Dew Drop was still the warm, wonderful, welcoming place it had always been.

There was comfort in that, and despite her tangled thoughts about Morgan, Jolie settled in for an enjoyable evening with the girls. Maybe hanging with these wise friends would give her some much-needed clarity.

Monday morning arrived with the resounding confirmation that Morgan hadn't just dreamed Jolie was back in town and teaching at the ranch. Like a bad headache pounding on the back of his eyes, she'd stayed on his mind all night after she'd taken down that steer and won the heart of every boy on the ranch.

Even the grown-up ones.

It went without saying that he wasn't in the best of moods when he parked in front of the chow hall. As luck would have it, Jolie came striding out of the building, a cup of coffee in her hand.

Setting his resolve, he climbed from his rig and tipped his hat at her. "Mornin'," he said, taking in the excitement in her eyes despite the dark circles she'd tried to hide with makeup.

"Good morning. It's wild in there." She motioned toward the chow hall. "I thought I'd go get my head on straight before they show up."

The sudden need to pull her to him, to feel her pressed against his heart, again slammed into him, looking at those circles under her eyes. The woman needed some rest. She'd said she was having nightmares—how bad were they? Obviously bad enough to be damaging.

"Sounds like a plan. They'll be over there soon enough and then all bets are off for the day. If you have any trouble, I'll be in my office most of the day."

Her smile put a catch in his breath. "There will be no trouble. I promise—though I haven't taught since student teaching, I'm a whole lot less gullible. It'll be fine."

Giving him a wink, she headed down the plank sidewalk that ran the length of the chow hall. He just stood there, like a fool, unable to move.

At the end of the sidewalk, she stepped onto the gravel, paused, turning, then gave a hesitant smile. "Thanks, Morgan."

He watched her go, her long cinnamon hair loose today, swinging like waves of warm spice tea midway down her back.

His jaw tightened. It took him a minute to catch his breath and pull his gaze away. He was one messed-up cowboy—that was the long truth of it all.

The chow hall was buzzing as he strode inside. Excited conversations were easy to pick up on as he headed toward the buffet table—"Jolie" this, "Jolie" that. Their new teacher filled the airwaves.

Not only had she successfully beat Joseph in the mugging—something they all aspired to do—but they were also excited about her kayaking, just like he'd suspected. Yep, it was more than clear they thought she was pretty awesome.

But would they still think she was awesome when she headed off into the sunset, leaving them all behind, standing in the dust?

A sudden poke in the ribs halted his downward-spiraling thoughts. Turning, he found his grandmother holding a spatula in her hand.

"Those eyebrows of yours are going to grow together if they get any closer. And that frown is never a good sign this early in the morning."

Morgan grunted. "Mornin', Nana. It sure smells good in here."

Nana's cheeks were rosy red from the kitchen heat. Tilting her head to one side, she crossed her red-sleeved arms over an apron that proclaimed, *Cooked with love— so hug me!*

"At least you noticed." A teasing undertone matched the twinkle in her eyes. "I wasn't sure you were even with us. Saw you talkin' to Jolie out there. If her being back has got you this shook up, then I'm not sure you're going to make it till the end of the semester."

"Nana."

"No one *heard* me. Now, really, are you okay?" Her Texas drawl was thick as the syrup the boys were fighting over at the end of the buffet line.

"Just concerned for the boys."

"They're doing fine. Stop worrying." She looked over at Sammy and B.J., whose syrup tug-of-war had gotten a little out of hand. "We'll talk about this later," Nana said, then turned her attention to the boys. "Hey, fellas, hold your horses! Do y'all think that syrup is the last syrup on earth?"

The boys halted in their battle, blinking at Nana in confusion, still clutching the syrup bottle between them.

"Well, don't just blink at me like a couple of owls. Answer my question like gentlemen. Sammy, what do you think? Is that the last bottle of syrup on earth?"

The kid swallowed like he had a biscuit stuck in his throat. "I don't figure so."

"Ma'am," Nana reminded him.

"Ma'am," Sammy added quickly.

"And what about you, B.J.—what's your answer?"

The younger boy cleared his throat. "Ma'am, Ms. Nana, it probably ain't. Only it's the only one I see."

Nana put her hands to her hips and her lips twitched at the corners. "You are both right. There is a lot more syrup in the kitchen, so I don't think you have anything to fight over. Thank the good Lord for your blessings and share that bottle or you'll both be eating your pancakes with no syrup at all."

Sammy was the first to let go. "Yes, ma'am. Are you sure there's enough?"

Morgan patted Sammy's shoulder. "There's plenty, so no more fighting."

"Sammy started it," B.J. offered, dousing his pancakes. "But he's new and ain't learned we got it good here."

Nana met Morgan's gaze with grateful eyes. He knew that it meant so much to her to be here for these boys and all the others who'd come through the foster care program to live here with them. He felt the same way. But he had his work cut out for him with Sammy.

He had to get the kid acclimated to the ranch. Small things like fighting over syrup didn't bother Morgan. But struggling to fit in did. He'd seen the look in Sammy's eyes as he'd let go of the syrup. Fear laced everything the boy did. Something about Sammy seemed different, but Morgan just couldn't put his finger on it.

Maybe Jolie would be able to help with that. The notion struck him as totally counter to what he'd been thinking since she'd arrived. He was still worried about her leaving—more so since seeing how the boys, especially Sammy, had taken to her.

But he knew he had to ease up. Fact was, Jolie was here and there wasn't anything he could do about it. Except pray that she did more good than damage before she left—and that his heart was still intact when she went.

Chapter Seven

The week flew for Jolie. She and the boys settled into a routine, though it did take some getting used to. Jolie wasn't teaching just one or two subjects, or even one age group. She was teaching all subjects to sixteen boys in grades one through twelve, all at varying skill levels—even those in the same grade.

She had every available teaching tool at her fingertips, though, and access to whatever she needed. The purpose of the private school was to give these boys a step up when it came to academics. Some of them had had such terrible home lives before coming to Sunrise Ranch that they either hadn't gone to school much at all, or their grades were far below passing. Morgan's mother had dreamed of not only giving boys the opportunity to live and experience life on this beautiful ranch, but also to see to their spiritual needs and provide the chance for them to thrive in all aspects of life. The boys Jolie had gone to school with had gone on to become doctors, lawyers, businessmen, ranchers, rodeo champions—the list went on. There were even a couple of preachers in the mix, and a missionary, too. Lydia's vision had been a blessing in so many ways, and this week Jolie had gotten to experience it from the other side of the desk.

She was tired, but her spirit felt peaceful. She'd come to the decision that she needed to move into the farmhouse that Randolph had offered. Maybe if she settled into a real home for a few months it would help ease the nightmares and she could get some much-needed rest. Despite the lingering worry that Morgan might have a problem with her moving to the property, she was excited to make the move that evening.

Friday had come quickly. She was cleaning off the chalkboard prior to heading to the inn to grab her meager belongings. The creak of the front door had her looking over her shoulder, to find Morgan.

Immediately her pulse skipped as it had on the mornings she'd run into him briefly at the chow hall. Each time she'd been unable to gauge what was going on behind those deep blues of his.

Her nerves jangled, and it felt as though butterflies had taken flight in her stomach.

"Hey," he said, closing the door. He crossed the room in a few quick strides, coming to stand beside her desk with his hat in his hands. "Are you done for the day?"

The butterflies fluttered more. Morgan McDermott still had the ability to shake up her world. It was maddening—the man should be outlawed. Dressed in worn jeans and a loose turquoise button-up shirt with rolled-up sleeves showing off his corded forearms…Morgan was all cowboy.

"Yes," she forced herself to answer, trying to get her focus off just how handsome a man he was. "And I might add that my first week as teacher has been a success in my book. I *loved* it." She pushed on, ignoring the butterflies. "It felt so good reaching for ways to ignite those curious minds." Wrapping her arms around her waist, she tried to find the right words to express her feelings. "Your mother, she had such vision, Morgan. I'm just so glad to have this opportunity."

She thought she saw shock flash in his eyes, but the shield he seemed to wear when he was around her clicked into place almost instantly. Except for the mornings she'd run into him in the chow hall, he'd stayed clear of her since the mugging. The connection she'd felt between them—if only for a moment—had disappeared just as he had.

"I've heard from the boys that you are one cool teacher."

"Ooh," she cooed, giving him a teasing grimace. "I know it had to hurt you to hear that. Worse having to *repeat* it."

That actually won her a smile that tickled her insides—and suddenly she was remembering being kissed by Morgan.

As if she'd ever forgotten it.

She'd been kissed a few times over the years by the men she'd dated, but there hadn't been many, and their kisses had been like cola without the fizz. No one had ever appealed to her—or affected her—like Morgan. Her gaze shifted to his lips and her pulse paused. She leaned slightly toward him, drawn by an invisible cord.

"The boys expressed what I've been worried about from the minute I learned about this deal you and my dad worked out," Morgan said.

Jolie prayed for patience with capital letters. Looked as if there was no reason for her to be thinking about Morgan McDermott's kisses after all.

"Morgan, come on. This bad attitude…"

She let her words trail off. She'd had little sleep, leaving no patience for this.

"I'm just worried—"

She pinned him with a glare and cut him off. "I *get* that you are worried that I'm going to run off and they will feel abandoned. But I'm here to help them, not hurt them. I've signed a contract for the semester and I plan to honor that."

Clamping his mouth shut, he said nothing, instead absentmindedly tracing a finger across the front of her desk. Despite her anger, Jolie shivered, thinking of his fingers tracing her cheek as they had so many times, so long ago. When he glanced up at her, his expression was less guarded.

"Look, I'm sorry. I didn't come here to fight. I've been watching Sammy ever since the calf wrestling and I think you're helping him," he admitted.

Had she heard him right?

"I came to tell you that I'll do whatever I need to do to help you help him," Morgan continued. His amazing blue eyes softened—he was actually conceding.

"G-good," Jolie stammered. She thought about trying to apologize again, telling him that she hadn't meant to hurt him. But she knew he would only deny that she'd hurt him in the first place. "That's the way it should be. Our past, what happened between us—"

"Is the past," he said firmly.

"Yes. We should still be able to help these boys even though we once had feelings for each other and it didn't work out."

What else could she say? She'd just come up against one wall after another with him—he'd made it clear there was no sense in rehashing old history that he had no desire to revisit. So she stopped trying. For now.

They stared at each other as if both trying to figure out where they went from here. He raked his fingers through his black hair and she could almost feel the sensation on her skin.

Slapping his hat on his thigh, he nodded, then strode out the door. On the steps he turned back toward her.

"I hear you've decided to move into the farmhouse." Topic changed. "Do you need help moving?"

"No, I'm fine. I didn't bring much with me, and your dad told me it was semifurnished."

"Yeah, it should be okay to get you by till you leave at the end of the semester. If you decide you need help, call and I'll bring some boys over to lend a hand."

Jolie rubbed her temple, watching Morgan stride away into the distance. Oh, what a tangled web they'd woven.

She missed him. She'd not only given up her fiancé, but her best friend, too. Had she chosen the wrong road that day?

The question was irrelevant—she'd had to leave. She just wished it hadn't cost her Morgan's friendship. She'd hoped that coming here to apologize would give her back her friend.

A soft bump and then a creak sounded from the back storeroom. She headed to investigate and found the back door standing open. Someone hadn't closed it properly, she thought with a smile. Kids.

Deciding it was time to be practical— no more drifting back to the past—she locked up and headed out. She had a house to move into and a man to boot from her thoughts.

Good thing she'd worn her riding boots today.

"Guys! Hey…guys," Caleb huffed when he finally made it to the horse stable where the other boys were tending to their horses. "Sammy…" He paused, taking a deep breath. "I think Morgan likes Jolie!"

Joseph spun around, the cool-down brush he'd been using on his horse still in his hand. "Whoa, slow down, slick."

"Yeah," Wes urged, putting a hand on Caleb's shoulder. "Breathe, dude, before you keel over."

Caleb gulped air, feeling as if his eyes were going to pop out he was so winded. He needed to tell this, to make them understand!

"Now, what were you saying?" Wes asked after Caleb had sucked in a couple more huge gulps of air and calmed down a little.

"Okay," Caleb said slowly, looking around the group, trying to harness his excitement. "I was over at the school, and I heard Morgan and Jolie talkin'."

"And?" Joseph urged.

"And guess what? I think they used to have a thing."

"A thing?" Sammy asked. "What's a thing?"

"Yeah, what thing?" Wes asked.

Caleb grunted, impatient for them to get it. "You know, a *thing*. For each other. Back when they were young."

Caleb noticed Joseph and Wes look at each other all serious.

"You sure about that? Like, what did you hear?"

"Jolie, she said— She was talkin' to Morgan and said, just because they used to like each other and it didn't work out, that shouldn't stop them from helping us."

"Well, what do you know." Joseph crossed his arms and got that look in his eyes that told Caleb he was thinking something over.

"Swweeet." Wes grinned.

Joseph looked thoughtful. "You know Morgan's been like a dad to us for a long time and he's never been sweet on a girl."

"Well, there was that woman we saw him with once in town." Wes hooked his thumbs in his belt loops. "We never saw her again, so I figure that didn't work out so good."

Joseph nodded. "Yeah, he never talks about anyone."

"I heard he got left at the altar or something one time and it gave him a broken heart," Tony offered. "I'm just sayin', you know, like, do you think it coulda been Jolie?"

"Naaah, she wouldn't do something like that," Wes scoffed.

"I wonder, though." Joseph's eyes widened. "I heard Nana saying she left six years ago, then I got here not long after she left. And, you know, back then we didn't see much of Morgan."

Caleb waved his hands. "I ain't much on knowing what love looks like. I can tell you that Jolie looked real sad, though. And well, Morgan, he kinda looked weird, like he'd just swallowed some nasty cough syrup. Then he told her that that was the past and it should stay that way."

Wes whistled. "This is good. I feel *romance* in the air."

"That'd be cool." Joseph's grinned at Caleb as all the other kids started talking.

"You mean like if they fell in love," Sammy said, looking weird, too.

"But," B.J. piped up, "you said Morgan wanted it to stay in the past and he looked all mad."

"You'd have to have seen Jolie, the way her shoulders were all hunkered down like she'd just lost the rodeo or something. She was sad. That's all I know, though, because I got out of there. Fast."

"Sounds good to me." Wes wiggled his eyebrows.

"Yeah." Caleb grinned. "I think it would be neat to see Morgan with a girlfriend. Oh! She's moving into the farmhouse, too, and Morgan said something about how it would be fine till she left at the end of the term."

"It'd be like having a mom," B.J. said.

Caleb heard the wish in his voice and knew what he meant. Morgan and his dad were like their dads—they were the ones involved in running the foster care program. The house parents were great, but they were more like grandparents than dads. It would be nice to have a mom around the ranch.

"Yeah, until mine comes back to get me," Sammy said. "I like Jolie."

Caleb felt bad for Sammy. They all knew his parents weren't coming back. He'd find out eventually, just as they all did. "Then it's done." Grinning from ear to ear, Joseph looked at everyone. "So here's what we're going to do."

Good. Joseph had a plan. He always did—the boys counted on that.

"What are we gonna do?" Sammy asked, and Caleb nodded because he wanted to know, too.

"Whatever it takes." Wes cocked an eyebrow at Joseph, who laughed.

"Yeah, that's about it. We're gonna make those two spend as much time together as possible." Joseph winked at Sammy. "Short Stuff, if you like Jolie, we're gonna make it so she sticks around."

Tony, who was tougher than all of them put together, frowned. "My sister used to love this old movie about some twin girls who did all kinds of stuff to get their divorced parents back together. I think my sis thought it would work on our parents. There wasn't any saving that train wreck, though."

"See, that's the thing. If Morgan fell in love with Jolie, then she might stay and we'd have a cool teacher. Maybe then she'd teach us to kayak, too." Wes had been talking a lot about kayaking. He craved adventure and wanted to ride bulls, only that was the one thing on the ranch the boys weren't allowed to do.

"You did good, Caleb," Joseph said, clapping him on the back. "Real good."

Caleb grinned, feeling as if his chest was going to explode. "You really think we can do this?"

Wes and Joseph hiked their eyebrows at each other before looking at the rest of them.

"We're gonna give it our best shot," Joseph said.

"And that's a promise." Wes had a twinkle in his eyes that meant one thing: they were going to have fun doing whatever it was they were going to do. That twinkle *was* a promise.

And hopefully it was a promise to get Jolie and Morgan back together so Sunrise Ranch could feel even more like a home, with a dad…and a mom.

Chapter Eight

Jolie eyed Salty, the black mare she was about to ride. She hadn't been on a horse in years and hoped she didn't embarrass herself.

"You sure are taking your time getting in that saddle."

Morgan walked up beside her looking all-too-good in his beat-up cowboy hat and checkered shirt. His jaw was scruffy with a five-o'clock shadow and there was some challenge in his eyes as he studied her.

"I'm about to climb up there. I'm just wondering if you could have given me a bigger horse to ride." Salty was huge—at least sixteen hands tall and very broad.

"She's a good horse. Not as salty as she used to be." His lips hitched into a grin. "You can handle her and you know it."

"If it's like riding a bike, then yes, I'll be just fine."

He turned serious as he studied her. "You look worn-out, Jolie. Are you still having nightmares?"

Lately, Jolie had been fighting hard against the urge to try to knock down the walls that Morgan had put up between them. She knew she *wished* there were no walls between them. Wished she felt free to talk to him. But would that be a mistake? If there was no wall she might fall for him all over again, and where would that leave her…them? But despite her uncertainties, when he looked at her with such concern, she knew she was fighting a losing battle to keep the wall up between them.

"I don't want to talk about that right now," she replied. "I'd like to hop on this horse and see if I still have what it takes to be a cowgirl."

"Uh, yeah—you're being a little too humble. You're a natural-born cowgirl and that doesn't ever leave a person."

She gave a discordant laugh. "My composure is a bit shaken, so that's all the more reason to hop on this baby and join this roundup. The boys were pretty persistent in getting me to come along. Sammy truly wouldn't take no for an answer."

"That's the reason he's sitting up there on Cupcake looking like he's about to toss his cookies."

She laughed. "Poor kid. The good thing is he's doing it, and that is a really big step for him. If helping in this roundup gets him to push himself, then I'm all in."

Morgan tipped his hat at her. "Good for you. Load up. You sure you don't need any help?"

The twinkle in his eye caught her off guard for an instant. Was he teasing her, or...flirting? Seeing the old Morgan for a second dumbstruck her. "I think I can manage. Do *you* need a helping hand?"

He laughed at her offer, shot her a wink

and strode off with his cowboy swagger. Watching him swing into the saddle, a sigh escaped her. Berating herself, she jammed her boot into the stirrup, grabbed the saddle horn and hoisted herself up with ease. It felt like old times. A sense of excitement washed over her—this was going to be a good day.

Only after she grabbed the reins did she notice the boys watching her. Maybe it was her imagination, but they'd sure seemed interested in her past on the ranch this week during class. They'd asked all kinds of questions, even some about kayaking. She'd been happy to have made it through those without falling on the floor again.

She'd been able to put off their push for kayaking lessons, but that wouldn't last forever—the boys wanted to learn. She hoped she could eventually find her way toward teaching them.

Along with all those questions came some about growing up on the ranch. Even though she hadn't told them everything, she had given them small peeks into her life. And her life on the ranch couldn't be explained without stories of Morgan. They'd been inseparable as kids, long before he'd noticed her as a teenager. Long before she'd begun to panic that if she stayed at Sunrise, she would never find out who she really was and what she wanted out of life.

Long before she'd fallen in love with the feel of conquering a raging river, and long before she'd made the mistake of falling in love with Morgan, threatening her dreams of seeing the world one river at a time.

The boys were definitely getting to her. There was no way on earth she could look at those grins and tell them she didn't want to hang out with Morgan all day. So she'd agreed to come, and now she was suffering the consequences by having to corral the pitter-patter of her heart when he was near. No doubt about it, she was wrapped tightly around their wily fingers.

Giving them all a thumbs-up, she was rewarded by a grin from Sammy. B.J. giggled and Joseph returned the thumbs-up, then tipped his hat, copying Morgan. The kid was determined to walk in Morgan's boot prints. Jolie couldn't blame him—Morgan was a good, good man.

"Let's roll," Morgan called. Jolie took a deep breath, and off she went to spend an entire day with Morgan. She just hoped her heart could handle it.

A couple of hours later, Jolie rode over beside Sammy and Morgan just as Joseph charged after a steer that had cut and run for the gully.

"Catch it, Joseph!" Sammy yelled, startling the steers around him and making his horse jump.

Jolie's heart skipped some beats but regulated when Morgan grasped the reins of Sammy's horse before she bolted.

"Easy, Sammy." His deep voice rumbled with gentle concern that pulled at Jolie's heart strings. "Don't go yelling like that and yanking on your horse's bit. You'll scare her. Okay, son?"

"Yes, sir." Sammy's knuckles were white

as he clutched the saddle horn. "I got excited. I sure wish I could ride like Joseph."

"You will someday. But until you're more confident, you'll have to remember to take it easy when you're out here in the middle of a bunch of cattle."

They all watched Joseph racing through the tall grass and around scraggly mesquite trees in pursuit. Whipping his rope from the saddle, Joseph had his loop instantly twirling circles above his head as he chased the steer.

"He's really good," Jolie said, watching the rope land in a graceful arch around the runaway's head.

"Awesome!" Sammy exclaimed in a loud whisper.

"He's a natural," Morgan agreed. "Joseph took to cowboyin' like a duck to water. Kinda like someone else I know. She just had more duck in her than cowgirl."

Jolie tucked a stray strand of hair behind her ear as she took his half-teasing, half-serious words into account. "Funny. But there is some truth in that."

He nodded. "Believe me, I know."

Better than most. Even though he didn't say the words, Jolie heard them loud and clear.

All morning she'd been glimpsing the old Morgan, but now his shields slid back into place.

"I guess you do," she said. It was all she could say, because they both knew it was the truth.

Their gazes caught, like magnets pulled to each other. Jolie wanted to say so much to Morgan—

"Are you gonna teach us to kayak?" Sammy's question broke the moment— and it was a good thing, too.

"I'm not sure, Sammy. Like I said in class I'll have to see how things go."

"What things?" he persisted. "Wes said it looked real fun. We watched you on the computer and it was cool."

It struck her that he'd said teach *us* to kayak. He was getting braver.

"It's very dangerous." She forced herself to remain calm. They were simply *talk-*

ing about kayaking, she reminded herself. She wasn't in the water, wasn't near the water....

She wasn't under the water fighting for her life, finding the thrill of the ride not so thrilling when she held it up against being alive.

Sammy patted Cupcake. "Wes said I was too much of a scaredy-cat to ride a rapid."

"That wasn't nice of Wes to say," Morgan interjected, his tone saying he wasn't pleased with Wes. "He's a lot bigger than you and he likes doing things that are risky. You have to do what's comfortable for you, Sammy. *Not* what someone else wants you to do."

"That's right," Jolie said, relieved that the conversation was heading away from kayaking. "We're so glad you wanted to ride a horse this morning and help with the roundup. However, if it was something you really didn't want to do, then we would have respected your choice."

Sammy looked serious. "My momma was going to buy me a horse when I got older—I mean, she's *gonna* buy me a horse. She's probably trying to get the money to do it right now. So—so I need to learn to ride so I can be ready."

Jolie didn't know what to say. Maybe his mother *had* told him she was going to buy a horse. And what right did Jolie have to tell him he might never see his mother again?

Morgan shifted in his saddle. "It's good for you to learn to ride. It will help you join in with the others. Now, ease on over to the outside of the left line and stay on the outer edge. That'll help keep the cattle moving forward and not out. If a stray busts loose, let Joseph or Wes handle it. Got that? Today, your job is just to get used to the saddle and the cattle."

Sammy let go of the saddle horn and took the reins. He nodded, looking intently at the cattle. "I'll try."

"You'll do fine. Just do as I ask and stay safe. Okay?"

"Okay, Mr. Morgan."

Jolie smiled at him. "I'm so proud of you, Sammy. You're doing great."

Sammy's eyes widened as if he'd never heard a compliment before. "Thanks. I've been praying about my fears just like you told me. 'When I am afraid, I will trust in you, O Lord!'" As he repeated the verse Jolie had taught him, he finished as if he were a fire-and-brimstone preacher. Jolie laughed and Sammy, grinning, tapped Cupcake with his heels and headed off.

Jolie watched him go, pride swelling in her as if he were her own child.

Morgan eased his horse closer to hers as they started moving with the cattle, keeping Sammy close by. "What's the real story on why you won't teach the boys to kayak?"

Jolie had known this was coming. She'd known it ever since she'd passed out.

"I have reservations about teaching them is all."

"I've figured that out. But something's going on here that isn't right. Like I said in the arena, you leave your career, you're having nightmares, you look like you haven't slept in months. You get faint at the mention of kayaking—yes, I noticed exactly what we were talking about when that happened. And now you avoid even talking about teaching the kids the very thing that makes you tick."

His expression had hardened as he spoke and his words were matter-of-fact. It was as if he had placed her inside a glass jar, and he was on the outside looking in without emotion.

She hated it.

And the realization that she hated it hit her like a cannonball.

"Like I told you, I'm having a little trouble."

"And?" he prompted. He'd always had a way of pulling the truth out of her if he wanted it.

"I'm afraid—" She'd no more gotten the words out when they heard shouting at the front of the cattle drive. Another steer had broken loose from the pack and was heading for the hills as hard as it could run.

This time it was Wes who took off after it, his rope spinning in the air. Suddenly his horse reared straight up, then began bucking wildly. Wes dug his heels in and hung on. He kept his hand on the reins and fought to control the animal that had suddenly turned into a bucking bronc.

The second the ruckus began, Morgan spurred his horse forward, as had Joseph and Rowdy. Jolie knew instinctively what was in the grass before she saw the rattler strike out at the horse's legs.

It was *huge*—its head was as big as her fist!

The horse bucked far enough away that the snake missed its target. Morgan tugged his rifle from its holder and fired before anyone else could get close.

He didn't miss his target.

Morgan had always been steady with his aim and a sure shot, just like his dad and brothers. It was a known fact out here sometimes it took a bullet to protect the herd. Or the kids.

"Yee-haw!" Wes yelled. Getting his horse

under control, he whipped his hat off and grinned as if he'd just won the bronc-busting event at the National Finals Rodeo. She remembered Wes mentioning he wanted to ride bulls, but it wasn't allowed on the ranch. Even though she completely understood why the ranch wouldn't put the guys in danger like that, she wondered just how good he might be if given the chance.

Morgan's gun was back in its sheath before the smoke cleared and Jolie breathed a sigh of relief, sending up a prayer of thanks. It had been a very close call. If Wes hadn't been as good a rider as he was, he'd have been on the ground with the rattler and things could have been really bad. Of course to him, it was all a great adventure.

She remembered being that way. Before.

Jolie let the idea of God's goodness and protection wash over her. She knew in her case He'd been there for her, but she still couldn't seem to let go of her fear. She wondered what it was going to take to find her courage again.

She rode up beside Sammy, who'd halted his horse and sat frozen, watching the scene play out in front of him.

"You okay?" she asked.

His smile took her by surprise. "That was *awesome!* Did you see that? Did you see how Morgan shot that snake?"

Jolie chuckled. "Yes, I guess it was pretty awesome."

In the distance Morgan put a hand on Wes's shoulder and grinned. Now that everyone was safe and sound, Jolie had to agree it was like a scene straight out of the movies. The way Morgan had charged to Wes's rescue—he protected the boys in his care as though they were his own flesh and blood.

He *was* awesome.

Snared by his gaze across the distance, her whole being seemed to hum. Her breath caught and she suddenly felt lost. Why had she really come home? Was it to apologize to Morgan? Or was it to find out if she'd made a mistake leaving in the first place?

And the biggest question of all: Was it possible that she was still in love with Morgan McDermott?

Chapter Nine

Morgan nearly had a heart attack when Wes's horse spooked. Standing there talking to the boy, he gave thanks that the snake hadn't bitten the horse, and Wes hadn't been thrown to the ground.

"That was some great riding you did," Rowdy told Wes. "You can be proud of that. No doubt about it."

"Yes, you can," Morgan added. "That right there shows why it's good to be prepared with your skills. And God had His eye on you, too. Don't forget that."

"I won't, sir." Wes's wolfish grin faded for a moment. "I was ridin' and I was prayin' at the same time." His smile popped back in place. "I was prayin', 'Good Lord, get me out of here!'" He chuckled as only Wes could, and the rest of them did, too.

After the excitement, Morgan didn't get to finish his conversation with Jolie. He and Rowdy split up, each riding the perimeters of the herd, away from the boys, watching for any other rattlers. When they made it to the last watering hole, it had been a long day. They still had a way to go, but the longest part of the drive was done.

The guys were tired and hungry and the cattle were thirsty.

Nana and her "truck wagon," as they'd named her version of the chuck wagon, were a welcome sight. The bed of the truck was rigged with all the essentials to fix a meal out on the range, and Nana also towed a barbecue pit behind the truck. This morning she'd started them off with a hearty breakfast in the chow hall, but they'd had only jerky and water in the saddle for lunch. The delicious smell of roasting meat and baked beans wafted through the air as Morgan dismounted.

"Want me to take your horse to the river for water?" Sammy asked. Morgan noticed he was riding with a little more confidence than he'd shown earlier. Riding all day could do that.

Morgan handed over his reins. "Thanks."

"I think Jolie's sick," the kid said, worry in his tone. "She didn't look like she felt good when she got off her horse. Caleb took it to the river for her."

Morgan looked up and saw Jolie trying to hide a limp as she headed toward Nana. "Thanks for the heads-up, Sammy. I'll check on her."

Sammy grinned. "*Yes!* I mean, good. That'd be a *real* good idea."

Morgan watched the kid lead the horses toward the river, a little confused but mostly amused by the kid's over-the-top reaction. Then he headed toward Jolie. He knew she'd bitten off more than she could handle today with this long drive. She was in great shape, no doubt about it, but there was a difference between riding a rapid and riding a horse all day. A shorter drive to start on would have been better. But she'd let the boys talk her into coming today, even knowing what it would cost her. The thought that she would do that for them—well, it did his heart good. Real good.

"Sore?" he asked, striding up next to her and grabbing a paper cup to pour himself some of Nana's sweet tea, which was a blessing all the way down.

Jolie cringed. "Just a little."

Nana clucked her tongue at her. "Honey, I'm not going to say I told you so, but I will say you're probably not going to be walking tomorrow. A long salty soak tonight might save you."

"Oh yeah," Jolie groaned. "I may soak all night."

Morgan's hand tightened on his cup. Laughing in the face of pain was pure Jolie—the Jolie he'd fallen for. He halted that line of thought and shoved it out of his head.

Massaging her thigh, she crinkled her nose, grinning at him. "There are just some muscles that are only used when riding a horse."

"Yup." Morgan fought being drawn to that grin with every ounce of strength he had. "But I have to say you've been a real trouper about it. Sammy's worried about you, though."

She clapped a hand to her forehead. "He saw me ease out of the saddle. I tried to throw my leg over the horn and hop off, but the leg just wouldn't cooperate. It was pretty pathetic."

Nana handed her the plate she'd fixed as they were talking. "Take this over yonder beside the river and hang your toes in the water while you eat. Take a load off."

Jolie took the plate. "I wanted to help you, Nana."

"You will do no such thing." Nana shooed her with her hands. "You've been doing your part all day. This is pretty self-serve for everyone and little work on my part. Now go." She shooed Jolie again. With a grateful look, she headed not toward the river but away from it, going to a stand of trees where the shadows of the evening settled.

Nana quickly stacked another plate high with brisket and beans and thrust it into Morgan's hands and ordered, "You go with her."

His boots dug in, drawing a stern look from Nana and leaving him no choice but to go. Crossing the grass, he caught some of the boys watching him.

"Enjoy," Rowdy said with a smirk plastered on his face.

Morgan didn't bother to reply to Rowdy's teasing—he was too focused on continuing his conversation with Jolie. She'd been about to tell him why she wouldn't teach the boys to kayak, and what exactly she was afraid of. He'd been thinking about it all afternoon.

Joseph crossed his path before he got to Jolie. The kid was fighting a grin and an odd glint lit up his eyes as he shot Morgan a thumbs-up.

What was that all about?

Continuing on toward Jolie, he caught

sight of Caleb, so busy watching Morgan that he tripped on a log and fell flat on his face in the dirt. Jumping up, the lanky boy dusted himself off as he grinned at Morgan.

Something wasn't right here. They were all looking too...happy. Watchful.

He sat down beside Jolie, then set his glass of tea between them on the flat rock she'd chosen.

"I'm thinkin' Nana is right. I'm going to be in a world of hurt in the morning even with a salty soak."

Morgan stabbed a piece of brisket. "I'm sure you're used to being pretty beat up after a river run."

"So right," she answered, rolling her eyes as she scooped up a small forkful of beans and chewed. "These are so good."

He watched her enjoying her food for a couple of stretched-out moments and suddenly he felt like a goldfish in a very small aquarium. Glancing around he caught the boys watching him, although they immediately became very busy when they saw him catching their curious gazes.

What was with all the watching?

Ignoring them, he cut to the question he'd been turning over in his mind all day. "You were saying, before Wes tangled with the rattler, that you were having some trouble and that you were afraid." Jolie didn't take the bait and start talking. Quietly he continued. "What are you afraid of, Jolie? What's got you so tied up in knots that you're struggling with nightmares?"

She toyed with the meat on her plate, finally expelling an exasperated breath. "Okay, I'm only telling you this because we used to be…good friends. And I know you're going to pester me till I tell you and even pull the boss card, if needed."

"Yup." His mouth lifted at the corner— she knew him too well. "Right on both counts," he agreed.

"So here it is—the ugly truth of it. I can't bring myself to get back into my kayak."

What?

She couldn't have startled him more if

she'd slapped him. She'd lived and breathed kayaking from the day he'd first introduced her to it when she was twelve—she'd already been after him to teach her for a year. He knew how dangerous it was when the water was up and had refused to take her out, but she finally convinced him, and they'd played around with the small rapids during the dry season, when the river had been low and slow. He wasn't into crazy thrills—he'd used his kayak more for fishing—but he'd taught the kid a few things. Nothing fancy, because he didn't know anything fancy. And he warned her to steer clear of the rapids when the rains came.

The next summer when the river was up, she sneaked down to the water and experimented on her own. He'd been hotter than molten lava when she told him she'd taught herself how to roll—which was no small thing—and several other tricks of creek kayaking.

But what could he do? There had been

no stopping her. She'd had no fear of the water and she'd felt invincible.

Until now.

Staring into her clouded eyes, he realized he'd not had any idea how badly her brush with death on that river in West Virginia had affected her.

He studied her face. "I knew it was bad," he said, quietly. "But to make *you* afraid of the water? I can't grasp that."

She gave a humorless laugh. "Yeah, unbelievable. The girl you couldn't keep off the water is now afraid to go near it." She released a heavy sigh and rubbed her temples. "I can't get things straight in here. My head is so messed up. I'm in jeopardy of losing my sponsors if I don't get back out there soon."

Like the quick snap of a whip, anger ripped through him. "Don't they understand what you've been through?"

"I'm a professional. They pay me to compete with their logo on my shirts. I'm a billboard to them, and when I'm not on the water or doing press for an upcoming competition, they're not getting their money's worth out of me. It's understandable."

"*Understandable?* Yeah, I understand. You nearly died! They should have some sympathy for that."

"They do, to a point. I have to be back by Christmas, ready to shoot a commercial and test a new kayak for my biggest sponsor. We have to leave the country to shoot it in a warm climate, so they have to start making arrangements."

He had to admit that her life was interesting. She grew quiet, staring at the river that was just barely visible from where she'd chosen to sit. "If you're afraid to get in the water," he asked gently, "how are you going to train?"

"I'm still weight training, and I run each day before work."

"But you have to be in the water. You have to stay conditioned to it." Even he knew that jumping back in without being sharp would be suicide.

Jolie put her fork down. "I'm not sure if I'll ever be able to get back in the water,

Morgan. I—I *lost* something when I was pulled under and I couldn't come up. I left part of me down there. I've had close calls before—that's part of the sport. This, this was different. It's like I lost my heart beneath the water."

Her eyes were huge, haunted. And he reacted on instinct as much as anything else when he slipped his arm around her shoulders and tugged her into hug. She responded by laying her head on his shoulder. "It's going to be all right, Jolie. Coming here, getting away from everything was probably a good idea. Distance sounds good to me."

It hit him that he could run with this. If he wanted her back in his life, then he could milk this for everything it was worth—and get her to stay here on the ranch.

His own thoughts startled him. Did he want to do that?

He still had feelings for her—he couldn't deny that any longer. He might have buried them deep, but right now they were pounding at the steel plate encasing his heart.

Could he finally have what he'd wanted six years ago? Could he talk her out of trying to go back to life on the water?

His conscience pricked. This wasn't the way he'd want to be with her, no matter how tempting the option was. It wasn't honorable, and that was what he'd promised God he would be.

"It's going to be all right. You're the toughest girl I know, and I've never seen anything keep you down or hold you back."

She straightened, lifting her head off his shoulder. "Thanks for believing in me. I'm just not sure if I want to continue." Her beautiful green eyes shimmered. "I came back to reevaluate my life. And I'm not sure, Morgan, but I think I might have made a mistake when I left here six years ago."

A *mistake?* Morgan stared at her, shaken by the emotions richocheting inside him. His heart pounded as he tried to form a coherent string of words. None came. She *thought* she'd made a mistake when she'd handed him back his heart—did she get that? Did she get that she'd been holding his heart in her hands when she'd held that ring?

He shot to his feet. "I have to check the horses," he managed to say with reasonable calm. Then before he could say anything stupid, he strode away.

There were moments in a man's life when the best course of action was to keep his mouth shut.

This was one of those moments.

Chapter Ten

Jolie's words were on Morgan's mind the rest of the week. After she'd dropped her bombshell, he'd gotten as far away from her as he could get.

And he'd stayed clear ever since.

Actually, he'd stayed clear of pretty much everyone. Because there were times a man couldn't hide how angry he was.

Four days after the drive, his dad met him coming out of his office.

"All week you've been about as ornery as that stallion we sold last year. What's bothering you?"

"You brought her here," he snapped, scowling at his dad. "What do you think?"

Randolph raked his hand through his hair in frustration. "Look, I know this is a tough situation. Nonetheless, I'm trusting God that it'll work itself out."

"That's mighty good of you," Morgan grunted, feeling no better for his father's answer. *He* was the one who'd done this to him; *he* should be the one to fix it.

"Morgan." His father's voice stopped him as he started to leave. "You're going to need to forgive her, you know. For *your* sake."

Morgan kept on walking straight to his truck, started it up and drove. He just needed to *go*.

Forgive her? His dad had no idea what Jolie had said to him. She *thought* she might have made a mistake. A *mistake!* So, what if she hung around here, he let her back into his heart and then—boom!— she realized that the water was pulling her back? Where would that leave him?

Right back where you were when she left the first time.

After what seemed like forever, he ended up at Tucker's office in Dew Drop.

His brother had chosen to run for sheriff after his tours of duty in Afghanistan with the marines were done. There wasn't much happening in the tiny town, but there was still a need for the law since the county was fairly good-size. He had several deputies and Tucker led them well. He was steady as a rock and the brother Morgan went to when he needed good solid advice. Rowdy was more reckless—and the last thing he needed right now was reckless. Morgan entered the sheriff's department and went straight to Tucker's office, knocking on the open door. Tucker was pouring himself a cup of coffee. "Hey, Tucker, got a few minutes?"

His brother grinned and held up the pot. "You are right on time. Want a cup?"

"Do you have to even ask?" He walked in and took a seat in one of two hard-cushioned chairs. Tucker filled two black mugs and handed him one before taking his seat behind the desk.

"How's the situation going out there?" he asked, not one to beat around the bush.

Morgan knew he meant Jolie. "Is it that obvious why I'm here?"

Tucker hefted a shoulder. "You have that deer-run-over-by-a-semi-truck look. But then again, I'm trained to be observant." He waved at the wall of credentials behind him and gave Morgan a wiry grin before taking a sip of his coffee. "Talk to me before you explode."

Morgan told him, in confidence, some of what Jolie had revealed to him. He needed Tucker's black-and-white view on things. Even before he'd gone into law enforcement, Tucker had always had a clear view of the world around him.

"That's a tough one," Tucker said, a slow whistle escaping him. "It must have really messed Jolie up if she's thinking that way. Trauma has a way of cutting deep. Changing a person."

Tucker had experience with this—he'd seen lots of action on hostile soil and lost comrades during an especially brutal attack. He had a slight limp from the bullet that had sent him home, and scars that he didn't talk to anyone about. Not even Morgan.

"She's scared and she's not sleeping well. Still, when the boys aren't asking her to teach them to kayak, she's herself. Well, almost. But I don't know if I can—or want to—try again."

Tucker nodded although he didn't interrupt.

"But if I did, I could talk her straight into thinking quitting was the thing to do. Tucker, this fear could guarantee that she stay here on the ranch."

"Sounds like it." Tucker's brows met over serious McDermott blue eyes. He frowned. "You'd have it made."

Morgan set his coffee on the desk, stood up and crossed to the window, where he stared out at the main street in Dew Drop. From here he could see the Spotted Cow Café on the corner. When they were teenagers he'd bought plenty of pie there just so he could tease Jolie while she worked.

She'd loved it. Life had been perfect then. He'd believed they had a future stretching before them.

"I'd be lying if I said the thought wasn't flip-flopping around in my head, and that'd be pretty pathetic." He swung around as Tucker let out a gruff laugh.

"Yup. So what are you going to do? No, what do you *want* to do?"

Morgan's eyes narrowed. "Hey, you're supposed to be giving me some advice, not acting like a shrink."

"You're doing fine on your own. So?" Tucker pressed.

Morgan shook his head, hating what he was about to say. "She needs to get back in that water or she's going to regret it for the rest of her life."

"I agree. Sounds like she needs help from a friend."

Was he that friend? Dropping his head, Morgan felt his chest squeeze tight. When he looked up, he met Tucker's watchful eyes. "That water is what took her from me in the first place."

"Yeah." Tucker's eyes shadowed and he seemed lost in thought for a moment. "Life comes in circles sometimes. This might be rough."

Morgan just nodded, letting the truth settle in on him.

"You can handle it. Morgan, she came back here for a reason. She could have gone to her family in Houston, but she came here. That says something to me." Tucker looked down into his coffee cup for a few seconds, and then back up at Morgan. "When I was out there—when things were at their worst and I thought I was going to die before anyone could get me out—all I could think about was coming back here. Coming *home*. It wasn't just the ranch. Don't you get it, brother? Jolie came home. Maybe she doesn't even know why, but she came. Give this to God and see where it goes. You only live once. Maybe you need to take a chance and have no regrets."

Morgan knew Tucker was right. But that

didn't mean doing what he suggested was going to be easy.

In fact, it was probably going to be the hardest thing he had ever done in his whole life.

Days had gone by since the cattle drive and Jolie felt at loose ends since Morgan had walked away from their conversation. The boys had tried several times to get her to join in on other activities with Morgan, but she'd always managed to have something else to do, enabling her to make an honest excuse. The last thing she wanted to do was make Morgan uncomfortable again.

It hadn't taken any gifts of discernment to figure out he hadn't liked what she'd said. The man had jerked to attention and stampeded to the farthest corner away from her—and he'd stayed there.

She didn't blame him really. She was confused herself. She hadn't even meant to say what she'd said—the words had just come out, like they had a will of their own.

But it had just felt so right, sitting there with him like old times. There had been such comfort in being with him, in telling him what she was going through.

And then she'd gone too far.

Exposed too much.

Well, at least now she knew that her being back at Sunrise Ranch hadn't softened his heart to her at all. It was good information for her to have.

So this morning, she decided she'd throw herself into teaching to distract herself, and it was the perfect day for it—it was science day, and she was teaching the boys how to make a volcano.

"A volcano!" Sammy exclaimed when Jolie told them what they were going to do.

Not ever having taught science—or ever thought she would have to teach science—Jolie had been a little intimidated by the subject. But she was actually enjoying the class. She told them they were going to build the volcano with just a two-liter bottle of diet soda, sand and water. And they jumped right in, sculpting the wet concoction around the bottle, which not only resulted in the volcano but in a few muddy teens as well.

After it dried, Joseph poked it. "Hey, that does look good. I hear they just foam a little, though."

"That's why we're going to add these candies to the soda. I read online that it will make things a little more exciting," Jolie said with a wink.

"Really? What's it going to do?" Sammy asked, intent on the project. He'd become Jolie's personal helper, and the happiness it seemed to bring him helped her heart.

Smiling at them, she opened the Mentos candy. "Now, I'm ready to show y'all what happens when these two chemicals are combined."

"Let 'er rip!" Caleb yelped. He was so excited to see the eruption that he could hardly hold still.

"Stand back, everyone," she said, looking around the room. If anything, they all crowded closer.

Wes backed up, giving her a wink. "Bombs away!" he called.

Joseph gave her one of his thumbs-up and chuckled, "Let 'er rip."

The younger kids giggled with glee as she poured the entire tube of candy into the mouth of the volcano. It erupted instantly—spewing everywhere! Foam and gunk hit the ceiling and splashed down on everyone. Jolie yelled and the boys whooped in delight.

And at that very moment, Morgan strode into the classroom.

"What is going on?" he yelled above the laughter of the boys.

"It exploded, Morgan! Look!" Sammy yelled, pointing at the ceiling and wiping liquid from his face.

Morgan looked up just in time—a glob of foam fell right smack in the middle of his forehead. Eyes flaming, he wiped it off with his shirtsleeve and glared at her. And with good reason. The room was a mess.

He'd avoided her all week, so why had he picked *today* of all days to show up?

"I thought the volcano was supposed to spew a *little*," she said. "I had no idea it was going to erupt like Mount St. Helens."

Just great. He was going to give her the worst-teacher-ever award. She knew this just made him think of the mishap during her student teaching.

Hair dripping, she looked around the room. The boys stopped laughing and watched her warily, as if worried she was about to cry. She took in their expressions, and suddenly Jolie couldn't help it—she laughed.

Yes, she might look like an inept fool to Morgan, but this *was* funny. She laughed harder. The kids looked at Morgan and to her surprise, his lip twitched and then he, too, began laughing. And then the boys joined in.

When the laughter died down, Jolie slipped her arm around Sammy's shoulders, giving him a hug. "Now we have to clean up this catastrophe."

"We'll help," Caleb offered.

Jolie grabbed paper towels and began

wiping the sticky soda from the computers. Thankfully, she'd had sense enough not to set the volcano too close to them and the soda had only splattered on the keys.

"So, were you trying to trump your classroom adventures as a student teacher?" Morgan's voice was warm with teasing and his eyes warmer as he looked at her. But the tingle that raced up her spine was the warmest of all.

"Just trying to keep things interesting."

He chuckled. "Always."

She stopped scrubbing computer keys and he stopped wiping the desk. Funny how that simple word affected her—*always*. What would *always* be like with Morgan? She'd given that up with him and yet she'd never stopped thinking about it.

Standing with him so close, feeling the warmth of him and smelling the scent of his woodsy cologne, she began wondering full throttle about him, about feeling his arms around her and his lips against hers....

Great, Jolie. Just great.

"You almost missed all the fun, Morgan." Joseph broke into her daydreaming.

"Almost," Morgan drawled, looking at Joseph. "Thanks for inviting me to come to the show. It was a bit more exciting than you'd said it was going to be."

So that's why he was here.

"If your teacher would read her instructions a little more closely, maybe things wouldn't get so crazy."

"That would be boring!" Sammy defended her, and everyone agreed. "I didn't even jump when that foam blew out of there," he continued, big eyes beaming and smile flashing.

"And that's saying something." Joseph gave him a teasing push on the arm. "You're comin' around, short stuff."

Goodness, Jolie loved these boys. In just a short few weeks they'd dug deep into her heart as if they'd been in her life forever. How had that happened?

This feeling must be embedded in Morgan even more deeply, she realized.

"Well, I guess I'd better get back to work," Morgan said, making no move to go as his gaze latched on to hers again.

She felt breathless.

She also felt the boys' full attention on them. Morgan must have, too, because he broke for the door, snagging what was left of the volcano experiment on his way out. "I'll toss this in the back of my truck and put it in the Dumpster. Unless you want to use it again." He held it toward her with a half grin.

She smiled. "You might want to save it. That volcano will probably become part of Sunrise Ranch legend. It could be valuable someday." When he chuckled, she said to the boys, "Clean up a little more, fellas. I'll be right back."

And she followed him outside.

Morgan tossed the volcano in the back of his truck and then turned to face her as a soft breeze sent wisps of hair splaying across her face. To her surprise Morgan lifted his hand and gently brushed them off her cheek. A wave of emotion made her heart race and suddenly she was thinking about kissing him…and wondering if he was thinking the same thing.

His eyes darkened as he caressed the strands of her hair between his fingers. Butterflies fluttered inside her chest—no one had ever made her feel the way Morgan did with just such a simple touch.

"I better go," he said suddenly, letting go of her hair and reaching for the door handle. "Hold it down in there," he added with a wink, then climbed into his truck and drove away.

Jolie didn't move as she watched him go. She was unsure exactly what she was feeling…but it felt like hope. Could it be that there was a chance for them? Was she crazy to even think it?

As she turned to head back into her classroom, she was startled to see the windows full of grinning faces.

Unless she was mistaken, she wasn't the only one wondering if she and Morgan had another shot at love.

* * *

Morgan entered the stable, on his way to take a look at the new foal. It was quiet and sunlight filtered in through the windows, giving the stalls a glow.

The foal was a beauty. He was lanky— all legs with a sleek body that promised one day to be a beautiful cutting horse. If he was as talented as his daddy, they might have another champion on their hands. Rowdy had won the title on the foal's daddy two years in a row.

"He's looking good, isn't he?" Rowdy said, coming from the barnyard.

"Yeah, he looks just like Pep." Pep's bloodline was famous and a good building base for the ranch.

"Good ol' Pep, he knows how to mark 'em. Now if we could just get a few of his colts with some of his talent, we'd be in the money."

Though Rowdy grinned, Morgan knew he was serious. On a ranch the size of Sunrise, they pursued multiple avenues that could generate revenue as well as give the ranch a reputation for quality in every way. It also gave the boys exposure to different aspects of ranch life, and different possibilities for their future.

"Jitterbug's going to do us proud. You know he is," Morgan said, hanging his elbows over the stall gate next to his brother.

"He'll do. So, how's it going with Jolie? Y'all sure were looking cozy at supper during the roundup."

"We were just talking."

Rowdy studied him. "You going to throw in with her again? Forgive and forget and see where it goes?"

Morgan studied his boots. He'd almost kissed Jolie. But he was a grown man with responsibilities—he needed to have a clear head, and he wasn't sure he could do that around her.

Tucker had told him to give it to God and have no regrets.

Today he'd been tempted to do just that.

"I'm just asking," Rowdy said when Morgan remained silent. "I'm not sure I could do it in your situation. I like Jolie—

always have—but that was harsh the way she led you on like she was going to marry you and then the minute she got the offer to join that kayak team, she jumped ship and bailed. My question is, can you ever trust her again?"

Bingo.

Morgan rubbed his jaw—startled by Rowdy's unexpected advice. Instead of being reckless it was on target with Morgan's thoughts. "She's here to teach the boys and work out a few issues she's had since the accident. I'm not going to kid myself into thinking she's sticking around this time. I'm not throwing in with her."

But I am going to help her get back in the water.

Rowdy slapped him on the shoulder. "Be careful."

"It's under control, but thanks for being in my corner." Morgan hadn't thought Rowdy was in his corner, and it felt good to know differently.

"What are brothers for?" With that, Rowdy sauntered out of the stable and disappeared into the bright sunlight. Morgan turned back to the foal.

Can you ever trust her again? Rowdy's words echoed in his head—and his heart. Truth was, he couldn't. He didn't.

And that was the answer he'd been searching for. The attraction was obviously still there, but without trust, it didn't matter.

He was going to help Jolie get back in the water because it was the right thing to do. But it didn't mean he'd give her his heart on a platter again.

Morgan had a good life and he'd come to enjoy it. If it got lonely sometimes, so be it, because finding a woman to share his life had proven to be more trouble and heartache than he ever wanted to risk again. First Jolie and then Celia—though truth be told, Celia had hurt far less than Jolie. Still, he'd opened up to both of them, bared his soul and let them into his life—and they'd both left.

Nope, Morgan wasn't ever going to trust a woman with his heart again.

He would help Jolie, and ensure that she moved on at the end of the semester. And it would be the best thing for both of them.

Chapter Eleven

Gulping air into her burning lungs, Jolie leaned forward and grasped her knees. She'd been doing sprints for thirty minutes and was covered in sweat, her muscles on fire. She'd let herself get out of shape in the month since she'd arrived at the ranch, and now she was paying for it.

Straightening, she wiped her brow with her fingertips and continued to breathe heavily. The hill she stood on was steep—pure torture, and excellent for a workout.

She smelled the sweet scent of pure country air. It was hot air—even though it was now September, the temperature still hovered in the low nineties—but it was Texas country, her country, and she'd missed it.

She hadn't told Morgan the whole truth last week when he'd asked her how she was staying in shape. She'd exercised a bit, but not like she needed to in order to be in ultimate physical condition to hold her own against the rapids. Her endurance had to be in top form. If it wasn't, it could mean life or death.

Embarrassed by her half truth, she'd begun a rigorous exercise routine the very next day. She'd needed to work out her frustrations over how Morgan raced away from her when she'd told him she thought she'd made a mistake in leaving six years ago. That the workouts helped her to feel more like herself was an added bonus.

The feel-good endorphins were definitely working their magic, and she needed them. Until today, she'd thought there was no hope for Morgan and her. But standing beside his truck earlier, he'd thought about kissing her—she'd seen it in his eyes. And she'd thought about kissing him. Thinking of that moment sent shivers through her.

Heading through the woods toward the farmhouse, she made herself think of everything she had to be thankful for instead of thinking about kissing Morgan. Being alive was top of the list, and coming home to the ranch, and meeting the boys. And Morgan was up there, too.

Since she'd been back, Jolie realized a bunch of things, including the fact that she'd felt adrift even before the accident, as if caught in a backwash. What had driven her for so long had come to mean less and less, and things she'd put on the back burner had begun to tug at her.

In the beginning of her career, it had been different. Driven by the need to conquer as many rivers as possible, she'd been hard to stop in those first four years. Regrets over how she and Morgan had parted always trailed her, but her desire to be the best female professional kayaker in the field overshadowed her regrets.

Not so these last two years—things had

begun to change. When her friends and competitors began slowing down, getting married and beginning families, she'd become restless. And sad. It took two for her dream of a family to become reality. Her love life had dwindled to almost nonexistent after she gave up dating, which had been nothing but disappointing. And she'd begun to really regret her past...and regret hurting Morgan.

After the accident, she'd known she couldn't run from it any longer. She'd told herself she was coming here to make amends, but now she knew she was here for more than that. Much more.

So here she was, her entire life in flux, so full of unrest that she was confused. And so full of longing, she was toying with fire.

The white wood and cheerful red shutters of her house came into view through the trees. Nothing fancy, but homey. And after being on the road so much, homey was exactly what she needed.

Stepping onto the back porch, the loud

rumble of a diesel pickup signaled she had company. Going to investigate, she rounded the corner just as Morgan got out of his truck looking tall, dark and dangerous for her heart. Jolie sent gravel flying skidding to a stop.

She knew after a workout in scalding heat that she looked like a red lobster. Still, her pulse jumped despite her sweaty self.

"Jolie," he said, his eyes moving over her, probably taking in just how terrible she looked. "I was on my way to check some mares close to foaling and the boys told me I should see if you wanted to go." He grinned. "Just for the record, *I* thought you might want to come, too. I know you used to love the baby crop."

Jolie clapped her hands together. "Oh, Morgan, I would love, love, *love* to see the babies—are there any running around yet?"

"A few." He chuckled.

So the boys had sent him, but Morgan had thought it was a good idea. If she'd been wearing any boots, that fact would have just about busted them clean off her feet. "I'm a mess. Can you wait while I change?"

"You're fine. I mean—"

"Are you kidding? *I* don't want to be closed up in a truck with me right now, so I'm pretty certain you wouldn't want to, either. Give me ten minutes. Okay?"

"You got it." Following her to the porch, he sat down on the old wicker rocker that had been there when she moved in. "I'll be right here," he said, looking up at her with those blue troublemakers. Jolie almost tripped over the doorstop.

Her mind going wild, she raced into the house. Morgan had come for her. Heart pounding, she made quick time in the shower, not even giving the water time to warm up. Then she proceeded to sling clothes all over the place in search of the right thing to wear. The clock was ticking when she finally decided on the fourth shirt she'd tried on, along with the second pair of white shorts. Slipping her feet into her sandals she hurried to yank her wet hair into a ponytail, put on some moisturizer, a hint of mascara. Finally she gave herself a nod in the mirror, noting the tint of pink from the sun.

Or was it from being flustered?

With a minute to spare she raced from her room and ran hard into an end table with her knee. *Ouch.*

Through the screen door, she glimpsed Morgan fingering his Stetson between both hands, studying the hat like it held the secrets of the universe. Her heart clutched as he raked a hand through his ruffled hair and took a deep breath.

Was he nervous?

The very idea sent a tingle zipping through her. It was a good feeling to know she wasn't alone in this.

"All done." She pushed open the door, forcing herself not to sound too breathless, too eager. "Ready if you are."

Who am I kidding? she thought when Morgan looked up at her with those perfect blue eyes. *I'm not ready for this. I'm not ready for this at all.*

* * *

"Great, let's get this show on the road," Morgan said, jumping up from the chair. A little shaky in the knees, he caught the scent of her freshly washed hair. Whatever she'd used made him dizzy it was so sweet.

Get a grip, he told himself. He was in trouble and he knew it. Better to get this over with. He turned and headed for his truck, then remembered his manners and hurried back to open her door for her.

"I am so excited," she said, looking up at him like she had at the school the day before. Her eyes were so luminous he could practically see his fool face in their reflection.

He gave a stiff smile and put his hand on her elbow, assisting her into the truck. His fingers tingled as he touched her soft skin. Hurrying back around the truck, he slid behind the wheel. He'd never been happier that truck manufacturers had started making trucks bigger—he needed as much space as possible between him and Jolie.

Driving down the lane, the trees hung

over the paved road like a canopy. It was a beautiful, sun-dappled section of road that he loved. And apparently so did Jolie.

"I've always loved this part of the road. When I was in Kauai, I saw a road with magnificent canopy over it. It's been painted and photographed an unbelievable amount of times. Every time I drove it, all I could think about was this little stretch of road in Texas and how much I'd loved it."

He glanced at her. "I didn't know there were any rapids in Kauai."

She shook her head. "I was there for a promotional event. My sponsor also makes rafts and wanted shots of me on the Na Pali Coast rafting. I *loved* it there—it was so gorgeous. And I got to swim with dolphins—one of the cool perks of my career."

"It sounds great." What else could he say? She certainly wasn't going to get that kind of perk here on the ranch. All the more reason to be cautious. In the end, he was certain Jolie would pack her bags and go back to the life that took her all over the world and let her swim with dolphins.

"It *was* great," she said. "And yet, Morgan, it's so good to be home." Her voice wavered slightly. They cleared the tree canopy, turning into the drive that led to the mares. When they stopped, she quickly pushed open her door and hopped down, as if to get away from what she'd just admitted. "Let's see these mommas and their babies."

Sliding from the truck, he followed her to the fence where she studied the mares and their rounded forms.

"They are beautiful." She pointed out some of her favorites, talking a lot about each one. She was as nervous as he was, he realized. "You always did have a great eye for a good horse."

They were standing close again, as if drawn to each other. "Thanks," he croaked, his nerves getting the best of him. "It's just a talent God gave me."

"Well, we all have different talents. Yours is definitely cattle and horses."

And hers was riding a river in a plastic banana, as Rowdy always called her kayak.

"You have a wonderful talent with the boys, too, Morgan. They love you so much." She turned so that she was facing him, leaning her shoulder against the wooden fence post. The sunlight sparkled off her drying hair in a way that he liked.

"I try." It was the truth—he really did. "We've had some great kids come through here. I thought about leaving a few years ago, then decided instead to take on more responsibility and become involved. It's been a blessing to me."

In more ways than he could ever tell her. When his life had crashed around his feet after she'd left, he'd jumped into his relationship with Celia too quickly. After that had fallen apart, he'd almost left Sunrise. But deciding instead to be more involved with the ranch had been a turning point in his life, and the only way he could describe it was to say that he'd found his calling.

And now he would help her get back to *her* purpose in life so that he could continue on with his own. Maybe even take a chance on love without being on the rebound this time.

"And you've been a blessing to them," she said, breaking into his thoughts. "I think of Sammy and how lost and alone he must have felt when he came here. But you and this ranch, and Nana, and Randolph and Rowdy and everyone here…you're rebuilding his life, and the lives of all the boys. You know that, don't you? You're putting a new foundation of love beneath their feet." Her voice broke and it touched his heart.

He couldn't speak.

"Morgan," she said, her eyes brimming with sincerity, "I have to thank you for letting me stay. I love being a part of all this." When he still didn't say anything, she turned back to the horses and pointed at a very pregnant chestnut mare. "I predict she's next. What do you think—tonight?"

He forced himself to disengage from her and look at the mare. "I might have a good eye for horses, but you're the one who always had the eye for due dates. We'll see if you're right. I'll have Pepper bring her into the stalls just in case."

Opening the gate, he led the way into the pasture. Jolie spent the next little while patting and talking to all the mares. Morgan stilled his heart against how much he loved seeing her with the horses on Sunrise Ranch. He reminded himself that this was not her dream.

"Oh, what a sugar you are," she said, laughing when a gentle bay tried to nibble at her ponytail. Each mare she talked to got some sort of encouragement along with a gentle, loving touch of her hand.

It made Morgan more jealous than he wanted to think about.

About ten horses later, he realized visiting the mares had been a bad idea. Clearing his throat, he decided, purely for self-preservation purposes, that it was time to talk about getting her back in the water.

"Can we go over there to that tree? I'd like to talk to you about something."

Curiosity lit her eyes. "Sure. Lead the way."

Pushing old memories from his mind, he led the way to the tree, checking for snakes before letting her sit. She placed her palms on the trunk behind her and leaned back to study him, her lanky legs crossed.

"Shoot. Tell me what's on your mind."

"I want to make you a proposition."

"Oh really? And what would that be?"

Dinner and some stargazing.

"I want you to listen to me before you jump in."

Cocking her head to the side, her eyes narrowed. "Sounds a little sketchy."

Morgan sat beside her. "I've been thinking about what you said, about being afraid of going back in the water. And also that you may have made a mistake when you left."

She inhaled a shaky breath and looked away.

"Jolie, I'm going to be honest with you. I don't want to get into whether your leaving was a mistake or not. I've moved forward—things change." Her shoulders stiffened. "But what I do know is that you've never shied away from a challenge. Fear has never defined you. If you don't get back in that water, I think you will regret it for the rest of your life. And you can't live with regret like that."

Jolie blinked several times, looking solemnly at him. "You know, it was fear of regret that drove me to leave all those years ago."

"Yeah," he forced himself to say. "And I understand that now. I'd be lying if I said it hadn't hurt back then. But you did what you had to do. And now you have to do it again."

She looked at her hands and then into the distance before finally looking back at him. This evasiveness wasn't like her, which gave him more insight into what the accident must have done to her.

"I've been thinking. Soul-searching. I'm not sure I want to continue kayaking."

"That's just fear and you know it," he said. "What about the guys? They are going to hound you until you teach them, you know."

She bit her lower lip, thinking. "I can't talk to them about the accident."

"All the more reason to just get back in the water and do it. Where's the girl I knew?"

She gave a humorless laugh. "I don't know if you've noticed but I'm not that girl anymore, Morgan. I'm almost twenty-eight years old."

"I've noticed." Oh yes, he had. "Look, you couldn't have kept up your competitive edge if you didn't still have the drive that you had before."

"Maybe I *don't* have that edge or that drive anymore. Maybe that's the problem. Did you think of that?"

"I don't believe it," he said gruffly, not liking the defeat he was hearing. "Not you."

She stared at him unsmiling. Seconds ticked by.

He fought off the urge to pull her into his arms and tell her that he would keep her safe. "Here's my proposition," he said instead.

A furrow appeared between her brows. "Shoot."

"I take you to the river and we work on your getting back in the water. No one has to know. We can get you over this hump and on with your life."

"Why are you doing this?" Anger tinged her words.

"So you can help the boys. And get back to the life you love."

Her eyes flashed. "You just won't believe—"

"No, I won't, Jolie," he snapped, losing patience. "You're afraid. And I don't want you here just because you're afraid."

Now he'd done it. The truth was out and he couldn't pull it back. Well, so be it.

She stiffened. "I see." She stood up and paced a few feet away from him. With her hands on her hips, she kept her back to him as she contemplated her situation. Finally, she swung around about as angry as a wildcat. "I'll do it, for the boys. I'll show them that letting fear keep you down isn't what we do. That God will help overcome. I just hope He gets with this program soon."

"That's okay with me." He knew she was still hot at him but holding it in check.

"So, when does this start?" Her hand was on her hip, her chest heaving with anger.

Feeling drained, he stood. "How about tomorrow afternoon? The boys have chores after school, so that's a good time to get away. I'll pick you up around four, if that works for you."

"Fine." Jaw clenched, she turned and stalked back across the pasture.

That was his cue—the conversation was over. She was not happy with him, but at this point, he didn't care. He was doing what needed to be done. Because the sooner she got back in the water, the sooner she got out of here. And the sooner she got out of here, the better it would be for both of them.

Chapter Twelve

The sound of the rushing water set Jolie's nerves on end. Before the accident, it had made her adrenaline pump and her energy level skyrocket. Now she was terrified by the sound, and by the thought of stepping into the swirling water and climbing into her kayak.

She'd had to push her anger at Morgan aside this morning so she could teach class. But last night she'd fumed at the high-handed attitude he'd had when making this proposition. For him to *assume* he knew what was best for her was irritating beyond comprehension—he didn't have a clue.

Okay, to be fair, he *was* right about the fact that the boys would hound her until she was forced to tell them the truth, and she didn't want to admit she was afraid. Especially not to Sammy—what a hypocrite she would be. So that was why she'd finally agreed to do this.

Before the accident, Jolie had really been afraid only once in her life, and that had been the day she'd handed Morgan back his engagement ring and driven away from him. God had given her the strength to do that—to reach for something more in her life, to dare to go beyond the boundaries of what was comfortable.

God was going to have to give her the strength to do the same here.

Only, right now she felt nothing except the cold edge of panic. Palms as wet as if she'd been dipping them in the river, her heart racing with anxiety, she marched down the path behind Morgan.

What am I doing? The question echoed in her mind.

Fighting came the answer, pricking at her like a thorn.

Jolie hadn't faced the possibility that her real reason for taking a break from kayaking was fear—it was easier to make it about needing to set things straight with Morgan. But the idea that Morgan could be right about her fear *bothered* her. More than she wanted to admit.

She was scared spitless, as Chili Crump would say. Both he and Drewbaker had fought in two wars and yet they both said crawling off in that yellow banana she rode over waterfalls would scare them spitless.

Long ago she'd thought they were just teasing her. Now she understood exactly what they'd meant.

"Are you all right?"

Morgan stopped a few feet ahead of her. She hadn't even realized she'd halted in her tracks until he'd turned around.

They were on their way to the spot where he'd first taught her to kayak.

"I'm fine," she lied, catching up to him. It wasn't as if she was the first person this had ever happened to. Her friend Rita had gotten tangled upside down a couple of years ago and hadn't come back to the sport yet. She was a ski instructor in Colorado and guiding white river rafting expeditions in Tennessee. At least she was able to get on the water in an eight-man raft. Jolie hadn't so much as gotten her big toe back in the water.

"You don't look fine," Morgan said gently, studying her face.

So much for his not seeing her terror. Tears were welling way down deep, threatening to surface.

"Come on, talk to me, Jolie. Tell me what you feel. It didn't used to be hard for you to talk to me."

"I'm fine." She passed him on the trail. "I really am." *Liar, liar, pants on fire.* Her heart pounded, threatening to explode.

"No, you're not," he snapped, storming toward her, eyes blazing.

"Morgan McDermott." She swung around, glaring at him. "Stop telling me how I feel." Angry at herself for being a wimp, and at him for forcing her to do this, she lashed out. "How *dare* you!"

Tramping down the path, she could practically feel Morgan breathing down her neck. Despite her defiant spirit, her steps faltered the closer she came to the water, and her knees weakened. Her mouth went dry and her stomach hollowed out.

Crazy. This is crazy...and embarrassing. When she came to a sudden halt, Morgan slammed into her.

Grasping her arms, he kept her upright on the steep incline. His touch tempted her to throw herself into his arms, to bury herself in the security she knew she would find there.

Instead she forced herself to continue toward the sound of rushing water.

You don't have to do this! the wimp inside cried out to her.

Right. She was finished with kayaking anyway, wasn't she? Teaching full-time was the new plan. So she didn't have to be bullied into this. Panic gripped her like a choke hold and she spun, intent on fleeing.

Instead she found herself pressed against Morgan's hard chest, looking up into his dark eyes so full of concern.

"Whoa, take it easy," he urged, his tone softer than she'd ever believed possible.

Shaking her head, she backed away from him as though he was a hot frying pan.... The rest of the saying slipped her mind as his hands wrapped around her arms and his calm eyes searched hers.

She had to tell herself to breathe or she'd have suffocated right there as Morgan gazed into her very soul. "I—" *Breathe.* "I'm going back. I don't need to do this. It's ridiculous." The rush of the river seemed to get louder. She pulled away, trying to free herself from his grasp, but he held on tightly.

"Jolie, you can do this. Come on, babe. You can." His voice was full of compassion. "I know what happened to you must have been horrifying. But I also know you, Jolie. You can overcome this."

Swallowing cotton, she shook her head. Humiliation was the worst. Blinking fast, she fought off tears. *Please, no crying!* She hadn't cried at all since the accident—she'd held it at bay, even at its worst. Now a tear slipped from the corner of her eye.

The tenderness on Morgan's face made things worse. The pad of his thumb brushing the salty drop aside did her in as the tears she'd refused to cry for so long began to spill from her eyes, one by one.

"Don't cry, Jolie," Morgan said tenderly.

"I'm not," she denied.

His eyes twinkled but he didn't laugh. "Whatever you say."

She dropped her head to his chest and flat-out lost it.

If Morgan hadn't already figured out the seriousness of Jolie's situation, he clearly knew it now. Jolie wasn't a crier. He'd seen her get dragged and stomped by steers that would make a man cry, and she'd only gotten mad. She might look delicate, but she was cut from tough stuff. The fact that her sobs were soaking his shirt and her shoulders trembled in his hands shook him to his core.

"I'm sorry, sugar. I didn't mean to make you cry." He gently placed his hand on her head and stroked the length of her silky strands. "You don't have to do this today."

As she rested her head on his chest, he was certain she could feel his heart thundering away.

"No," she said in between sobs. "You're right, I need to do this, but as mad as it makes me…I can't…seem to make the last step into the water. I can't even make it *to* the water." Her eyes sought his. "I honestly think I'll pass out before I get my toe in the water. Isn't that a twist?"

Even though the last words were an attempt at humor, there was nothing funny about the situation. "If you make progress every day, it will happen."

"What will? Me passing out?" She attempted a grin.

He didn't. "No. You'll eventually get in the water, and then get in the kayak…"

She took a deep breath, finally getting

a handle on her tears. She nodded, the hint of a smile still quivering on her lips. Morgan's heart stopped and every cell in his body went on alert as he stared down at her. She blinked—once, twice—and her lips parted. He felt her heart quicken against his own.

"Morgan." It was a mere whisper and it drew him like honey as he lowered his mouth to hers.

Instantly the years slipped away and it was just like it used to be between them. He hugged her close, wanting to feel the warmth of her against him. When her arms slipped up and around his neck his knees nearly crumpled beneath him.

Trouble. The tiny word wedged its way into his head.

This was supposed to be all about getting her back in the water so she could leave to pursue her passion, passion that wasn't for him.

She will *leave. She has to.*

Pulling away, he heaved a breath as they stared at each other. The world slowly tilted back into place. "Are you feeling better?" he croaked.

A twinkle lit her eyes and he was glad he'd helped put it there, if nothing else.

"How could I not be?"

He found himself pushing her hair behind her ear, his fingers lingering, sliding down to her nape. She trembled at his touch and it took every ounce of his strength not to lower his lips to hers again.

"We'd better get back. We'll do this again tomorrow if you want—I mean, we'll try to get you in the water. Not—" He shut his mouth before he said anything else.

"Yes, you're right. If I'm ever going to be able to look at myself in the mirror again, I need to be able to conquer this. Tomorrow is a deal."

"No, wait. We're taking the boys out to build fence right after you let them loose tomorrow. I forgot." Understandable that he'd forget—his brain was fuzzy after kissing Jolie.

"Sure," she said, moving a step away from him. "I remember the boys mentioning that. They asked me to come along. I told them I graduated from fence building a long time ago."

Morgan chuckled, seeing that just the idea of not having to get in the water tomorrow was a relief to her. "You never thought you'd be back here teaching, either."

"True. But believe me when I tell you that stringing barbed wire in hundred-degree weather is *not* on my bucket list."

He wanted to ask her if kissing him again was. Afraid of her answer, he kept his mouth shut.

They headed back down the trail, and he talked sense into himself the whole way while clanging warning bells continued to go off in his head. They'd kissed once, and based on the way he'd reacted, he knew it could never happen again. Because if it did, he was a goner for sure.

Chapter Thirteen

"Aw shucks, Jolie, do we have to learn to cook?"

Jolie had to fight the urge to scoop B.J. up in a big hug. "Cooking is a skill that even boys need to learn."

"We'd rather be ridin' and ropin'," Sammy groaned, trudging along beside B.J. They were trailing the rest of the boys, making their way across the pasture toward the chow hall.

"You'll both live. Nana, Ms. Jo and Mabel are excited to teach you. I want you two to be nice to them and appreciative of the time they're spending to do this for you."

Sammy squinted up at her in the sunlight. "You been tellin' me not to lie, Jolie. If I tell them I'm likin' it, then that'd be a big fat lie."

Jolie almost fell over in a heap of laughter.

"Me, too," B.J. added. "I ain't but eight. Don't that make me too young to fiddle with a stove?"

Anything to get out of cooking or baking.

"Believe me when I tell you that you will be well supervised." Both boys' frowns practically dragged in the dirt under their feet.

Nana was holding the door open for them when they finally got to the chow hall. "Well, boys, glad you could join us," she said, a grin in her voice.

"Do we have to do this, Nana?" Sammy asked, as if he was going to get a different response from the one Jolie had already given him.

"Yes, you sure do, little man. And by the

time we get through today, I bet you'll both be the fried egg kings."

"Eggs," Sammy said in dismay. "You mean we ain't even cookin' cookies?"

"'Aren't' cooking," Jolie corrected. She was his teacher after all.

Nana hooted. "You're cooking pies *after* you learn to cook something that'll actually put nutrition in your system."

Meeting Nana's laughing eyes, Jolie shook her head in dismay. "The other guys seemed excited about coming. I thought that was a little surprising, but these two, they take the cake."

Nana hustled them along toward the kitchen. "The other boys have been through this before and know we have a good time in the kitchen. These two ruffians weren't here last year."

Jolie thought back to when she'd gone to school on Sunrise Ranch. "We didn't cook when I was here."

Nana dipped her chin. "Randolph wouldn't hear of it. Thought it was for girls. That man." She shook her head and rolled her eyes as if to say he'd been stuck in the dark ages. "I've since changed his mind. I convinced him that many of these boys might have to cook for themselves one day and need to know the basics. And, well, then he saw firsthand with his boys. Not a one of my grandsons has a wife to cook for him yet and I had to help them all out with what goes on in a kitchen. You'd have thought those handsome cowboys had two left hands when it came to knowing the first thing about working a kitchen."

Jolie got a comical image in her head of Morgan elbow-deep in dishes with pots overflowing and the stove on fire. "I struggled a bit myself when I went off to college." She chuckled. "My poor mom didn't think I was ever going to eat anything except cereal and power bars."

The gloom hanging over Sammy's and Jake's heads was almost visible as they trudged into the kitchen several steps ahead of Nana.

"What in the world is wrong with you two?" Ms. Jo demanded in her no-nonsense voice, a twinkle in her eye. She had her fist on her hip, her gray head cocked to the side and a get-your-attitude-straight look on her face. Jolie grinned.

The boys were young but they came up to Ms. Jo's shoulder. When they didn't smile, she whipped her crooked pointer finger out and hiked her brow at them. Jolie knew they were in a heap of trouble—trouble that would be good for them in the long run.

"I didn't just ask that question to the air, boys. We're going to have ourselves a mighty fine time in here baking and cooking, so I'd surely like to see a little enthusiasm. You only get out of life what you put into it."

Sammy's eyes were big as saucers. "You ain't gonna whip us, are you?"

Ms. Jo's thin brows practically banged together and her eyes flashed with indignation. "*Whip* you? Why would I want to go and do that? I know for a fact that once you dig your fingers into the pie crust I'm going to teach you to make, you are both going to want to bake pies for a living because you're going to have so much fun."

"Fun. Cooking?" B.J. looked far from convinced.

Joseph had already tied an apron around his midsection and came striding over, his ever-present grin on his face. "Come on, little slowpokes, get your aprons on and let's get this show on the road. I'll show you my skills from last year."

Ms. Jo winked at the cute teenager. "Now that's a great attitude. B.J. and Sammy, right?" she asked and they immediately nodded. "Y'all go with Joseph here and he'll get the two of you all set up. Do you trust me?" B.J. nodded instantly, but her question clearly startled Sammy. His expression was guarded. "Trust is something earned, son, and I'm aiming to earn your trust so remember what I've said. Deal?"

Sammy thought on it. "Deal," he finally said. There was no doubt in Jolie's mind that Sammy would be watching everything Ms. Jo did. And when it was all said and done, he'd have a verdict.

And a very tasty pie to call his own.

Who knew cooking could build trust in a little boy who really needed a good experience in that department? As they walked off, Ms. Jo pivoted to her. Nana and Mabel, who'd been across the room handing out aprons, came over to join them.

"So, how are things?" Ms. Jo asked without so much as a blink of the eye.

"Things?" Jolie pretended ignorance.

"Now, Jo, easy does it," Nana chuckled.

"Easy does it, my foot," Jo balked. "I've been waiting for a little news and haven't seen hide nor hair of her."

"That makes two of us," Mabel harrumphed. "And I've had to put up with Jo's constant complaining because you've been AWOL. It's enough to make an old woman crazier than she already is!"

Jolie laughed. "Y'all knew exactly where to find me, so don't think I'm feeling sorry for you." She hoped the boys would return and they'd have to turn their attention to the baking at hand, but the boys were fighting over who was going to have to wear the apron with the big strawberry on it, and there was no telling how long that was going to go on. "I haven't been AWOL. I've been working."

Ms. Jo's brow cocked. "Is that all?" She sounded suspiciously like she wanted something more than that to be going on.

"Yes, that's all. And exercising—keeping my training up takes time, too."

"And going on roundups and birthing colts, too."

Nana was not helping the situation.

"Sounds like fun to me," Mabel cooed. "It is so romantic on the trail—once you get past the dirt hanging in the air and the heat. And the sweaty horses. On second thought, maybe the trail isn't a place to foster a budding relationship."

"Budding? Who said anything about a budding relationship?" The words were out of her mouth before she could clamp a hand over the traitorous lips—she hadn't intended to talk to them about any of this at all. "The last time I checked, you three were all against my starting anything up with Morgan." The words were hissed quietly so that the boys wouldn't overhear.

"True," Ms. Jo said. "However, there have been a few indications that maybe we were a bit hasty being protective of our boy."

"We're all set," Joseph called.

Praise the Lord for the intervention!

Joseph and Wes had lined up the motley crew like they were about to compete on the *Iron Chef* television show.

Jolie grinned. "Look, ladies, the boys are ready to cook."

"Bake," Ms. Jo corrected.

"Cook," Nana said, giving Jo the eye. "Eggs and sausage are necessities."

Ms. Jo gave a snort. "Depends on who you ask."

"Then I guess it's both bake and cook," Jolie chirped, escaping from the interrogation huddle. She had a terrible feeling that things were just about to start heating up.

The thing was, she hadn't seen much of Morgan since their kiss. They'd agreed to meet again and attempt to get her in the water, but it hadn't happened. She'd gone home and immediately gotten cold feet. Obviously Morgan had, too, because he hadn't called yet to reschedule the date. And that had been fine with her.

At least she'd kept telling herself it was fine. But just thinking about the feel of his arms around her and the heat of his kiss made her cheeks warm.

So far the only good thing that had come of the day beside the river was that her nightmares had eased up. And that was probably just because thoughts of Morgan were keeping her from sleeping in the first place. But that was a piece of info that she and she alone was privy to. And she planned to keep it that way.

Morgan was late. On purpose.

"You better hurry up," Rowdy teased as he threw a leg over his horse and jumped to the ground, his spurs jangling on impact. "We don't want to let the pies get cold."

Morgan deliberately took his time getting

out of the saddle. When Nana overheard the boys begging him to come join their cooking class, she'd basically demanded that he and Rowdy sample the food with the boys. He'd groaned, knowing full well that the boys had an agenda—they were always trying to get him and Jolie in the same room. Knowing he was going to have to face Jolie for the first time in a week scared him.

He'd arranged his every move over the last few days with the sole purpose of staying out of her range. And with good reason. She was far more dangerous to him than he'd ever suspected. He'd naively thought that what she'd done to him would insulate him from the feelings that he'd had for her; he'd thought his heart would be protected. And then he'd gone and kissed her.

And completely messed up his world.

One wrong move and he was mincemeat.

Rowdy was having a lot of fun teasing him. The slug was supposed to have his back, not enjoy watching him hotfoot it across coals without his boots on.

"Payback is going to be sweet, just you wait, little brother."

"Hey, I don't have anything on the burner right now, so don't get your hopes up." His lips curved into a lazy smile.

"I wouldn't get too smug if I were you," Morgan warned, striding past him. "I'm a patient man."

Rowdy's chuckle followed him as he headed toward what he was certain would be a circus—with him as the main attraction. He knew Nana had keyed in to the fact that he was avoiding Jolie. She had asked him a time or two where he'd been hiding out at lunch—he might as well have admitted his guilt flat out. All the more reason for her to join forces with the boys to get him here today.

And she had backup—Ms. Jo and Mabel would be watching his every move, expression and twitch.

He was doomed.

And Rowdy wasn't helping him at all.

The last thing he needed was everyone in that room realizing what a vulnerable spot he was in. A rock and a hard place would have been better than this—at least he'd have had somewhere to hide. But no such luck.

Steeling himself for what was to come, he shot the good Lord a plea for help, pulled open the door and stepped into the center ring under the glaring spotlights.

"Morgan, look what *I* did!" B.J. yelled, instantly alerting Jolie and everyone else that Morgan had entered the room.

"Hey, I'm here, too," Rowdy clowned, pretending to be hurt, following Morgan into the kitchen. The room seemed to shrink with the two tall cowboys in it.

The instant Morgan's gaze sought out Jolie, all the air disappeared. Jolie dropped her metal spatula on the stainless-steel worktable, splattering meringue everywhere—including on Sammy—before it clattered to the floor. Every eye turned her way.

"You kinda like him, don't you?" Sammy

whispered, blinking through globs of fluffy white meringue on his eyelids.

Jolie gasped, as much from having splattered the kid with pie topper as from his keen observation. "Why would you say that?" she whispered, concentrating on cleaning the sticky stuff from his face with the skirt of her apron.

He squinted as she held his chin. "'Cause you get all nervous when he's around. That's what happens in all the gushy movies."

"No, I do not like him." She scrubbed harder.

"At all?" Sammy asked, looking confused now.

Guilt slid over Jolie. She stopped her scrubbing so she could leave some skin on the poor kid's cheek. "Yes, I do like Morgan. As a friend," she added quickly. *Nothing more.*

"Well, you're pink right now and they do that in the movies, too, when they like the guy a lot."

She was about to ask him when he had

time to watch all these gushy movies, but Morgan was coming their way.

"B.J.'s pie looks great. How does yours look, Sammy?" he asked, his eyes landing on her for only a moment before turning to Sammy. She wondered what was going on behind those pools of blue as her pulse cartwheeled through her body and memories of his kiss played havoc on her senses.

"We're about to put it in the oven. See?" He proudly pointed at the chocolate meringue pie. He'd been helping Joseph and finally decided to make his own, so they were running late on getting his into the oven.

"That looks mighty tasty." Morgan placed his hand on Sammy's shoulder. "You did a fine job."

"I didn't want to at first. You know cooking ain't for boys. But Nana showed us how to cook egg-and-sausage breakfast tacos so us boys won't starve when we go off to college."

Morgan chuckled. "She taught me the same skills before I went off myself. It came in real handy. And pie making—now that would have really come in handy for a college man."

A grin spread across Sammy's face. "I liked it. Jolie helped me and she did good. Till she dropped her spatula when you came in." He leaned toward Morgan. "And she turned kind of pink. You know what that means, don't you?"

Heat stung Jolie's cheeks. "Hey!" She gently tugged on Sammy's ear and he laughed mischievously.

"You tell me what it means, Sammy," Morgan teased, crossing his arms.

B.J. was suddenly glaring at Sammy. "You aren't supposed to say anything," he hissed in a low whisper that caused Sammy to grimace.

"Oh yeah, I forgot." He looked contrite, but then the words came flying out of him in a rush. "When a girl turns pink, it means she likes a boy. And when she drops stuff, too."

Morgan took in her hot cheeks, which she was certain were fire-engine red. "So I guess that means you better go tell Rowdy she likes him."

Both boys looked confused. Jolie was relieved—instead of being embarrassed, she found the scene touching. In their minds, the boys were just trying to help out the clueless adults.

"Morgan." B.J. spoke carefully as if explaining something to a two-year-old. "She likes *you*."

Sammy shoved him. "You weren't supposed to *say* it!"

B.J. glared at him. "*You* did and Morgan had it all mixed up!"

Rowdy sauntered over, bringing Ms. Jo and Mabel with him. Nana came from the other side of the room with the older boys trailing her. Jolie suddenly wanted to crawl into a hole.

"Did I hear my name? Morgan, what's up? You walk in and the kiddos start to fight?"

Ms. Jo didn't miss a beat. "You two looked like you just choked down a live cat for lunch. And I'm not talking about B.J.

and Sammy. Jolie, why are you so pink? If I didn't know any better, I'd think you're a little flustered."

She did not need this. She really, really didn't. Fighting a river was easier than this.

"Do you feel well?" Mabel chimed in. "Maybe you have a fever, honey. Maybe Morgan needs to take you home."

"Good idea," Nana chimed in. "Morgan, why don't you take poor Jolie home."

"Whoa!" Jolie boomed, stopping the chatter erupting around the room. She knew a hoodwink when she saw one. "There is *nothing* wrong with me. I certainly don't need to go home. Now, weren't Rowdy and Morgan invited here to taste-test these goodies? Because I'm in the mood for pie!"

It was one thing for her to be having thoughts about Morgan. It was altogether another thing for this entire room of folks knowing it!

Thankfully Mabel led the boys away to set up for the tasting. Only problem, that left her standing alone with Morgan. "That was awkward—talk about being on the hot seat," she said, forcing herself to look at him.

"Is that what that was? Felt more like a frying pan." He chuckled.

Jolie's traitorous thoughts went straight to thoughts of the kiss beside the river. His gaze dropped to her lips and she knew he was thinking about it, too.

"I'm sorry I haven't gotten back to you about us going back to the river," he said.

"We better get over there before they start up again." Jolie knew this was not the time or place to discuss what had happened between them.

Besides that, she wasn't sure at all what to say about that day…which was exactly why she'd been avoiding him. She'd been a disaster that day. It was embarrassing, and the fact that she'd been so distraught that she'd thrown herself into his arms and cried like a baby—that was the worst.

Chapter Fourteen

On Monday morning a few days after the pie fiasco, Jolie drove up to the schoolhouse to find the boys huddled in the front yard in deep conversation. The instant she stepped out of her Jeep, they busted apart, looking like guilty puppies that had just torn up her flower beds. Something was up.

"Hey, guys." She strode over to them as if she suspected nothing. "How are y'all today?"

"We're good." Wes grinned, excitement glistening in his pale green eyes. The teen looked more like a grown man than any of the kids, even Joseph, though he wasn't as tall. He was muscular and serious, unless he was thinking of an adventure. He was ready to finish school and get into college on the roping team. Life on the ranch had been good for him.

"How are you?" he asked her, stuffing his hands into his pockets. "You doing okay?"

She wasn't sure what to make of his line of questioning. Did she hear concern in his voice?

"Yeah, how are you?" Sammy asked as all the other boys chimed in.

"I'm fine, fellas. What's with all the worry?" She looked at Wes and then Joseph for answers. "What's going on?"

Wes shifted his weight from one scuffed boot to the other. "Well, I, ah, I was surfing the Net last night looking at your YouTube videos," he added. "And well, we've looked at it before, all the amazing stuff you can do in a kayak. It's really cool seeing you coming down those rapids and over those sixty-foot falls. It blew me out of the water. You're awesome, Jolie. But, man…" His words trailed off…worry filled his eyes.

Dread filled Jolie.

"We came across your accident." Joseph was the one who said the words, his lips tight with concern. "We hadn't seen that. You almost *died,* Jolie." He raked his fingers through his too-long hair, reminding her of what Morgan did when he was upset. "It was bad."

Bad didn't begin to tell the story.

"It was," she said, trying to figure out what else to say but coming up empty.

"People were screaming on the video," Wes said, "going crazy when they thought you weren't coming up. Then your kayak came loose and it seemed like forever before you surfaced."

Jolie's stomach rolled. Inhaling slowly, she counted to ten, fighting hard to keep her nerves steady. Falling apart in front of the boys twice was unacceptable to her. She was stronger than that.

Please, God, hold me up. Take me past

this moment when I'm unable to hold myself up.

She searched for words of assurance for the boys who were so concerned that most of them couldn't speak. Their care steadied her.

"What happened?" Sammy asked, touching her arm. "How did you live through that?"

"By God's grace, Sammy. By God's hand." It was true. "Only God could have given me the extra air it took to be under the water all that time. There are things in life that can only be explained by God's interventions, guys. And me surviving my accident was one of them."

"I don't see how you can get back in your kayak after that." Coming from Mr. Thrill Seeker himself, Wes's words startled her.

"In all honesty, guys, it's time for me to come clean with you. I *can't* get in my kayak. I came here to try and get my head on straight, but the thought of getting back in the water is rough. I'm trying, though. It's just taking some time."

"That's why you haven't been too keen on teaching us," Tony said.

"That's why."

"It's kinda like getting back on a bull," Wes said. "Only, a bull is more controllable than a river."

Jolie's nerves had calmed down a bit and she found Wes's words compelling. "Why do you say that?"

"Well, you can study a bull, know its habits and in some manner, predict his moves. A river, like the one you were on…" He hiked a shoulder, his brows crinkling skeptically. "You have no way of knowing what's beneath the surface. If that log hadn't come downstream from somewhere and lodged in that spot, then you'd have done your roll, come out of the water and finished that run. No preparation could have saved you from that log being there."

Jolie knew his words were true to some extent. Her training was similar to a bull rider preparing for the arena. However, there was always the element of surprise.

"I think that's the way it is in life, too.

We have to prepare and then give it to the Lord. That's what I did. I'm going to get over this and move forward, with God's help. And the time I'm spending here with you good-looking cowboys is helping me do that."

That won her some grins. Looking around at the group—at "her boys," as she'd begun to think of them—a lump formed in her throat and she ached with love of them. They were helping fill a spot that desperately needed filling in her soul.

"We like you being here," Sammy said, slipping his arm around her waist. "I'm glad you didn't die in that water."

She gave him a reassuring smile. "Me, too, because I'd have missed being here with you."

Sammy's expression was so full of hope that it stunned her. This child needed her.

The thought cut deep through Jolie. No one had ever needed her. Not like this. Yes, her team members needed her for her skills, and the points she could bring them. But the way Sammy needed her was different. He needed her for security, for support…for the love she could give him.

Thank You, God, for bringing me here.

She closed her eyes momentarily, the prayer filling her soul. Looking about the group, she realized that there were others who needed her, too.

Excitement surged through Jolie. She needed to talk to Morgan—to tell him what she was feeling. To share this new emotion with someone she cared for.

With the man she loved.

Morgan leaned back from his desk, weary from reading all the legalese that came with running the ranch. Taking in sixteen wards of the state did not come without an overabundance of paperwork. Keeping the ship running required staying on top of the forms that needed to be filled out. He'd taken on that part of the business when he'd signed on as partner with his dad.

Rubbing his eyes, Morgan was actually glad to have the office to hole up in for now. With Jolie being everywhere he was, it was hard to keep his head straight. Hard to keep his distance. Hard to stop thinking about kissing her.

That had been a gargantuan mistake on his part. Then, after the fiasco in the kitchen with the "spectators" watching their every move, he'd felt like even more of a fool than he had when he'd kissed her.

A man had to have a backbone.

Especially with an audience watching.

A knock on his door had him looking at the clock on the wall—nine-thirty. It had gotten late. "Come in," he called, expecting to see his dad, his brother or just about anyone other than Jolie.

So much for hiding out.

"Hi," she said, moving just inside the door. "Do you have a minute?"

Nope, all out of minutes. "Sure. I was just doing paperwork."

She glanced around his office, taking a few more steps into the room. "I like your space. It's you."

The walls had heavy, rich paneling. He

had a cowhide rug on the floor, and Western art on the walls as well as pictures of boys with their animals at the county fair. Some of them holding championship banners and some were not. The projects weren't about the winning—they were about the experience of seeing something through. While Jolie's gaze had taken in the entirety of his office, it was the pictures of the kids that she had focused on.

"Thanks. I enjoy looking at those photos and seeing on their faces the satisfaction of a job well done."

Smiling, she perched on the edge of the leather chair across the desk from him. She wore jeans and a pale yellow blouse that caused her cinnamon hair to look darker and her emerald eyes to glow like jewels. They seemed less weary today, more alive. He hoped she was sleeping better.

He realized he was going to have to find some strength to handle being alone with her, or risk losing his pride.

"I thought we needed to talk. About several things. For starters, I need to apologize for falling to pieces down by the river. I—" She shook her head and closed her eyes briefly, drawing his attention to her long lashes against the warm golden skin of her cheeks. His gut clenched, remembering the soft feel of her skin.

"I'm not used to being so emotional. I'm sorry you had to pick up the pieces afterward."

"I should have kept my mouth shut and let you deal with your problem in your own time."

"No," she said. "I mean, you did the right thing making me try and face up to my fears. I'm glad I at least took a step toward the problem. Even though I ran away."

He cleared his throat. "I'm sorry I kissed you when you were…in a rough spot."

It's out there where it needs to be. Now move past it.

"About that. I'm sorry I threw myself at you."

That took him by surprise. The woman had been in a world of hurt. "I didn't see you do anything except need a little support. I was glad to give it."

Their gazes held as relief came over her face.

"Okay, then, we'll mark it up as 'I'm not sure what that was' and move on. Deal?" Her smile was warm.

"Deal."

"So, we need to discuss the boys."

The boys? "What's up?" he asked, trying to recover from the effect her smile had on him.

"The boys have been looking at videos of me competing. They finally came across the accident."

He should have known this would eventually happen. "What was their reaction?"

"Of course it scared some of them—all of them, actually. They wanted to know how I'm doing. I told them the truth—that I was having trouble. And they all understood. I told them I was trying to get my nerve back, that I'd come here to do that. Morgan, they were so sweet. I have to tell you that they've touched me deeper than I ever dreamed they could."

"They have a way of doing that." He took in his office for a moment. "That's why I'm here."

"I told them with God's help, I'd get back out there. I just wanted to tell you, and to thank you for trying to get me out there. I was a little miffed at you for pushing me. Maybe that was one of the reasons I got so…intense. I mean, when you're angry, it ups your emotions, so that could explain my anxiety."

"Were you mad at me the day you passed out?"

She frowned at him. "Okay, so maybe I'm just overly sensitive to the thought of getting in the water."

"That'd be my thought on the subject."

"Time will help. Anyway, I wanted to come and tell you what it means to me to be sharing time with the boys. Thanks for letting me be here."

What was he supposed to say to that? She was still leaving eventually, and they were still going to suffer because they'd all bonded to her. What did she expect that was going to do to them? "You're welcome." It was all he had.

Awkward silence filled the space between them. "Okay, then, I guess that's all I came to say." She stood to leave.

Say something.

Everything knotted in the pit of his stomach.

She headed toward the door. At last, impulse drove him out of his chair, skirting the desk in three strides. "Jolie—"

She'd spun at the same moment. "Yes?"

They stared at each other. Here they were *again*.

"I'm glad you came by. I've been swamped with paperwork that needs to be filed this week. So I've kind of been scarce."

She chuckled. "Well, that's a relief. I thought you'd been avoiding me."

"That, too," he admitted and smiled, loving her laugh. "Is there something else on your mind?"

"I'm thinking Sammy is better. We had a long talk today. That video gave me the opportunity to talk to all the boys, especially to Sammy, about how God is with us even in the bad times."

"Thank you for talking with him. Time will make everything better. Time and love."

Jolie's eyes brimmed with unshed tears. "Well, that is one thing the boys get here, that's for certain. Y'all are doing a great thing here, Morgan, and I'm proud to be a part of it. I've never been needed like I feel I am here. Today it hit me that I'm actually making a difference."

She got it. That dug deep into Morgan's soul. "Pretty cool feeling, isn't it?"

"It is. Well, I guess I better go and let you get back to work. Good night, Morgan."

"Good night, Jolie," he said. She was already heading out the door. He watched her cross the waiting area and push the door open. She didn't look back as she closed it behind her. The click of that door cracked like a gunshot in his head.

Jolie was falling for the boys and the boys had fallen for her. Raking his hand through his ruffled hair, he realized it was trembling.

So much for holding it together.

Jolie drove through the gate, headed toward her temporary home, her mind spinning in so many directions she wasn't sure what to think about first.

Morgan had looked tired but heartbreakingly handsome as always. She'd wanted to ask him more about his day, ask him how he'd been doing since he'd kissed her. Maybe kiss him again...

Nope, she was definitely not going to think about that. Pushing her hair out of her face, she was glad the top was rolled back on her Jeep—she needed as much fresh air clearing out her muddled brain as possible.

Her mind shifted to Sammy. She wanted to do more to make Sammy feel comfortable on the ranch; something that was special, and would involve the other boys, as well—something to give them all a sense of ownership in this ranch that was their home. What could it be?

She would seek the advice of Ms. Jo and Mabel. Nana, too.

Maybe she'd just ask the boys if they had any ideas about something they could do. Like maybe a festival. Maybe a reunion? Something they could enjoy…something that would keep them—and her—busy.

Something fun. Something different.

Something they could call their own.

Something that would let Morgan know she was serious about being here at Sunrise…serious about working with him.

Chapter Fifteen

When Jolie asked the boys the next day at school what kind of event they'd like to hold at the ranch, they took hardly a second to think about it. In fact, she was so startled by their quick response that she wasn't sure they'd understood what she was asking. But they had, and their answer was clear as day: they wanted to have a fishing tournament on the big lake.

"Wow, that was the quickest consensus I've ever seen among you fellas! Have y'all had fishing tournaments before?"

"Us older guys have." Wes grinned. "But it's been a while."

"We hear them talking about how fun it

was all the time," Caleb interjected. "And Mr. Macintosh—you know Mr. Macintosh and Mr. Crump? Well, they have done some funny stuff."

"Yes, I know Mr. Macintosh and Mr. Crump. And I'm sure they do have some stories to tell," Jolie said, smiling as she thought of the town pot stirrers.

So it was decided that they were going to put on a fishing tournament and invite the town of Dew Drop to participate. The boys figured they'd charge a small fee and donate the money to the church's youth fund. Jolie thought this was an excellent idea—she was proud of the boys for wanting to donate to a good cause.

"What about you around the water?" Sammy asked.

She told him that they'd picked a good event, and it would be one more step toward getting her in the water. She didn't add that it wasn't the calm waters of the lake that shot her blood pressure sky-high—it was the raging sound of rapids.

By the end of the day Jolie had a plan

and was pleased with how excited the boys were about the fishing tournament. They were even saying they could start having it every year. She liked that—loved it, in fact. It was exactly what she'd been after— an idea of their own that would tie them to the ranch in a special way.

Now she just had to run it by Morgan, but she was sure he would be all for it.

"Are you going to come work cattle with us?" Joseph asked, as they were all exiting the building. To her surprise, instead of racing off and claiming freedom, they lingered.

"I hadn't thought about it," she said. "I really need to see Morgan."

"Oh, then it's your lucky day—he's gonna be with us," Joseph drawled in his best Morgan imitation. "Come on. We're gonna vaccinate and tag 'em, and brand some, too."

Sammy grabbed her arm. "Come on with us. *Please.*"

Jolie could do nothing other than agree when the boys took her arms and pulled her along to the barn. Saddling up her horse, she listened to the excited chatter filling the stables as all her boys saddled up, too. Jeans were a staple on the ranch and she wore them to work most days, so at least she was prepared for this spontaneous change of plans. Slipping her foot into the stirrup she boosted herself into the saddle. It creaked beneath her weight as she settled into it, and joy settled into her.

She was glad the boys had insisted she come.

Riding out of the barn with the guys, Sammy came up beside her on Cupcake, his control better than it had been. "Goodness, you're looking like a regular old grizzly cowpoke. Awesome job, little man."

He grinned proudly. "I don't even need any help anymore. Joseph or Wes or Mr. Pepper have to cinch the saddle up for me usually, but I got under there myself today."

Sammy's pride in his accomplishment put a smile on her face that was so big it nearly hurt. "You're a regular cowboy now, Sammy."

"I know, and who woulda thought it? I mean, I never even saw a horse except in pictures before I came here. And now I'm a cowboy."

Jolie laughed. The sun was bright in the indigo sky as it beat down on them. As beautiful as it was, it couldn't begin to compare to the joy that filled her watching Sammy snap his bootheels against his horse's belly, urging it into a trot to meet Wes and Joseph at the head of the gang.

Thank You.

The prayer of thanks eased out of her. And as she rode out with the boys, looking like a posse from an old Western, she conversed with the Lord all the way, thanking Him for the blessings in her life, for the renewing of her spirit, which she hadn't even realized needed renewing, and for the way He took bad situations and made them good.

One of God's many promises whispered

through her mind. *I will never leave you or forsake you.* It was true.

By the time they made it to the corral where the cowboys were working a huge herd of cattle, she'd finished praying and moved on to a loud, excited conversation with the boys about all their plans for the fishing tournament.

Life was good.

The instant the men came into view, Morgan—unmistakable in the way he sat in his saddle, so erect and proud—broke from the herd and loped in their direction. His straw Stetson tugged low over his penetrating eyes, his face covered in a sheen of perspiration and dust, he looked rugged and powerful. He set Jolie's pulse galloping as he took his hat off, smiled a welcome at the boys and rode straight to her.

"This is a nice surprise." A gorgeous smile cut across his tanned face—a smile just for her, cutting deep into her heart.

"The boys hijacked me and wouldn't take no for an answer." She grinned back at him. Mercy, mercy, mercy, she was going to have to hug each and every one of them for it, too.

Life, Jolie realized as Morgan spun his horse and took up beside her, still grinning, wasn't just good—it didn't get any better.

It was a scorcher of a day, although September was racing by faster than a wild mustang charging for open pastures. Morgan knew it would start cooling down over the next few weeks, but for now, summer was stretching out and taking everything it could get.

Jolie didn't seem to mind the heat as she worked right alongside the boys and men. She'd been branding and tagging with Sammy, encouraging him the whole time. Watching her made his chest feel tight.

She looked up from where she had a knee on a calf, holding it so Sammy could brand it.

The faster summer went by, the sooner she'd be gone.

The sooner he'd be safe.

The sooner he'd miss her again.

The caustic scent of burning hair signaled that Sammy had been successful.

"Great job!" Jolie exclaimed the instant Sammy had done the deed and she let the calf up to jog away. Sammy had been worried about hurting the calf, and Jolie had explained that God had made cattle's hides thick for a reason. After that, the boy had had no problem wanting to learn the age-old trade of cattle country. Now, he was grinning from ear to ear.

"I did it!" he yelped, giving Jolie a high five. "You're one good cowgirl, Jolie. Let's get another one."

"Send out the signal and Wes will cut one from the group for us."

Sammy whipped off his hat and whooped and Wes nodded his way, lifted his rope and sent a loop flying through the air. He and Joseph were bringing in the calves while the younger boys helped the ranch hands minister brands and vaccines, ear tags and whatever else the calf needed.

Jolie had jumped right in there, not minding the grime that went with the job.

She was a tough cookie with a soft interior—and he had a weakness for cookies.

Morgan struggled with wanting more from Jolie every moment he was awake, and even while he was asleep. After seeing her last night, he'd had a very restless night.

"You sure do look like a man in need of a little distraction," Rowdy said, drawing up beside him. Morgan hadn't even realized Rowdy was riding over from where he'd been overseeing the action on the far side of the corral.

"What's that supposed to mean?" he grunted, not happy that he'd been lost in thoughts about Jolie—and even more unhappy that he'd been caught.

Rowdy laughed. "Morg, you're in la-la land."

His eyes narrowed to slits. "The sun is in my eyes."

What a stupid thing to say, McDermott!

It just made the goofy grin on Rowdy's face get goofier.

"So, you've got it bad again, haven't you?" he asked, turning serious.

"Last time I looked I felt fine. Didn't know I had anything."

"You know what I'm talking about." He thumped his heart with his fist. "Right here, looks like to me. I'm not sure how to react to it, either."

So his brother was a wise guy with eyes of a hawk. "Okay, so I'm a little messed up."

"A *little*. You better shore up those leaks in the dam if you don't want everyone who looks at you to know you're 'a little messed up.'"

Morgan rubbed his jaw, stubble stiff against his fingertips. "I've got my feelings cinched up tight, Rowdy. She's going to leave again—there is no doubt in my mind that she will, come December. And I'll be a big part of getting her ready to do that." Morgan took a moment to look at her before he went on. "I've been praying about this and I know that she's meant for bigger things. She's reaching a multitude of folks out there. Last night I saw a video of her at a children's hospital, encouraging kids who have stars in their eyes over her. A kid's mother took the video and posted it because Jolie went there without an entourage or a camera crew. She went because she wanted to. She's the real deal, Rowdy. Too much ability to be here wasting away on a ranch in the middle of Texas."

Rowdy shook his head. "Don't belittle what you do here on this ranch with these kids. You're not wasting away doing what you do, are you?"

"No," Morgan denied emphatically. "I love every minute of making sure the boys get what they need."

"Then why should it be any different for Jolie?"

"It's not the same. Here she'd have no spotlight and no chance to do the work she does, inspiring people. It's just not the same." And it wasn't.

Nope, come the end of this term, she'd be gone, and he'd have helped her get back out there where she belonged. It was time to head back to the river. And this time, she was getting in.

Chapter Sixteen

"It was awesome today!" Sammy gushed, pulling a feed bucket over to where the fellas were gathered at the back of the stables, covered in dirt, their faces streaked with sweat. He'd had more fun today than ever. And Jolie had hugged him and been so excited for him.

"Sammy's right, that was awesome. I *l oved* it. But, so, what do y'all think?" Caleb asked, looking at Wes and Joseph.

"I seen what y'all been talkin' about," B.J. said, rocking on his bucket, his face still red as an apple from all their hard work. "Morgan, he was watching Jolie a bunch. Does that mean he loves her?"

Wes was chewing on a long piece of hay and he pulled it out of his mouth and grinned. "It's a start. I was watching him, too, and he's got it bad."

"Got what bad?" Sammy asked. "Love?"

He pointed at Sammy with his hay. "I think so, my man. I think so. Don't you, Joseph?"

"I hope so. We've been trying hard to get them together on the quiet, and they seem to like each other most of the time. But I'm not sure about all the time. That worries me."

Tony hung his leg over the rung of the stall. "Then we just got to try harder. Keep it up, man. In them romances, love takes time. Morgan don't look at anyone else like he looks at Jolie. Don't forget the day by the truck after the volcano. They were seriously thinking about kissing. You all know it."

"And Jolie was all pink in the kitchen," Sammy reminded them. "Remember?"

"Love's about more than just wanting to kiss or turning pink," Joseph said. "But I agree with Wes—let's keep finding ways to get them together. This fishing tournament is going to fit right in. Can y'all keep on keepin' this a secret? Everyone raise their hand who thinks we should keep trying to help Jolie and Morgan fall in love."

Everybody raised their hand, and Sammy and B.J. grinned at each other.

"Good," B.J. said. "'Cause I want Jolie to be my mom. Even if she is scared of the water. I don't care about that. I can still love her just as good. You can, too, right, Sammy?"

Sammy nodded, his insides feeling all funny thinking about it. He knew he could love Jolie, but he wasn't real sure she—or anyone—could ever really love him. If his parents didn't stick around... He stopped himself. His parents would come back—they would. But until then, it would be nice to have Jolie and Morgan be his ranch parents.

"Yeah, B.J., I can love her, too," Sammy finally said.

Two weeks after they'd come up with the idea of the fishing tournament, Jolie headed to the newspaper office in town with the official advertisement in hand.

Since they'd first thought of the idea, the tournament had morphed into a really big day—it wasn't just about fishing anymore. There were going to be all sorts of competitions and events. And the boys also wanted to add a little arena fun for the kids who didn't want to fish.

They'd decided to have the tournament the week before Thanksgiving, which didn't give them long with the weeks flying like they were.

As she pulled up in front of the newspaper building, Chili and Drewbaker were sitting on the church pew outside.

"Stupendous idea about the fishin' tournament, Jolie. Folks are talkin', excitement is abuildin'," Chili commented as she closed her door and stepped up onto the sidewalk.

"That's the truth." Drewbaker sliced off a sliver of soft wood from the elaborate bird he was carving. "I even heard we're having a competition on who's got the most decorated boat. Whoever thought about decorating a boat?"

"Well," Jolie chuckled, "that came from Nana, actually. She thought it would add a little something to the pot to have a bit more competition. She thought she'd put you fellas on the spot with decorating."

"Sounds like something she'd do." He scratched his chin with the knuckles of his hand, holding his knife. "I bet ol' Jo and Mabel are gonna have a doozied-up dingy."

"Don't you know it," Chili grumbled. "I 'spect they're already patting themselves on the back in congratulations on winning that part of the tournament."

Jolie saw the competitive wheels turning behind the two men's watchful eyes. "Well, you know them, I'm sure they have big plans."

Drewbaker squinted, drawing his bushy brows together, his face the picture of a man who loved a good contest. "I hear there's a paddle rule. No motors. I'm thinking y'all need to renege on this no-motor policy. Maybe give the teams whose ages add up together to be more than, say, a hundred and twenty-five, the opportunity to use a trolling motor."

Jolie laughed. "Boy, you've got this all figured out, don't you?"

That won her a hoot from Chili. "When two old codgers like us are fighting for our lives with the young studs you've got out there on the ranch, then you betcha we're getting things figured out. This takes strategy."

"And I can tell you're good at that."

Two wide, mischievous smiles spread across their faces. Jolie loved that everyone was having a good time with this, and she was thrilled that folks wanted to help out the kids. Many ranches around had offered the use of their boats because they knew that the ranch wouldn't have enough for all the boys to be on the water at the same time.

Morgan had teamed the boys up so that those with less experience had someone more experienced in the boat with them.

Morgan himself was competing with Sammy and Jolie was very thankful for that.

Wes and Joseph had been disappointed that they hadn't gotten to team up together, but they made her proud by being good sports about helping out the younger fellas. Plus now they had their own competition going—Jolie was holding her breath to see which of the two would bring in the largest bass.

"Don't you be giving away any secret tips to the likes of them," Ms. Jo hollered from across the street. She'd come outside and was glaring their way with her fist on her hip.

"I'm not, I promise," Jolie called.

"Hey, you just stay over there and let the woman talk to us all she wants about this," Drewbaker returned. "Y'all are goin' down."

Chili hooted again. "Like a lead tank."

Jolie shook her head. "Boys, you do know Mabel and Ms. Jo fish together out at Patrick Lake all the time. They even have an alligator they've named."

"We know. That don't mean we're scared of them."

"Surely don't, Drewbaker," Chili agreed. "It surely don't."

Jolie excused herself before she got into any more trouble, and made her way to the newspaper office to drop off the ad. A little while later she was headed back home with plans to work out. She nearly drove her Jeep into the ditch when she saw Morgan's truck parked in her driveway with him leaning against the tailgate, boots crossed at the ankles and a long strand of grass sticking from between his teeth as he waited with arms crossed. Her pulse skittered to life as if it had been dead to the world until right now.

"Well, hey, there, mister," she said, hopping from her Jeep. "You sure are lookin' lazy all propped up by the tailgate."

A slow smile eased its way from one corner of his lips to the other beneath the shade of his hat.

Her toes curled and her stomach tilted.

"If you think I need something to occupy my time, then you need to give me something to do," he drawled.

"Hold on to your hat, bucko, or I just might do that." Not in any of the ways that were flying through her mind, of course. No hugging or kissing the cowboy. Nope, none of that.

"Sounds like a plan. Or if you don't have one, I'll tell you what mine is."

"I'd be willing to hear yours," she said, slamming the door. She strode to lean against the tailgate beside him, forcing herself to be at ease. His husky chuckle did nothing to help settle her butterflies.

"I'm here to see if you'd like to go down to the river for a rematch."

She gave him a grimace. "Talk about messing up a perfectly good afternoon."

He leaned so that his shoulder was pressing against hers. "I come in peace. You realize it's been nearly a month since we tried this? You're sleeping better, I think."

"That's true. Not always, but for the most

part I am. The nightmares are only a few times a week now instead of a few times a night."

"So don't you think it's time to push yourself some more?"

Jolie took in some air—it was time to tell Morgan about the decision she'd made. "Morgan, maybe we should talk."

He shifted to face her, still leaning against the tailgate. In the past few weeks they'd worked together to get the fishing tournament in order and they'd relaxed around each other somewhat. Jolie was certain that Morgan felt the anchor load of attraction that she felt, and had always felt. And yet they'd never mentioned the kiss they'd shared on the banks of the river again, not since the night in his office.

She thought that was probably the way he wanted it.

There was still a no-trespassing sign on his heart, and she was trying her hardest to mind the sign. But she knew it was useless. Her heart belonged to Morgan McDermott, even though she'd trampled his years ago.

What Ms. Jo, Mabel and Nana said was true—Morgan had never been the same after her. It hurt knowing what she'd done to him.

She was praying that time would heal the wound between them. God could handle this, even if she couldn't.

"I decided last week that I'm retiring from competition."

Morgan looked like she'd hit him with a soggy fish, he looked so shocked. "That's a mistake and you know it, Jolie. I've told you before you would regret doing something rash like that. You'll always know you let fear have its way with you. What kind of example is that?"

His words were what she'd expected, to a degree. "I didn't say I wasn't getting back in the water. But I don't want to compete anymore." She took a deep breath, preparing herself to reveal the next part of her decision to him. "I want to be here on the ranch. I'd like an extended contract."

"No."

For a moment, Jolie wasn't sure she'd heard him correctly.

"Haven't you been pleased with what I've been doing?" she asked.

He looked torn for a moment and she felt her heart sink. She'd been working her hardest, trying to do a great job because the boys deserved it. She'd also wanted to prove to Morgan she could do it. She'd been hoping for a firm "You've been doing a great job, Jolie," but that was most definitely not what she was getting.

"Well, that was eye-opening," she said. "Not sure what you expect out of your teachers, but when a girl gives it her whole heart and that's not good enough, that's pretty rough. Especially when I know I've been doing a knock-out job—the boys' grades and their attitudes reflect that."

"There is no denying you've done an excellent job. But this is about you, Jolie. I won't be a part of your not doing what you need to do."

"Excuse me, you don't know what I need to do and what I don't need to do."

"That so?"

"That's so." They'd moved within inches of each other, which is what always happened when they argued. How it happened was beyond Jolie, but it always did.

He searched her eyes. "I know you," he said, his breath warm against her skin, sending a shiver racing down her spine.

She shook her head, both to clear it and to deny what he was saying. "Not so. Or you'd know being here with these boys means the world to me. Being here…with *you*." There—she'd said the truth. It was barely audible, but she'd said it. "It means the world to me, Morgan."

He lifted his hand and it hovered for a moment, then gently touched her hair. Like a featherlight kiss, his gaze rested on her lips, making her step toward him.

"No." The word flew from him as he stepped back, breaking the pull between them. "I won't let you do this. You love what you do. You're afraid to admit it, though, and I won't let you use me and this ranch as a crutch."

"I *love* you, Morgan." It was true—she'd never stopped loving him. She was certain that what she felt for him now was the love of a grown woman who knew her own mind. "Coming back here and being near you, seeing the man you've become, watching you with the boys and witnessing the dedication that you have to them and this ranch, it just makes my heart ache with regret that I wasn't here to help build this with you."

Her heart felt swollen inside her chest.

Morgan's eyes flashed. "This would never work, Jolie." Grabbing his hat, he tore it from his head and slapped his thigh. "This will not work," he said again, and in one swift motion he pulled her into his arms and covered her mouth with his, stealing her breath. Jolie could feel the years of loss in his kiss, in the iron clasp of his embrace as he crushed her to him. And she returned his kiss with all the regret of lost years and the joy of homecoming. She trembled in his arms and was glad to have them for support. Her heart thundered in time with his and when he suddenly broke free and backed off, it felt as if a part of her had been ripped away.

He glared at her, swallowing hard as if there was a boulder lodged in his throat, his chest rising and falling. "I watched you leave once and had to pick up my heart." His voice was gruff. "I tried to be fine with it. Even thought I was in love with Celia. But she called me on it the night before we were to marry. Did you know that? She didn't marry me because she realized I was still in love with you."

She shook her head. "I knew the wedding had been called off, but I didn't know why. I'm not sure anyone did."

Are you still in love with me now? she wanted to ask, only the words wouldn't come. His glare held them off like a shield.

"She was right. But Jolie, I picked up my life and I've moved on. I was happy finally. And then you came back." He shook his head again, and bent and picked up his hat from the ground where it had fallen, forgotten in the midst of their embrace.

"I won't be renewing your contract, Jolie. You need to get back to the life you love. I'll help you all I can, but I can't do this— I can't go backward."

She couldn't breathe, couldn't speak as she watched him stalk to his truck and slam the door behind him. He was already halfway out of the driveway before she could move.

Numb, she walked to the porch and sank to the step, too dazed to do anything else.

Chapter Seventeen

He'd really done it this time. He had completely lost his mind.

Yes, sir, no doubt about it, he was a raving lunatic. Why else would he have been fool enough to kiss Jolie after she fired a bombshell right at his heart?

Crazy—therein lay the problem.

Crazy *and* a fool.

Now he knew what had been wrong all along. There was obviously something in his brain that was broken when it came to Jolie.

He didn't like it one bit.

But he didn't have a clue how to fix it.

Gravel spewed behind him as he drove

like the lunatic that he was down the road leading to his house. He'd built the place with his bare hands the year after Jolie left. He'd put a lot of sweat—and yes, tears—into the house. It had been a refuge away from the eyes of everyone in Dew Drop. Driving into the yard, he was relieved when he saw the stone-and-log fortress—home. It was sturdy. It had clean lines and hard edges. Just like his heart.

His grandmother kept telling him it needed a woman's touch to soften it up—some flowers, and a couple of trellises of roses and morning glories.

It was fine like it was, he'd told her.

He walked in through the heavy door that he'd made himself from the oaks in his woods, with hand-sanded planks and bold, strong hinges that were meant to last a lifetime. Strong, dependable, reliable.

Slamming the door behind him, Morgan's steps echoed as he walked straight through the empty house and out the back door onto the deck that overlooked the river.

Had he built this house to keep her memories at bay? Or had he built this house on the crook of the river to remind him of her?

The question slammed into him the minute the sound of the flowing water reached him.

Grasping the deck railing, he glared down at the river twenty feet away. His life had been in order. It had been settled.

And now this.

I love you.... Her words reverberated through his thick skull. *Coming back here and being near you, seeing the man you've become, watching you with the boys and witnessing the dedication that you have to them and this ranch, it just makes my heart ache with regret that I wasn't here to help build this with you.*

Regret. He knew a thing or two about regret. He closed his eyes and prayed for God to throw him a lifeline.

Part of him clamored to go back and tell Jolie he wanted her here. However, he'd learned that love was about letting them go. It was about helping Jolie do what she was meant to do.

He wasn't giving in to any weakness this go-around. Because if he gave in, if he opened his heart again and then she left, he knew the pain would be worse than the first time.

No. Girding up the door was the best thing.

But the kiss. His pulse kicked up like a buckin' bronc just thinking about that kiss. How was he ever supposed to forget it? He couldn't and he knew it.

When she left…at least he'd have the memory. But it was going to take everything he had to stay strong and let her go.

Jolie went through the week—which was blessedly busy—on remote much of the time, but to her surprise, she was able to enjoy the boys' excitement in getting ready for Saturday's fun.

Focus, Jolie, she kept telling herself.

Focus on the fishing tournament, on keeping sixteen boys in line, on putting Morgan's rejection on the back burner.

The boys weren't the only ones who were excited. Nana, Ms. Jo and Mabel had prepared all manner of goodies for the occasion with help from Edwina, T-Bone and many others from town. No one would starve come Saturday—that was for certain.

Dew Drop and the surrounding area had been invited and a huge number of folks were going to turn out. Thirty-two teams had applied for the tournament, which was a great number—not too many and not too few. The boys had been figuring out how to decorate their boats and for the most part, they had kept it simple, not wanting to distract themselves from the main goal, which was to hook the biggest fish.

Many of the boats had forgone the decorations completely, because it had been optional, but some were done up in style. There were boats with umbrellas, including one that had an inflatable palm tree sitting next to the trolling motor, which, of course, would remain off because they had to use paddles. Another had an American flag flying. Sammy and Morgan had mounted a set of sun-bleached cow horns on the front of their boat and Sammy was proud of it. She'd laughingly offered to put a big red bow on the horns for added decoration. Horrified, they'd declined her offer.

Morgan had been around some, keeping busy with the boys and keeping interaction with her to a minimum. She was fine with that. She still wasn't clearheaded about what had happened between them. She'd told Morgan she loved him, and he hadn't said it back. They'd shared the kiss of a lifetime and she'd felt certain his whole heart had been in that kiss, and yet instead of telling her he loved her, he'd refused to let her stay. This really confused her, and by the end of the week it was becoming increasingly hard to focus. Best bet was to do as they were doing and let it steep—for now.

But it was not a foregone conclusion that they were done. Oh no, not by a long shot.

Saturday dawned, cooling off at eighty-five degrees—perfect for Texas in November. As up-and-down as the weather was in the fall months, it could easily have dawned at sixty degrees and wet. God had given them a beautiful day, though, and for that Jolie was thankful.

The lake area was beautiful, too—a steep hill sloping down to a picturesque lake surrounded by large oak and cedar trees. Upon Jolie's arrival, a group of deer lifted their heads from eating acorns beneath the oaks and raced for cover within the nearest stand of trees. She took a moment to enjoy watching them before driving the rest of the way down to the dock.

It wasn't long before things started rolling. The boys' boats had been carried down the night before and sat ready to slide into the lake, palm trees, cow horns, flags and umbrellas included.

Rowdy, Tucker, Randolph and most of the cowboys who worked on the ranch showed up to help direct people and offer assistance where needed. They were also in charge of the arena event, which the boys had decided was going to be a cow-dressing competition. Jolie could only imagine the fun the kids were going to have treating cattle like Barbie dolls.

Nana and Ms. Jo were unpacking a truckload of goodies and Mabel was setting up the drink station, with the help of several of their friends from church. Jolie realized early into this fundraiser that the folks of Dew Drop were just as generous with their time and money as they'd ever been. A feeling of peace filled her—it was nice to belong here.

She only wished Morgan felt it was nice for her to belong here, too.

"Where in the world are those two loud-mouth whittlers?" Ms. Jo asked about thirty minutes before it was time for the boaters to put in. The grounds were crowded with folks milling around and kids running and playing. Everything was set—everything except Chili and Drewbaker. They hadn't shown up yet.

"I don't know. This isn't like them, is it?" Jolie asked, checking her watch one more time.

"Not on your life. Those two are usually first responders when it comes to being on time."

Ms. Jo's words were barely out of her mouth when a honking horn drew everyone's attention. Drewbaker's dusty blue, sixty-something Ford pickup topped the hill, heading slowly down the big slope toward everyone. Both men were grinning as everyone gaped at what they were pulling on the flatbed trailer behind the truck.

It was a round metal watering trough, about six feet across. It had two folding chairs sitting in it with a cooler in the center. On the edges they'd mounted fishing pole holders, and several poles stood at attention.

"Heavens to Betsy, what is *that?*" Ms. Jo snapped, marching to meet them as they eased to a halt.

"Here we are, secret weapon in tow," Drewbaker said jauntily as he climbed from his old truck with a grin.

Chili's cheeks were pink with excitement and cheer as he hurried around the front of the truck to where a crowd had gathered, studying their contraption. "Ain't she a beaut?" he bragged.

"She's a beaut, all right," Ms. Jo snorted. "Secret weapon—ha! I'll have to see it to believe it."

"Does it float?" Wes asked, sauntering up, eyeing the contraption with interest.

Drewbaker's mouth dropped open. "Does a dog wag its tail? Sure it floats!"

"But will it tip over?" Joseph asked skeptically.

"Well, now, there's an interesting possibility," Chili chuckled. "Me and ol' Drewbaker might just be takin' ourselves a little bath if it tips one way or the other." He tugged out two life vests and held them up. "Just in case."

Morgan stepped through the crowd, brushing past Jolie as he went. The woodsy scent of his cologne teased her senses. *Unfair,* she thought.

"Fellas, I'm not sure what to make of this, but I have to say I'm interested in seeing what happens when y'all climb in it."

"How do you get it in the water?" Caleb asked.

"Yeah," called a few people in the crowd.

Good question. Because the trough wasn't on a regular boat trailer and there was no curve to the bottom, she assumed they would have to get the boys to carry it down to the water.

"If we could get a little assistance," Drewbaker said. Climbing up on the flatbed trailer, he began gathering the fishing poles from their holders. He handed some to Sammy and Caleb and B.J., who had raced to help.

Drewbaker then lifted the fold-up chairs out and handed them off to a couple of boys, and the ice chest, too. When the boat thing was empty, he had Morgan, Tucker and Rowdy help him and Chili lift it to the ground, then tip it on its side and simply roll it down the hill to the end of the dock. Once there, they turned it upright and eased it into the water.

"Well, I'll be," Jolie murmured.

Chili used a rope tied to the handle to secure it to the dock. Now all that was left was their managing to get in the thing.

Ms. Jo and Mabel watched with squinted eyes.

"I have to give it to the old codgers, it's original." Mabel chuckled, shaking her head.

"They'll probably drown themselves before the day is done," Ms. Jo retorted. "Come on, Mabel, let's go show these fellas how it's done."

And so the day began.

The tournament was officially started with the wave of a flag, and everyone jumped into their boats and pushed out into the water ready for battle. Everyone, that is, except Drewbaker and Chili. They eased into their circular contraption very carefully, keeping their weight evenly distributed, grinning the whole time. Once in their seats they pushed off from the dock.

Drewbaker gave a salute, and to the amazement of everyone watching, they floated out onto the lake like a dream!

Nana paused beside her. "I don't know about you, but I have a feeling the boys will vote that funny dinghy the winner."

Jolie chuckled. "If those two get dunked in the lake, it's a sure winner."

Nana's eyes widened. "I wouldn't put it past those two to do something like that on purpose if they aren't having any bites today."

A sudden squeal from the lake had them both zeroing in on Sammy and Morgan.

"I got one! I got one!" Sammy called. Morgan was sitting beside him in the small two-man boat, calmly showing him how to reel in the fish. Once he got it reeled in, he waved his pole in the air, the small fish dangling above their heads until Morgan grabbed it and took the hook from its mouth.

"That's good for both of them." Nana tilted her head to the side. "Morgan has been preoccupied and fairly irritable this week—more so than anytime since you got here. You wouldn't know anything about that, would you?"

Not wanting to discuss their situation even with Nana, Jolie hesitated. "Let's just say I might know something about it, and I don't know how to fix it."

Nana gave her a sympathetic smile. "This is what I was afraid of. I remember the first year after you left. I couldn't help Morgan with the pain, and I had to watch him work through it in his own way. 'He heals the brokenhearted and binds up their wounds'—I clung to that verse for Morgan, Rowdy and Tucker after their momma died. And I did it again for Morgan after you left. I knew he didn't love Celia." She shrugged. "I couldn't tell him that, though. Thankfully the poor girl had the gumption to realize it herself and do something about it." Her kind eyes looked steadily into Jolie's, and Jolie couldn't speak. "This can't be easy for either of you. I've been praying God's will—and you know He does have one. Even if we don't understand it. God's got a plan, Jolie."

Patting her on the arm, Nana headed toward the goody table. Jolie took a deep breath and studied Morgan from a distance. Sammy was keeping him busy, fidgeting on the boat seat and hooking his shirt almost every time he tried to cast his line. Morgan patiently worked with him.

Dear Lord, what is Your plan for my life?

"Please tell me," she whispered in the

slight breeze. It was the first time that Jolie could remember actually asking God that question.

Morgan was trying hard not to laugh as Chili and Drewbaker were having a terrible time with a leak in their tub.

"They're biting better on your side," Chili said, poking his buddy in the shoulder with the tip of his pole. "And it's time for you to bail water and me to fish."

"Hang on to your horses. I think I have a bite," Drewbaker grumbled, keeping his fishing pole steady over the water.

Morgan and Sammy had been hearing bits of the fellas' conversation off and on all morning. It was entertaining, that was for sure. Fishing was normally a quiet sport, but not today on this lake. When a kid caught a fish, he whooped and his boat rocked with excitement—Morgan was glad he'd insisted on life vests. When a grown man caught a fish bigger than his neighbors', he whooped, too, and taunted them with his catch.

"I sure am liking this fishing," Sammy said, grinning when he pulled in his third bass of the morning. Holding it up proudly, Morgan chuckled.

"That's because you're whipping the pants off me."

Sammy shrugged. "I got the moves."

"Yeah, I guess you do."

"Hold on to your hat, Chili, I've got a bite! A big-un, too," Drewbaker yelped excitedly, drawing everyone's attention. His line stretched out and he began reeling in his catch. It was a fighter and the bass did a flip out of the water.

"Whoa, Nellie! That's a big-un," Chili said, halting his dipping. He shot to his feet in excitement, making the tub rock with force. It would have been fine except Drewbaker's chair tilted when Chili slammed back down in his seat. Hanging on to his pole, Drewbaker rode his chair as it slid with the rocking tub. To Morgan's surprise the tub stayed afloat as Drew-baker managed to get his good-size bass into the tub without bashing his buddy.

"I thought for sure they were goners," Sammy said, laughing.

Morgan was thoroughly enjoying fishing with the boy. Sammy was doing well in general, and seemed more settled now. The fact that he hadn't freaked out over the thought of the tub tossing the two whittlers into the lake was a good sign, too.

"Catch him," Drewbaker demanded, drawing their attention again. Chili was bent over, grasping at the bottom of the boat. "What's going on now?" Morgan called to the duo.

"The fish got loose in the bottom of the boat!" Chili yelled.

Drewbaker looked up, over the edge. "There's so much water, he's swimmin' and thinkin' he's found a new home. We can't catch him!"

"You two need to just take that contraption to the shore right now," Ms. Jo demanded. "Serious-minded fisherwomen can't even think straight for all y'alls lolly-gagging and jammer-jawin'!"

Sammy grinned at Morgan, his big eyes bright. "This is the most fun I've had since I got here. I sure am glad I'm with you."

If that didn't get to a man, Morgan didn't know what would. "Kiddo, it's the most fun I've had in a long time, too."

It wasn't lost on him that all of this had been Jolie's idea. She was a good teacher, with an eye for making things special for the boys. He had to admit it—she would be a blessing to the program if she were to stay.

The question was, could he handle it if she did?

Chapter Eighteen

The fishing tournament was a success. The boys could not stop smiling and teasing each other after they got back on dry land. And they were thrilled with the results of the boat-decoration contest—it was no surprise when Jolie counted the votes from the jar and announced that the galvanized tub had won unanimously.

Jolie loved seeing everyone have a good time. Kids were running around playing kickball, and people were visiting and catching up while Morgan and his men unloaded the young cows for the cow-dressing contest. She felt a rush of pride that her boys had made this day happen, with a little help from her. And from Morgan.

She and Morgan made a good team.

Pushing the thought from her mind, she went over to help organize the kids into six different groups—there were about seventy in all, in a vast range of ages. After they were organized, she lined them up around the temporary arena Morgan had hauled in for the occasion. She put Sammy in a group with Wes and several kids who were his age and younger—she hoped he would feel like the leader of the younger ones.

"Jolie, can you help?" Rowdy called to her. Climbing through the portable railed panels of the temporary corral, she crossed to where the cowboys were gathered around Morgan. His gaze landed on her and he lifted his chin in greeting.

"Your job is to pick a cow, stay by her and help out if needed. The object of the game is for the kids to dress the cow using the clothing they have on. Your job is to make sure no one takes off anything they shouldn't."

"Seriously?" Jolie asked. This was a new event for her.

Rowdy chuckled. "You'd be surprised just how inventive kids can be during a cow dressing."

"I hope we don't end up with a bunch of streakers running around."

"It will be fine," Morgan assured her, speaking directly to her for the first time that day. They had spoken a few times during the week, but their conversations had been quick and strictly about business. His eyes were distant, the wall between them firmly in place. Jolie looked away, not wanting him to see how much this hurt her.

"Okay, take your places. Two men to an animal," Morgan said. Cowboys scattered instantly.

Jolie didn't move quickly enough and to her dismay ended up beside Morgan and his cow.

Of all the luck.

Looking about as happy as she was about

their situation, he continued giving instructions through a megaphone. "Okay. Here we go. Dress your cow."

Like a flood of ants attacking a bowl of sugar, the kids came over the railings of the arena and headed straight for the cows. The teams had to wrestle the cow to the ground, then dress it. Laughter and hooting erupted as the clothes went flying—kids stuffed colored socks on cows' hooves, stripped off long-sleeved shirts and tried to pull them over the cows' front legs and wrapped shirts around the animals' necks. By the time Morgan blew his whistle, the animals were running around with clothing flopping everywhere.

Everyone was laughing hard by the time it was over, and kids were jumping up and down with excitement. When Jolie met Morgan's eyes, she knew he was thinking the same thing she was: they'd done a good thing.

And for today, she was satisfied with that.

"Good job, Jolie." Morgan tipped his hat at her.

"Thanks. I was glad to do it." She pinned him with a steady look. "We make a good team."

Before Morgan could say anything else, Jolie turned and headed for the goody table. She needed some chocolate chip cookies to keep her mouth busy—the last thing she wanted to do right now was say too much.

With any luck, Morgan McDermott would spend some quality time thinking on what she'd just said.

When Jolie returned home from three days in Houston for Thanksgiving—where she'd been forced to answer endless questions from her parents about being on the ranch with Morgan—she headed straight for Randolph's office. She'd loved her visit with her family, but she'd missed the kids and she'd missed Morgan so much it hurt.

Driving up to the office, she was relieved to see that Morgan's truck wasn't there.

She entered the small lobby. Randolph's

door was open and she rapped gently on the door frame to get his attention.

"Jolie," Randolph said, standing and waving her inside.

"I know I've done a good job," she said after explaining why she'd come.

Randolph, who looked so much like an older Morgan, leaned back in his chair. "You've done a fantastic job, Jolie, but Morgan is a partner in the ranch. He has a say in who will teach the boys on a full-time basis. If Morgan isn't on board, I can't give you the contract. I'm very sorry about that."

She'd known what he'd say, but she had to at least ask. In her heart of hearts she knew this was where she belonged. She'd been praying, and listening for God's will, and she had to see if He would open a door through Randolph.

Forcing down her disappointment, she rose. "Thank you for everything. I understand." Turning, she headed for the door.

"Jolie," Randolph called, his deep voice stopping her. "'Many are the plans in a man's heart. But it is the Lord's purpose that prevails.' That's Nana's favorite proverb."

"Yes, I've heard her quote it before."

"God's will is at work in your life. Remember that."

The words hit deep. "I will." She left, offering him a smile on her way out that probably looked as sad as it felt.

She hoped God let her in on the plan soon. Because she felt as if her life was here, on the ranch with the boys, and with Morgan. Without it, she had no idea who she was or what she was supposed to do.

Or how she was supposed to handle letting go of Morgan a second time.

"Something is wrong with Jolie," Wes said, looking at the group assembled around him behind the stables. He'd called the meeting because it was time to do something.

"Yeah, she's been quiet and real distracted this week." Joseph had his boot propped on the corral rung and was tapping his fingers on his knee. "I think she's worried about not being able to get in the water."

"Yeah," Wes agreed. "I heard her talking to someone about an advertisement she's supposed to shoot over the Christmas holidays. And she didn't look too happy when she got off the phone. It sounded like she's got her back up against the wall."

"She doesn't have to do it if she don't want to, does she?" Sammy asked.

"She's a professional kayaker," Wes stated. "She gets paid to do these ads. Her job is on the line, I think."

"But what about her being our teacher? And our ranch mom, like y'all told me?" B.J. asked.

The guys all looked at each other with uncertainty.

"Look—" Joseph pulled his boot off the rung and stood straight "—we want Jolie to stay, but she's got priorities. She's got to get past this bad thing that happened in her life. It's kind of how we've had to do it a little bit. I mean, we've each had some bad stuff—we know how hard it is to get past it."

Sammy looked sad. "Will she come back to us if she gets back in the water?"

"I don't know, Sammy," Joseph said.

He and Wes stared at each other for a long moment. Wes knew Joseph hated the look on the little kid's face as much as he did. And the other boys', too. They had to do something and they both knew it.

"Sometimes a person doesn't know what's in front of them till they face their fears."

"How do you know that, Joseph?" Sammy asked.

"I don't know. I heard it in a movie. It sounds right, though. I'm thinking Jolie and Morgan have this thing going on. Y'all have seen how they've been lookin' at each other lately."

"Kinda mad," B.J. said.

"And sad," Sammy added with a sigh. "When one isn't looking and they don't know we're watching."

"Yeah," everyone agreed at once.

"Couldn't Jolie teach us and still compete in kayaking?" Tony piped in.

"Maybe." Wes thought hard. "I'm just not sure."

Panic lit Sammy's face. "I don't want her to go."

"None of us do," Joseph said.

"Isn't there something we can do?" Caleb asked.

"Yeah." Tony stepped up. "We have to do something."

"We can pray that she stays," Joseph replied, perking up.

Sammy looked down at the dirt. "If we're good, maybe she'll stay."

Wes raked his hands through his hair, his heart hurting bad. He knew prayers didn't work. He'd prayed hard for his family not to fall apart, but God didn't always listen to prayers. He knew he couldn't tell the little kids that, though. They'd already been through enough, and it wasn't easy being a bunch of misfits that nobody wanted.

"Hey, you guys start praying. Me and Joseph will come up with something. Meanwhile, fellas, keep your ears and your eyes open. Anything you see or hear that could help us with a plan to get those two together, you tell us. If we get them to fall in love, then I betcha Jolie will stay."

Joseph and Wes looked at each other over the little kids' heads as they began to pray, hoping against hope that Wes was right.

Chapter Nineteen

A cold wind blew in from the north right after Thanksgiving. It matched the chill in Jolie's heart.

Blinking in the wind, she urged her horse to pick up speed as she rode across the open range. She needed the feel of the wind in her hair and the thunder of hooves beneath her. She hadn't been to the river's bend since she'd gotten back, and she had to go, even if she didn't want to.

Too many memories were there. It was where Morgan had asked her to marry him. It was where she'd said yes. It was there, on the banks of the river, that they'd fallen in love.

Today, feeling lost and confused, her time on the ranch almost up, she'd suddenly thought that if God was going to give her answers, maybe she would be able to hear Him at the river's bend. Or at least maybe she would be able to think clearly.

Nearing the curve in the gravel road leading to the river, she slowed her horse and rounded the corner at a slow trot.

Her heart stopped at what she saw. A log-and-stone house sat where she'd once dreamed of a having a home—and Morgan's truck was parked in the drive.

He'd never said a word.

Heart thudding, she slowly climbed from the saddle, tied up her horse and walked to the front door. It was beautiful, and looked hand-crafted. She ran her fingertips across the smooth surface, then, taking a fortifying breath, she knocked. Her heart pounded and her head was spinning with questions.

She'd never thought to ask where he lived. She'd never dreamed...

When there was no answer, she found

herself walking around the beautiful house to the back—she had to see what it looked like. She halted when she saw the deck. It was exactly as she'd dreamed when she was seventeen—built on the edge of the steep hill with a beautiful view of the river below, and the setting sun. Morgan stood with his back to her, his elbows resting on the deck railing, a mug cupped between his hands.

Walking up the steps, she stopped on the last one.

"Morgan," she said, barely audible over the gentle sound of the river. It struck her then that she hadn't hyperventilated or freaked being close to the water. It had been part of her plan, coming here, hoping this would be the place she could make peace with her past—all of it. But she hadn't planned on finding this.

At the sound of his name Morgan straightened and swung around. "Jolie."

He took her breath away. He was the only man who'd ever made her feel the way she felt now, and the most handsome man she'd ever seen.

"You built our— A house. Here."

He set his mug on the railing. "I always said I was going to build a house here."

"Yes, you did." She stepped up onto the deck and walked past him to the railing. "It's still as beautiful as it ever was."

White foam rolled over the rocks at the river's curve. She braced her shoulders and forced herself to look at the rushing water curling over the rocks.

"Why?" she asked.

The question was simple. Why had he built this home, here, where they'd sat on the grass and dreamed young dreams together. Turning to him, she searched his guarded eyes.

"I built this house here because it wasn't just *our* dream, it was also *my* dream, Jolie. Just because you left didn't mean I had to stop dreaming. I wanted a house here on this spot and so I built it."

She crossed her arms, a conscious effort to shut out the pain this confrontation was causing. Was pain the only thing they had left to give each other?

"Y-you did a good job," she admitted, studying the house's lines. "It's a beautiful place."

He looked at a loss for words at her admission. "Thanks," he said curtly. "So why are you here?"

"I came to see the bend. To think…about things."

"You didn't know my home was here?"

She shook her head.

"It's a good place to think. That's what I do best out here."

Her stomach felt like it was turning upside down doing airscrews, which used to be her favorite kayak trick. She knew it was time to just lay her cards out on the table and come clean. "Morgan, I wish you'd give us a second chance."

"There is no us anymore."

Fire flamed inside of her. "You wouldn't know it from that kiss—"

"Not fair, Jolie. That was a mistake."

"I think you're afraid of us. I think you're

just as afraid of letting me back in as I am of getting back in that water."

She expected him to deny it. He didn't.

"Maybe." His eyes were hard and as dark as a moonless night sky. "We've been over this."

"No. We've been over the fact that you won't let me teach here because you think I need to go back to competing. What we haven't been over is that you won't open your heart to me and admit that you still love me."

She held her breath. Of all the brazen assumptions to make, she knew this could be the most presumptuous. When he said nothing, she somehow found the strength to continue.

"You think it's so easy to tell me to get back in that kayak and do what I love, yet you won't risk—"

"I don't have to risk anything, Jolie. I'm fine the way I am. You're not."

"You don't know what I am."

"Jolie, I've told you before and I'll tell

you again. I will not give you a place to hide."

She started to tell him it wasn't his responsibility either way, that if she wanted to quit kayaking, that was her choice. But she couldn't have that conversation with him again—she just couldn't.

"Have you told the boys you won't be coming back?" he asked. "They need to know, and it needs to come from you."

"No, I haven't. I was hoping…" One look in his eyes told her there was no point in finishing that sentence.

"I'm not renewing your contract and that's final."

She stared at this man she loved, this man she didn't understand. That was that; it was done. She'd done everything except beg and she wouldn't do that. Not that it would have done any good anyway.

"I'll tell them, Morgan." She turned and walked to the steps.

"I do love you, Jolie. Always have, always will. There just is no *us* anymore. You don't get to always make the rules.

You don't get to just walk out when you want and then walk back in when you want."

She glanced over her shoulder, wishing—regretting. "You're right," she managed, then walked down the steps. What more was there to say other than asking if he'd ever thought about forgiving her—but he'd probably thought of that and rejected it. Asking him would feel like begging, and she just couldn't do it.

It was time to move on—yes, time to figure out a plan for her life and move forward.

This was over.

Morgan was elbow-deep in paperwork when Randolph walked into his office the next morning and laid a form on the desk.

"Jolie's official application."

"I told her I'd never hire her."

"She told me that when she dropped it off at the house yesterday morning. She said she still wanted to make it formal. She wants this application in her file."

"Why?" Morgan rubbed the bridge of his nose. She'd dropped the application off before she'd ridden out and discovered the house. And him. Before they'd talked yesterday evening. "I won't change my mind."

Exasperation lined his dad's brow. "I know you were hurt, son. I guess I can admit that after watching the two of you together these last few months, I'd hoped there might be a chance for reconciliation. But that won't happen if you aren't willing to take a chance. Son, let go of your pride if you love her and fight for this relationship."

Morgan pushed back from his desk and stood. "Do you think watching her go again is easy? Because it isn't. Dad, the *easiest* thing I could do would be to sign a new contract and let her stay. But I won't do that."

"Morgan, when your mother died, I didn't have a choice but to let the Lord have her. And I'll admit I was angry about that. Some people in this life get miracles—we didn't when it came to your mother. And when Jolie left you, it was one more time in your life when you didn't get the miracle. I hated that, son. But this time, you're getting the chance to have it. Now you just have to take it."

Morgan glared at his dad. "No." He couldn't be more plain than that.

"Then you may lose her forever. Are you really prepared for that? I think in the back of your mind you hoped she'd come back some day. That's why you built that house where you did, and that's why you haven't moved on and found someone else."

"What ever happened to 'when you love someone, let them go'?" His jaw jerked as he spat out the question.

His dad looked sad. "'If they love you, they'll return,'" Randolph said, finishing the quote for him. "What do you think is happening here, Morg?"

"The boys are going to need support after today," Morgan said, closing the door on the topic of him and Jolie, and moving on to what counted. "She's telling them she's leaving."

"They're resilient. They'll survive. It will be hard, though. They've bonded with Jolie like nothing I've ever seen."

"And that was what I was afraid of all along."

His dad pinned him with sharp eyes. "Morgan, you're harder than even I realized." Randolph turned and left Morgan to himself.

It had been all he could do not to go after Jolie yesterday when she'd left his home, telling himself one more time that this was for the best. If he gave her any kind of encouragement, she'd stay. And he would always be afraid—yes, he admitted to himself that he was afraid—that she would regret walking away from kayaking.

His dad believed Jolie coming home was a miracle, that all Morgan had to do was reach out and accept it. But Morgan was more afraid of seeing regret in her eyes down the road if she stayed.

And he was more afraid of that than losing her.

Miracle or no miracle, Jolie regretting coming back to him was the one thing he couldn't live with.

Chapter Twenty

Jolie knew it was time to tell the boys that she wouldn't be around next year. They needed time to adjust to the idea. And so did she.

So the last thing she was expecting was to walk into a classroom decorated for a party. There was a large sign that said "We love you, Jolie!" covering the projection screen. Colored ribbons from the storeroom dangled from the ceiling fans, whipping around as the two fans turned.

"Surprise!" the boys yelled when she entered, all smiles as they surrounded her.

"What's all this?" she asked, her hand

on her heart as she looked around at her classroom. It was a sight she'd never forget.

The smaller boys were all talking excitedly. "Hold on, buckaroos," Joseph said, laughing as he calmed them down. When they quieted, he grinned his lopsided smile. "We wanted to make sure you knew how much we appreciate you being here, coming on at the last minute to take on a bunch of ragtags like us. You didn't have to do it but you did."

"Yeah," Wes said, looking a little worried. "It's good to be appreciated. We just wanted you to know."

Jolie bit her lip, tears brimming in her eyes. She sucked in a hard breath. "Thanks," she croaked like a frog. "You have no idea what this means to me."

That had all the boys beaming. They looked so proud that her heart clutched in her chest and she had to close her eyes.

"This is the sweetest thing anyone has ever done for me. And I mean that. And you are not ragtags. You are the kind of kids a woman could call her own—and I do. I want you to know that."

Their smiles faded, and she knew they could hear the sadness in her voice.

"I need you to sit down. I have to tell you something."

"Not that you're going to leave," Sammy blurted out, panic in his eyes.

Jolie hated this. He'd recently lost his family and now he'd formed an attachment to her and *she* was leaving. What would that do to him?

"Yes, I am. I have to. I'm sorry. Listen, Sammy, everyone, there are just some things that can't be changed. But my leaving has nothing to do with all of you. I have loved every minute of my time here since the first day I hopped out of my Jeep and saw you standing there. I love all of you."

Wes and Joseph looked down at the floor, not meeting her gaze.

Dear Lord, help me.

"If you loved us, you would stay." Sammy's brown eyes held unshed tears, his chin trembled and his voice was a faint whisper.

Jolie went to her knees in front of him. "I can't stay."

"Why not?"

How could she tell them Morgan hadn't renewed her contract? They would resent him, and that would be terrible because they had to have a good relationship with him. She had to preserve that no matter what.

What Morgan was doing, he was doing out of a misplaced concern. At least that was the assumption that was getting her through this.

Morgan was trying to do what was right for her.

The realization slammed into her as she looked into Sammy's dear face. This wasn't about not forgiving her…it was about doing what he believed was right. Jolie's heart raced at the realization.

Trying to grasp this new information she continued, "This was always a temporary position. You knew that, Sammy. All of you did. As much as I love being here, I have commitments that I have to keep."

And it was true, she did. Morgan had been right about that.

But you can come back...?

The words whispered through her. She heard a horn honk outside and she smiled. "It's going to be all right, guys. I promise. Sammy, it will be okay. Don't be afraid. Okay?"

He nodded. "Okay."

She hugged him tightly, then stood. "I didn't know y'all were fixin' things up for a party—it goes to show you great minds think alike because I was planning on having one myself. If I'm right, that horn is Ms. Jo and Mabel out there with a truckload of homemade pies. I ordered them for an end-of-term celebration."

"Awesome." Wes jumped up and headed to the door. "I'll help bring them in."

Jolie chuckled. "Y'all have worked so hard, you deserve it."

Ms. Jo's pies could make anyone smile, and she sure hoped it was true today as she watched the kids race outside to help, including Sammy after she'd urged him.

Glancing around the decorated room filled her with determination. No way could she just walk away. There had to be another alternative. And she planned to find it.

"What do you mean you can't do anything about it?" Ms. Jo demanded a few hours later after Jolie let the kids head out early for the day. She'd managed to turn the day around somewhat, though Sammy had remained quiet. He'd participated but kept asking her questions that told her he was still worrying. She just prayed that time would help.

"Yes, who does Morgan think he is making you leave if you don't want to?" Mabel snorted.

"I tell you what, I was miffed at you for what you did to him, but now I'm equally miffed at Morgan. That man needs a knock upside the head, if you ask me."

"Whoa, there, aren't you two the ones

who were telling me not to get any ideas? To just be friends?"

"Well," Ms. Jo snapped, "what else were we supposed to say? We didn't want him to get hurt any more than he already had been. We were just trying to be cautious."

"That being said," Mabel added, swiping another forkful of leftover coconut pie, "I agree with Jo. Who is he to tell you you have to leave?"

"He's the guy holding the teaching contract."

Ms. Jo and Mabel gaped at her.

"What?" she asked, bewildered.

Ms. Jo glared at her with impatience. "Who says just because you don't work at Sunrise that you have to leave Dew Drop?"

The door crashed open before Jolie fully processed Ms. Jo's declaration, and Caleb rushed into the room. "Jolie, come quick. We can't find Sammy. He ran away!"

Some of the boys had stopped by the office and told Morgan Sammy was missing, so he was already on the phone with

Tucker when Jolie and Caleb came racing out of the schoolhouse, Ms. Jo and Mabel hotfooting it behind them. They all hurried toward him across the pasture.

Tucker had told him that he'd be there in a few minutes. Morgan had never been happier that his big brother was the sheriff of Dew Drop County. And Rowdy and Chet were on their way with their group, too.

"Caleb said there was a note," Jolie gasped, grabbing his arm as she arrived.

He handed her the note, and his gut clenched watching Jolie, her eyes glistening while she read the words Sammy had painstakingly printed out on a piece of white notebook paper.

Jolie, I'm going to make you proud enough of me that you won't leave.

"What does this mean?" She blinked hard, fighting off tears.

"I'm not sure. He's got a plan, it sounds like. We'll find him," Morgan assured her. "Tucker and Rowdy and the men are on the way. Dad, Pepper, Wes and Joseph are already out there on the roads leading out from the ranch."

She bit her lip. "Okay. We'll find him," she said as if to herself.

Clare and John, Sammy's house parents, hurried from the chow hall with Nana, clearly worried.

"He's crazy about you," Clare said, squeezing Jolie's arm. "He's just come alive since you showed up. Well, all the boys have, actually. They were devastated that you're leaving. But this…" Her words trailed off and she dabbed at tears.

"Leaving, that's the stupidest thing I've ever heard," Ms. Jo snapped, shooting Morgan a stern look as she and Mabel joined Nana in giving Clare some comfort.

Morgan tried not to think about his part in this—not right now. Now he had to hold everyone together and find Sammy. His gaze locked on Jolie. "We'll get a search up once Tucker gets here. We'll find him," Morgan told her again, wanting to give her a hug and ease the alarm in her eyes. But

Jolie crossed her arms and nodded once, as if to block him out.

He couldn't say he blamed her.

Jolie fought to stay in control as the sound of Tucker's siren in the far-off distance signaled they would soon be taking action. But it wasn't happening fast enough for her. She needed to do something soon or she'd go crazy.

"Caleb," she said. "Who was the last to see Sammy?"

"Me. We were going to play in the hay barn, but he said he had to do something, so I went with Tony instead. We decided to go see what he was doing and found the note on his bed."

Tony piped in. "We took it down to Ms. Clare right when we found it."

"Do you guys have any idea where he might have gone?"

They all shook their heads. Jolie felt helpless as Tucker's SUV pulled into the yard and came to a quick halt. Turning off the lights and siren, he stepped from the vehicle and strode their way. Even though his aviation shades hid his eyes, the hard set of his jaw said he was taking this seriously.

"Tucker, glad you're here," Morgan said, looking just as grim as his brother.

"Any word?" Tucker asked, pulling his shades off, looking from Morgan to Jolie.

"None so far," Morgan answered.

Jolie wrapped her arms around herself. "Tucker, if he's walking off the property, the guys would have found him by now. A little kid like him couldn't have gotten far on foot in less than an hour."

"True. We'll start searching the ranch. But we need some facts first."

"These three were the last to see him." Morgan placed an arm around Caleb's shoulders. Jolie found herself wishing his arm were around her instead. "They came straight to us when they found the note."

"Do you have it?"

"I do." Jolie thrust it at him, anxious for his trained eye to see it. She watched as he read it, meeting Morgan's gaze for a brief moment. "Any hints in there that we're missing?"

"Sounds like he has something to prove. Any thoughts about that?"

"He's been better about being scared," Caleb said.

Just then, Randolph drove up with Joseph and Wes from scouting the roads. Randolph shook his head as he strode toward the crowd. He, Morgan and Tucker went off and had a discussion, and Nana came and put her arm around Jolie.

Within minutes cars began to arrive full of folks from town, like Chili and Drewbaker. Walter Pepper and the other ranch hands came soon after, having had no luck searching the immediate area. More law enforcement with a team of search dogs was on the way. Within the hour they had a full-blown search going.

Jolie had been going over her conversation with Sammy from that morning, and the note he'd left. Her gut was trying to tell her something…he'd asked her where she was trying to kayak and she'd told him about the trail behind her house that led down to the river where she had been going to picture herself getting in the water. She'd confessed that she hadn't been able to get in so far though. Surely he wasn't trying to prove—Jolie halted in her tracks.

Proud enough of me that you won't leave.

Spinning around Jolie searched for Morgan. He was getting on his horse on the other side of the pasture, about to start a mounted search. Racing toward him, Jolie had never been so happy to be in shape in all of her life. He spotted her and rode out to meet her.

"What's up, Jolie?" he asked as he brought his horse to a halt.

"I think he might be at the river behind my house. I think he's going to kayak."

"Seriously?"

Jolie nodded. "He wants to make me proud. Maybe he thinks if he can do what I can't, I won't leave."

Morgan's brows knitted beneath his straw Stetson. He held a hand out to her and pulled his boot from the stirrup. "Come on, let's go check it out."

Jolie didn't waste time. She reached for his hand, rammed her boot in the stirrup and let him hoist her up behind him. They were heading toward her house almost before she got her arms around his waist. Jolie clung to Morgan, her heart racing with hope as they galloped across the pasture.

"You sure you can face this? Do I need to get someone else to help me?" he asked over his shoulder.

"I'll handle it," she said with no hesitation. If they found Sammy in that river current—she prayed he hadn't done such a foolish thing, but if he had—he would need her. "I'm the best person for this."

"That's my girl," Morgan said. His words dug deep—it had been a long time since she'd been his girl. A long, long time.

Too long.

This wasn't the time to think about the past between them, but as they rode, memories crowded in alongside the worry for

Sammy. Like a kaleidoscope of past, present and a future yet untold, everything shifted in and out of focus, bringing new images to her mind's eye.

When they made it to the cabin, Jolie's heart stopped as she looked at the spot where her kayaks sat. "My yellow kayak is missing," she said grimly. "He's out there, Morgan."

"Looks that way," Morgan said.

"I need to grab my gear." She jumped from the horse, raced inside the house and grabbed her backpack from where it rested in the corner, forgotten. Inside it was her kayaking gear, and her rescue ropes. Outside again, she went straight for one of her other kayaks, hoisted it to her shoulder and without waiting for Morgan she hurried to her Jeep and stowed it across the backseat, not bothering to attach it to the roof rack.

Morgan helped straighten it and then hopped in as she cranked the key and rammed the gearshift. "Hang on," she warned, and punched the gas. Wheeling through the backyard and onto the faint trail, she cut through to the clearing.

When they hit the steep hill, the Jeep's wheels left land for a moment as they surged forward, soared through the air and hit hard before racing downhill.

They didn't say much as they scanned the land while they drove, hoping to find Sammy before he made it to the water.

How long had he been gone?

When they made it to the trail that led to the water, Jolie jerked the Jeep to a halt and grabbed her kayak.

"I can carry that for you," Morgan offered.

She shook her head. "I always carry my own load."

It was part of the sport—her kayak was as much a part of her as her arms. "It's okay," she assured Morgan over her shoulder. "Thanks for the offer."

She jogged down the path where she'd had her meltdown that day that had ended in the kiss she couldn't forget. Morgan didn't ask her if she was all right again—

he just jogged beside her and kept up. They topped the hill, bending down to miss a couple of low-slung tree limbs. She could hear the river now, the rush of rapids downstream from where they would put in. It was an ominous sound to Jolie. Her heartbeat became erratic and her skin clammy.

Thinking of Sammy, she never slowed down, refusing to give in. She was going in if Sammy needed her. No question about it.

Bursting through the last of the trees she headed straight down the embankment, scanning the water anxiously. And praying hard.

Her heart stopped. "There!" she shouted, spotting him on the far side of the river clinging to a tree branch, just past the first set of rapids.

Instead of holding him under, the vortex had spat him out when he'd slipped out of his kayak. She thanked God for that.

And for giving her a window of opportunity to get to him.

But there was no way to get down the

rocks to Sammy. Going through the rapids was the only way.

She'd have to hold the kayak in control while maneuvering to him. And once she had him, they'd have to make it through the worst rapids together in a one-man kayak.

"You can do this, Jolie." Morgan's penetrating eyes told her he had faith in her. Even having seen what a basket case she'd been, he had faith.

Her head was swimming. "You better get downstream and be ready in case you have to grab him," she advised as she started moving again. Morgan would know the spot she meant—it would be his only shot to grab Sammy if she missed, or if Sammy lost his grip on the tree before she got to him. If they both missed, the river would sweep him into the worst section of the rapids. His only chance then would be in God's hands.

Jolie prayed.

Glancing over her shoulder she saw Morgan racing down the path. He'd be standing between two large rocks in a shallow section that had a slippery fast current, just bypassing a pool of calm water to the right, perfect for a takeout.

At the water's edge, Jolie fought her demons, thinking only of Sammy. She was in the kayak within seconds—no hesitation, paddle in hand and moving. She found her line in the water quickly and set herself up to hit the rapid perfectly. She took the first set with no problem, a warm-up for what was to come.

Keeping her line, she set herself up for the second set of rapids, this one was the money spot, as they called it in competition, the one that counted...

This one's for Sammy.

The water was cold as it washed over her, the current swift, strong from the rain they'd had up north two days earlier. She prayed God would keep Sammy's strength up, and thanked Him for giving her the ability to do what needed to be done to save him.

She took the rapid, a mad vortex of powerful, churning water with the means to pull a person down and not spit her out until it felt like it. She wished for her yellow banana—her old friend—but this kayak would have to do.

She cut through the rocks with skill honed from hard work and God's gift... and then she maneuvered a perfect roll, dipping head-first beneath the surface then rolling out and flipping the kayak into the air. The move required strength as she twisted her body, forcing the kayak to alter its course. She landed it perfectly and with a swift push of her paddle was right next to Sammy beneath the tree.

Jolie held the boat still with the paddle against the rocks behind him. She reached with her free arm, muscles burning from the effort, and she got him. His eyes were huge, glazed with fear, his lips purple from the chill.

"Y-you came for me," he gasped, clinging to the limb.

"I'll *always* come for you," she declared, voice hoarse with emotion, knowing it was true. "Let go of the tree," she urged against the roar of the water. Thankfully, Sammy was thinking clearly enough to respond with a nod and do as he was asked. He took her hand and she pulled him toward the boat. It was hard to do, since she was having to use the paddle to hold the boat steady and keep them out of the current. If she wasn't careful she could be swept away from him. "You have to climb up by yourself, Sammy, okay? I can hold you steady, but you have to climb on your own."

There was no place for him except on top of the kayak in front of her, with his feet on the stern. This wasn't a normal situation—it was a tricky balancing act. God's hand and His alone steadied the boat as she held off the current with one hand on the paddle. She felt her strength waning—she knew she wasn't going to last much longer.

"When you get up, lean back against me, hold on to the deck line and keep your feet on the kayak in front of you. Can you do that?"

"Y-yes, I can." Even though his teeth

were chattering, there was power in his voice now. Jolie was so proud of Sammy as he scrambled up the kayak and eased into place.

"We're going to make it," she told him as he leaned against her. "Hold on, buddy, here we go," she said, and let the current have them, sweeping them back into the dangerous flow.

Chapter Twenty-One

Morgan prayed harder than he ever had in his whole life as he watched the rescue. Jolie was amazing—her strength and skill awed him as she held it all together and came through the last set of rapids with Sammy in front of her. Once it was clear they'd make the trip without flipping, he moved to the calm pool where he knew she was headed.

Morgan steadied the kayak, then took Sammy into his arms. The boy looked slightly dazed as Morgan hugged him hard, thanking God. "You're okay, little man," he said, looking into his tense face. Limp as a rag, Sammy nodded and rested his head against Morgan's heart. Jolie climbed from her kayak, her exhaustion evident in the way she moved.

"We need to get him to a doctor," she said, hoisting her kayak to the shore and leaving it behind as she assisted Morgan in getting Sammy up the steep incline to the path.

"I got them on my cell. An ambulance should be getting to the woods' edge soon."

Hurrying along the path, Morgan kept talking to Sammy as Jolie held branches out of their way. Sammy looked up at him, his eyes bright with tears. "I didn't mean to mess up. I tried to make y'all proud of me. I tried to make Jolie see that I could help her in the water so she would stay. You won't send me away now, will you?"

Morgan held him closer, and kept his pace. "Never. You're going to be fine, Sammy. We're not sending you any-where—you are part of our family."

Jolie placed her hand on Sammy's head as they continued to hurry along the path. "I was scared for you, Sammy, but God kept you safe out there today. You're going to be all right. I'm crazy about you, don't you know that?"

And Morgan was crazy about *her*. Hearing her say those words to Sammy made his heart stop in his chest. It was going to be almost impossible to let her go.

She'd proven she could get back in the water, and she could do it with style. Jolie belonged out there—it was evident to anyone who saw her in action. After today, he had no doubt.

Sammy obviously didn't want to see her go any more than Morgan did.

But they would have to let her.

They were just coming out of the woods when the emergency vehicles came across the pasture with Tucker in the lead. It was like the cavalry was coming. Morgan had never been happier to see his brother in all his life.

Sammy had been through a harrowing experience and it was a miracle he'd survived long enough for Jolie to get to him. It was God who had held Sammy to that tree, no doubt about it. And it was God who was going to have to give Sammy—and Morgan—the strength to see her leave.

A few hours later, Jolie held a cup of coffee in her hands, letting the warmth sink into her bones. She wasn't sure the chill would ever leave her. Sitting on a bench on the porch of the chow hall, she watched the boys laughing and playing a game of football in the yard. Morgan and his dad and brothers were sitting together at the picnic table, talking to various people from town who'd come out to help with the rescue and then stayed to celebrate. Sammy sat on the bench between Morgan and Tucker, looking a little stunned that so many people had come to make sure he was safe.

Nana, Ms. Jo and Mabel were hustling around making sure everyone had something to eat and drink. Everyone was so relieved that Sammy was safe that the rescue party had turned into a regular party.

Jolie's role as the hero was making her uncomfortable. She'd had to repeat to

Tucker what she'd done, then defer to Morgan. Morgan had a version of the tale that was so full of praise she couldn't listen, but his version pleased everyone more than her clinical retelling of events had.

"I gotta say one thing," Edwina said, stopping beside Jolie, topping off her cup of coffee without bothering to ask. "You got some nerves of steel, Jolie. You done good savin' that boy. You know I ain't never made it no secret that I ain't got a lick of use for men. But Morgan's got himself some good qualities aside from bein' drop-dead gorgeous—yeah, I do have eyes." She gave Jolie a grin. "But truly, you could do a whole lot worse—believe me, if you were to meet Lester or Darin or even Marv—any of that bunch of losers I married—you'd have a clue how much worse it could *get*."

Jolie smiled, chuckling. Edwina had not been lucky in love.

"There you go. If my love life won't pull a chuckle out of you, nothing will. But honestly, maybe you need to rethink this leavin' thing. If that man looked at me the way he looks at you, I might be tempted to dip my toe back into the matrimonial waters. Somethin' to think about." She winked and was gone, off to spread her cheer elsewhere.

If she only knew that this time, it wasn't Jolie who'd chosen a different life. It was Morgan.

Jolie looked over at Sammy, who had stayed away from her since they'd made it back to the ranch, sticking close to Morgan's side. It was as if he needed to shut her out.

And she hated it.

But there was a huge positive here—Sammy had come so far. He wasn't lying anymore, and he'd taken a risk today. However misguided his actions had been, he'd left his fears behind and tried to be strong. Jolie knew she'd had a part in his growth. Looking at him now, she was filled with pride of accomplishment like nothing she'd ever felt on the river.

Jolie had no doubts now about what she

was going to do with the rest of her life. What she didn't know was how Morgan was going to handle it.

He thought he'd figured out the rest of her life for her.

But he was wrong.

Standing, she dropped the blanket on the bench and walked over to where he sat. "Morgan, may I speak to you?"

When he looked up at her and saw her serious expression, elation slid off his face and his eyes darkened.

"Sure."

Jolie led them away from the crowd, to the quiet of the stables. The smell of hay and feed greeted her, and from the cool shadows she heard the soft nicker of newborn colts. She slowly turned and faced an unsmiling Morgan.

"I'm staying, Morgan. I'm retiring from competition," she said quietly. "I know where you stand on all this, but I know what I want, and I know what's best for me."

"Jolie, I saw you out there today. You

were magnificent. To leave that beauty and skill behind would be a waste. You are meant for great things."

She smiled. "Yes, I am. And so are you. Here on this ranch is where the great things happen. Watching these boys flourish, and loving them. This is the great thing I'm meant for now. This is what I choose." She studied his face as he stared down at her. "I'd like your blessing, Morgan, but I don't need it. My plan is to move to Dew Drop and get a teaching job at the public school, and volunteer on the ranch, if you'll have me."

Morgan had grown still. His jaw jerked and his eyes cut through her, searching for the truth. "I don't know what to say," he said. "I know for me the boys are enough. At least, it satisfies me. But you're going to regret—"

"I already regret, Morgan. I regret leaving you. I regret hurting you. Yet I know that God had a plan back then and it was meant to be. And now I know *this* is meant to be. So I'm here to stay, and I'm praying that at some point you will trust my love for you and let me into your heart again."

She stepped close to him and placed her hand on his heart. It was racing.

"I love you, Morgan McDermott, and you love me. You told me so. Can you let me back into your life?"

He didn't say anything, and her heart sank. She'd hoped if he knew she wasn't leaving it would change his mind. But as she stepped away from him, she knew her plan wasn't going to change one bit. Dew Drop was where she was supposed to be.

"I hope one day you'll be able to accept my being here, Morgan, and even let me help out with the boys. It would mean a lot to me." Jolie turned, not knowing what else to say. She'd made it to the double doors of the stable when his hand on her arm halted her.

"Jolie."

She faced him, framed in the doorway with the soft breeze in her hair. She knew she must look a sight after all they'd been through on the water, but she didn't care.

"Don't you know it would be easy to agree? The hard part is to let you go. I hope you understand that."

She lifted her hand to cup his strong jaw. "I do," she whispered, nodding. "I truly do. But this is where I *want* to be. Where I need to be. With you. And the boys. And no regrets. None."

She could see the war in his eyes, his beautiful, deep, fathomless eyes. His forehead crinkled and his jaw tensed as he struggled with the right thing to do. The right thing to do by *her.*

"You have to trust that what I say is true, Morgan. I love you, and if you open your heart to me I will never, ever leave you. Please trust me."

He nodded ever so slightly. His eyes calmed and a slow smile eased across his face as he turned his head to kiss her palm. His hand came up and took hers, and Jolie's heart cracked open with love. And hope.

No words were needed as his arms came around her and his lips met hers. "I love you, Jolie Sheridan. Will you marry me?" he whispered.

With tears in her eyes, she nodded. And behind them, whoops, cheers and clapping erupted.

"Well—" Morgan chuckled "—it's a done deal now. You're stuck with us. Because I'm not telling *them* any different."

Jolie looked across the grass to her boys. "Good. This is my *family,* and I'm not going anywhere."

Squeezing her hand tightly in his, Morgan looked at her with love in his eyes. "Then let's go make it official."

She smiled, her heart in full bloom. "Lead the way, cowboy. Lead the way."

Epilogue

"*Hubba, hubba,* come to papa," Wes croaked from the front pew where all sixteen boys were standing in the church.

Morgan would have gone over and thumped him on the ear if he hadn't been standing beside the preacher and thinking a more polite version of the same thing as Jolie entered the sanctuary on the arm of her dad. She was so beautiful that he could do nothing but hold her gaze and watch her walk down the aisle toward him. He'd been waiting six long years for this day.

After she'd convinced him that she wanted a life on the ranch with him and the boys, they'd wasted no time setting the date. Jolie had wanted to get married immediately, but they'd given themselves a month.

It was a cold day in January, with a fine layer of snow on the ground and the wind rattling the church windows. He'd hoped for a sunny day for Jolie, but she'd said even a blizzard wouldn't keep her from becoming Mrs. Morgan McDermott.

For Morgan, the sun had come out the moment Jolie said yes. He'd gotten down on his knees in front of the boys so they could see how it should be done. She'd laughingly agreed, and her laughter had filled every space in his heart.

He thanked God for bringing her back to him in *His* time. Morgan recognized that Jolie had needed the time away, and even though he wasn't real high on thinkin' it, he'd needed the time she was away, too. Although he'd loved her, he'd tried to corral her when what she'd needed was space to find her way and become her own person.

Now she could live life with him on the ranch with her whole heart and no regrets.

"She looks like a fairy princess," B.J. whispered so loudly the whole church heard him.

Morgan had to agree. To get a good view of her coming up the aisle, the two boys had moved over to peek around Wes, who was standing on the end.

Her long, white dress was soft and kind of sparkly as it moved about her. She practically looked like she was floating. Her eyes were shining with happiness and locked to his as the space slowly disappeared between them. Her lips trembled with a soft smile.

"She *is* a fairy princess," Sammy said, puffing his chest out. "She's ours and she's here to stay."

Joseph had moved up behind them. "Yes, she is, boys," he said quietly. "Now let's move on back to our seats and let the preacher marry her up with Morgan."

Beside Morgan, his best men—Rowdy and Tucker—chuckled.

"That'd be a good idea," Rowdy murmured low. "Because Morg here has been waitin' his whole life for this moment."

"You're up next, Rowdy, my man," Morgan heard Tucker tease their little brother.

"Me? Nope, that'd be you, big brother."

Morgan met his dad's steady gaze from the front row and they shared a moment, both thinking it would be interesting to see which one would be next.

The piano drew to a halt as Jolie and her father stopped in front of him.

"Who gives this woman?" the preacher asked.

"Her mother and I," Mr. Sheridan said, and placed Jolie's hand in Morgan's.

Jolie smiled that hundred-watts-of-pure-joy smile of hers, aiming it straight at him as she squeezed his hand, their eyes locked on each other. "I love you," she whispered, and as one they turned toward the preacher.

"This is gonna be *goooood,*" Sammy whispered.

"It already is," Caleb hissed.

"We got her for always now," B.J. said, his voice loud and clear, making the congregation chuckle.

Jolie turned and shared that killer smile of hers with the boys. "And I've got y'all," she assured them.

Morgan chuckled and cleared his throat. "Preacher, the floor is officially yours. Let's get rollin' so I can put a ring on her finger."

"At last," Rowdy said with a chuckle.

Morgan shot him a warning look—he hadn't forgotten that payback was owed to his little brother. And he was a patient man.

Jolie turned back to the preacher and nodded. "Okay," she said. "Make me the happiest woman in the world."

"Finally," Morgan grunted. Laughter

rumbled behind them as the preacher proceeded to make Morgan the happiest man in the world. At last.

* * * * *

*If you enjoyed this story
by Debra Clopton,
be sure to look for the other
Love Inspired books out this month!*

Dear Reader,

Thank you for joining me at Sunrise Ranch deep in the heart of West Texas. I have to say that I loved creating this new bunch of characters. As you can tell from reading this book, I wanted to keep you on your toes with them, so that you'll never know what to expect when you visit the ranch or the small town of Dew Drop and the Spotted Cow Café.

Just like my Mule Hollow series, I love never knowing what my characters are going to do next. So I'm busy working on the second story and having fun seeing what mischief everyone is getting into… stay tuned!

I so enjoyed telling Morgan and Jolie's story, and I hope you are looking forward to watching the other two McDermott brothers meet their matches later in the year.

The theme verse of this book, John 14:18, is one of my favorite of God's promises:

I will not leave you comfortless—I will come to you.

I loved using the theme of comfort in this book. Sammy needed comfort, and Jolie and Morgan were there for him, helping him through his grief. Jolie needed comforting, and so did Morgan. For all of them, God was the ultimate comforter, and He put them all in place to comfort each other.

I pray that if you need comfort today, you'll bow your head and talk it over with God. He is there to comfort you, too.

Until next time, live, laugh and seek God with all your hearts!

Debra Clopton

Questions for Discussion

1. Morgan's mother's vision for creating the foster program at Sunrise Ranch was to share the beauty and blessing of this West Texas ranch with less fortunate boys who had no place to call home. How did Morgan feel about his mother's dream? What are his plans for the future?

2. Why did Randolph McDermott hire Jolie Sheridan when she'd hurt his son, Morgan, so badly?

3. Despite what he is feeling when he learns what his father has done, Morgan is determined to be a good role model for the boys of the ranch. What does this say about him as a man?

4. Why do the boys of the ranch react in such a heartfelt and wistful manner when they watch the mother horse care for her newborn?

5. Jolie has regrets despite the fabulous life she has lived and the adventure and success she has known. She is torn between two worlds—the one she chose and the one she left behind. Have you ever felt torn between two choices? Did you pray for God's guidance in making the right choice?

6. How do Ms. Jo and Mabel react to Jolie's return to town? They love Jolie and Morgan and are not even thinking of matchmaking. Why?

7. Sammy is certain his family is going to come back and get him. Even in his time of need and distress, when his parents abandoned him, God was taking care of Sammy. What did God do for Sammy?

8. Putting his personal reasons for not wanting Jolie at the ranch aside, what is the main reason Morgan thinks her teaching the boys is a bad idea?

9. Jolie realizes, as she and Morgan have their first battle of wills outside the classroom under the oak tree, that God has given her a purpose in coming back to the ranch. She realizes she can help the boys. How does this make her feel?

10. When Morgan realizes he still loves Jolie and that she is afraid of the water, what is his reaction? What does he contemplate doing? Are you glad that he makes the choice to help her? Why?

11. Jolie is terrified of the water, and the nightmares haunt her. She is struggling and asking God to help her, but it isn't an overnight fix. Sometimes in order for God to help us, it takes time. Have you ever had to have patience while you waited for God to act?

12. When Sammy needs her, does Jolie hesitate? What does she do?

13. Why is helping Jolie get back into the

water an act of love and sacrifice on Morgan's part?

14. Jolie is forced to take a stand when it comes to choosing to leave or stay. What does she realize when she has to make the choice on her own without Morgan's help?

15. Sammy thought if he was good, Jolie would stay. Like Morgan knew in the beginning of the book, he needed stability and commitment in his life, as did all the boys. When Jolie makes up her mind to stay, it's about more than her love for Morgan. It's about finding her purpose in life—what is that? Sometimes it takes a while to realize our purpose. Do you believe that God has a purpose for each of us? Have you asked God to help you find your purpose?

REQUEST YOUR FREE BOOKS!

2 FREE INSPIRATIONAL NOVELS IN TRUE LARGE PRINT
PLUS 2 FREE MYSTERY GIFTS

Love Inspired
TRUE LARGE PRINT

YES! Please send me 2 FREE Love Inspired® True Large Print novels and my 2 FREE mystery gifts (gifts are worth about $10). After receiving them, if I don't wish to receive any more books, I can return the shipping statement marked "cancel." If I don't cancel, I will receive 3 brand-new true large print novels every month and be billed just $7.99 per book in the U.S. or $9.99 per book in Canada. That's a savings of at least 33% off the cover price. It's quite a bargain! Shipping and handling is just 50¢ per book in the U.S. and 75¢ per book in Canada.* I understand that accepting the 2 free books and gifts places me under no obligation to buy anything. I can always return the shipment and cancel at any time. Even if I never buy another book, the two free books and gifts are mine to keep forever.

117/307 IDN FVZK

Name _____ (PLEASE PRINT)

Address _____ Apt. #

City _____ State/Prov. _____ Zip/Postal Code

Signature (if under 18, a parent or guardian must sign)

Mail to the **Harlequin® Reader Service:**
IN U.S.A.: P.O. Box 1867, Buffalo, NY 14240-1867
IN CANADA: P.O. Box 609, Fort Erie, Ontario L2A 5X3

* Terms and prices subject to change without notice. Prices do not include applicable taxes. Sales tax applicable in N.Y. Canadian residents will be charged applicable taxes. Offer not valid in Quebec. This offer is limited to one order per household. Not valid for current subscribers to Love Inspired True Large Print books. All orders subject to credit approval. Credit or debit balances in a customer's account(s) may be offset by any other outstanding balance owed by or to the customer. Please allow 4 to 6 weeks for delivery. Offer available while quantities last.

Your Privacy—The Harlequin® Reader Service is committed to protecting your privacy. Our Privacy Policy is available online at www.ReaderService.com or upon request from the Harlequin Reader Service.

We make a portion of our mailing list available to reputable third parties that offer products we believe may interest you. If you prefer that we not exchange your name with third parties, or if you wish to clarify or modify your communication preferences, please visit us at www.ReaderService.com/consumerchoice or write to us at Harlequin Reader Service Preference Service, P.O. Box 9062, Buffalo, NY 14269. Include your complete name and address.

LITLP13TR

REQUEST YOUR FREE BOOKS!
2 FREE RIVETING INSPIRATIONAL NOVELS IN TRUE LARGE PRINT PLUS 2 FREE MYSTERY GIFTS

LoveInspired®
SUSPENSE

TRUE LARGE PRINT

YES! Please send me 2 FREE Love Inspired® Suspense True Large Print novels and my 2 FREE mystery gifts (gifts are worth about $10). After receiving them, if I don't wish to receive any more books, I can return the shipping statement marked "cancel." If I don't cancel, I will receive 3 brand-new true large print novels every month and be billed just $7.99 per book in the U.S. or $9.99 per book in Canada. That's a savings of at least 33% off the cover price. It's quite a bargain! Shipping and handling is just 50¢ per book in the U.S. and 75¢ per book in Canada.* I understand that accepting the 2 free books and gifts places me under no obligation to buy anything. I can always return the shipment and cancel at any time. Even if I never buy another book, the two free books and gifts are mine to keep forever.

124/324 IDN FV2K

Name	(PLEASE PRINT)	
Address		Apt. #
City	State/Prov.	Zip/Postal Code

Signature (if under 18, a parent or guardian must sign)

Mail to the **Harlequin® Reader Service:**
IN U.S.A.: P.O. Box 1867, Buffalo, NY 14240-1867
IN CANADA: P.O. Box 609, Fort Erie, Ontario L2A 5X3

* Terms and prices subject to change without notice. Prices do not include applicable taxes. Sales tax applicable in N.Y. Canadian residents will be charged applicable taxes. Offer not valid in Quebec. This offer is limited to one order per household. Not valid for current subscribers to Love Inspired Suspense True Large Print books. All orders subject to credit approval. Credit or debit balances in a customer's account(s) may be offset by any other outstanding balance owed by or to the customer. Please allow 4 to 6 weeks for delivery. Offer available while quantities last.

Your Privacy—The Harlequin® Reader Service is committed to protecting your privacy. Our Privacy Policy is available online at www.ReaderService.com or upon request from the Harlequin Reader Service.

We make a portion of our mailing list available to reputable third parties that offer products we believe may interest you. If you prefer that we not exchange your name with third parties, or if you wish to clarify or modify your communication preferences, please visit us at www.ReaderService.com/consumerschoice or write to us at Harlequin Reader Service Preference Service, P.O. Box 9062, Buffalo, NY 14269. Include your complete name and address.

Reader Service.com

Manage your account online!

- Review your order history
- Manage your payments
- Update your address

> ### **We've designed the Harlequin® Reader Service website just for you.**

Enjoy all the features!

- Reader excerpts from any series
- Respond to mailings and special monthly offers
- Discover new series available to you
- Browse the Bonus Bucks catalogue
- Share your feedback

Visit us at:
ReaderService.com